CABAL

PRAISE FOR THE SERIES

"Sean Hagerty's debut novel, JONES POINT, is a powerful story that draws you in from the start and keeps you locked in until the very end. Fans of military thrillers are going to want to keep an eye on this new author, a hard-hitting special operations insider who can still tug at the heartstrings."

TAYLOR MOORE, former CIA intelligence officer and bestselling author of *Cold Trail*

Cindy,

CABAL

A DANE COOPER NOVEL

Thank you so much for the support. I hope you enjoy.

RLTW
Send Me
Sean

SEAN HAGERTY

BLUE HANDLE PUBLISHING

The characters and events in this book are fictitious.
Any similarity to real persons, living or dead, is coincidental
and not intended by the author or publisher.

For information, address:
Blue Handle Publishing
2607 Wolflin Ave. #963
Amarillo, TX 79109

For information about bulk, educational,
and other special discounts, please contact
Blue Handle Publishing.
www.BlueHandlePublishing.com

To book Sean Hagerty for any event,
contact Blue Handle Publishing.

Design and editing by Book Puma Author Services
BookPumaEdit.com
Cover image by Robin Mackey of Robin Mackey's Photography LLC

ISBN: 978-1-955058-31-5

To my father
Paul Edward Hagerty VII
(June 17, 1946 – October 29, 2024)
Taken from us too soon.

There was not a soul on this planet that my father could not charm. He treated everyone as an old friend. And there was not a place on this earth we could visit where he wouldn't bump into someone he knew. He made friends easily with what he liked to call his "Irish wit and wisdom." My dad used to always say he was sorry that he gave me his smart mouth but not his height. (He was six-foot-five). He said that I should thank him for not naming me Paul Edward Hagerty VIII. Thanks, Dad. I appreciate that.

His obituary remarked on his final days: "Although Paul's passing was untimely, the family has taken great solace in knowing he faced the end on his terms. He had spent the last several weeks visiting each and every member of his loving family. Everyone got their final memory of him laughing, joking, and otherwise filling every hearth with his enormous presence. Once complete, he retreated home to the villages and his love/hate relationship with golf. He often loathed the game, but he cherished the time with all his golf buddies and friends. He smacked the little ball around the greens as fast as he could so as to finish the game quickly and enjoy cocktails and laughter in the clubhouse with the love of his life, Ann, and his closest friends. Many may imagine him playing a round in heaven. However, Paul has swung his last club. He is reconnecting with lost friends, telling tall tales, and enjoying jovial banter over a rousing game of cribbage."
https://www.afterall.com/obituaries/PaulHagerty

The day you bury your dad is the day you will realize that you have lost the only man who wanted to see you succeed more than him. — Unknown

PROLOGUE

Kunar Province, Afghanistan, 2006

The fluctuation of weather was unlike anything he had experienced before. The lowlands suffered severe heat, draining every possible ounce of water from the human body. But that same water froze moments later at the extreme peaks of the mountains, bringing with it the possibility of hypothermia and death. And in this God-forsaken country, those extremes could be enjoyed daily thanks to the rigorous operations to subdue the ungovernable masses. Why would anyone fight over this hellhole? It hasn't worked for centuries. Conquering armies left bloodied and defeated. Just ask the Mongols, the British, the Russians, and probably the United States one day.

The Soldiers of Second Battalion, 7th Psychological Operations Group called Asadabad their home after nearly three years of warfare throughout the country. From province to province, they had worked their magic to convince the Afghan population that not only was Al-Qaeda a threat to their nation and American soldiers were here to help, but that buildings such as the Twin Towers of New York did indeed exist and had been destroyed by the terrorist organization.

None of that mattered. Help was not appreciated, especially when it was help building something the Americans had inadvertently destroyed in the first place. Fighting and rebuilding and fighting and rebuilding. Cities and villages destroyed and reborn. A war without an end.

The fact that Al-Qaeda was a global threat eluded most of the local population. The nationalism rooted throughout the modern world was a foreign concept here. Al-Qaeda wasn't bad for them, they claimed, since the group did not operate in their village. Plus, the group never hurt anyone. It was the same story in every village.

Most Afghanis spent generations confined to a single valley, never venturing beyond its steep slopes to the rest of the world, let alone the rest of their country. Their neighbors on the other side of the mountain were alien to them, besides the occasional encounter tracking wayward livestock.

It reminded him of his home in the hollers of West Virginia. Or rather, how his ancestors had lived once they migrated west from the overcrowded eastern seaboard in the eighteen-hundreds. It was a feeling of confinement, the feeling of isolation that enticed a young boy to leave the comfortable predictability for adventure that only the United States Army could provide. The suppression of free will and lack of any other opportunities helped him excel in the armed forces. A drive to succeed and never-look-back attitude pushed him harder and harder.

First, the infantry. He easily mastered the basic skills, rising rapidly through the ranks, but found himself wanting more. And to get more, he needed authority. Power. The power he sought with officer candidate training. But even that wasn't enough. He was never enough. Someone was always better. Special Forces? Why not? He was unstoppable.

Or was, until he went through the qualification course affectionately called the Q-course. He just didn't have the right stuff. He was a good soldier, just not good enough to wear the green beret. He was crushed.

But wait, his commander said. There was another Special Operations organization that would be a perfect fit for a soldier of his talent and skill.

And that is how a young captain from the hollers of West Virginia found himself back in the same hollers, halfway around the world in Afghanistan. He was leading a team of PSYOPS soldiers trying to convince the Afghans of the truth. Yes, buildings could be built without mud and twigs, reaching for the skies as the Twin Towers once did.

The posters they distributed depicted pictures of the towers before that horrific collapse. The local Afghans would argue and claim that the pictures on the posters were not real. Buildings could not stand that tall. They would fall from the wind. They would crumble upon themselves. Allah forbade it! That was his favorite answer from those ignorant goat herders. Whenever there was a concept they couldn't understand, they would turn to their religion to refute it. Or they'd turn to that religion to affirm something.

My family is sick. It must be Allah's will.

Our herd is dying. It must be Allah's will.

The crops are dying. Allah has willed it.

Or it could be that they hang their diseased animals for slaughter over their precious water supply with blood dripping into the river. They travel upstream to defecate in that same water, then wash themselves in it. All the while, the women are downstream washing their clothes and collecting their drinking water. Allah has made them sick, but once they recover, it must have been Allah that cured them. Certainly could not have been the medications the various teams handed out like candy to prevent the spread of disease among the people. His contempt for them grew steadily each day.

This contempt clashed with yet complemented his current assignment. He mentally justified the dichotomy. His job was to persuade, to convince the Afghans that the American cause was righteous and just. He recalled the phrase he had heard too many times: Capture the hearts and minds. However, he had no interest in hearts or minds. No faith anymore for this cause. His contempt hardened his heart and cemented his resolve. These people were beyond salvation.

They were beyond hope, stuck in their centuries-old, ignorant ways. Ignorant of how the world really worked. Ignorant of the doings of man outside their rock huts and muddy fields. Generations wasted. Blind adherence to a vision formed by religion, formed by the lands, and formed by their ancestors that left them in a perpetual state of poverty. Poverty of the body. Poverty of the mind.

He couldn't capture their hearts and minds. He had no sympathy left. He was in psychological operations and would have to persuade them with lies and deceit. Play on their ignorance to obtain their assistance in eradicating the terrorist threat to his country. No, fuck his country. To protect himself.

The only hope was the next generation, the children still curious about the world. These children were benefiting from exposure to the soldiers; the children were unaware of the listlessness around them in their parents, their grandparents, and their leaders. They were the only hope for Afghanistan, the only hope for the world. They were the only light. Corruption had still not tainted their souls. Souls still submersed in innocence.

CLICK . . . CLICK . . . CLICK.

The digital card in his camera captured their hope. Captured their fleeting joy. Captured the truth of their souls. Captured? Not the right word. Captured implied a glimpse of their progression before they descended into the abyss. Captured meant a simple recording of their decline.

He needed to do more—collect. By collecting, he would freeze their moment in time to keep their purity. Collecting was protecting them from losing that innocence and falling prey to the endless cycle of their parents. He was protecting them. He was collecting their souls.

1

THE MOUNTAIN

Old Rag Mountain, Virginia

`Keeper: I have another task for you.`

`Devotee: I really wanted to start collecting.`

`Keeper: You will when the time is right. Your other skills are needed for now.`

`Devotee: Okay. Whatever you think is best.`

Dane had a dentist to kill today.

As dawn broke over the mountain, Dane smiled to himself and sipped the instant coffee from his metal canteen cup. It had been a cold night at that elevation, but Dane had the right gear for his hide site. When he arrived at the unit, he was given quite a large sum of money to procure all necessary civilian camping gear, similar to his military issue, for assignments where it was not desirable to openly proclaim *AMERICAN MILITARY.*

He had also chosen the perfect location along the western ridge of Old Rag Mountain. He was nestled among an outcropping of boulders, providing him protection on three sides and overhead. His poncho and sleeping bag retained the warmth from his body heat throughout the night. More importantly, the site provided him anonymity. He was away from any major hiking trails and his particular location was not a destination for those visiting the mountain. The best views were along the eastern ridge. This was crucial to the mission. That was why he hiked to this location the day prior to await his prey.

It seemed like only yesterday when Dane's life was turned upside by the club. All the mystery and intrigue that led him to that Bellevue Forest mansion in Arlington felt so fresh. He met the president, Charles, and his right-hand man, Jack. They explained how the club worked and its singular focus to hunt the monsters who hunt our children. That day, he entered into a world of violence and revenge. A world that allowed him to channel all that grief, all that anger, all that rage for a single purpose.

There were others. Faceless members that provided tools, weapons, and even intel. The logistical support this club offered would make most three-letter D.C. agencies jealous. And, of course, there were also others like him at the tip of spear conducting finishing operations. Sam Turner had become a lifelong friend, bonding over their cathartic intensity while punishing these monsters. Without Sam and Jack's help, the club never would have stopped the Pupil—Wilson Simmons—and rescued those two children from his basement dungeon.

Dane had killed Wilson without a single shred of remorse. And ever since, he had been killing his way through every pedophile, molester, and kidnapper he could find. He wouldn't stop until he found his baby girl, his Angela.

Dr. Kevin Webster appeared to the world as an honest, upfront, productive member of society. He was fit, attractive, and operated a thriving dental practice in Fairfax, Virginia. He attended all the right parties. He made appearances at all the right civic events. He dated beautiful women while cruising around town in his silver Mercedes. And to top it all off, he was a humanitarian. He spent countless hours working with the homeless shelters in D.C. and the surrounding Maryland and Virginia neighborhoods. He cleaned teeth, provided dental hygiene classes, and donated supplies of brushes, floss, and paste. His bright, welcoming smile could be seen on billboards through the northern Virginia and D.C. area. But Dane and his team knew the Edward Hyde side of his persona, the one Webster tried to keep hidden from the world.

There had been a string of kidnapping and sexual assaults in metro D.C. over the last several months. Young girls were grabbed, assaulted, and then dumped back onto the streets. Rarely did they seek medical attention, and it was seldom reported when they did. Most politicians and activists gravitated to other urban issues. Those who investigated found underfunded police departments with higher priorities. Crime among the homeless community was endless.

The fact that the assaults took place over a wide swath meant patterns never emerged for investigative links. Dr. Webster pursued his prey, believing that he was safe from exposure. He was wrong.

Dane and the team identified Webster's patterns. Combing through the limited records, they determined the homeless shelters where each of the young girls stayed temporarily or visited for medical services. Dane postulated that their sexual predator hunted at these locations. He requested further analysis, and Charles connected him with the group's National Security Agency (NSA) member.

By running names and phones numbers through the databases, several people emerged with connections to those clinics. Add in several more exhaustive searches, a compilation of an offender profile, and one expunged record that she wasn't supposed to find, and out popped Webster. He had access to all the facilities, his cell phone was present in the vicinity of all the known attacks, and his sealed indictment as a sixteen-year-old boy described a bipolar narcissist with the desire to dominate and shame those he deemed weak.

Dane and Sam quickly established a pattern of life for the doctor. It was fairly simple, due to his office hours at his dental practice. As Webster filled a cavity, the two men methodically searched his luxury condo. They found evidence, trophies, and even the zippered leather mask several of the reporting victims remembered. The victims stated that he never removed it, so they could never provide a full description.

The two men also found the hidden room where Webster indulged his urges. They noticed some unusual empty space in the corner of the living room and a nearby bathroom. A wall of shiplap concealed the door. Unless you were specifically looking for such a place, it would never be found. However, Dan and Sam were looking, and the find sickened them both. The ten-by-ten crimson room housed all of Webster's sick obsessions for domination and torture. This was the nail in the coffin, so to speak.

Hence the bitter mountain cold on the crisp Monday morning. During their search, they found printed directions and a day-use ticket for Old Rag Mountain in Shenandoah National Park. Webster happened to be an avid hiker, and he closed his office each Monday to pursue that and other endeavors. The mountain was a popular spot on the weekends, but would be virtually empty on Monday.

The location was perfect for Dane, compared to Webster's other legal hobbies. The country club greens were not a suitable place for an assassination. And although they could work with Webster's fondness for sailing, it was hard to clandestinely stalk your prey on the open water.

The two men drew straws. Sam would enter Webster's condo, remove all evidence of his crimes, and disable the shiplap opening for the red room. Dane would make sure the good doctor befell a fatal climbing accident in one of the most dangerous areas of Virginia. Problem solved, without a messy police investigation that might lead back to the club.

On the surface, the task appeared fairly straightforward, but Dane needed Jack's assistance. "I have two problems," he told Charles.

"How can we assist, Mr. Cooper?"

"Cameras and cars are my biggest threats. This area is remote. And to get there, I need to avoid Interstate 66 and 95. Too many cameras. I don't want my vehicle or my mug shot captured heading toward a potential crime scene."

"That makes perfect sense. Are there no alternate routes you could utilize?"

"There are, but even small towns are devoting more and more of their budget toward community safety. It is difficult and costly to hire and train more officers. Cameras provide cheaper solutions to monitor the roads while their limited forces handle direct contact with the populace. Jack driving for me would be the preferred option since cameras are aimed at drivers and license plates. It also solves my second problem."

"You have nowhere to park," Jack answered. "I was looking over maps of the area. Permits are required, some lots close at night, and a lone vehicle would be reported as abandoned. You would stick out in those tight rural communities."

"Correct. I figure we make our way to Luray. From there, we move south and east as much as possible using back roads. We find a discreet spot for a drop-off and I move out smartly."

Jack smirked at the old phrase *smartly*. "And the pickup?"

"Sperryville. I don't want to have any electronic devices chirping while I am out there. Pick me up on Water Street heading east out of town. I will be near the intersection where you turn right on River Lane to head to Copper Fox Distillery. It closes at six. I am thinking of a late-morning visit with Webster, so we can link up around dusk. Let's do a seven o'clock pickup. If I am not there, wave off and I will find my own way out or find a pay phone."

"Think you will look out of place?" Jack asked.

"Nah, I have been there a few times. Hikers all over the place accessing various trails. I won't even be noticed."

Charles concluded the meeting. "Well, gentlemen, it appears you have everything you need. Good luck."

Sam had joked that since he won the straw draw, he got the better end of the deal. He got to spend time in the expensive condo, then return to his warm bed at home while Dane slept on the rocks. Although it had been a long time since he had slept on the ground, Dane enjoyed reconnecting with some of his earlier survival training. And this time it was on his terms.

Deployments with the unit rarely involved sleeping in the wilderness, but Dane had plenty of chances with the Rangers. His platoon would hump enormous rucks around the woods and swamps of Fort Stewart, Georgia. Patrols, battle drills, live fire exercises, and airborne operations filled his early career. Each of those tasks individually could be somewhat enjoyable, if not exciting. Not in the Rangers, though.

Let's conduct all these activities at once, one after another, and throw in some helo operations, maybe an obstacle course or two. Let's take two weeks every month and see how much we can make it suck. Jumping out of a plane? Here is an eighty-pound ruck and a Gustav tube. Camp for the night? Nowhere dry—sleep in the swamp where the enemy can't find you. Train as you would fight. And God forbid you put on anything for warmth without permission from leadership.

Dane never understood why all that snivel was on the packing list, yet they were forbidden to bundle up for comfort. He smiled to himself. *Wouldn't have changed it for the world.*

He tried to pass those skills onto his kids, John and Angela. They would explore the woods while camping, and he attempted to teach them the skills they would need if they ever had to survive. They built fires, plotted routes on maps, and even purified water. Both kids knew how to read a standard map. They could navigate by compass needle or identify terrain features along their route that coincided with markings on their map to determine their location. But they avoided the suck. Tents were warm and dry from the roaring fire they had every evening. Everyone wore their snivel.

As Dane quickly packed up camp, dark thoughts began to loom. It was happening more and more as memories of Angela swirled in his mind. The work with the club had tempered his rage, but it was returning slowly with each dead end. He knew he couldn't let it consume him. He had been down that road before. Ever since the killing of Wilson Simmons, his demons had returned. He had known there was only the slimmest of odds they would find her in that house. But his heart had still dropped when she wasn't there.

He took the tiny chain and pendant from his front shirt pocket. He knew it was dangerous to carry personal effects on clandestine operations. Those could be accidently dropped and used as evidence of involvement. But the risk far outweighed the calming effect it had on him. He was always carrying a little reminder of his Angela.

The chain was simple and crude, bought at a street market in Bamako, Mali. It was the pendant that held the true value. Dane had found a small jewelry-maker, sitting on the ground before a large tree stump amid the throng of stalls. Atop the stump was a metal mold of the African continent with a heart carved out over Mali. He watched the man use a simple gas torch to melt the French Franc coin and fill the mold. Such a simple thing could have given Angela so much joy, but he never got the chance to surprise her. She was gone when he returned.

The only positive from the Wilson Simmons operation was seeing those two precious faces behind the cage doors. At least he was able to save someone else's children and to make Wilson pay. That had fed his soul. Temporarily.

Now, it felt empty again. The lead to the Keeper went cold. He and Sam had to accept the temporary setback and concentrate on other efforts. Dane needed to continue the hunt for Angela. He was like an alcoholic constantly reminded of his thirst. He was going to temporarily quench that thirst with the good doctor. He tucked the jewelry back in his pocket. *Time to get to work.*

Dane spent the remainder of the morning scouting the area, identifying locations for the kill and routes for his egress. The area was desolate. The light dusting of snow from earlier in the week had melted, yet the ground was still frozen enough to conceal his presence. He wasn't really expecting investigators to put much effort into Webster's death, but it never hurt to be careful. He didn't need to have boot prints left behind or any other trace evidence that could place him in this area. He checked and double-checked. He was alone. Alone with his rage. Until he wasn't.

Webster crested the top of the mountain just before noon. Water bottle in hand, Dane saw his heaving chest and flushed cheeks. He was in good enough shape to climb Old Rag Mountain, but not good enough for what was coming next.

Dane watched Webster drink greedily. The doctor removed his pack and dropped it to the ground. Between gulps, he fished around in his backpack for a camera that he then slung around his neck. Webster placed his water bottle next to his pack and moved to the cliff edge to record his achievement.

Dane moved noisily out from the woods to announce his approach, lest he startle the doctor and cause a fatal fall. Dane wanted the pleasure. "Morning. Don't mean to intrude. I thought I would have this place to myself."

"I thought the same." Webster turned and offered Dane a weak smile before returning to his view.

"You been up here before?" Dane asked. "Any other good spots for a view?"

Webster lowered his camera. He appeared aggravated and dismissive. "Yes and no. This is the spot. Everyone comes here to enjoy the splendor and relish the isolation that can be found among the mountains. That is why I come here a few times a year. For solitude."

Dane scanned his surroundings. He double-checked the trail head Webster had climbed. Empty. He moved closer to the man. Rage building, he had to will his hands silent. "Sorry. I didn't mean to bother you."

Webster didn't even turn this time. "Then why are you still doing it?" he asked, the firm tone of his voice chastising Dane.

The wind filled the vacuum created by the paused conversation. Dane let the rage grow. The whole eternity of a minute passed. Webster smugly snapped photos of the mountain and took exaggerated breaths of the fresh mountain air.

"I guess I am trying to figure out why a piece of shit like you is allowed to share the air I breathe."

Webster turned in rage and let the camera fall to his chest. With gritted teeth and clenched fists, he closed the final distance to Dane until they were just inches apart. Froth clung to Webster's lips. "I don't know who the—"

Rookie move, Dane though as he smashed his forehead into Webster's face, obliterating his nose. *Never get that close to an opponent unless you are attacking.*

Blood erupted as Webster stumbled back before he was steadied by Dane's grip on the camera strap.

Webster howled in pain. "What the hell are you doing? What the fuck!" His hands covered his shattered nose, but failed to stem the flow of blood. His eyes widened as he took in Dane's wide grin.

"You see, assholes like you think they can do whatever they like. Hurt whoever they like." Dane remained cool, calm, and even-toned. "You think you are untouchable. I have now persuaded you otherwise."

Dane pointed to the cliff. "Jump."

Webster was clearly dumbfounded. "Are you insane?"

Dane slapped Webster on the ear with a cupped hand. "You like to rape little girls. So, I'd like for you to jump." Dane moved closer.

"No. No. I never did that. Whoever told you that was lying. I have lots of enemies. They are jealous of me. They make up stories."

Another well-placed slap connected with the opposite ear. "You like to leave them underneath a bridge to die. Leave them at a rest stop. Maybe even dump them in a vacant playground or field." Dane moved even closer. "Jump."

"Those were accidents. I found them injured. I didn't hurt anyone, just gave them a ride. Dropped them where they wanted. I didn't want anyone blaming me!" Webster began to cry. He cowered with each blow.

"Those were no accidents. You are a complete piece of garbage. Jump."

Webster was backed up to the very edge, squatting with nowhere to go. "I c-can't. I can't jump. Turn me in. I'll confess." His sobs drowned out his words. "Please, I need help. I need—"

"Doesn't work like that."

"I'll do anything. Anything you want," Webster cried. He could get no closer to the edge without falling over. Still in a squatting position, he hugged himself tightly, rocking back and forth like a frightened child, as if that would make this all go away.

"I want you to suffer just like your victims." Dane booted the doctor hard in his chest. "Goodbye, Dr. Webster."

Webster's screams the entire way to the base of the cliff were music to Dane's ears. And the crashing of the body through the boulders and scrub brush was the encore.

I DON'T WANT TO DO THIS. THE MAN SAID I MUST WRITE EVERY DAY. HE SAID IT WILL HELP ME. HE SAID HE WON'T READ WHAT I WRITE, BUT I DON'T WANT TO. I DON'T WANT TO JOURNAL. I DON'T WANT TO BE IN THIS PLACE. I DON'T UNDERSTAND WHY I AM HERE. I WANT TO GO HOME. I WANT MY MOM AND DAD.

2

THE BENEFACTOR

Occoquan, Virginia

Jackson Lentz settled comfortably in the leather seats of the helicopter. He knew that it was a short trip from Washington Dulles International Airport to his home on the Occoquan River, but he was weary from all the recent travel and the day was just beginning.

Flying on the helicopter was the most soothing part of his workday. He flew to nearly every meeting or engagement, yet found the familiar and repetitive countryside beautiful each time. He never tired of the views. Something new was discovered each time he stared out the window, especially flights over the Occoquan on the final approach to his home. He always instructed the pilots to follow the river as much as possible from the beginning in the Manassas Bull Run area until they arrived in Belmont at the mouth of the river. Sometimes, the regulatory agencies allowed him this indulgence. As long as they steered away from Fort Belvoir and Quantico, the Department of Defense was happy. But he never knew when some executive government flight would divert his route and rob him of those fleeting moments.

The twenty-one-hour trip home from Hòn Tam, Vietnam, was exhausting. The private jet afforded far more luxuries than commercial airliners, but sitting for that long was still the same. *Albeit, a much larger chair*. Contrary to what most people thought about him, the billionaire didn't actually own a private jet. People assumed he did based on the enormity of his financial estate.

However rich he was, Jackson still tried to make prudent decisions with his wealth. He remembered his father's words of advice when he was the CEO of the burgeoning, small tech company: *If it flies, floats, or fucks, rent it!* Jackson tried keeping a straight face after that when he had inquired about purchasing his first car. His father would hear nothing of it.

"You are going to lease your car, son. Although you may be able to buy it outright, in doing so the car loses its value the moment you drive it off the lot. Twenty percent is left behind. You are then stuck with all the maintenance and upkeep costs. You are also giving all that money to the dealership. Money that you could be investing at a higher rate of return. Lease. Small monthly payments. The dealership covers all but routine maintenance, and you can just walk away after a few years and lease another vehicle. The dealership eats the devaluation."

Those sage words of advice and others stuck with Jackson to build the foundation of his empire, an empire that turned a small, inherited tech company into a force to be reckoned with. Jackson Lentz was one of the richest men in the world. He could afford to purchase the airline company, let alone the Gulfstream ferrying him to and from Southeast Asia on a monthly basis. But no. That money was invested, and not in the failing airline industry. It was put to better use.

Jackson did not have the hours available in the day to watch the stock market's every tick. He could not oversee all the finest details of his multiple companies. What he could do was hire the right people. Another of his father's lessons. *Hire the right people, give them the freedom to make decisions, and incentivize their efforts. They will work harder if they are able to increase their earnings. If you don't give them a way to climb the corporate ladder, they will go somewhere else that does.*

One investment, however, did not turn a profit. It was the club he had founded with Charles Thornton, for which he was the sole contributor. The club was the reason for his frequent trips to the small Pacific Island off the coast of Vietnam.

Hòn Tam is renowned for its lush tropical forests, pearly white beaches, and a stunning blue ocean. It attracted tourists from all walks of life. Those worshipping the sun were scattered along the shore. Anglers tried their luck luring in the exotic sea life the waters had to offer. And the truly adventurous explored the ocean bottom, diving among the coral reefs and the numerous caves along its cliffs. It was said the island's cave network traveled for miles along the coastline.

Jackson visited for a completely different reason. He might occasionally enjoy a dip in the warm waters, a relaxing on a sunset sail, or a round of golf on the championship course, but his main interest was the lax banking practices of the island.

Many entrepreneurs used the island to manage their financial portfolios. They assumed Jackson also moved his well-deserved gains throughout the world market to this island, avoiding a majority of U.S. taxes and maximizing his returns. They assumed incorrectly.

For one, Jackson was not interested in avoiding his taxes, despite the reporting of the mainstream media. They could accuse him all they wanted of "not paying his fair share," but he knew it was all bluster. He certainly didn't shy away from the tax breaks afforded him under the U.S. tax code, but he did not come to Vietnam to hide his earnings. Well, at least not for personal gain. He came to Vietnam to secretly move the funds he needed to support the club. He considered this moral dilemma manageable since it could be argued the funds for the club represented the public interest. The public just didn't know it.

He and Charles had met over a decade ago. At the time, his company had exploded on the national and international scene. Jackson took the tech company from chips and processors to robotics, artificial intelligence, and biotechnology. These advancements drew the attention of the federal government and others in the defense industry. Charles was the face of one of those three-letter government agencies, and Jackson created a consortium among private industry to develop the technology Charles required.

Breaking into the defense contracting world was huge for Jackson. The giants like Raytheon, Boeing, Lockheed Martin, and others had firm control over the market and would throw only table scraps to the little guys. He broke through and was well on his way to getting a seat at the adult table. It was his turn to throw scraps. That was the circle of life in the corporate world.

Charles was a man who lived in the shadows. He had serious connections, evident by the scope of the projects requested along with the ample purse for funding. But the rest of the man was an enigma. Jackson asked, pried, and practically begged, but Charles was always tight-lipped about his true role in the government. His business cards supported this charade with the ambiguous title of assistant secretary of defense for research and technology. Jackson knew there was more to the conservative, southern gentleman with a sharp mind and a determined demeanor. He just couldn't figure it out.

Then, one evening after working together for over three years, Charles lowered his guard.

The two men shared a late dinner and a few cocktails after a particularly grueling conference in Tampa, Florida. Jackson and the team had been working with Special Operations Command out of MacDill Air Force Base on a peculiar requirement. Charles was the broker on behalf of the Department of Defense. The Special Operations community had concepts and prototypes for their requirements. They needed help bringing those concepts to life and produce them at scale.

The men's conversation was mostly consumed with the normal rambling and observations from their recent interactions with colleagues and peers. As the waiter cleared the dishes, though, a TV over the bar streaming the news presented a gloomy story of yet another abducted child. The mother, half crying, half begging, pleaded alongside the Hillsborough County Sheriff's spokesman for her son's return. She pleaded directly with her community to help her find her child. It was heartbreaking. Jackson was stunned to see the stoic features of his friend morph into a mask of pure hatred.

"How about a nightcap and a nice Cuban on the patio?" Charles asked.

"Sure," he responded. Jackson wasn't known to be a prolific drinker, but he sensed a determination in Charles. More than usual.

Charles raised two fingers toward the waiter, then gestured toward the patio. It was a cool summer evening, and the view of Tampa Bay was breathtaking. Yet the area was completely deserted. On Saturday nights, the hotel's clientele obviously preferred to sample all the nightlife offered by downtown Tampa.

Once seated, Charles removed two cigars from his interior suit pocket along with a cutter and a torch. He expertly snipped both ends of one cigar and handed it to Jackson. He leaned forward with the lit torch as Jackson puffed greedily, engaging the tightly rolled Cuban tobacco. Charles sat back, tending to his own cigar. The waiter set two glasses of brown liquor on the table between the men and quickly departed. Charles stared ahead at the ocean as he began to speak, almost as if Jackson wasn't the intended audience.

"Jackson, I wanted to talk with you about the past and then discuss the future. I will fully understand if you are reluctant to participate in my proposal. You may even be repulsed. Be that as it may, knowing the details of the tragic passing of your wife and daughter, you of all people may be sympathetic to my proposal. However, if you decline, I would appreciate you keeping this conversation private, which I would adamantly deny anyway if made public."

This was surely an evening of stunning events. Jackson's mind raced with possibilities, but he restrained his emotions. Thoughts of Jessica and Sarah crept to the forefront. Dread and loss flooded back in. He sipped from his glass, allowing the whiskey to roll around his mouth and tongue as he fought to control his emotions. He simply nodded.

"Most people do not know that I lost my son many years ago," Charles revealed. "It seems like a lifetime ago, yet only yesterday at the same time. I was working out of the embassy in Paris. My wife had passed a year earlier. Cancer."

"My condolences."

"Thank you. My son was ten at the time, and I thought the temporary move to France would help him. New start for the two of us as we put our lives back together. We were virtual strangers due to my work. His mother was an amazing parent who I could never replace. I needed to adjust to fill that void from her passing as best as I could. Everything worked wonderfully at first. We had a small flat in the city, and he attended The American School nearby. Well within walking distance. He was thriving. He made new friends and was exposed to an entirely new world. We were even able to do a little traveling. I would let him choose the locations for our weekends excursions. Skiing in the Alps. Visiting the World War II battlegrounds in the Cotentin Peninsula. We even explored the Mediterranean by sailboat. He was healing, and I was, too."

Charles paused as the waiter returned with fresh drinks. He took a long pull off his cigar while staring out over the bay. The patio lights had come on as the sun disappeared into the ocean. A few remaining sailors whisked upon the bay making for home port. Jackson remained motionless. He was afraid to break the connection between them and lose the relevancy of this tragic story.

Charles continued. "I was working a joint task force with the French, targeting financiers for the growing radicalism in the Middle East. Money was flowing from Europe, assisting start-ups such as Al-Qaeda and Hamas and even Al-Shabaab. I won't bore you with the details of the investigation, but suffice to say, we were making great progress. Too good. The money was slowing to a trickle. That is when the terrorists decided to derail the task force. They waited one afternoon outside my apartment. As Johnathan approached on his way home from school, they grabbed him right off the street in broad daylight. His body was found days later in a field outside the city. It was riddled with bullets."

"Oh my God, Charles. I am so sorry. I never heard of an American student being killed in Paris by terrorists."

"That's because we covered it up," Charles said, looking straight at Jackson for the first time. "We covered it up for a variety of reasons. Mostly political. Both countries did not want an international incident to give rise to panic among the citizens of the European nations nor provide validity to the terrorist groups. We didn't have any family, no real friends to notify, so I took my son home for a private burial at my family estate alongside my wife."

"Did the French authorities find the killers?"

"No. I did."

Jackson stared at his friend and colleague, willing him to continue. Charles obliged.

"I had befriended a young military operative who was part of our task force, on loan from the Department of Defense. He worked for a shadowy unit out of Washington D.C. and was more than willing to go off book. He had previously been our main surveillant for the task force on the streets, tracking the financiers and their goons' movements. They never knew he had eyes on them more often than not. Recording their illicit activity to inform the local authorities and often Interpol. He also knew Johnathan well. He was a regular at our flat. The two of them would talk baseball to no end. It was difficult to view games on the French TV. Anyway, he reached out. Offered a plan. I accepted and I went back. Unofficially."

"Unofficially?"

"I flew to London four months after the funeral to take up a new post. My friend arranged anonymous transport to and from Paris across the channel on several occasions. I believe a total of five trips. During each of those trips, he and I visited individuals who were of interest to the task force I previously managed. I didn't know which group sanctioned my son's abduction and murder."

"How did you figure out who was responsible?"

"I didn't. He and I hunted everyone on our list from the task force. They were from several different terrorist organizations. We executed every single one of them."

"I am sure the French became concerned with that many bodies piling up in their city. Especially since they were bodies they were interested in for legal reasons."

"They were not exactly pleased, but at the same time, the French authorities have a different cultural view then Americans often have: One less terrorist for them to worry about."

That night, The Cabal was born.

Jackson snapped back to the present as the Sikorsky S-76 slowed and its nose rose about twenty degrees on descent after crossing Richmond Highway. Its destination was a hidden cove on the north bank of the river. Jackson smiled as he gazed upon the Occoquan River out the starboard window. This was his paradise. He watched the tranquil river flow into Belmont Bay and then out into the mighty Potomac River. He had found this little oasis decades before when he and Jessica first moved to the area. They adored the town itself and were frequent visitors. *But that is gone now,* he thought.

All he had left of both their memories was this modest home tucked away among the trees along the river. The locals knew someone important dwelled among them due to the Sikorsky's frequent flights overhead. But Jackson had strategically omitted any personal information when acquiring the property. The world believed he lived in some sprawling mansion in Malibu or Maui when, in fact, one of the richest men in the world called the quiet shores of Occoquan, Virginia, home.

Jackson thought back again to that night The Cabal had been born. Charles had laid himself completely bare at Jackson's feet, his soul naked to the core. Charles held nothing back. But Jackson had.

It bothered him that he didn't open up as well. The timing had been perfect. Now, it was too late. Too much time had passed, and revealing his secret to Charles after all that had happened between the two of them would seem like a betrayal at this point. He told Charles that the murders of Jessica and Sarah were never solved. However, he omitted one tiny detail: The murders would never be solved. Jackson had used every means available to him to ensure the two carjackers would never harm another person again. The private team he had hired were known for their extreme discretion.

Those were two bodies that will never be found.

3

THE PORT

Savannah, Georgia

```
Zealot: I found one I like.

Keeper: This will be your first.

Zealot: I have done this before.

Keeper: You were sloppy before. Untrained. Remember what you have learned.
```

"You got eyes up, Sam?"

"Covered, Dane. You guys are clear."

"Okay. Security here seems weak, but I still don't want to tangle with any guards. We have no beef with them."

Dane gently placed the lock and chain in the grass alongside the access road. He had sprayed the hinges with lubricant, eliminating any possibility of noise. As he had told Sam, the guards and dockhands had nothing to do with the mission this evening. *Well, that is not entirely true,* he thought. The smugglers had to have someone on the inside to pull this off. But without any way of positively identifying the accomplice, he needed to treat everyone tonight as friendlies.

"We good to go, boss?"

Tony's whispered question annoyed him. It was his first mission with the club, and Dane felt he was just not ready. Actually, not even really qualified. But the President had insisted that Tony was operational and, more importantly, the Benefactor was persistent that they attack this underage human smuggling ring as quickly as possible. Sam and his sniper rifle sat atop the abandoned cement factory across the river, providing overwatch, Dane's back would be exposed without anyone alongside him on the ground. He would be vulnerable maneuvering through the labyrinth that was the port of Savannah. There were two other semi-qualified members of the club, but one was on the injured roster from a bite in the calf and the other was under law enforcement scrutiny for a bar fight in downtown D.C. last week.

Phil Pratt joined the club a few months back, and was wounded on his first mission. He was a retired Ranger like Dane and had spent a decade with the U.S. Marshals. During his time with the feds, he lost his son during a drive-by shooting in his D.C neighborhood. The once safe neighborhood had dissolved into chaos and Phil had not moved out in time. The Marshals Service would not investigate the crime, leaving it to the D.C. Metro police, citing jurisdictions and authorities. This had not set well with Phil, who began investigating on his own. Apparently, the Metro police were not too happy about that. Neither were the Marshals when the complaints began pouring in. Phil was told he had two options: Stop or be transferred to a less-than-ideal posting. He chose option three and quit on the spot.

Dane was not present during Phil's first mission, but he heard that Phil had located a suspected pedophile wanted on a warrant in South Carolina. Accused of multiple incidents, the man was off the grid, hiding along the loose border between West Virginia and Virginia. However, Phil had a lifetime of tracking those who did not want to be found, first with Regimental Reconnaissance Detachment of the Rangers and later as a Marshal. He found the small backwoods cabin easily and prepared to finalize the job. There was not a soul in sight that would bear witness. What Phil did not count on was the perp's mastiff running loose in the woods as an extremely effective security system. As much as it pained him to do it, Phil had to neutralize the animal before it tore him in half. Since the pedo's victims were all known, the club had no further use for him. There were no more loose ends. Turning him over to the authorities would have resulted in a light sentence, and the pedo would have been back on the street in no time. Phil simply had to dig a slightly larger hole to accommodate the target and his mastiff. The grave would never be found.

Jed Kent was recruited from none other than the New York Police Department. After a twenty-year career with Army Special Forces, he began a second career accumulating nearly ten years of experience with the NYPD. A friend of a friend had gotten Jed an age waiver and a status well above entry-level officers. Instead of working patrol as a rookie, his federal time with the Green Berets earned him a spot in the city's newly created multi-jurisdictional task force. The task force was meant to take a holistic approach to crime throughout the city. Jed worked the streets in tandem with other law enforcement agencies, utilizing unconventional techniques for tackling the city's overwhelming crime problem. He said he was happiest driving around in his hooptie with a trunk full of guns looking for trouble.

His life came crashing down when his teenage daughter went missing during a spring break trip to Jamaica. She had been staying in a luxury resort in Ocho Rios with a group of friends when she and another girl decided to explore some of the island's culture. The two girls were never seen again. Jed was devastated. He had cautioned the girls that the country has been embroiled in civil war throughout its history and that pockets of violence could erupt at any moment. He warned them to stay in large groups within the relative safety of the resort or with an official tour group, but they had not listened. Like Dane, his world collapsed. Alcoholism and suicidal thoughts plagued his life.

Jed rebounded with membership in The Cabal. He started his own protective security company, hiring quite a few disgruntled former cops looking for a career outside of law enforcement. He also rebuilt his crumbling marriage and defended that renewed love when his wife, Cindy, was smacked on the ass at a D.C. nightclub. Jed put the man through a window and into the hospital. That man happened to be a fed with the Department of Homeland Security.

Jed wasn't out of hot water yet, but due to all the witnesses and failure of the man to identify himself, Charles was confident the club's legal team on both sides of the bench would resolve the problem. Jed wasn't worried either. And he would have done it again, even if he knew the man was a federal officer. Everyone else on the team agreed.

Having a badge doesn't protect you from facing the consequences of your actions.

Fortunately, Dane had Sam on this mission with good glass on his rifle. He would clear paths and call out threats, but he couldn't do that while covering Dane's six. Dane needed a number two on the ground. With Phil and Jed out, Tony was it. He wasn't necessarily a bad guy; maybe Dane was being too harsh. Tony Carter was just young, immature, and impatient. His background was a little questionable, too.

He had served for six years in the Air Force as a special police officer. Once separated from the Air Force, he was hired by the Bureau of Alcohol, Tobacco, Firearms and Explosives. Tony had dreamed of becoming a member of one of the ATF's special tactical teams, but he was not chosen after his first audition at their selection course. That in itself was not uncommon. Quite often, as with most high-level selection courses, applicants made several attempts until they finally passed. Younger candidates in particular were often told to get more experience, sharpen their skills. And that was exactly what Tony had been doing.

Tony was preparing himself for the following year's selection course, but fate had other plans. His wife of eight years and his four-year-old son were killed in a robbery. They had stopped at a local convenience store on their way home from the mall, which at the time was occupied by a low-life strung out on drugs and trying to make a quick score. Several rounds, fired from a stolen handgun, changed Tony's life forever.

A broken man, he never tried out for the special teams again. He accepted this fate and the cubicle to which he was assigned in the main headquarters in downtown D.C. The club eventually found him and offered him the same redemption presented to its other members.

Tony was by no means an amateur, but tonight would require precision honed to a sharp edge by experience. Intelligence indicated that a shipment was on its way to the port this evening slated for immediate departure to the Middle East. The ship was fired up and ready to sail, simply awaiting this last-minute cargo delivery. It was that cargo the team was here for. In addition to weapons and explosives, the ship was to transport underage girls destined for the brothels of

Europe, Asia, and Africa. Sex slaves. Dane's blood boiled just thinking about it. He had lived here in Savannah once, beneath the Spanish moss of the southern oak trees. Was this going on under his nose when he was stationed here?

The Rangers of First Battalion of the Seventy-Fifth Ranger Regiment called Hunter Army Airfield home. It was a small base on the southern edge of the city housing the Rangers and elements of the elite Night Stalkers Aviation Brigade, along with general support units. The base was tiny and without the normal amenities found on larger installations. It had limited base housing, a clinic instead of a hospital, and no real training areas.

The Rangers had to travel to Fort Stewart for anything more robust than basic rifle marksmanship or static line jumps on a brutal tarmac that claimed the ankles of many Rangers, young and old. That was, of course, if you were fortunate enough to hit the runway. On several occasions, the Air Force seemed determined to kill the entire group or stick of jumpers by illuminating the green jump light a few seconds too early. That illumination indicated it was clear to jump, and sometimes the jumpmaster was just not paying close enough attention. Or maybe the jumpmaster was aware that they were not over the airfield yet, but trusted in the Air Force calculations that the wind speed and direction at twelve hundred feet would carry the jumpers safely to the airfield. Either way, the jumpers would miss landing on the base entirely. Abercorn Street was just outside the base with the typical row upon row of shopping centers. Those parking lots would be littered with Rangers and parachutes due to the early exit of the aircraft. Sometimes that was better than trying to dodge that strange radar dome in the middle of the airfield which, at times, seemed impossible to avoid.

Although many of the young soldiers lived in the barracks, the officers and senior noncommissioned officers were scattered throughout the oldest city in Georgia. The coastal town, hosting the largest port in the state, sprawled over one hundred square miles with a variety of neighborhoods. Some Rangers enjoyed living close to the river in the historic district, home to a vibrant nightlife along River Street. Others preferred the sleepy eastern neighborhoods that allowed quicker access to the ocean from the shores of Tybee Island. Wherever they chose to live, the rich and often-macabre history of Savannah permeated the entire city.

Since its inception in 1773 by General James Oglethorpe, there was something mysterious about Savannah. The transatlantic slave trade brought great prosperity to the city, but also murder, the supernatural, and hoodoo. Dane initially thought it was misspelled or mispronounced by some of the more eccentric locals, but he was mistaken. They meant hoodoo, not voodoo.

Centered on an elaborate belief system inherited from the African continent, hoodoo encompassed a deep spirituality, ghosts, and the conjuring of magical spells. Not a single tour of Savannah neglected this "casting of roots," as it was called sometimes.

The plan for the evening was simple and straightforward. The cargo ship was moored in a secluded section of the port. The pier was scattered with shipping containers and other storage units, providing excellent concealment for Dane and Tony. The van would travel through the port security checkpoint, at which point Sam would hone in on the interaction for entry. Through his scope, he could easily observe any bribery for passage. It was entirely possible that the guard could be lazy and neglect to inspect the vehicle. *Highly unlikely,* Dane thought. He doubted these traffickers would gamble their entire operation on the off chance that they would avoid inspection upon entering the port. They needed an inside man.

Sam would need to confirm culpability of the guard before any action could be taken. If guilty, no punishment would be visited upon the guard this evening. If necessary, though, they would pay a call to guard Billy Carter another time.

Dane realized that his frustration with Tony was not Tony's fault alone. When the President had discussed this mission with him and Sam a few weeks ago, both had been visibly frustrated.

"Wait, you are taking us off the Keeper case?"

"Mr. Cooper, the trail has gone cold. Forensic analysis of Mr. Simmons' computers has provided us nothing as to the Keeper's identity or whereabouts. We need more data."

"The trail will only go cold if we allow it to go cold," Sam offered.

"I am sorry, but in the meantime, the Benefactor would like us to investigate the shipment of young girls from the port of Savannah to the East African Coast."

"That should not be us!" Dane began to get angry. "I really don't care what this Benefactor wants. Tell him to give the evidence to the authorities. Savannah police. The FBI. Even Homeland Security! They are better equipped to handle these types of things."

"Mr. Cooper, the Benefactor is the reason this club exists in the first place. He provides funding and guidance. I oversee that guidance. As of now, the guidance is for one of our other members to conduct a deep analysis of the kidnappings similar to our cases from earlier this year. This woman has extensive research and analytical experience. She will pore through all the case files and hopefully provide us with new threads to pull."

"So, after this is done, are we back to working the Keeper cases again?" asked Sam.

"Gentlemen, I assure you that none of these cases will be forgotten. They are simply in the hands of others providing their expertise. I need your expertise in Savannah."

Dane and Tony hid among the sea of containers, ready to ambush the van. This was the third night straight they visited the yard in preparation for this mission. Rehearse. Rehearse. Rehearse. The latest intel suggested two men were in charge of the delivery—one armed driver and one guard. Once the van stopped, Dane and Tony would approach from both sides, leveling suppressed pistols at the two smugglers. Ideally, Dane intended to capture them alive. He and Tony each had thick zip ties and bandanas for cuffs and gags.

Once the two men were secure and thrown into the van, Dane would drive out of the area along the path that he and Tony entered on foot, to link up with another club member. This member was with law enforcement and would ensure the girls found their way to a shelter. Dane had even left the gate ajar for a quick exit.

With the girls safe, he, Tony, and Sam would have plenty of time to interrogate their prisoners before disposing of them in one of the numerous nearby swamps and visit Billy Carter, if necessary. The alligators would feast tonight.

Dane had boarded the ship the previous night to lay the foundation for contingencies. He had hidden a small explosive device in a critical location within the berth and another to disable the Automatic Identification System. Once the tanker was far enough into her journey on the open ocean, the devices would be activated, and the remaining traffickers would permanently reside along the ocean floor. Lastly, he left a small hatch near the stern of the ship ajar. Located several feet above the water line, it was a last-ditch option in the event the entire plan went to hell, and they needed to fight aboard the vessel.

In the event the traffickers in the van decided to resist, Dane hoped the silencers paired with the subsonic ammunition would be quiet enough among the metal jungle of the shipyard to avoid drawing unwanted attention. Hollywood had a knack for misrepresenting the sounds of suppressed weapons. In real life, the noise was much louder and would be amplified throughout the artificial echo chamber created by the shipping containers. The rifles they each carried were a last resort in the event of a catastrophic outcome. Dane hoped it didn't come to that.

He and Tony were in position when Sam called out on the radio to announce the start of the show. "Well, well. Van is here, and it looks like little Billy Carter just accepted a nice fat wad of cash."

"Roger. We will deal with him later. Shift eyes to us."

"Roger. Wilco. You are both clear. Van is less than one mike out."

Dane watched the van's headlights travel in a swooping arc as the vehicle made its final turn, heading parallel to the dock. Sam shifted his focus to the ship, looking for any signs that the crew was alerted to the activity below. The van slowed and rolled to a stop, perfectly poised for Dane and Tony to intercept. The operation was going as planned.

4

THE CHURCH

Washington, D.C.

The car idled quietly at the curb while Special Agent Roger Patterson waited patiently for his partner, Special Agent Patricia Stills. He didn't know what he dreaded most: The crime scene they were heading to or the possibility of some God-awful cup of coffee Pat was about to bring him. He had gotten the call about the murder at the worst possible moment and was unable to grab his normal brew of choice. He would have to settle for Patricia's concoction at this trendy coffee shop.

The pair were notorious for not agreeing on anything. They couldn't decide on restaurants, routes to take to crime scenes, or even the music playing in the car. Since Roger was the senior, he controlled the music and the driving. Classic rock and any route that avoided I-95 won out. The food was another story, normally ending with a bottle of Tums and quick stops at local police and fire stations for the bathroom. *That woman has a gut of steel.*

Roger had been attending a celebration of life for a childhood friend. He couldn't fathom why we as a society stopped calling these services funerals. *Do we have to change the entire English language to help assuage everyone's feelings?* Regardless of the moniker, the atmosphere was somber. His friend, Eric, had died from a heart attack. He was in his early sixties, ate healthily, didn't smoke, hardly drank, and walked several miles a day for exercise. Dead nonetheless. No warning signs. He went to bed one evening and never woke up.

Roger sighed after looking at his extended belly nearly reaching the steering wheel. *I need to do better. I could be next if I don't turn things around.*

His self-reflection was broken when Pat entered the car. She noted the frown on her partner's face when she placed the coffee in his cupholder.

"Don't worry. Nothing fu-fu with pumpkin spice. Straight black."

"Oh, thank God."

"You are so dramatic. It wouldn't hurt you to try different things, you know."

"I am fine with black coffee."

"Fine, be that way. I checked my phone. The freeway should be clear from here."

"Negative. I'll jump on 395 at the last minute when we have to cross the river."

Roger pulled away from the curb, merging into the morning traffic. There was no need for lights and sirens. The victim was already deceased, and the coroner was at least thirty minutes behind them, thanks to a nasty accident on Theodore Roosevelt Bridge.

Roger had no desire to attend this scene, and definitely didn't feel like rushing. Washington, D.C., was out of their jurisdiction, but the Metro Police had extended an invitation since the victim was part of their ongoing investigation. Reverend John Anderson of the Humane Hands' D.C. chapter had been murdered.

The case from the previous summer still remained with the Virginia Bureau of Investigation and the Pennsylvania State Police. The reverend and his church were at the heart of the investigation, both the beginning and the end. The new case began the moment Holly Jones and Jon Parker were discovered at the church in the early morning hours. Since that time, the case had gone nowhere. It had come to a full halt. No evidence. No witnesses. Not even a possible lead provided by a nearby camera. The person or persons who rescued and delivered those children were ghosts. He and Pat, of course, had to follow up on the possibility that the children had escaped captivity from a nearby residence. House-to-house and door-to-door checks in the surrounding area had turned up nothing. Not a single resident in the area had anything helpful to offer the investigation.

As that case went cold, the detectives were left with the reality that Carl Blanchard of the FBI may be right. Someone, or a group of people, had rescued those children. It was the only explanation for how those children found themselves in the church.

Roger struggled with this concept. As a newly badged detective decades ago, he would have insisted that the world had no place for vigilante justice. Society needed structure and rules to function. The law must be followed. Dedicated law enforcement officers and the courts were all that stood between a functioning society and anarchy. But the Roger of present, more seasoned, could no longer define the world in black and white. Social tensions were brimming. Violent crime was reaching record peaks while law enforcement budgets were cut. The honor that the badge once held was being tarnished by a few bad apples. Those bad apples needed to be tossed in the trash, not the whole bushel. Law enforcement should be held to a high level of accountability, but the criminals no longer were. Police were vilified in the press as much as possible while criminals were excused due to the unfairness of life and societal shortfalls. The whole Defund the Police movement caught like a brushfire. *Literally,* Roger thought, as he had watched American cities burn every evening on the nightly news. Society had changed.

He and Pat had conducted several interviews with Jon Parker and his family. The boy was obviously traumatized, and specialists in child psychology typically joined those meetings. However, little Jon would rarely offer any new insight into the case as he listened and answered the same repetitive questions, sequestered between his mother and grandmother and nervously petting his new puppy. The community had celebrated Jon's safe return with a pit bull puppy to replace his lost faithful companion, Shelly. Shelly, who had suffered fatal wounds, did everything possible to protect little Jon, but couldn't withstand the cruelty and ferociousness of the abductor.

Jon's recollections were sporadic and vague. He remembered cages. He remembered Holly. And he remembered the scary man, but not particular details. The asked about unusual markings. Roger had rolled up his sleeve at one point showing his forearm tattoo, asking if the man had any markings or paint markings. The boy marveled at the faded green pentagon with a small red rat at its center but shook his head. It was too dark for him to get a good look at his captor. Plus, he remembered sleeping a lot. This was not surprising due to the levels of fentanyl found in the little boy's bloodstream.

The Pennsylvania State Police faced the same dilemma. Holly was drugged as well. Additional details she mentioned offered little on the abductor's identity. A table with puzzle pieces, bins with toys, and the horse on the stairs. The last one had the investigators confounded. Toys and puzzles to occupy the children's minds made sense, but the horse on the stairs reference didn't fit into any conceivable scenario. Notes were shared and each team meticulously scoured the reports for any leads. However, there was nothing there. No crime scene. No evidence. And no suspect.

Roger and Stills maintained close tabs on the two cases, but without any new leads, they were obligated to place the case on the back burner while new events required their attention. Three separate jackets sat on Roger's desk. Three new cases. Three more lost souls.

The glaring lights and commotion in front of the church jarred Roger into the present.

"What a zoo, Roger. Looks like we can park over there," Patricia said, motioning to a roped-off area manned by a single officer.

Roger lowered his window as he presented his badge to the officer. "Special Agents Patterson and Stills."

"Just park here, sir, and you can enter the scene on the side of the rectory."

Roger eased the car to the curb. The pair made their way around the side of the church. The Humane Hands of D.C. structure was a historic site dominating the entire corner. Humane Hands was an enormous enterprise spanning the globe with churches, education centers, and outreach programs. The D.C. chapter was its official flagship. Its gothic architecture belonged on the narrow streets of European capitals more than in Southwest D.C. The rookie stuck at the access point recorded the special agents' presence in the crime scene log while handing them booties and gloves. He pulled open the massive oak door to afford

Roger and Pat access.

They entered a long, narrow vestibule that led into the nave just behind the altar. Monstrous organ pipes adorned the rear wall, draped in various tapestries woven among the brass. Candles behind the altar flickered and danced erratically, illuminating the dark church. All the windows were comprised of dark stained glass that allowed in very little light from the outside world. The feel of the room was still warm and inviting. The pulpit was a place of comfort, votive candle stations its hearth.

That mood was quickly extinguished several rows down among the pews along the western edge of the church. Harsh light stands pointed at the feet of the chatting officers. Roger and Pat headed in that direction.

The center of all the activity was the former Reverend John Anderson, lying on the floor between the pews. His body was covered in lacerations and blood. Around him spread a large pool of blood that crept along the church floor. The scene was an absolute nightmare. From an initial look, the reverend appeared to have suffered greatly.

"Special Agents Patterson and Stills?" A man broke from the group and removed a latex glove before shaking each of the agents' hands. "Detective Fletcher, District 6, 605th."

The special agents nodded in acknowledgement.

"Thank you for coming out," the man continued. "I figured since the reverend is part of your ongoing investigation, you should be present on the scene."

"We appreciate that," Roger replied. "What are your working theories?"

"Well, we found forceable entry on one of the lower windows on the back of the church. It leads into the kitchens. The suspect, or suspects—no ruling there yet—appeared to have moved throughout the church and systematically removed anything of value. The basement was used for meetings, so it is basically empty except for tables and chairs. It appears untouched."

"It appears the main level here was trashed," Stills commented.

"This and the second floor are the only locations for anything of value. You can see they pulled anything they could off the walls here. The second floor is more for administrative purposes. A few more classrooms, storage, and the reverend's office."

"I take it the third floor is the residence?" Roger asked, trying to remember the layout from when they were last at the church.

"Correct. We think the reverend heard some noise and came down to check it out. Hence the nightshirt and bare feet. He probably surprised the intruders."

"All those cuts look like a little more than a simple burglary," Pat commented, nodding toward the deceased holy man.

"We thought so at first. But then we found the looted storage room and the open safe. There was supposedly a large sum of money in there for all of the Humane Hands charities and outreach programs. Working theory is that Reverend Anderson was tortured for that safe combination."

"Why did they have large amounts of cash?" Pat asked.

"Let's just say some of the generous donors may not all be from respectable professions, yet still want to do good for the community."

"Criminals? Drug dealers?" asked Roger. "Are you kidding me?"

Fletcher slowly nodded. "There are several who have ties back to those communities. And we are not talking street dealers or gangbangers skidding around corners and shooting up neighborhoods. These are respectable high-class business criminals. Plenty of politicians, lawyers, and lobbyists with a penchant for snorting shit up their noses in this town. Business is good for a lot of these guys that think with their head instead of their hands."

The smirk was clear on the detective's face. "Some of these dealers are looked at like Robin Hood. Nobody around here cares if some politician or bigshot lawyer dies of an overdose as long as the community recreation center gets that new baseball field."

Roger and Pat thanked the detective and stepped away from the immediate area as the crime scene photographers finished. The medical examiner had arrived and was preparing his initial assessment before transporting the body back to the labs.

"I can see the robbery angle, Roger."

"On the surface, it fits and torture for a safe combination could explain the cuts. But it seems excessive. Need to get an idea of how much money we are talking about here."

"Of course. The reverend didn't want to give up the money, let the community down."

"That doesn't stick with me. As long as we have this swamp in D.C., there will be people searching for products. Something to go up their nose. Some to share with others to demonstrate power. I am sure the money is flowing in. Plus, if someone did steal from the church, who better to scour the underworld than the very criminals that filled the coffers? I am certain many of them would stop thinking with their heads and get guys for their hands."

"I see your point. If whoever did this knew about the money, they must have known where it came from. Pretty stupid to steal from that group."

"Exactly. This feels more personal. Something the reverend did not want to reveal. Something more than a combo."

Roger and Pat watched as the medical examiner's team processed the scene. Photographs and sketches were complete, capturing the moment for study. They examined the body from head to toe. Clothing was bagged. Samples from fingernails collected. All available fluid sample were extracted. The reverend's chest and abdomen lacerations, although painful, seemed superficial. When the team rolled the body, the cause of death and the source of the larger pool of blood became obvious.

Roger eased the car into the busy D.C. traffic toward the freeway that would take them south into Virginia and to the office.

"I still can't believe that hole Roger. Did he really say it could have been made by a narrow cutting tool or a drill?"

Roger nodded.

"A fucking drill? What the hell? I have never heard of anything like that. It is sick."

"I need to do some research when we get back, but I remember some stories from the eighties and nineties. Jamaican and some Russian gangs were known to use drills on their victims during interrogations.

They would bind them to a chair and drill holes in their hands, feet, or kneecaps."

"Well, in case you weren't paying attention back there, this wasn't hands or feet. That was a hole straight to the spine. I can't imagine the pain. How could someone do that? Who could have done this? Too extreme for a simple burglary. They rarely go beyond some milder violence if they interact with the home or business owner at all."

Concentrating on the road, Roger nodded. He wasn't ignoring Pat, but rather allowing his mind to process everything they had just learned.

I DON'T KNOW WHERE I AM. I DON'T KNOW WHAT TIME IT IS. THE LIGHTS COME ON IN MY ROOM WHEN I WAKE UP. THE LIGHTS GO OUT WHEN THE MAN TELLS ME TO SLEEP. I GET TO GO OUTSIDE EVERY DAY. THERE IS GRASS AND SWINGS. THE MAN SAYS IT IS GOOD FOR ME TO PLAY. HE CALLS IT RECESS, JUST LIKE IN SCHOOL. I CAN'T SEE ANYTHING OVER THE TALL FENCE. I WANT TO GO HOME. I WANT MY MOM AND DAD.

5

THE MEET

Arlington, Virginia

```
Keeper: Did you get any answers from the reverend?

Devotee: I did. A female. I will contact her next.

Keeper: Good. Let me know if you develop any additional leads.

Devotee: Okay. And then can I start collecting?
```

"Can I bring you anything else, gentlemen?"

"We are good. Thank you, Jack."

The two men sat before a roaring fire, each holding a glass of their preferred whiskey. Charles Thornton enjoyed his with a splash of water. Jackson Lentz preferred one large cube. Each man believed his method of adding water to the twenty-year-old single malt Scotch whiskey was the best to unlock the rich flavor.

They were enjoying robust Cuban cigars that lingered in the air before the smoke was extracted by the powerful filtration unit installed the previous summer. The system quietly summoned the smoke upward and out of the dwelling through a series of vents. Charles normally selected the rear veranda for his evening cigars, but a strong breeze and light layer of snow removed that option this evening. The fire provided the perfect setting for two old friends to catch up on one another's lives.

Jack turned to leave.

"Please stay. We have business to discuss, and your insights are critical due to the state of current events."

"Is this your attempt to gang up on me, Charles? Two against one?" asked Jackson, speaking for the first time.

Charles simply shook his head as he indicated to Jack to pull up a chair. Jack did so, but not before he returned to the bar. He poured himself two fingers of the single malt. *Neat,* he thought to himself, *the way it is meant to be drunk. If you needed water to improve the taste, then the distillery would have added more to the bottle.*

"I have not invited you here to create tension. And Jack's presence is necessary as my chief of operations, my number two, and quite frankly, my closest confidant. His operational roles have also vastly increased as we have expanded our efforts."

Jackson eased himself back into his chair. The slightest noticeable tension left his body. A small sip from his glass after a long pull from his cigar brought a smile to his face.

"But you do want to talk about the direction of the club? The Cabal, as you have become fond of calling it."

"I do." Charles answered. "As I have reported to you over the last several months, we believe to have uncovered a unique and disturbing truth."

"Yes. I understand completely. You think there is some sort of ringmaster of these kidnappings, and this sicko is mentoring others when it comes to abductions. If this turns out to be true, we will put our full resources against this person. You know we have the same intentions and always will."

"We don't just think. We know this man exists. Our operative uncovered this connection among these monsters during his last assignment. An assignment that, I may mention, resulted in the return of two children to their respective families."

"You mean Dane, right? I don't think we need to talk around names here at your home. I also don't think it is necessary at all. Our communications are quite secure. I think what that man did was nothing short of amazing. What all of you did. I know Jack here and Mr. Turner played a key role in—How do you spymasters say it?—

taking a player off the board."

"Close enough, Jackson. And you are correct that we are completely secure in this house. However, there may have been a compromise somewhere. We are still looking into the matter. I am sure you heard about the reverend from Humane Hands. He was not one of us, but that is where the children were placed. We need to ensure all of our members and communication channels are secure."

"First off, I heard on the news that the reverend was the victim of some sort of hate crime against the church. It was reported that the church was vandalized and he was brutally attacked. I don't see a solid connection to us. It is not located in the safest neighborhood to begin with. Secondly, Dane did an incredible job. Hats off to him and the others. But the computer drives he recovered erased themselves, including the link to this chat he witnessed. Correct? Some sort of malware code that was activated when Dane engaged with this Keeper in a chat session?"

"Well, yes, but—"

"But nothing, Charles. That lead is severed. The case is cold, unless there are some new developments that we have not yet discussed. When those developments come, they can rejoin the hunt for this Keeper."

"That particular lead is cold, so we need to focus our efforts on establishing another. We have quite a bit of information about the former Mr. Simmons. If we can find another member of his group, we can do some link analysis for possible patterns and connections. Plus, we have identified several other individuals that require our attention."

"Charles, I agree completely. However, I don't believe that it requires all your resources. There are some very powerful people that have highlighted just what is happening with the child sex trafficking trade. Right now, it is the bigger threat to our children. It is also a national security threat, since it is directly funding known terrorist organizations overseas. And these human smugglers have tried and tested routes that can be used for drugs, weapons, anything really. Imagine what else they could be smuggling in and out of this country."

Jack spoke for the very first time. "Sir, with all due respect, we have a limited number of people addressing these threats. It took three of us to catch Simmons and even then, we almost missed him. These are complicated operations that require precise planning and expertise."

"Gentlemen, I appreciate everything you are saying. And I want you to continue investigating this Keeper. But I also want you to address these smuggling rings. Savannah for now. Miami can wait."

"I don't have enough people. As Jack said, it took three of them to take down Simmons." Charles responded.

"Then make more of them. The threats are growing. We need to grow as well."

"Sir," Jack said, "it is not that simple. To remain in the shadows as well as we have for so long takes particularly cunning members. They are rare. They need to be ghosts. These are skills developed over a lifetime of work in the shadows. None of us were just trained and then set free on operations. We watched our mentors, we experienced operations, and we faced failures. All of these are acquired by practice and repetition."

Jackson appeared agitated. He rose from his chair and approached the bar. After a long pour into his rocks glass, he returned to his seat. He had made no offer to either man for a refill. He stared at Charles, willing him to speak.

The old spymaster sighed. "We have worked well together over the years. You provide the financial security of the club. I handle operational oversight. I am telling you operationally that we are stretched thin."

"And I am telling you to do both missions." Now Jackson was clearly frustrated. "You have good people in other roles. If you can't recruit more operative-minded professionals, then train the folks you have."

Charles sighed. "Easier said than done, old friend. Like Jack mentioned, we select people for their particular skills. Training one of my logisticians to be a shooter would be as practical a use of talent as using Dane to provide transportation needs for one of the finishers. I still think these trafficking organizations should be addressed by law enforcement. Maybe even the military. They have the manpower."

"Oh, they are going to get more involved. Tell Mr. Cooper to make sure he checks in at work after the Savannah job. There is a direct connection to the Horn of Africa. And France."

"France?"

"Yes." Jackson placed a thick binder on the end table. "Everything is in there. I would like to be present for the final briefing, finally meet Mr. Cooper in the flesh."

Charles slowly flipped through the binder. The intelligence seemed solid and accurate. The analysts that had put it together gave it a very favorable rating for accuracy. They were certain. Jackson obviously still had quite a long reach into the intelligence community to obtain this kind of information. "I appreciate this, I really do. But I didn't ask you for this, and I certainly cannot put my needs above those of others or the safety of my people."

"This benefits all parties. The fact that it may close a chapter in your life is simply an added bonus. You deserve to have justice as much as any other parent."

Jack sat in silence. Charles had handed him the folder, but he wasn't sure what exactly the two men were discussing as he read. He knew these two men guarded one another's secrets and that those secrets were the foundation of the club today. He had never asked Charles about his past. It was up to the man to entrust in him, and Jack was patient. When the time was right, Charles would confide in him, especially as this mission progressed.

"I need you to trust me," Jackson said. "I am not trying to wrest control of the club from you. I firmly believe in the scope and direction you have taken past operations. Let's see where events lead us. We both want the same thing. We just may have to divide and conquer."

With that, Jackson departed. Charles stared into the fireplace as if the flames would summon forth old memories. He appreciated Jackson's intentions, and he knew that the proposed operation wasn't solely about him. He was still hesitant. Law enforcement had ramped up their efforts against the club. They needed vigilance now more than ever. New operations brought increased scrutiny. He turned to Jack. "Sorry, lost in thought."

"Not an issue, sir."

"Let's table this current topic. Talk to me about the reverend."

"It was gruesome. The reverend suffered. Metro PD thinks it was a burglary gone wrong and that he was tortured for a safe combination."

"But you think otherwise?"

"I do, sir. And so do our friends with the Virginia Bureau of Investigation and the FBI. The torture does not add up. The little I can find about the reverend shows that he was actually a very pious man. People scoff at that due to the elegance of the church and his residence. But he did not indulge in any extravagance. His quarters were simple with a single bed, a desk and chair for his writings, and a small wardrobe for his clothes. Yes, the church was wealthy, but he did not spend any of that on himself. It stands to reason he would apply that same mentality with the church members."

"He catered solely to his flock?"

"Yes, and he knew what amount of money was in the safe. Although a large sum, he doesn't seem like the type of man that would resist at all costs to protect it."

"And if the church was that wealthy, they could always refill their coffers."

"Exactly. I believe the reverend would have been more concerned about vandalism that would delay or prevent church or humanitarian services. If criminals were demanding access to the safe before they left, it would appear that the faster he gave in, the sooner they would be gone."

"That makes sense, Jack."

"Also, the method of torture. The exact weapon has not yet been identified. The medical examiner on site noted wounds consistent with a small cutting tool. Possibly a drill."

"Did you say a drill?"

"Possibly a small drill, yes. I am hoping more information will emerge from the medical examiner's office over the next several days, but that is all we have for now."

"Have you heard of something like this before, outside of Hollywood movies?"

"There are obviously the rumors about the mafia back in the day, taking hammers and picks and even drills to the limbs of their competitors. And in the late eighties, the Jamaicans were known as ruthless torturers with swords, axes, and picks."

"You are certainly not suggesting some old gangster has come out of retirement to rob a church and torture a reverend, or a Jamaican drug lord is rising from the grave."

Jack smiled. "No, sir. There were other rumors before and during the Afghan war of certain instruments being used to interrogate terrorists."

"Torture conducted by our military, or our alphabet soup brothers and sisters?"

"Both, but definitely agency-led. Lots of stories about torture in villages throughout Afghanistan. Later, it was whispered that prisoners were taken to third party countries that provided even less oversight on *enhanced interrogation techniques*."

"And these techniques?"

"I never personally witnessed these interrogations, but I had mates who swore up and down that the agency issued small electric drills to their operators in the field. Small, compact, and easy to charge, they would use thin drill bits to bite into a suspect's skin. Running at a high rate of speed, incisions would be small, precise holes that could go straight into the bone. Running the drill at a slower speed would shred muscle and skin. All in all, a barbaric yet simplistic means to garner information."

"So, the reverend may have been killed by a former operative or soldier?"

"It is one possibility that we should not ignore as we build a profile of this guy."

"In light of recent events and the information provided by Jackson, my hands are forced in how we face these threats. You're the chief of operations, Jack. What are your plans?"

"It sounds like Dane is going to be busy for a little while with Uncle Sam. I just got word that Jed was cleared of those assault charges, so he is ready to get back to work. And Phil's leg is mostly healed. Tony is out for a bit, but Sam is good to go. I want to put Sam on the Keeper with Jed in support. Phil can handle a couple of our stings until he is one hundred percent, and then move to Sam's team. I will follow up on the reverend and check on the Scout. She is the only link we have to the church. She may be in danger. I will consolidate the team if necessary to protect members of the club. Sam can handle our loose ends, such as the hotel sting operations."

"I have tried to reach the Scout with no answer."

"Then I better get moving."

6

THE BUST

Savannah, Georgia

Dane prepared himself as the van stopped. His pistol was at the ready, and he was poised to leave his last position of cover to overwhelm the driver when he opened his door. Dane saw Tony out of the corner of his eye in a similar location on the opposite side. They were ready.

The van was large enough to have sliding panels on both sides, obviously designed as a delivery vehicle. The door on Tony's side opened first. His reaction was not as anticipated. Dane watched as Tony holstered his pistol and transitioned to rifle. The barrel spit fire before the sound of the shot caught up with Dane's ears.

Tony put four rounds into unseen targets. That was all Dane saw, since he had to engage his own enemy. The panel on his side opened a split second later than Tony's and he was faced with five assailants. Rather than transitioning, Dane engaged immediately with his pistol. Unlike Tony, Dane didn't have the element of surprise. The smugglers on his side came out firing and Dane was caught in the open since he had surged forward. There was no turning back for a better shooting position.

Dane's first shot caught one smuggler in the chest, the second finding its home in another's thigh. Dane's remaining rounds would have to wait. He sprinted across the open area and dove behind cover, bullets piercing the air around him. He couldn't risk inadvertently striking one of the hostages with a wildly inaccurate shot. He heard Sam over the radio calling out hostiles and casualties. As soon as he saw Tony engage, he had jumped into action.

"Shit, Eagle, whatcha got?"

They were fairly certain their communications were secure. However, they took the additional precaution of call signs, nonetheless. Badger for Dane, Eagle for Sam, and of course Tiger for Tony. Tony hadn't found it funny.

"Lots of hostiles, man. This is a hornet's nest. I count ten total from that van. Five on each side."

"Tiger?"

"He's down. He got one and then took a round in his thigh. I put two more down but then they pulled the girls out. Two of them moving toward the ship. I have no target. Repeat, no target."

"Roger. Are they clear of my line? Can I safely engage?"

Sam checked Dane's location with respect to the fleeing smugglers. "Hostages are at your nine o'clock. Clear to engage from the eleven to the two. I have no immediate shot on your hostiles. Will re-engage once I do. Transferring to the ship."

Dane holstered his pistol and drew up his rifle in one smooth motion, thanks to hours and hours of training. He retrieved a small grenade from his left utility pouch. Pulling the pin, he tossed the device around the corner. The flash bang ignited and completed three series of small explosions. Dane had selected the three-banger for this operation, knowing that if he needed them, then all hell had broken loose. He would need the distraction of the little device to regain the advantage.

Dane rounded the corner with the butt of his weapon firmly in his shoulder and his left hand gripped around the front of barrel, elbow pointing straight out to the side, vertical with his shoulder for maximum stability while he moved forward and engaged. He flicked his selector to fire and got to work. Sam's last words were about his engagement of hostiles on the ship. They were shooting at the van from the upper decks, ostensibly to provide cover for the remaining smugglers to usher the girls onboard. Sam systematically dropped them one by one with well-placed shots. Those still at the port were now Dane's responsibility.

The first smuggler received rounds to the chest, throat, and face as Dane sped toward the van. Unlike the movies, Special Operations warriors knew that automatic fire was for machine guns, preferably mounted on a tripod or vehicle. Although the function existed on the rifle he carried, it would be erratic fire, wasteful of precious ammunition on the smaller and lighter weapon platform, especially while moving.

Dane's brain was shifting to the next target while processing the last. Armor. That first shot to the chest hit armor. Adjusting his point of aim, Dane released several rounds into the thighs of the remaining men. He continued to sprint forward and reached the van as all three hit the ground. He gave them two apiece to the head and then finished off the injured man from the initial engagement. He knelt behind the van engine for maximum cover while changing mags and called Sam for an update. Shots from the ship onto the van had ceased.

"Eagle. Status."

"Shit, Badger. They got the girls inside. Ropes are being pulled. I am running out of targets."

"Roger. Tiger, you up?"

Tony's voice came through strained and ragged. "Here, boss. Took one in the thigh. Got a tourniquet on it though."

Dane raced around the van to where Tony had fallen. He was propped up against one of the shipping containers, wrapping an Ace bandage around the wound.

"Badger, you two had better hurry. Lights and sirens just lit up all over town, heading your way. Mine too. Another five mikes and I need to displace."

"Roger. Good copy," Dane replied. "Tony, grab my shoulder. Getting you out of here."

Dane dragged the man to his feet, and they shuffled over to the van. Dane pushed Tony into the driver's seat and gave him simple instructions. Get out of here fast. Link up with the Cop. Burn the van. Don' t do anything stupid. Tony grunted. Fortunately, his right leg was uninjured, and he began driving the vehicle toward the originally planned exit point.

"Tiger's clear."

"Move your ass. Ship is pulling away. I don't think you can reach that open hatch from earlier, but some piles of cargo are close to the pier at your one o'clock. You can make the jump onto the lower deck opening if you move now! Let's see if you really are as ferocious as a honey badger. Sprint—don't think."

Dane didn't even question the instructions from Sam. Shipping containers blocked the view of the ship's lower-level platform, but he would blindly follow that man anywhere and let him be his eyes. He erupted into a dead sprint and leapt upon the cargo Sam had identified. Without slowing momentum, his leg muscles exploded as he sprang from the dock, the ship a blur as it motored by.

Sam had been correct. As the lower deck opening appeared, Dane's momentum was enough to clear the open water. The timing was not perfect, but good enough. He missed the side of the ship and crashed onto the lower deck. As he caught his breath, Dane remembered a quote from his training days: *Perfect is the enemy of good.*

"Holy shit. That was some Hollywood movie shit. Done poorly by someone who obviously is not a stuntman, but damn. I wish I recorded it."

"Glad you got a laugh," Dane groaned. He slid behind some cargo to assess the situation. "All right, talk to me, Eagle."

"I think you're good, man. Nobody saw your Evel Knievel shit, but the police are not happy. I am moving. Will check in when in my next perch."

"Roger."

As Sam prepared to break down his sniper position, he scanned the area once more. The ship was almost under the bridge, which would soon block any view he had. He still had a clear view of the port and the guard post where the van initially entered. *Huh,* he thought. *There is that little son of a bitch, Billy.* Sam settled the crosshairs just above Billy's left ear and slowly depressed the trigger. He was rewarded with the spray of red mist through his scope, indicating that Billy was no more.

Upon inspection of his gear, Dane realized that his optic on the rifle had been smashed by his heroic leap of faith. The weapon itself would still function and the iron sights were zeroed, so not a total loss. In case other portions were damaged, Dane slung the weapon across his back, refreshed his pistol mag, and press-checked the slide. He carried more than enough pistol magazines for this fight. Dane was unfamiliar with fighting aboard ships but figured the pistol would be more manageable in tight corridors and spaces. *Where were the SEALs when you needed them?*

They had planned for this contingency. If there were too many gunmen, they would sneak aboard and wait until they were out to sea. After eliminating the smugglers, Dane and Tony would free the girls and rendezvous with Sam via a prepositioned cigarette boat capable of holding a lot of people. That contingency did not account for a firefight at the port and a possible run-and-gun along the Savannah River. Surely, by now, the Coast Guard was alerted and moving to intercept when the ship cleared the main thoroughfare of the city and they had room to operate. Or they might come directly up the river as fast as possible.

Either way, Dane's time was limited, He had to ensure the girls were safe, and that meant eliminating every hostile onboard lest they use the girls as human shields or remove any evidence of them completely. Dane took several deep breaths, forcing as much oxygen as possible to his brain.

The ship was large, but laid out in a simple pattern. Corridors ran the length on each side with periodic stairwells allowing for access to higher or lower decks. Dane's first instinct was to disable the ship and remove any guards around the girls. He would then clear floor by floor as he made his way topside. He much preferred fighting down a flight of steps. Retaining the high ground was a centuries-old tenet, but he had limited options. Up it was.

He found the engine room easily. Hallway signs were helpful. Two men were working the boilers, and Dane hesitated. *Could these be innocent ship hands with no knowledge of the smuggling? Doubtful, but . . .*

The sight of firearms secured to their sides confirmed his final judgement. They are hostiles. Dane shot them each in the head. Just as he was about to destroy the control panel, he stopped. *Damn it, you idiot. If they lose steering, the ship could crash into town. You can't disable the ship now. That will have to wait until open water or a more desolate area.*

Dane exited and moved up another floor to the ship's man interior hold. This would be the most logical place to imprison the girls. And that logic paid off. Two men sat at a small table smoking, their rifles propped against a wall behind them. The movement of the ship gave them a false sense of security. Two quick pops had both men on the floor. The girls were caged in the center of the room in a space equivalent to a police drunk tank. Cots were scattered about, and one small section was blocked off by a sheet. Probably the bathroom. The girls' reaction to the gunfight was minimal at best. They barely moved, obviously drugged. They were safest here anyway as Dane continued the hunt. He would leave them for now.

The next floor up was obviously living quarters. He doubted anyone would be in their room sleeping, considering what was happening. He moved quickly past. Two more rooms were at the end of the hall across from one another—the galley and the infirmary, according to the signs. Like shooting fish in a barrel. None of the men had time to even make a sound as bullets tore through their heads and throats. Those in the galley were grabbing snacks and water before moving out to their posts. Those in the infirmary were prone on small beds, bleeding onto the floor. Not a single one of them innocent. All died.

One more floor remained. Dane silently entered the bridge. *This should be the last three.* One manned the wheel. One scanned the area with binos. One screamed into the radio. Wheel and bino man were dead before anyone noticed he entered the room. However, radio man stiffened, his back to Dane. Dane noticed that the ship was steering out of control. It had passed the Talmadge Bridge and was chugging along River Street. He could not let the ship crash into the town.

"So, here is what we are going to do. You are going to drop that radio. Then, you are going to raise your hands above your head and turn around slowly."

"Allah Ak—"

The man couldn't finish his outburst as he swung the pistol toward Dane. A single round penetrated the smuggler's forehead, and he dropped immediately to the floor. The film industry often exaggerated people being shot and the force throwing them across the room. Not accurate in real gunfights. Dane's 9mm round passed cleanly through the brain and literally turned off all of the man's bodily functions, including his leg muscles. The result was the body collapsing like a machine that had been turned off.

Shit, he thought. *I need to stop this boat.*

"THIS IS THE UNITED STATES COAST GUARD. YOU ARE ORDERED TO IMMEDIATELY GO TO FULL STOP. PREPARE FOR BOARDING."

"Eagle, you got me? What is going on out there?"

"Yeah, man. Coasties got here fast. In case you can't see them, they are on your port side. That's your left."

"I know what port is, jackass. Guess I am going over the other side."

"I don't know, man. That current is bad. Lots of folks have been killed."

"Well, either that or I stay and get arrested by the Coast Guard. I would die of embarrassment. But I need to stop this boat first. Any advice?"

"You should see a throttle at the helm. Near where a person would steer. Big wheel. Straighten it. There should be some sort of joystick or set of levers close by. Pull them all the way back for full stop. Boat that large will still take a hot minute to slow but hopefully it will clear the town."

"Thanks. Done. Going for a swim."

"Good luck."

THE MAN IS MAKING ME GO TO SCHOOL. I HAVE A SMALL DESK. THERE IS A TV THAT PLAYS CLASSES. THE TV SHOWS ME THINGS AND PROBLEMS FOR ME TO DO. I HAVE PAPER AND PENCILS. I WANT TO GO BACK TO REAL SCHOOL. I WANT MY MOM AND DAD. THE MAN LETS ME USE MY OWN BATHROOM. HE TELLS ME TO SHOWER ONCE A DAY. HE GIVES ME TOWELS AND NEW CLOTHES. THERE IS A BUCKET IN MY ROOM FOR EMERGENCIES. THE MAN TOLD ME TO YELL OUT IF I NEED TO GO TO THE BATHROOM. HE WILL OPEN THE DOOR FOR ME.

7

THE TASK FORCE

Washington, D.C.

Devotee: I paid the female a visit.

Keeper: Did you get any answers?

Devotee: I did. I have another one to visit. This is more complicated that it originally appeared.

Keeper: Stay vigilant. Contact me at the slightest hint of an emergency.

Carl had spun his chair away from his desk to enjoy a brief view of the city while finishing his morning coffee. He had already worked through his morning emails, sorting the mundane from the meaningful. He had to meet with the deputy director at one, so his entire morning was free.

Ken, his assistant, was in the archives retrieving the last of some records they planned on reviewing. There had been several suspicious events since last summer, which led him to believe this vigilante group was not laying low after their spectacular win with the two children.

The details of the rescue of Holly Jones and Jon Parker were nonexistent. The means by which they arrived at Humane Hands completely unknown. Their return was being credited as some sort of miracle. But Carl and his team knew better. Several more pedophiles had been quickly removed from society. Carl knew in his gut the group was still active. Neighbors by day, killers at night.

Carl couldn't understand how they had not slipped up thus far. *Could they be growing?* Carl silently hoped they were. Not because he approved of their actions, but because more people meant more mistakes. More evidence. More clues. More links.

Sam Turner was a complete bust. They had apprehended him in connection with the death of Arthur Camp. Camp was found dead in Fort Hunt Park, the result of an apparent suicide. The scene was suspicious from the start. Camp, a convicted felon and registered sex offender, had somehow been hired as an elementary school janitor. His death sparked an investigation into his background, revealing sordid details of his activities at the school. A second janitor was wanted for questioning, but he was nowhere to be found. With his fingerprints found at the school, Carl was certain Sam Turner was their man. Planted at that school to determine Arthur Camp's guilt and then mete out punishment.

The Virginia DA refused to bring any charges after a plausible explanation for the prints and had ordered his immediate release not one second before Holly and Jon were found. Quite possibly the strongest alibi in the land. Sam Turner had been in police custody when the children arrived at the Washington D.C. church. Airtight alibi. That is, of course, unless he had a partner or partners acting on his behalf.

Keep your smirk, Mr. Turner. We are not done with you yet.

The Virginia AG became involved. She had no jurisdiction over the FBI, but she was still a powerful player in D.C. She did not appreciate the FBI "witch hunt" into one of her more "connected" constituents.

Sam Turner had provided protection at one point or another for anybody that mattered in Northern Virginia. Hence the lunch with the deputy director regarding an inquiry from the Office of Professional Responsibility. Complete bullshit. Carl knew nothing would come of the complaint against him. It just annoyed him that he had to listen to these whiney political appointees.

Ken interrupted his thoughts as he entered the room, placing the last of the boxes upon the conference table. "I think that's everything, sir."

Carl turned his chair back to its traditional position and joined Ken at the table. The thought wall adjacent to them continued to grow. It was still covered with his theories and assumptions under the Art column, while only confirmed facts made it to the Science section.

Sam Turner and Dane Cooper were still listed under Art, but Carl knew deep in his gut they belonged under Science. With Turner clear of any direct connection with the return of Jon and Holly, Carl became more interested in Mr. Dane Cooper.

His whereabouts were unknown that day and throughout the night when the children were rescued. A quick check with the landlord had confirmed that the basement apartment had been dark all evening. He also confirmed that Dane's motorcycle, normally parked at the rear of the house under a tarp, had also been absent for a few days. The landlord was doing a lot of yardwork that week and noticed its return three days later with damage to the right side of the fuel tank. It appeared that Mr. Cooper may have had an accident. No reports could be found in a hundred-mile radius concerning any crash involving him. Mr. Cooper may not have reported it. Certainly, he would want to make an insurance claim.

Several boxes were neatly arranged along the table. Ken had done some brilliant research. The first box contained files on the other possible candidates stalking pedophiles and meting out street justice. Ken had prepared them last summer, which brought Turner, Cooper, and former police officer John Ferguson to the limelight. Carl had Ferguson surveilled by an old friend down in Fredericksburg on the day in question. The retired agent confirmed that Ferguson was clean. Turner was in custody. That left Cooper and the seven other possible suspects in Ken's files.

The second box was labeled Anomalies. This category was large and spilled over to a second box. There were quite a few anomalies. These were unsolved cases or cases where a ruling was made against the advice of the lead investigators. The rulings mostly included suicides or unusual accidental or natural deaths. That was where Carl was going to find his killers. One or more of them had to be guilty. He needed to tie just one of them to an anomaly and the case would crack wide open. Carl paused and stared at the board.

"What is it, boss?"

"We cleared Ferguson because we had people watching him."

"Correct."

"What if those two kids were not his case?"

"Not tracking what you mean by his case."

Carl stepped over to the board where he had some space and drew ten tiny boxes, all aligned vertically. He wrote one to ten in the boxes.

"These represent our suspects."

Ken nodded.

To the right of the boxes Carl drew about forty or fifty small random circles in a cluster.

"These are our anomalies. We have been looking at suspects on a case-by-case basis. Maybe Turner and Ferguson were on different cases. Maybe Cooper was working the one with whoever is file number eight, for example. Maybe Ferguson was the janitor in that school. Maybe Turner whacked the sicko in Fort Hunt Park."

"You think we are being too narrow and singular in our approach? This team could be bigger than we thought."

"Exactly." Carl snapped his fingers. "We need to cross-reference our ten suspects against a batch of our best anomalies. How many do you think is manageable?"

"I would say ten to start. More if we got help, but this is going to be a full-time analytical gig. Lots of manpower. Lots of PED—processing, evaluating, and disseminating. Where are we going to find that kind of help?"

"I have an idea," Carl said as he returned to his desk. "Start looking through the anomalies. Pick the best twenty-five." He picked up the phone and rang his secretary out in the front office. "Can you get me Rich Jenner over at the academy down at Quantico?"

"Right away, Mr. Blanchard." Carl replaced the receiver and stared at his board. A minute later, the phone rang.

"Blanchard."

"Kinda gruff to be answering your phone like that, since you more than likely reached out to ask a favor."

"Sorry, Rich. Lost in thought. Question for you: Do you still teach that intel analysis course over there? The advanced one for senior analysts?"

"Yup. A few weeks into the course right now."

"You still have them do a capstone project on real crimes?"

"They get their assignment midway through the course. In about a week. Why?"

Carl could hear the suspicion in his old friend's voice. "How many students?"

"Twenty-six."

Carl held his hand over the receiver. "Ken, pick out one more anomaly!"

"What are you up to, Carl?" Rich asked.

"I need manpower. I have a hot case, and I need advanced analysis on twenty-six cases cross-referenced against ten suspects."

"Oh wow. Exactly twenty-six? How convenient that it matches my number of students."

"All right, I had twenty-five. You caught me."

"It's that important?"

"Do you remember the two children recovered at Humane Hands last summer?"

"I do."

"It's that important."

"Okay, okay. Send me the files."

The TV along the wall caught his attention. "Thanks, Rich. I have to go." Without taking his eyes off the screen, Carl dialed the number from memory.

Roger sat at his desk in the Pit and stared at the dry-erase board. Everyone thought that the nickname for the VBI's Violent Crimes section must be some sort of creative acronym, but it was simply short for the Pit of Misery. The department dealt with crime throughout the state. Violent Crimes landed the worst ones. Its agents were exposed to degradations of the human race that most people could not even fathom, nor should they.

After leaving the church, Roger dropped Pat back at her place. She had a late-morning appointment, after which she would join him in the office. Roger saw no reason to return to the funeral he had left earlier.

He could not shake the church scene out of his head, his mind running multiple scenarios and trying to sort out every possibility.

The most logical was the initial Metro Police theory. Robbery turned to torture and murder. People have certainly killed for less. But the level of cruelty suggested only two feasible options to him. The killer knew the reverend and unleashed all the rage and fury he could muster. Or it was a complete stranger, a stranger who is a complete psychopath with absolutely no respect for human life. Both scenarios kept agents like Roger up at night.

He and Pat had two other open abduction cases, not to mention the cold case concerning Angela Cooper's whereabouts and the murder of Dana Chase at Jones Point. And although they primarily handled crimes against children, they assisted the entire section with their overwhelming caseloads. He and Pat had to close out the morgue report next week on some hiker that fell to his death. Some moron dentist was probably trying to prove how tough he was by climbing one of the most dangerous mountains in the state.

The phone rang with an all-too-familiar number. "Good morning, Carl. What can I do for you?"

"Hey, Roger. I didn't know if I would get you. The reverend thing is all over the news. Figured you two would still be there."

"We were. Just got back. D.C. is going to work the scene. We are going to assist, and they will be an open book to help our investigation."

"Sounds like red tape. Wanna cut it?"

"How so?"

"I have the green light from the higher-ups to create a task force. The return of those children this summer convinced the seventh floor that there is a real issue here. This death of the reverend is going to accelerate that timeline."

"I don't follow. Metro's working theory is robbery gone wrong."

"Don't tell me you believe that bullshit. The reverend was tortured for more than drug money."

Roger was slightly surprised. "How did you know about that?"

"Money laundering. Our section down here knows about the donations to Humane Hands from the local gangs. Many think it is not technically illegal since the dealers are not receiving compensation from the church. We could try to put together a RICO and state illegal gains go to the church and then the church invests in community service, but why bother? The money from some rich asshole politician or CEO is going for something good instead of the gangs buying more guns and bullets."

"Don't try to sell me on that moral balance bullshit, Carl. You can positively track that money, which helps your boys discreetly monitor the entire financial network to include not only the dealers, but their wealthy clients in the District."

"Guilty. And that is why I want you and Pat as consultants to the task force. I am bringing in Homeland, NSA, a few other alphabet agencies that have some law enforcement authorities, and the U.S. Marshals. They are good at tracking."

"First off, Capt. Ivers would shit. Our workload here is insurmountable."

"He will be getting a call from the deputy director of operations asking for a slice of your time."

Roger shook his head. "Secondly, I don't see the connection with the reverend and this mysterious club you are hunting. The Turner arrest put egg on everyone's faces, mostly ours. The AG is pissed."

"I know. I have an engagement later over the incident. I will smooth it over and take the blame."

"It *was* your idea! We have been throwing you under the bus as much as humanly possible."

Carl laughed. "Fair enough. But that is why I want you as consultants. The task force will be doing the heavy lifting and analytical support. I want you guys to check our math. Plus, we would want full access to all your ongoing abduction investigations."

"I would have just given those to you if you would have asked. No need to call my boss on me." It was Roger who got a laugh this time.

"It's a win-win. If I am right, you and your team are working parallel efforts with this club. It is inevitable that your paths will eventually cross. That's where the task force will step in."

"Sounds like I don't have a choice. Do the work and let you swoop in to take the glory."

"You don't. I am heading down to Savannah this afternoon. I will hit you up when I get back, and we can talk further details."

"Savannah? You mean that drug shootout at the port. It's been all over the news. Is this new task force going to branch out now?"

"Don't believe everything you read on the news. We got dead Somalis all over that port and ten underage girls recovered. And here is the kicker: Not a single law enforcement entity knew anything about this smuggling ring."

"Carl, I am really starting to regret the day I met you."

"You're welcome, Roger."

I SAY THE PLEDGE OF ALLEGIANCE EVERY MORNING. THE TV THEN PLAYS THE NATIONAL ANTHEM. THE MAN SAYS IT IS IMPORTANT. THERE WAS A NEW TIRE SWING OUTSIDE TODAY. IT IS TIED TO THE ONE TREE WHERE I PLAY RECESS. I WANT TO PLAY IN MY YARD. I WANT TO GO HOME. THE BATHROOM WAS DIFFERENT TODAY. THE FLOOR WAS WET, AND THE MIRROR WAS STEAMY. I THINK SOMEONE ELSE USES THE BATHROOM. NOT JUST ME. MAYBE I WILL GET TO MEET THE OTHER PERSON. I MISS MY FRIENDS. PLEASE COME GET ME, MOM AND DAD. I WANT TO GO HOME.

8

THE UNIT

Washington, D.C.

Dane jolted awake. He sat up quickly, heart racing and covered in sweat. The dream felt so real. Felt like he was back in that hellhole of a country. War had broken out overnight and the country had been waking to a new normal. Soldiers were everywhere but not with the intent to protect the citizens; they would rather rape, maim, and kill any perceived enemies of the new military regime.

That checkpoint on the way to the embassy came out of nowhere. Baby-faced soldiers with AKs pointing everywhere. Dane had been fortunate, rolling through the city in an armored Toyota Hilux. The soldiers' rounds could not reach him. His fellow commuters were not as fortunate. He had pushed his way through the obstacles, past the riddled bodies that had received the wrath of the mutinous soldiers.

Dane shook his head. It had been a while since nightmares had invaded his dreams. He stood quickly and immediately regretted that decision.

His swim the other evening in the Savannah River had been brutal. He had secured all his equipment to his body as quickly as possible before leaping into the river. It was easier to avoid the Coasties than he thought, but that was not due to his physical prowess. The current snatched him up, tumbling him over and over. He was swept past the Coast Guard cutter before they even noticed a man overboard. The police copter that arrived on station focused its powerful light on the container ship, not the water. Dane was free and clear—once he survived the dangerous waters.

The struggle to swim to the northern shore had been brutal. All of his energy was depleted, not to mention he was barely recovered from the broken arm several months ago. If not for Sam's quick reaction and ability to find him among the marshes, Dane never would have left the river.

The aching pain from his head to his feet reminded him of his brush with death as he made his way to the bathroom. The weather was less-than-ideal, which would make a motorcycle ride to work miserable. He was more than happy to walk. Dane was not sure he had the strength to handle the bike anyway. *Damn, that mission had been a close one. Even closer for Tony after taking a round in the thigh.*

He had no doubt that Tony's wound had already been properly addressed. The damn club seemed to have an answer for every problem. Except, of course, Angela. He needed to speak with Charles soon about picking up this Keeper's trail. Dane was convinced that he was the key to Angela, maybe Sam's daughter Rachel as well. They had also agreed on the ride home from Savannah to speak with Jack as well. He seemed to be more sympathetic and would be a valuable aid in pleading their case. The disruption of trafficking young girls was beyond important, but that was work that could be done by others.

He and Sam needed to find their little girls. Dane's mind began to wander as he walked along Independence Avenue and across the Anacostia River. He saw a softball game. He watched a school concert. He took another trip in his mind to the beach. A trip to visit Angela. To watch her grow and learn and explore the world. To watch her live.

The gloomy weather fed him. Dane could feel the fire building inside him: the rage begging for release. Dr. Webster felt that rage. The Somalis at the port had a taste. It was the Keeper's turn. But first, Dane planned on hitting the gym. No matter how sore he was, hitting the bag would soothe that rage. For now.

"What's up, Dane?" Tyler said while extending his hand.

Dane stood up from behind his desk in the Operations shop. "How you been, Ty?"

"Good, good. Just got back from some training. Went down to Benning for some long rifle work. Army Marksmanship Unit gave me a little tune-up. Some of those guys are phenomenal shots."

"Not surprised. What's up next?"

"I am heading up to the Pentagon. Briefing on the Russians and the current situation on the Wagner Group."

"Russian contract company. Didn't their boss die in a plane crash?"

"That's right, *plane crash*. If you get on the Russians' bad side, stay away from airplanes and open windows on higher floors of buildings."

Both men had a good laugh. Command Sergeant Major Reynolds stuck his head out of his office. "Coop, you got a sec?"

Tyler and Dane shook hands before Dane made his way across the room. "What's up, boss?" Dane said as he entered that office. He shut the door upon Reynolds' head nod. "Not tracking that I am in trouble or have fucked up lately, CSM."

"I am certain there are several fuckups that you have kept hidden from me. I hope this isn't one of them. I got a call from some Special Agent Blanchard over at the bureau. He was asking about your whereabouts the last several days."

"Yeah, guy is an asshole."

Reynolds was surprised. "You know him?"

"He was at one of my meetings with the Virginia investigators. Real condescending prick. I told him off."

"Why is he asking about you? Of course, I told him nothing, but it does give me pause when the FBI asks about one of my guys when it is not work-related."

Dane shrugged. "No idea."

Reynolds stared at him as if trying to read his thoughts. Dane knew that nothing in Savannah could be pinned to him if that was what Blanchard was seeking. The FBI probably combed through transportation records for Dane's travel to Savannah around the time of the incident. Thankfully, one of the club perks is the access to private transportation. Private jet to be exact, just like the New York job. But unlike New York, he had a target location in Savannah. Knowing that meant less time necessary on the ground. The jet was practically an Uber flying them back and forth.

"Not sure what you want me to say. I'm pretty sure we have seen each other daily here at the office all week."

"That is what's puzzling. Let's leave it for now."

"Anything else?"

"Yeah. Your number popped on the promotion list. You pin next month."

"Sergeant major? How the hell did that happen? I haven't been to the academy yet."

"New waiver policy for us. We just have to send you to the school in Tampa when you are able. We can determine an appropriate time later."

Dane stood up to leave. "Cool. Let's push as far out as possible."

"I'm not done. I need you in the conference room at fifteen hundred for an operational intel brief."

"Okay. Can you give me the five Ws?"

"Collection operation. Quick start. In country in forty-five days tops, hopefully less, then out."

"Where?"

"Hargeisa, Somalia."

Dane was surprised. "Wow. Okay. Who?"

"You. This is the second chance you were hoping for."

Later that day, Dane found himself seated at the large oval table in the operation section conference suite. The room was where operations and intelligence fused together for taskings and missions. The commander, Col. Joseph Alexander, sat at the head of the table. To his right was his S3 or operations officer. To his left, CSM Reynolds. The remaining chairs were filled with senior staff who were active participants for the briefing. Dane was seated next to Reynolds.

As per military protocol, the closer the proximity to the commander, the more senior your status. *Well, since this briefing is about my mission, I should be sitting at the head of the table,* Dane thought jokingly. He was still awestruck that the unit selected him for this mission. He also was overwhelmed with thoughts of his real work. *I can't believe I got pulled for a mission. I need to stay focused on the hunt.*

All eyes were clued to the far wall, the entirety of which was covered by a huge monitor. It was the kind of screen football fans would kill for. The S2, or intelligence officer, briefed off a large map display of

Somaliland, focused on the port city of Berbera. The officer explained that Berbera was the capital of the Sahil region of Somaliland, one of six administrative regions. Its importance was that it was the country's main seaport. Berbera Port had undergone major improvements over the past thirty years. Several countries and private companies invested in the port with the intent of establishing it as a regional hub. Even the Russians and the United States upgraded facilities to accommodate their navies. In 2020, Abadi International, out of Qatar, signed a multimillion-dollar agreement to operate a regional trade and logistics hub at the port. Hargeisa may be the country's capital, but Berbera was its link to the outside world.

The man continued. He explained that although the port had been modernized throughout its existence throughout the centuries, elements of illicit activities like smuggling remained. "The Somaliland government appears to turn a blind eye, which is no surprise due to the amount of money Abadi pours into their coffers. The general consensus in the intelligence community is that everything from drugs to weapons to chemicals and bioproducts are flowing through the port."

Col. Alexander addressed the briefer. "Let's move to the imagery, Tom. I want to give Dane some specific details. He can get more nuanced intel tomorrow up at NSA."

"Okay, sir. Next slide," the S2 requested of the presenter at the desk controlling the slides. "This is the port. Decent size, especially for a third world country with a limited economy. They do get quite a bit of business from Ethiopia, which helps. Not a lot of other African countries use the port. Puntland to the east uses Bossaso, and obviously, southern Somalia uses Mogadishu. However, what the others don't have that makes Berbera unique is the slaughterhouses and its close proximity to the Arabian Peninsula."

"That is on the east end of town, right?" Dane asked.

"Correct. They have animal quarantine pens. They have veterinarians, and they have a shorter distance to travel across the Gulf of Aden to Aden itself, making meat preservation easier and more cost-effective."

"I remember visiting the area when I was there." Dane said. "Herders would travel from the interior with their flocks, lock them up for the required quarantine time once the vet cleared them, and then right over to the factory for slaughter."

"Correct, and since they have limited cooling capabilities, they rely on salt and speed across the gulf to prevent spoilage."

"Area smelled awful. One time was enough for me."

"Second time's a charm, Dane," said Col. Alexander. "We need eyes and ears on that port and in that factory."

"What am I looking for?"

It was Tom who answered. "Bioweapons. We have fairly good intel that Abadi is heavily backed by China. And the PRC is interested in biowarfare. Infectious disease-type stuff. Some of the nastiest diseases have come from the African continent. We believe Chinese scientists are smuggling live samples out through Berbera to Aden. They know the Chinese port in Djibouti is being watched, but not Berbera. Stuff crosses on Somali boats, is off-loaded on Yemeni territory, and then picked up by the Chinese when they travel through Aden."

"They learned their lessons from Covid, then," Dane stated. "Obscure all transactions. It's the old deny, deny, deny, and blame others."

Tom nodded. "Next slide. This is one of the warehouses where we believe samples are being hidden in various cuts of meat. The viruses don't come in every day, nor do they stay long. They are packed and shipped immediately. NSA has a method for identifying when the shipments are coming through. Normally, they come in the late afternoon, early evening. The animals are slaughtered in the morning, dried, and then packed in the evening when it is cooler. Somali dhows leave just before the sun comes up."

"Can't their National Intelligence Agency handle this? Work with the police force. Much more efficient."

"We wish that were the case. However, we believe the government is complacent. We also have intel that they are smuggling support to the Houthis."

"Wait. You want me to go back there, re-establish my contacts to gain access to the port, and then double-cross them? I will have the entire Isaaq clan after me, not to mention the sub-clans."

It was Col. Alexander that spoke up. "Actually, that is not what we have in mind. When the government reorganized years ago, all of the old elites were purged. The new government had to make a showing of stamping out corruption to maintain the support of the people. It is highly doubtful any of your government contacts are still active. And, as of late, our country is not on great speaking terms with Somaliland."

"Is it because of the new Federal Government of Somalia trying to bring everyone together?"

"Correct," Tom answered. "Somaliland is not happy with the terms. They want to remain independent. The U.S. supports the new government. Relations are not good right now."

Col. Alexander continued. "You will be heading to the embassy in Djibouti. One of our guys has a reliable contact that will smuggle you and an NSA operative across the border."

"Why do I have a tag-along?"

"Two reasons. First is detection of bioagents. The NSA operative will be using some tech along the major routes into the city that will alert when certain biohazards are present. Secondly, we need samples, and I hardly think you are the best prepared person to handle the safe extraction of say, Ebola."

"Hmm, you have my attention. How soon 'til we leave?"

"Gonna need you in Djibouti in no less than four weeks."

Once the meeting concluded, Dane exited the building and headed across the quad to a separate warehouse. He hid his expressions well during the briefing, but he was not happy about leaving. Now that the Savannah job was done, Charles had promised they could dedicate more resources toward the Keeper.

Dane slammed the door as he entered the barn. He would definitely need to hit the gym tonight before going home. He climbed the second story and moved down the last row of cages. He couldn't remember why this was called the barn, since the two structures had no real similarities. No stalls. No tack rooms. Just floor-to-ceiling cages, divided in separate storage areas covering most of the usable surfaces, minus the narrow hallways. The barn was anything but.

Dane's seniority afforded him one of the larger corner units for his gear. Each operative was given a cage to store all their gear, minus weapons. Those went in the armory.

Dane opened his cage and secured the door with a bungee. There was nothing more annoying than having the cage door bang against you when you were going through your gear. Dane was startled when he looked up to see Tyler was standing in front of him.

"Boo."

"Goddamn ninja. You nearly gave me a heart attack."

"Damn. Sorry. I forgot about your advanced age."

Dane extended his middle finger. "I am only five years older than you, asshole."

Tyler laughed. "Been a rough five years from the looks of things."

"Are you finished? I got shit to do."

"Man, why are you in such a foul mood? Promotion. Mission. I figured you would be on cloud nine, brother."

"No, things are good. Just have some stuff going on."

"Are you sure? I have known you a long time. I saw you at your lowest, then watched you climb your way out. But now . . ."

"You think I am falling back into the abyss? Listen, every day is a struggle over Angela. I have good days and bad days. This happens to be a bad one."

"It's not that Dane. Don't try to bullshit a bullshitter."

"Then tell me, oh oracle, what does thou see?"

Tyler chuckled at his friend's attempt to lighten the conversation. He remained serious, but softened his tone. "Listen, man, I am just worried. Before, well, before you were broken. Angry, but defeated, like you were attacking yourself. Blaming yourself, which I can understand. You harnessed all that guilt, and you almost didn't come back."

"Well, I did, buddy. I came back. And like you said: Promotion. New mission. Things are looking up."

"That is a mask. You came back different. Darker. Like, you still harness that guilt, but instead of beating yourself up, you are containing it. Keeping it from getting out. I can see the rage, man. I know you."

Dane allowed the tension that had been building in his body to dissipate. "Look, Ty, I appreciate everything. Everything you have done for me. I promise you that I am good. Just working through some personal issues. I will hit the bags later and work off some stress."

"Okay, man. Just know I am here." Tyler turned to leave. "Maybe instead of the bags you need to find yourself a lady."

Later that evening, Dane pulled into the familiar driveway in Manassas. After Tyler left, he had spent the remainder of the day inventorying his gear. He would only need to request a few items for this new mission. But he pushed work from his mind, as he always did when he was with his family. It was something he found helpful over the years.

Separating work from his home life created a natural boundary, denying the stress from one crossing over and negatively affecting the other. And although John was the only family he had left, he would keep that practice. However, boundaries were becoming blurred concerning his third life. His frustrations with the lack of progress on the Keeper invaded his every thought. And although illogical and improbable, his mind somehow equated the finding of the monster with the return of Angela.

His thoughts were intercepted by the opening of the truck door.

"Hey, Dad! Am I driving?"

"Sure, buddy." Dane exchanged places with his son, amazed that the little boy he once knew was the young man beside him. Amazing how time flies.

"Where to?"

"It's nice out. I thought we could head over to Old Town. Hit the marina, grab a bite to eat, maybe hit the bars before heading back to my place. Couple of beers sound good?"

"Funny. I'm only sixteen."

"I know. I meant me, since I have my own personal designated driver." Dane chuckled.

The drive was short and fairly uneventful. Dane only had to caution John on his speed a few times and remind him to quickly check over his shoulder to ensure no vehicles were there when he changed lanes. However, his new driver parenting skills were put to the test during parallel parking on the crowded streets. John eyed a spot by Founders Park that he insisted could fit the truck. Dane knew otherwise, but

John inherited his stubbornness from his father.

He let his son spend ten minutes angling as best as he could before they gave up and found a parking garage. Dane smirked. *Well, it wasn't very sportsmanlike giving him this beast of a truck to practice with.*

They grabbed a couple of shrimp po boys at Vola's Dockside Grill and snagged a table outside.

"Not too bad with the driving."

"Thanks. Mom freaks out a little more than you do."

"I've been in more crashes."

John laughed. "I'll have my license soon. Then are we going to practice some cool driving stuff?"

"We can. I have a friend that owns a private racetrack in West Virginia. We can go there when I get back."

"Get back?"

"Oh. Sorry. I have to do a short trip next month for a few weeks."

"That sucks."

Dane's brow furrowed. "Tell me about it. I'm not too happy about it, either."

His thoughts immediately went to the club and how work was forcing him to take his eye off the ball. He patted the necklace in his breast pocket to calm himself. *I should just retire. I have over twenty.*

"You okay, Dad?"

"Huh, why?" Dane shook off his thoughts to look at his son, instantly regretting his curt response.

"You just looked really pissed."

"Sorry. It's nothing. Just work stuff."

"You sure?"

"Yeah, sorry. Didn't mean anything toward you. Work is at work. Let's enjoy the time we have."

The po boys arrived, and Dane watched John dive in. *Damn,* he thought, *this is not a side of me he ever needs to see.*

I DON'T KNOW HOW LONG I HAVE BEEN HERE. THE MAN SAYS I AM DOING WELL IN SCHOOL. I DON'T LIKE HIM. HE ISN'T MEAN. HE DOESN'T YELL. I WANT HIM TO LET ME GO HOME. I WANT TO BE IN MY ROOM AT HOME. I DON'T WANT TO BE HERE.

9

THE OFFICE

Fairfax, Virginia

Devotee: I found where our next contact lives.

Keeper: When are you going to pay a visit?

Devotee: I am planning for tomorrow.

Keeper: Okay. Let me know as soon as you find anything.

The crime scene photos Carl had sent were pretty gruesome, but Roger was no stranger to this. Even before his time on the force, he was exposed to the violence of man.

The jungles teemed with life until they didn't. The brutality of adversaries led to the abolishment of all breathing things. Man and beast all succumbed to the violence, and he had it worse than most. Why had he volunteered? The thin-yet-athletic version of himself had been the perfect candidate. Small enough to fit and brave enough to enter. Most didn't make it. Some were killed by snakes lurking in the tunnels. Others fell prey to booby traps meant to deliver a lasting and painful death.

And then there was always the Viet Cong. Burrowing farther and farther beneath the jungle. They fought ferociously to defend their homes above-ground. They were not different beneath. The labyrinths they had constructed could consume a man forever. And with all victories came another contest. Another chance to enter the lair of the enemy and dance with him again. Dance with him, playing by his rules. One more game until you lost or finished and went home. But when did it end? When did the mind let it end?

With knife, pistol, and the occasional torch, he would boldly enter, wondering whether this was his last race. Was it the last game in the maze before a gruesome death found him? Or worse, would he survive to live with the guilt?

"You okay? You are staring off into space."

Roger slowly entered the present, and his gaze drifted from the computer screen to Pat.

"I'm fine. Just doing a little thinking."

"You trying to stare a hole in the computer?"

"Just reviewing some new files."

"From who?"

"Our old friend Blanchard."

"What does he want now?"

"What does he always want? He is actively pursuing this club, Pat. He has even created a task force. He wants us as advisors. He wants our perspective on this, since it all ties closely with our abduction cases."

"Hah. Yeah, with all our free time. I mean, he is not wrong. Unfortunately, these cases could be woven together and pursued in concert. But the captain will lose his shit if we participate."

"A call from the deputy director at the FBI may change his mind." Roger picked up the remote and turned on the wall-mounted TV. As he searched the major news outlets, he saw that each was providing nonstop coverage of what they were calling the Savannah port mass shooting. He settled on CNN. Pat put some files on her desk and joined him to watch.

"We still have limited information and, as you can see behind me, the authorities have restricted access to the area due to the ongoing investigation. What we do know is that late last night there, a massive amount of gunfire was reported to the Savannah authorities. It was centered around a ship at dock 19. That ship, the Panama Merchant, is flagged out of Panama City, Panama. The ownership of the vessel is still unknown. Authorities believe a gunfight broke out between two gangs over a shipment of narcotics. The dispute continued from the port down the Savannah River as the ship left its berth. Bystanders on River Street also reported gunfire aboard the ship and from a nearby building in town. They both heard and saw flashes through windows on the ship as it passed underneath the Talmadge Memorial Bridge

and traversed the length of River Street. The Coast Guard was brought in to intercept the vessel as it passed through town on its way to open water. It is currently grounded near old Fort Jackson. We are still awaiting more answers to what led to this tragic event that left nineteen dead, including one Port Authority officer. That officer's name is currently being withheld upon family notification."

"Were assault weapons found at the scene?"

"Yes, John. Multiple assault weapons were found."

"Wow," Pat exclaimed. "I heard about it on the radio driving over here, but seeing it on TV really drives home the enormity of what happened. Did they say nineteen dead, Roger?"

Roger nodded. "But not injured. They always say how many were also injured. During something like this, you hear how many were hospitalized, in critical condition, etcetera." He frowned looking at the TV screen.

"I didn't think about it that way. Surely someone must have survived."

"If everyone is dead, then it means both sides were amazing shots or there is only one side's casualties left at the scene."

"So, a different player carried away the dead or injured? Or they didn't have any when it was all said and done."

"Well, Blanchard is on his way down. Said Somalis were involved. And underage girls were found, not drugs. Initial reports just don't add up. He is pretty sure it was our guys from the Parker and Jones cases. Our mysterious vigilantes."

"Well, he is starting to make a pretty good case. I thought he was a little off his rocker first time we met. But the facts do keep adding up."

"He is intent on finding something down in Savannah that the overwhelming law enforcement presence missed. Something only he can find, I am sure."

"I am sure he will tell us when he gets back and summons us to this almighty task force."

Roger chuckled. "What do you have there?" He indicated to the folders Pat had carried into the room.

"This first one is the autopsy on that dentist. Doc prioritized it quickly, since it was fairly clear what happened. Pretty gruesome. Recommend skipping the pictures."

Roger accepted the file from Patricia and glanced through the notes. Dr. Webster's remains were barely recognizable at the base of the cliff. "Over a thousand feet down?"

"Yeah, but not completely vertical. He smashed and scraped the cliff face the whole way down. Will keep the vultures happy for a while."

Roger made a face. "Thanks, partner. I guess I don't need lunch."

Pat pointed at Roger's belly. "You're welcome."

Head down reading, Roger extended his middle finger instead of answering. Once satisfied, he closed the file. "Okay, what is the medical examiner reporting?"

"Undetermined. Certainly wasn't natural. But could have been a suicide or an accident. He can't determine intent. He knows how he died. Just not why. That is up to us."

"Ruled out homicide?"

"Nobody was up there with him. Park ranger said Webster was there bright and early. Next closest hiker was over an hour behind." She looked at her notes. "John Curtis. He called it in on his sat phone."

"Maybe John pushed him."

"Nope. Both had those hiker-style trackers on them. Same company, too. Must be a popular brand. The company showed us both men's tracks. Webster was at the bottom of the mountain an hour before Curtis made the summit."

"Mr. Curtis did not hear a blood-curdling scream from the mountain trail? You would think that kind of noise would travel far."

"Curtis was on the trail coming in from the west. You don't weave your way up the face of the mountain. You come around from the side. He had a lot of mountain between himself and the cliff Webster went over."

"Could someone else have been up there hiking in from another trail? Isn't that near the Appalachian Trail?"

"It is east of the Appalachian Trail. Pretty rough hike from there to Old Rag. Also, it is very unlikely someone would go through all that trouble. Webster was clean. No past incidents. His condo was searched. Nothing out of the ordinary that would indicate he was targeted for any reason. Plus, this particular tracking company did not show any tracks from other hikers that morning. Could be someone else using a different company. Want me to search?"

"Agree with undetermined. See what you can pull from other companies. I just want to make sure we covered all angles. If nothing else, then close it out. I am assuming that other file is for the reverend."

Pat placed the Webster file in her outbox to be filed later. She opened the second file for Roger to see. "This is what Metro has so far."

Roger took a few moments to read the preliminary report and view several of the photos. "Where are they going with this?"

"Still robbery gone bad for now. Autopsy is tomorrow. They invited us to attend."

"Hard pass."

"I figured as much. They will give us the final report. The lab is running everything they found. FBI is helping as well. Prints are all over that church, so that is no help. Unless they find the murder weapon or get a DNA hit, they are stuck.

"Canvass of the area turn up anything?"

"Negative. No witnesses, sight or sound. Nothing so far on nearby cameras."

Roger stared off absently for a moment. "Two ghosts at the same church just months apart. One a savior and the other a demon."

"Don't start getting all biblical on me now."

"Ha, hardly. No way is this a coincidence. Blanchard is all over this."

"Well, I don't know how he can possibly weave all this together. We still haven't found anything tying the reverend to those kids. Nothing. Nobody from the church, either, as far as well can tell."

"I hear you. Carl has way more resources than us, and he doesn't have anything. Or at least anything he has decided to share."

"You think he is holding out on us?"

"No, but I also don't expect him to expound on his every working theory."

"Well, again, speaking with Metro, then can find nobody so far with a motive to hurt the reverend. He was loved by the community."

"So, what do you think, Pat?"

"Like we discussed before, the chance of these abductors working together is not so far-fetched. Just like the serial killer scenario where there was a mentor-mentee relationship."

"Like in *Star Wars* where Yoda talks about the Sith and says there are always two, a master and an apprentice."

Pat gave Roger an annoying look. "Can you take anything seriously?"

"I take *Star Wars* very seriously."

"I know, Roger. I am surprised you don't have posters adorning the walls of the Pit."

"The captain won't let me."

Pat rolled her eyes. "If this was the abductors, I see two scenarios." She walked over to one of the empty dry-erase boards and made two columns on the board: *Revenge. Intel.*

"Okay, partner. I see where you are going."

"Torture of this magnitude was done to punish or to extract information."

"Walk me through it."

"These sickos obviously know something went wrong, since the kids showed up at the church. They probably know more than us."

"They probably know that one of their brethren is dead."

"We don't know for a fact that he or she is dead."

"They are dead. There is no logical explanation at this point with regards to how those kids arrived at the reverend's doorstep, only Carl's theory. And if his theory is correct, I highly doubt a group would go through all this effort to rescue the children and leave the monster alive to do it again."

"I agree, but I have a hard time shutting that door mentally without having a body."

Roger laughed. "Well, you better, since that is one body I am fairly certain we will never find."

"Agree to disagree. Revenge fits, since this group wants someone to be held accountable. The Reverend was all over the news. He could have been their only known target."

"I can see that, but I am leaning more toward intel."

"Why?"

"Again, working theory, but if this is some kind of group, they have been fairly meticulous so far. Methodical, even. It seems that they use violence only when necessary. Look at Dana Chase."

"The guy smashed her skull and threw her in the Potomac!"

"I know, but remember it was one powerful, quick blow. The perpetrator limited the amount of violence. Controlled it. If you are insane enough to kidnap and then kill a child, then you are one mentally unstable individual. But with all that instability, the guy was still able to control his violence. That is all I am saying."

"Maybe if it is some sort of club, that doesn't mean all the members are the same. I bet these have pretty loose tryouts!"

Roger raised his hands. He could see Pat was getting worked up. "Okay, agree to disagree. It just seems like this was torture instead of an execution. They thought the reverend had information."

"So maybe they thought the reverend was part of Carl's mystery pedophile killers? Trying to get a line on the rest of them."

"As crazy as this whole thing is, that is where the evidence is leading us. And Carl."

"So, following that logic, if the reverend knew something, the possibility of identifying the killer's next victim would be virtually impossible."

"Easier if it was someone among his flock."

"Would the church give out that information? Hell, would they even have it? It is not like there is an attendance roster at the front door."

"I doubt it. There may be some sort of roster with close affiliates of the church. Big donors, volunteers, board members. Probably even those in the choir. However, there is a real possibility that the reverend didn't have any intel to give. It is a very real possibility that he had no idea his church was going to be used as a drop-off point."

"If that was the case—"

"Keyholders! Sorry to interrupt." Roger walked over to the board and wrote the word under intel.

"You think the killer wanted to know who had access to the church."

"Yes. Remember back to the original investigation. We asked about who had access, and he claimed nobody did. He would open his doors in the morning. Prayer, confession, etcetera. He helped set up the therapy groups in the evenings. He even let in the cleaning ladies on Tuesday and Thursday mornings. I always found it strange that he insisted nobody else had a key."

"Maybe he was protecting someone. Seal of confession and all that."

"Maybe, but maybe he honestly did not know that someone else acquired a key."

"We should probably share our thoughts with Carl. You said he is heading to Savannah?"

"Yeah. We can talk to him when he gets back. Regardless of this task force thing, let's stay abreast of this investigation. It is bound to complement ours."

Capt. Ivers stuck his head through the door. "Patterson, I need to see you in my office now about some task force bullshit."

10

THE SCENE

Washington, D.C.

The pilot announced over the Gulfstream's intercom that they were twenty-five minutes out from Savannah and would begin to prepare for landing shortly. Carl and Ken didn't even acknowledge the announcement as they prepared to pay a visit to the port.

The recent bloodbath definitely spiked on Carl's radar. As more and more reports poured in, it appeared that this smuggling ring had been quite active right under the noses of the collective authorities. Fingers were already pointing, and allegations were brewing.

Looking up from his notes, Carl glanced at Ken. "Double-check my count. Did they say they recovered ten girls?"

"Yes, sir. Homeland sent over the final findings an hour ago." The Gulfstream's wi-fi allowed the agents to stay connected to investigations and remain productive during long flights. "Ten females ranging from ten to fourteen. Three Caucasians, four Hispanic, and three Blacks. Identities are being established and families contacted. No apparent linkage among them at this time. They are all being treated at St. Joseph's Hospital. They cleared a ward for them and their families. Police are conducting interviews."

"Well, they have done a hell of a job keeping this out of the press so far. But that won't last forever."

"Agree. I talked to the public affairs officer before we left. They are not providing any details, just letting the press run wild with theories. They want to notify all the families before going public. They never mentioned the drug bust gone wrong theory. Press did that by themselves."

Carl flipped through grainy photos of the scene, courtesy of the local FBI office. The pixelation was deteriorated over email, but it gave him a good picture of the scene. "Damn. nineteen dead."

The ship was a smaller cargo vessel not normally used to cross the Atlantic. But that is where this feeder-type vessel was heading. The Panama Merchant's final destination was the Port of Aden in Yemen. Wasn't going to be going there any time soon.

"We are up to twenty-one, boss. They found two more in the engine room. Two Somali males, each shot once in the head. They were stuffed in a maintenance closet."

"That's a twist. What does that tell us?" Carl had his own thoughts, but wanted Ken to work through the problem as well. What good was being a mentor if you didn't actually mentor?

"Well, hiding the bodies is a little strange. The suspect or suspects left all the other bodies in plain sight. Why hide these two?"

"What are the two most important places on the ship? Places people may frequent more often to keep the whole thing running?"

Ken snapped his fingers. "The bridge and the engine room. Whomever did this started in the engine room and worked their way up to the bridge. They hid the bodies in case they missed someone before they reached the bridge. Before someone could sound an alarm."

"Exactly, he wanted to keep the element of surprise."

"He? One man?"

"A theory for now. Let's see where the evidence takes us."

The plane landed smoothly at the Savannah/Hilton Head International Airport. The Gulfstream taxied to the southeast corner of the airfield. Instead of entering the Gulfstream service entrance, the men entered the Air National Guard facility. It was quicker than the civilian entrance since they had planned ahead for support from the 165th Airlift Wing with regard to parking and fueling the FBI plane. A junior agent from the Savannah office picked up the pair for the short drive to the port and the absolute chaos that had descended upon the sleepy southern town.

Investigators from every government agency appeared to be in attendance, their vehicles overwhelming the streets around the crime scene. The port spanned for miles, reaching all the way to the city of Port Wentworth. Most people did not realize the volume of vessels traversing the river, since it was rather narrow compared to other waterways. The port itself was the third-busiest in the country. It was second only to the Port of Los Angeles for agricultural shipping. Certain areas remained somewhat cleared by the Georgia Port Authority to allow limited operations for the busy port, but Carl knew the investigation severely restricted their activity. *This must be costing the port millions,* he thought.

He and Ken did not initially seek out the lead investigators. He wanted to get a broad overview first before facts and evidence narrowed his perspective. If this was the club, as he had come recently to call these individuals, he believed they were secretly responsible. He didn't want to miss a thing. And he didn't want an investigator providing him with alternate theories until he had processed all the information provided by the crime scene.

His first stop was a guard station at one of several southern access points. Crime scene techs photographed and sketched the small booth, taking caution to avoid the tiny yellow evidence cards. The victims throughout the port and ship had all been removed, their bodies undoubtedly in a local morgue awaiting their turn under the knife. However, at this location, the blood evidence indicated a single victim. More than likely a fatal headshot.

"What happened here?" Carl asked one of the techs.

"Guard was killed. Single shot to the head. High-powered round. 308 slug was pulled out of that wall," the tech answered, pointing to the western side of the shack.

Carefully avoiding the dried pool of blood, Carl examined the wall. A wooden dowel had been inserted into the hole to determine the bullet's trajectory. It pointed in a southeasterly direction back toward the town, east of the Talmadge Memorial Bridge. *So, you guys had overwatch,* he thought. *Your professionalism does not disappoint.*

Next, he and Ken made their way deeper into the yard. Several officers were gathered around shipping containers clustered near one of the large docks. Bullet holes were all marked with smaller dowels. "Is this where they believe this little firefight kicked off?"

Ken looked up from his notes. "Yes, sir. Video captured a white van passing through the previous checkpoint. Cameras down here at the dock had gone offline, but the authorities believe the van stopped here to unload the girls. It makes sense, and from the casings on the ground, it wasn't a difficult guess."

"Of course, no cameras. Seven bodies here?"

"Eight, sir. Mix of 5.56mm and 9mm shell casings. The victims carried AK-47s, but we only found a few 7.62mm shells. They got off a few shots, but not as many as the other guys."

"Let me guess. A few 308 slugs were found as well."

"Four."

"Ambush point, but something went wrong. Maybe not expecting that many shooters. And over here?" Carl began walking toward the dock.

"Two more bodies. Same calibers."

Carl scratched his chin. "Okay, so I am guessing the bad guys got the girls aboard before our would-be rescuers could save them. The crew onboard was obviously alerted. Probably ready to depart as soon as the girls were aboard. Button up quickly and then the ship pulls away."

"Correct, but at least one of our guys must have made it aboard, hence the remaining bodies on the vessel. Plus all the reports about flashes and gunshots aboard the ship as it passed through the town. The town is never deserted. Plenty of spectators. They must have gotten a hell of a show."

Carl turned his attention to the pier. On request, the Georgia Port Authority retrieved the grounded ship. A tugboat had returned the vessel from the shoreline near Fort Jackson to its berth of origin. It had been partially blocking Savannah River access, but not affecting the Little Back River branch. The port had to allow navigation along the river. Moving the ship also aided the authorities in their investigation. The sheer volume of equipment needed could be easily brought to the dock. Not so easy out on the water or from muddy swaps. He studied the starboard side of the ship.

"How do you think they boarded, Ken?"

"Not sure, sir. May be an open porthole. Or some sort of rope ladder affixed ahead of time that they took with them? I have seen the SEALs and FBI hostage rescue teams practice with them during ship-boarding exercise. I think they are called caving ladders. Or, one of them could have already been onboard in case they missed getting the girls at the dock in the first place. Contingency plan."

"Maybe," Carl answered. "I doubt that the gangway was left down. It would probably have been severely damaged when they pulled away, yet it looks fine," he concluded as both men crossed the metal platform into the ship.

They spent the next hour roaming its rooms, bearing witness to the carnage unleashed just a day earlier. They spoke with detectives and crime scene techs to gather every little bit of the story possible. They were told the young girls were being treated at a local hospital and some had already been reunited with their families. From the initial interviews, investigators learned the horrifying stories of how each girl found themselves on the ship that evening. However, they provided limited details of the recent ordeal, except for the loud gunfire after exiting the van and later onboard the ship. Most of them described a lone man, covered in black from head to toe, attacking their captors. The investigators admitted to scratching their heads over that one.

Carl and Ken returned to the scene of the ambush at the pier. "Thoughts?"

"At least three shooters," Ken concluded. "Probably more, but we need to wait on ballistics to determine the number of guns fired at the scene. Sniper was probably to the east of the bridge. Somewhere high up downtown."

"Good. Not perfect math, but based on the rounds fired here and at the guard, they traced back to that general area. Investigators are combing both sides, but I think you are correct."

"So, the sniper is one, and at least two men to ambush the vehicle. Then, at least one man boarded the ship while the other moved the van."

"But why move the van? Why not just leave it and have another shooter onboard for the rescue?"

"Not sure, boss."

"And what are your theories on the guard?"

"Sniper shot him so he couldn't call for help when the shooting started."

Carl didn't answer immediately. He moved around the site, picturing the ambush in his head. He then walked over to the row of containers closest to the ship. Shell casings and a small pool of blood were marked by more little yellow tent cards.

Carl walked farther, over to an area of the containers out of a straight site line of the van and the ship. He squatted down for a closer look at the area. Another dried pool of blood was marked by a yellow tent card. "Ken, can you look up on the evidence sheet what was located here?"

Ken hustled over. He read from the file he carried, a copy provided by the local FBI office. "It says here, unknown African Male number six."

Carl frowned. He stood still, staring at the tent card. Ken stood patiently, realizing his boss was in his own thoughts and now was not the time to interrupt him.

Carl looked from the card back to the location of the vehicle. Back to the card and then back to the vehicle. "Huh."

"What is it, sir?"

Carl didn't answer. He slowly walked back to the scene of the firefight while studying the ground. He occasionally stopped and stared. Once he reached the vehicle location, marked by yellow tape, he stopped and turned. Again, he just stared.

"Why was one of the Somali terrorists over there?"

"I don't know what you mean, sir."

"They said a body was found over there," Carl said, pointing toward a tent card just out of sight.

"Yes."

"The body was moved. It does not fit that one of the smugglers would be over there."

"Moved?"

"Yes. Look at the trail from here to there. Small drops of blood—very faint, but there nonetheless."

"The Somali could have been shot here and then tried to get away and headed in that direction before succumbing to his wounds." Ken looked through the initial notes from investigators initially on scene. "Lividity checks out, so it appears he died in this location."

"Why would the injured man move away from the ship and his comrades? Not the greatest cover, either. If he was moved quickly, it wouldn't be noticeable. I would say less than ten minutes after he was killed. They probably just put him in the same position as he was when they killed him. Combine this with the missing van, Ken. They moved the van because one of them was shot. Out of the fight, he needed to leave quickly. Local police will find the van out in the swamp eventually, probably burned right down to the frame."

"Then why move the dead Somali?"

"Blood. One of them got shot. Probably lost a bit of blood before he could control it with a tourniquet or whatever. His partner got him to the van and got him out of here."

"But they still had the problem with the blood evidence?" Ken asked.

"Exactly. They probably didn't carry any chemicals to ruin the sample. So, our ingenious friends moved one of the bodies over the blood spill."

"I get it sir. With the body there, the crime scene tech would get a sample from the body rather than the ground. Why bother?"

"And even if the tech tested the blood, the flow from the dead smuggler would almost certainly ruin the sample. Have our FBI liaison notify the tech team to sample this blood. Probably too late, but it is something. Very clever. This club thinks fast on their feet."

"Will do. Anything else?"

"And I think once we receive the report on the gate guard, we are going to learn about a wad of cash on his person. And possibly some questionable activity in his past."

"A bribe?"

"Exactly. These smugglers wouldn't want to risk their precious cargo on a chance inspection. He was their inside man. He probably didn't know what to do when all the shooting started. If he called for backup, he would have to explain why he let the van through. I bet he was just frozen here."

"Then why shoot him if he wasn't going to interfere?"

"Punishment. Our sniper did not take too kindly to this young guard taking bribes and allowing child trafficking."

I THINK THIS IS A FARM. SOMETIMES I HEAR ANIMALS, BUT IT IS HARD TO HEAR. I THOUGHT I HEARD A COW YESTERDAY. I CAN'T SEE OVER THE FENCE. I CAN SMELL THE ANIMALS. IT SMELLS LIKE THE FAIR WE WENT TO WHERE THE COWS AND PIGS AND GOATS GOT BLUE RIBBONS. THE FOOD IS NOT BAD. THE MAN SAYS I MUST EAT EVERYTHING. HE SAYS I NEED TO GROW HEALTHY AND BE A GOOD ADULT. BREAKFAST IS MY FAVORITE. I LIKE THE EGGS AND ORANGE JUICE. THE MAN SAID THE EGGS ARE FRESH EVERY DAY AND THAT HE MAKES THE JUICE. HE SAID PEOPLE EAT TOO MUCH BAD FOOD AND THEY GET SICK AND FAT. HE SAID I WON'T GET SICK OR FAT.

11

THE ARREST

Fairfax Station, Virginia

Keeper: We have a problem. One of us was caught. Don't visit our other friend yet.

Devotee: We all know the risks. What do you want me to do?

Keeper: Take care of him. He is in police custody at the hospital. Be careful.

Devotee: I always am. Afterwards, I can attend to our other contact.

"Left here, Roger. On Hampton."

"Thanks, partner." Roger turned onto Hampton Road from Ox Road. The winding stretch through the trees was normally quite the scenic route. However, neither agent was interested in the scenery today. They rushed toward their destination. The call came in that there had been a bizarre kidnapping attempt at Fountainhead Regional Park along the upper Occoquan River. They did not have all the details, but chemicals were found on the suspect.

The use of chemicals or drugs on the victim was the only similar thread they had to pull for their open cases. They were alerted immediately. An actual suspect that may finally prove or disprove their working theory had been apprehended.

There had been very little evidence to go on, other than that old-fashioned gut feelings, but Roger was getting that feeling more and more. They were getting close. Hopefully, this was the break they needed.

They showed their badges to the park ranger at the main entrance. The park had been temporarily evacuated, and several park ranger vehicles blocked the gates. Other vehicles could be seen moving along trails in the woods to ensure no stragglers interfered with the active crime scene.

"Head all the way back, officers. Everyone is down by the fishing pier."

"Thank you," Roger responded.

Roger continued along the curving path through the thick woods. The sprawling park was situated above the dam along the Occoquan Reservoir. Unlike the lower portion of the river that enjoyed unlimited boating, the upper portion was shallow. It was home to canoes, paddleboards, and small flat-bottom fishing boats—nothing with any sort of engine that could drag along the bottom. Trees bordered it, at times creating a canopy across the waterway. It was hard to imagine this kind of wilderness just outside D.C.

He and Pat slowed as they neared the river. Several Fairfax County police vehicles were parked along the road in front of a cluster of restrooms. Roger hadn't been to this park in ages. He remembered the boat launch, which was farther east along this road, but he had never walked out to the fishing pier.

He had been here several years ago responding to a tragic accident. A group of young adults rented several canoes and decided to have a party on the water. They haphazardly tied multiple canoes together and began power drinking. They carried on all that afternoon. Several hours, in fact, which they admitted to the responding officers. Eventually, through the haze of alcohol, they realized their friend Danny was missing. He was found nearby along the shore, face down in the water. A massive contusion on his forehead explained why the young man had lost consciousness and drowned in the shallow water. The coroner had placed the time of death several hours before his discovery, his absence concerning none of the partiers.

Roger shook off those thoughts as he and Pat walked the final portion of their journey to the pier and took in the scene. Investigators photographed an older ten-speed bike leaning up against a rail. Others documented the contents of a tackle box and swabbed for prints on a nearby pole. It was surreal. This was literally the most docile crime scene he had ever attended. Everybody was going about their duties will very little haste. There were no flashing lights. No police tape. Just several technicians collecting evidence along the pier. Roger recognized one of the county officers.

"What you got, sergeant?" Roger asked, extending his hand to the officer.

"Pretty cut and dry scene, sir. Boy named Elliot Nobless was down here fishing this morning. Nut job comes out of the woods and stabs the kid with a needle, then tries to drag Elliot to his car." The officer pointed to an area behind where Roger had parked.

Roger nodded while he and Pat took notes.

"What the perp didn't count on was the two joggers that came around the corner from the direction of the boat launch." Again, the sergeant pointed to give the agents context.

"What happened next?"

"Not a good day for the perp. Two fit men in their thirties doing some CrossFit stuff down here in the park. They finished their workout on him. Perp is pretty messed up."

"Which hospital did they take him to?" Pat asked.

"Took them all to Inova up in Fairfax. The boy was unconscious from the injection, so the ambulance wasted no time. Uniforms drove the perp, since he didn't have life-threatening injuries. Just in a hell of a lot of pain. Both joggers were questioned, but released for now. We have all their contact information if a follow-up is necessary."

"Lead detectives are at the hospital?"

"Yes, sir. Standing by for when the boy regains consciousness."

Roger handed the sergeant his business card. "Please let them know we are on our way. They can call or text me the room number of our victim."

"Roger that, sir." He smiled at the unintentional pun as he read the agent's card.

Roger smiled back, then turned to Pat. "Let's get over there."

Once they were out of earshot of the others, Pat asked the question that was on Roger's mind. "Seemed to be a pretty docile crime scene. I would have thought there would have been more responders. Seems like they don't think it is a very big deal."

"I was thinking the same thing. But, on second thought, maybe it seems that way to us since we are so close to this case. They don't know that this may be tied to a group of serial kidnappers. It's not like we have exactly been putting that out to the press or even briefings for that matter. We have been pretty tight-lipped, asking only to be notified of abduction or attempts where the perp is trying to use chemicals."

"So, what are you thinking?"

"I am thinking that we need to discuss this with Carl. Maybe public assistance can be of help here with both of these groups. Keeping everything secret has not really worked. Maybe we need the media to help us find these guys."

"I see your point, Roger, but too much information out there could cause a panic. Especially with something new and unique. Serial kidnappers will cause quite the stir. Parents won't let their kids out of their sight."

"Well, maybe that is what we need for the time being."

Traffic was light, and they made good time to the hospital. Room number in hand, they entered the front doors and made their way to the fifth floor ICU. Throughout their careers, both investigators had visited this place more than they wanted. It was here or other local hospitals where they normally conducted their first interview with the victims they sought justice for. They easily found Elliot's room. Several family members were outside, talking to investigators. One broke away as they approached.

The man introduced himself. "Detective Clark. You must be Special Agents Patterson and Stills."

Roger nodded. "Is there somewhere we can talk in private? I don't want to further upset the family."

"Sure, sure. Follow me." Clark led them to a small waiting room down the hall. It was unoccupied.

"If we can start with the basics, that would be great. We talked to the folks at the scene and got a general summary, but not many details."

"Right. This is what we have so far from speaking with the boy. Our suspect can't really talk yet on account of having his jaw smashed. He should be out of surgery any time now. The doc will call us when we can have a little chat."

"You said info from the victim, Elliot Nobless?" Pat asked. "I thought he was drugged."

"He was, with fentanyl citrate. Docs aren't sure how much, but they brought him around."

"Never heard the second part of that drug name," said Roger.

"That's the interesting part. I will get to that at the end. Elliot was down at the dock fishing this morning. He goes every morning, rain or shine. He lives nearby and his parents explained the ritual. They said Elliot's therapist recommended allowing him this morning routine to help relieve stress that would build throughout the previous day."

"Is he on the spectrum?" Pat asked.

"He is. I guess the medical community keeps changing the diagnoses and labels. As his folks explained, on a three-level scale Elliot is at two, requiring substantial support. Social interactions are difficult unless it holds a special interest for him. Hence the fishing and repetitive behaviors. They encouraged his habit and were trying to use it to broaden his social depth. Fishing events, tournaments, that kind of stuff."

"Makes sense. So, what happened?" Roger asked.

"Suspect had parked near the restrooms, and Elliot saw him enter the men's bathroom. He thought nothing of it and went back to fishing. He felt a prick in his thigh, and someone strong grabbed him, cupping a hand over his mouth. He said he felt sleepy and didn't remember much else."

"Okay. Pat and I will need to talk to him at some point, but I am fairly certain now is not the time."

"Yeah, I would give him a bit. He is stressed to the max. Poor kid is a wreck. He keeps shutting down and moaning. The parents are obviously going crazy. Who wouldn't be? I only got the basics to. . ."

Detective Clark looked at his phone. "To charge our suspect, who is out of surgery and awake. One floor up. Shall we go upstairs?"

The suspect was in a recovery room on the fourth floor. The trio paused before entering the room. "I keep referring to him as the suspect because we still have not identified him."

"We figured as much. What is the holdup?" Pat asked.

"No wallet. No ID. Nothing. We are running his prints and tracing the car, so hopefully we will have something soon. It is taking longer than I would have hoped."

"Just so we are clear up front," Roger interjected, "the VBI will be taking over the investigation since it appears to tie into several open investigations. It is not meant to insult your department, but this case may very well be tied to even more investigations above the state level."

"No hard feelings at all. I follow the news and our internal briefings. I expected this. I also suspect this has something to do with those children found in the D.C. church. Anything to help with your open cases. We will offer all necessary support."

"You mentioned earlier that the fentanyl was important. Why?" Pat asked.

"Because it is hard to get. This isn't some street mixture. This was medical grade. Like the stuff you use for surgeries."

"So, this guy may be associated with the medical field in some way?"

"Let's go in and find out."

The suspect was seated partially upright in the hospital bed. His right hand was cuffed to the guardrail, his left a mixture of IVs and bandages. His face and jaw were severely swollen. Only one eye could glare at them. It was obvious that he had sustained several fractures.

The uniformed officer chaperoning the suspect stepped out for a break. The charge nurse remained, ensuring all the monitoring devices were operational. She changed out the suspect's IV fluids and turned to the officers to leave.

"He is slightly loopy but should be able to answer questions."

"Do we need to limit our time here since he just got out of surgery?" Detective Clark asked.

"He tried to kidnap a kid. I don't give a shit what you do with him.

We followed that Hippocratic oath crap with this scum. My conscious is clear. Do what you like." She then turned and left.

Pat closed the door after she left, only to feel resistance. "Got room for one more?"

"Blanchard," she remarked. "I should have known you would be here."

"I know this wasn't my vigilante club guys. Perp is too alive. Still, a lead is a lead."

Patterson and Stills introduced Blanchard to Detective Clark before approaching the hospital bed. The man looked spent. He looked like a defeated boxer, exiting a ring he never should have stepped into. The agents told Carl that they had not been able to identify him thus far. Prints had still not returned, and the vehicle was proving more difficult to trace than initially thought.

Clark explained that despite Vehicle Identification Numbers, or VINs, going in two places on every car since the eighties, the VINs had been intentionally destroyed. Many modern cars had them digitally recorded on internal electric systems, but the suspect's sedan was not one of those vehicles. Technicians were removing some of the undercarriage to check for a hidden VIN underneath. Many manufacturers often did that to aid police with recovering stolen vehicles.

Roger spoke first. "Let's start with your name."

The suspect groaned. His eyes fluttered as he slowly shook his head side to side.

"We know you can hear us," Roger continued. "And despite your broken jaw, the docs assured us you will be able to communicate after surgery. Even with the loose wires holding your jaws nearly closed. So, let's try again."

The man's eyes slowly opened. "No, I don't think so."

"No?" Pat asked. "We will eventually find out. We have your car, your fingerprints, even your DNA."

"It doesn't matter," he mumbled softly. "It doesn't matter. It's over."

"What is over?" Roger continued.

"He will come for me. I was told not to get caught. I was warned."

"Who is he? What are you afraid of?" Carl asked.

"If not him, then them. The hunters. They are everywhere. And nowhere. None of us are safe anymore." The man managed the semblance of a giggle through his broken jaw. His one good eye would not stay focused in the same place for more than a fleeting moment.

"Let's try again. Who is he? Does he have a name? Do you know where he is?" Roger asked.

"He has rules. I knew them. I made a mistake."

"Okay, then who are these hunters?" It was Carl's question.

"Not safe here. He can get me here. They can get to me here. Not safe."

"Listen, buddy, this will go a lot easier if you cooperate. If there is someone else involved, you need to tell us." Roger said.

"Not saying nothing. Nothing. Lawyer."

President: I need your help. A suspect was apprehended, and I would appreciate the delay of his identification in both databases.

Cyber Tech: I can delay the release, but not the identification process. That would crash each of the systems.

President: You can get a result, but delay the automated response system for fingerprint identification?

Cyber Tech: Yes. I can stall no more than twenty-four hours. I assume you would like the identity soonest. I can pull that manually.

12

THE BRIEFING

Fort Meade, Maryland

Dane tugged at his collar to relieve the pressure around his neck. He looked in the rearview mirror to adjust the tie trying to choke him to death. It was going to be the tie or this damn traffic that would finally do him in. The grim reaper must have sent both this morning to drive Dane into an early grave. This was going to be a long day.

Dane loathed the drive to the National Security Agency, or NSA, located on Fort Meade in Maryland. Traffic could change in a matter of seconds, and he had to get out of the hornets' nest first. Northern Virginia and Southern Maryland were not much better than the city, either. He never quite figured out which was worse—getting stuck on small D.C. side streets with the buildings closing in or sitting out on an enormous freeway complex only to be at a complete standstill, blocked in by a thousand fellow commuters. Google Maps might estimate the trip would take fifty minutes, and then suddenly jump to two hours. That was exactly what had happened this time, and Dane found himself in bumper-to-bumper traffic along the Baltimore Washington Parkway in a suit he hated to wear. Hopefully, the day got better from here.

Col. Alexander had early meetings at Fort Meade, so he would meet Dane at NSA headquarters. That meant Dane got to enjoy driving the government sedan both to and from the agency along the most congested roads in America. And it was some super fuel-efficient foreign car that was uncomfortable as hell. He could barely fit in the tiny seat, and his head bumped the ceiling whenever he hit a pothole. Around this area, that was often. *How can the U.S. government buy foreign cars as their service fleet? Makes no sense,* he thought.

Dane finally broke through the gridlock and approached the gates of the base. Now the real fun began as he tried to find the right access road that led to the correct gate. He got it wrong every time. It was as if Google Maps wasn't even trying. Dane was certain that the NSA and Fort Meade did this on purpose. It had to be part of their security posture. Can't break into what you can't find.

His frustration began to subside as he entered through the correct gate, which led to the NSA visitor center. Even though he was on a cleared access roster, the fun of the security checkpoint still awaited. *This is why I hate coming here. I have every clearance known to man, and I am constantly monitored in all aspects of my life to include social media, financial data, even travel habits. But I still have to take off my shoes and belt every time I go through a metal detector. Ridiculous.*

The protocol officer met Dane upon completion of his rigorous inspection and soundlessly led him to an adjacent building. Dane was tempted to share his favorite NSA joke with the man: *How do you tell if an NSA employee is an extrovert? They stare at your shoes instead of theirs.* Dane stifled a laugh. *Probably not the best time.*

The duo entered an enormous briefing room. There was a grand U-shaped conference table with padded leather chairs and carafes of water at each seat. Microphones were at each seating, obviously needed for a room this size. There was no way the unaided human voice could travel across. The remaining space was taken up by gallery seating on either side. The place could easily hold a hundred people. With the addition of Dane, it now held six.

"About time, Dane," Col. Alexander said with a grin. He introduced Dane to the director of the agency, along with his deputy. Next was one of the chief scientists and, finally, the operative who would be accompanying him on the operation. Her name was Nicky. Dane was sure she had a last name. He just didn't hear it. She was stunning. *Oh boy, I can't let this become a distraction,* he thought. The display screens came alive on the far wall with an enormous map of Africa. Countries were highlighted in various colors.

The chief scientist took the lead. "Good morning, everyone. I am

Dr. Reagan. I am going to provide a brief overview of the diseases we are tracking out in Africa. There have been several small outbreaks across the continent. The color coding here denotes the status of those outbreaks. Green is contained and eliminated. Yellow is controlled. And red is uncontrolled."

"What diseases are we looking at?" asked Col. Alexander.

"Several. However, we are going to concentrate on a few that we believe the Chinese are attempting to weaponize. These are the ones with the highest fatality rate and that act quickly."

"There are several deadly viruses on the continent," added the director. "Hepatitis B is a serious problem, but the use of it in warfare would require too much time. It attacks the liver and can eventually cause cirrhosis or cancer, but that doesn't help in the immediate fight. It could be something used to poison future soldiers, but still would not be very practical."

"So, you are looking at things like Ebola," Dane said.

"Yes, along with a few others." Dr. Reagan replied. "Specifically, those resulting in viral hemorrhagic fevers. These diseases are fast-acting and already difficult to treat."

"What is considered fast?" asked Col. Alexander.

"Within a matter of days. The average case for hemorrhagic fevers is death after ten days from the onset of symptoms. It will be a miserable ten days. Soldiers exposed to this would become combat ineffective with twenty-four to forty-eight hours."

"Shit, that's fast," Alexander replied.

The director spoke up. "That is the reason for the urgency of this operation. The Chinese have been researching bioweapons for decades. It's hardly a secret. But given the current state of affairs, confrontation appears imminent. We could be facing these weapons sooner than we think."

"I know we are tracking several of the facilities on mainland China. The whole community is ready to strike those targets when asked, but I never realized that they were collecting live samples overseas." Alexander shook his head. "Whatever happened to good old-fashioned warfare?"

"So what viruses are we looking to intercept?" Dane asked.

Nicky spoke for the first time. "Four. Ebola, Crimean-Congo Hemorrhagic Fever, Lassa Fever, and Marburg."

Dr. Reagan continued. "The fatality and incubation rates of hemorrhagic fevers vary. Intel suggests they are experimenting primarily with these four to lower those times. This is where the Chinese believe they will have the most success."

"Incubation?" Dane asked.

"That is the amount of time between infection and the onset of symptoms," Nicky answered.

"Okay, thanks."

"I will turn it over to Ms. Blackburn to discuss detection techniques."

Huh, Dane thought. *She does have a last name.*

"Thank you, sir. Gentlemen, I will bring three unique pieces of equipment for this operation. The first are bio sensors. We believe the Chinese scientists are using animal byproducts to conceal the samples and ship them back to China via Yemen. The sensors are sensitive up to around thirty feet and will need to be placed along likely routes of travel."

"There are three roads coming into the meat-packing warehouse district," Dane replied. "Maybe two for each road and then two more by the slaughter grounds' entrance for good measure. I assume they are man-portable and concealable."

"Yes," Nicky answered. "They are very light and relatively small. The entire package is the size of a coffee cup. Our modeling guys can conceal everything in plaster rock molds that will blend well alongside the road."

"Is power an issue?"

"Nope. We fixed that common problem with most of our stay-behind devices. The battery is very powerful, but obviously won't last forever. Our modeling guys came through again and developed solar charging properties in their plaster. Think of each rock as its own little independent power source. Also, as a last resort, I can remotely charge the device from my tactical autonomous modulation interface, or TAMI."

"How close do we need to get for an emergency charge, and how long do we need to be on target?

Nicky grimaced. "We need to be within thirty feet for around twenty minutes for a full charge. Not ideal."

"Yikes," Dane chuckled. "We can probably rule that out. Let's hope this plaster works. What are your other two items?"

"Well, TAMI is the second. It interfaces with the sensors, but also has detection capabilities as a standalone device."

"I assume this is also man-portable?"

"Yes. I can easily carry it in a backpack."

"Great. Can we bring two?"

"We can," Nicky answered. "But these devices are very complicated, and it has taken months of training."

Dane interrupted. "I have no intention of using TAMI other than in an extreme situation. I think we should plan a little more training so I can assist you. I will leave the tech to you. I just want to carry a spare. Two is one, and one is none."

"Done," Nicky replied. "The third pieces of tech are small containers to secure the viruses for transport."

The deputy director passed small folders around the table. "Inside you will find projected routes to and from the warehouse once inside Somaliland. We can make available any requested imagery. We have a modified Land Rover at the base in Djibouti. It is up-armored with specially designed containers for the virus."

"I don't think that will work. Can you pull up a map of Somaliland on the screen?" Dane asked.

Dane rose and walked to the front of the room to study the map on the big screen. After several moments, he turned back to the group, focusing on Nicky. "Are your portable virus containers meant to last for the entire trip home in case we couldn't use the ones in the Land Rover?"

"Yes. The Land Rover is a backup containment system."

Dane turned to Col. Alexander next. "My boat still around?"

The colonel smiled as if reading Dane's thoughts. "Why yes, it is. Any place in particular you want it?"

"The terrain will be too rough on a Land Rover. All that armor weight will bog us down and tear up the vehicle, plus using roads will be dangerous. Too few routes, and they are in terrible shape. They don't have any sort of road network cross-country in between cities. Even the cities are not the best. Plus, if something goes wrong at the port our exit roads will all be easily blocked."

Dane turned back to Nicky. "I don't suppose you know how to ride a dirt bike?"

Nicky led Dane down a series of hallways to her team's area. The director had other engagements, and Col. Alexander was needed back in D.C. He and Nicky would further refine the plan and reconvene the group in one week for training authorizations and final mission approval. Dane had a few ideas about training venues, but he had to gauge Nicky's skill sets. He smiled to himself. *Get your mind out of the gutter, man.*

"Here we are."

Dane followed her into a fairly large team room and was immediately struck by the efficiency of the layout. The center of the room was sunken, requiring several steps down to reach its level. A large square table dominated the space, with workstations scattered around its periphery. There were two private offices on the far wall, separated by a large video teleconference display screen. The elevated platforms around the outer walls contained cages similar to what Dane had in the barn at his unit. "Well, this doesn't suck."

Nicky laughed. "We do have a pretty good setup. Comfortably houses an eight-person team. We are short right now with six, but hoping to get some newbies soon."

"I like how your gear is right here if you need to grab or mess around with something."

"Yeah, they actually listened to us when they designed the place. Let's step into my office. Since I am the assistant team leader, I get my own space."

Dane stepped into a tidy little office. It had the bare essentials. Nicky was obviously a minimalist. She didn't even personalize the space. No pictures of family or a husband, or even a boyfriend. He already noticed her ringless hand. *Stop, dude. Keep it professional!*

"Please sit. So, what is this talk of motorcycles and boats? And yes, by the way, I can ride. Just need a refresher. And I am comfortable on boats. Just never operated one. Probably need to do a little more than sunning and drinking while floating on the river, though."

"Ha. Probably no bathing suits and beers this time around. A refresher course for the bikes is easy, and I have a place to train you up quick on boats."

"Oh, our first date sounds exciting." Nicky laughed.

Dane smiled. "We need to use dirt bikes for maximum flexibility. Main roads are a no-go. I don't feel like running into a militia patrol. The boat is ideal for exfil. It can accommodate the bikes, so we don't have to ditch them. Plus, Somaliland has no navy. Not that they could catch us anyway out on the open water."

"What do you have? One of those cigarette boats?"

"Ha, no. Better. A standard-looking fishing dhow. Looks just like the others, except mine houses a large modern engine. She's fast if we need it."

"I hope you don't plan on blowing up the port," she laughed. "I've heard about you cowboys."

Dane smiled. "Some of those stories are certainly true, but no. No bombs. I just like options in case things don't go exactly as planned. And they never do. The enemy always gets a vote."

Nicky nodded. "Okay. I like that. The water certainly gives us more wiggle room if things go bad."

They spent the next few hours going over the operational plans for the mission. Gear they would need. Timelines for execution. And of course, training. Dane would need a crash course in biothreats, while Nicky needed to brush up on motorcross skills and get some experience handling boats. They needed a remote place since, like any training event, marksmanship practice was crucial. Not that they were anticipating a fight, but they had to plan for the worst possible scenario.

Dane told Nicky that he would call her in a few days to set that training up and continue mission planning for their back briefs. They said their goodbyes. Dane knew his way out.

Dane glanced back as he left. Pencil clenched in her teeth as she studied a screen with those murky hazel eyes, Nicky tucked a loose strand of blonde hair behind her ear. *Boy, am I in trouble,* he thought. *Then again, maybe Tyler was right.*

THE BATHROOM WAS WET AGAIN TODAY. THERE IS SOMEONE ELSE HERE. I AM GOING TO WRITE THEM A NOTE. MAYBE WE CAN BE FRIENDS. I WOULD LIKE TO GO ON THE SWINGS AT RECESS WITH MY FRIENDS. I GO ON RECESS EVERY DAY. THERE IS A ROOF, SO I CAN GO OUT IN THE RAIN, BUT I DON'T HAVE ANY FRIENDS TO HANG OUT WITH.

13

THE SUSPECT

Fairfax, Virginia

Devotee: It is done.

Keeper: Good. Thank you. What update did you have about the woman?

Devotee: She was tough. Took a while. I have the name of a man I will visit next.

Keeper: Excellent. I won't forget this. When it is over, you can begin your own collection.

"Captain, I didn't ask for this. Carl sprung it on both of us. I told him our caseload could not support task force duties, but he insisted he needed our help since these cases are so intertwined."

"Well, what's done is done, Patterson. The feds talked to the chief, and he, of course, thinks this is great for the bureau. My hands are tied, no matter how much I don't like it."

"Well, I will at least talk to Carl to ensure our participation is kept to a minimum. Share files. Consult on cases. That sort of thing. But we have enough on our plate that we can't go running to him every time he calls."

"Right," Capt. Ivers answered sarcastically. 'I'll believe that when I see it."

Obviously dismissed, Roger rose and made his way back to his area of the Pit. Pat was laser-focused on an open folder spread across her desk. She didn't even see him come in. She was clearly startled when he sat down across from her at his desk.

"Damn. Didn't even hear you."

"That must be some pretty good reading."

"First, how did it go with the captain?"

"He's not thrilled, Pat. But he knows how this town works."

"No shit. Okay, catching up on stuff coming in from the Fairfax guys." Patricia slid a large stack of photos from the folder over to Roger.

"Is this from the lab?"

"Yup."

"Wow. Looks like a car from a war zone. And still no VIN?"

Pat shook her head. "The hidden one was removed. The mechanics are still looking, but they aren't hopeful."

"Did they get any trace evidence from the car? Something useful that could help locate this guy's abode?" Roger asked.

"Lots, but nothing that identifies him. Most of it is generic dirt and dust. Seems like our perp kept the car fairly clean. Appears to be vacuumed regularly, and there was no trash or anything left in the car."

"What, the lab guys can't test an obscure dirt sample found underneath the car jack and figure out the farm it came from where our victim broke down on the side of the country road a few weeks ago?"

"Real funny. Maybe you should write detective novels if this whole police thing doesn't work out. They are trying to match DNA from hair found in the car, but just like the prints, nothing yet from CODIS."

"What I don't get is why go through so much effort to conceal the car? I mean, taking it apart and removing the hidden VINs. Why?"

"I have two thoughts there. The first is maybe he got it that way. Bought it at a private sale and never recorded a new title. Or maybe he didn't expect to be caught, but he removed it just in case so it couldn't lead back to him. He may have some mad mechanic skills."

"Well, we need a full court press on this thing. I know we think this was his first time, but that may not be the case. He could have another child."

"I know. I am pushing the lab guys hard. Carl is pushing the fingerprint folks running the Integrated Automated Fingerprint Identification System hard. There should have been a hit by now. Hard to believe our guy wasn't printed at least once in his miserable life."

"Bizarre. In this day and age—"

Roger was interrupted by the phone ringing at Pat's desk.

"Special Agent Stills. Uh huh." She furiously began scribbling notes on a nearby pad. "Uh-huh. Okay. Uh-huh. Got it. Thanks."

Roger stared at his partner once the receiver was safely in its cradle.

Pat looked up from her notes. "Oh shit. Sorry. That was Barry over in operations. Seems like the whole IAFIS has been on the fritz for the last day. Nobody has been getting results. It's restored now and spit out a fingerprint match. Johnathon Tyler Basker."

"Now things can start moving!"

Pat ripped her scribbled note sheet from the pad. "And I have an address. Let's go. I'm driving."

"Like hell you are."

They arrived at the small home in Springfield and parked behind the litany of cruisers. They had called ahead to Springfield PD to secure the scene and conduct a cursory search. They had debated on whether to authorize entry, since the entering officers would bring contamination to the scene despite precautions, but they were willing to take that risk. Basker could have another captive.

Fairfax County was lead until the state authorities arrived. They contacted Roger and gave an initial description of the scene, along with several recommendations on processing the scene. It appeared that there were no other victims present, but there were indications of other potential victims for Basker. Roger had authorized them to start without them.

Roger and Pat signed in, gloved up, and entered the front door. It was a modest brick home built off I-95. It was just outside the beltway, and probably predated the freeway system around the capital, a system that frustrated every commuter for a fifty-mile radius. The homes in this neighborhood were solid, built for returning World War II soldiers and their nuclear family of a wife and two or three children. From the frontlines to the factory, they helped build the greater D.C.

area, including the monstrosity of a freeway now outside their front windows.

He and Pat flowed from room to room. Technicians were busy taking film and notes, meticulously capturing every detail of the home. It had a small living room with a gallery kitchen extending from the left side. There were two small bedrooms, one of which appeared to be a home office. Two IT techs sat at Basker's desk; myriad wires connected to every electronic device they could find. Two laptops, one computer tower, and several phones and tablets were arranged across the desk. The techs cloned all data first, lest they lose precious evidence while hacking into the machines. Roger and Pat left the small space and proceeded to find the basement stairs. Rounding the hallway corner, they got their first surprise at the house, which in hindsight was really no surprise at all.

"What took you guys so long? You really need to check out the basement."

"Lead the way, Carl," responded Pat.

Roger rolled his eyes but followed Carl and Pat down the narrow stairway to the basement. *Of course he got here before us,* he thought. *Probably sleeps with a police scanner in his bedroom.*

Their eyes were assaulted at the bottom of the steps by the overwhelming artificial light. The basement was otherwise dark and dreary, more like a bunker or a dungeon. There was no natural light, which made sense for homes built during the threat of a Soviet nuclear strike. The Cold War era created a hypersensitive population worried about the apocalypse, even going so far as instructing schoolchildren to shelter under their desks upon witnessing a bright flash. The bright flash of the police light stands stirred Roger to look for his school desk.

Once their pupils appropriately dilated, adjusting to the room, Carl showed the pair what had been discovered so far. They carefully avoided disturbing the swarm of crime scene techs as they began their somber tour of the basement dungeon. "So, what the hell is up with the FBI fingerprint database? You guys forget to pay your bills?" Pat asked.

"Funny, Stills. Actually, hold that thought to the end. I want to talk task force business with you both when we have a little more privacy."

Roger remained silent. As they moved throughout the basement, he willed his mind to capture and maintain every little detail. The main room was dark and unfurnished. Cabinets ran along the walls, untouched so far by the crime scene techs concentrating their searches on the three small bedrooms, or rather cells. Basker had previously worked as a general contractor and obviously had the skills for the modification of living spaces. It appeared that Basker planned for three guests. The rooms were approximately ten feet by ten with a sink and commode in one corner and a single bed in the other. A modest desk filled the last available corner. The final touch was the reinforced doors with a plexiglass window, along with a delivery tray for the transfer of items and food. Roger shuddered.

Pat and Carl had moved into the fourth and final room. It was clearly the space of a madman. One wall was covered entirely with pictures and writings and string, connecting streams of thought. One in particular drew Roger's attention. Several pictures of John Nobless covered the center of the wall. Strings branched out to other clusters. Fountain Head Regional Park. John's bike. His parents' home. Even the nearest police station. Although insane, this level of detail indicated a methodical mind.

"Super creepy," Carl noted.

Pat moved closer to the wall. "All these children. We need to start identifying them all. Make sure they are safe."

"Detective from Fairfax County upstairs told me about the pictures. His team prioritized identification. He has patrols ready to conduct welfare checks with the family. I told him not to wait on our say so. Just start and keep us informed," Roger answered. "Let's hope this was his first attempt."

"The initial sweep of the cells indicated they have not been used," Carl offered.

Roger moved from left to right, focusing on every image on the wall.

Pat recognized her partner's body language and intense focus. "Did the detective have anything else about the wall we should be aware of? I don't think I have ever seen anything like this outside of the movies."

"He said photographs only, so far. They haven't moved a thing. Once they are positive they have the sequence mapping all captured digitally, they will remove, catalogue, and reconstruct it in the lab. The are taking it to Fairfax County labs for the build, which is fine. They have space and are close by for us to access when we need. They will bring in psych consultants. I asked them to coordinate through our office as well."

Several minutes passed before Carl broke the silence. "Please keep my office informed, too. We have resources to offer. Let's head outside for a moment."

The three silently exited the house. It was a modest backyard enclosed with a tidy wooden fence. A single shed stood along the back fence. Very little privacy was afforded in the tightly packed neighborhood. It seemed like Basker didn't utilize this area. There was no grill, no deck, not even a couple of lawn chairs.

"Do you mind telling me why we are standing around in a would-be abductor's backyard?" Pat asked. "Most of the evidence seems to be on the inside. Unless we are going to tear apart that shed."

"Because Carl doesn't want to discuss his theory in front of anyone. He only trusts us on the state side when he should be looking at his own house."

"Carl, what is he talking about?"

"Roger is referring to the delay in identifying our subject. A delay caused by a glitch in IAFIS and CODIS. Someone didn't want a fingerprint or DNA match."

"Actually, I was more thinking a specific glitch with respect to the notification aspect of the system. The suspect was identified. Probably early on. The requesting agency was not provided that information, but I think someone else was."

Pat looked perplexed. Carl answered her look.

"We know the system was hacked. It caused nearly a twenty-four-hour delay. Whoever did this was good. I mean scary good. Our guys are clueless."

"Why would someone do that?"

"So they could search this place before we did. It strengthens Carl's theory about this club."

"What was it for you? What triggered that detective's nose of yours?"

Carl asked Roger.

"Several of the wall art was askew on the first floor. The techs had not powdered them yet, so I know they didn't move them. The queen bed in the bedroom was not lined up completely with the indents in the carpet. Most everyone is concentrating on the electronics and the basement. Cursory search of the bedroom to be followed by more in depth later. No way someone just knocked those bed legs out of the carpet indents. Bed was lifted. And the pictures on the creepy wall in the basement have been folded back slightly, as if someone wanted to look for writing on the back. Basker seems too OCD for those things, and I know our techs are more careful than that with evidence."

"Anything else? "Carl asked.

Roger turned back to the house and pointed. "Everything is locked up tight except that window. Our suspect entered there. It is one of those old flip locks. Easy to open, but a pain to relock. I am betting our home invader ran out of time and had to leave. Figured an unlocked window was not cause for alarm."

"Well, well. I am certainly glad we are on the same team. And that you are on my task force."

"So, you two think somehow this club was able to hack FBI database systems and get someone over here to search this place before us?"

"That's what we are saying, Pat. Carl's theory is starting to shine through."

"My theory is expanding. This club is more powerful and capable than I originally thought. And after seeing Savannah, I am more convinced that they are just getting started. They took out nineteen armed men and rescued ten underage girls."

"Wow," exclaimed Patricia. "Do you really think the club is that big? That is like eight or ten shooters."

"My theory is just three," Carl replied.

"Only three?" asked Roger. "Three? How did they manage that kind of carnage with only three people?"

"This club has some very talented players. Plus, if I am correct about the motivation of these folks, they will never stop until every one of these pedophiles, smugglers, or anyone harming children is in the ground. Unless we stop them first."

Just then a uniformed officer jogged into the yard. "Special Agent Patterson. Stills. Call from the hospital. Johnathon Basker is dead."

Benefactor: Are we still on for tomorrow night?

President: We are. However, I would like to avoid the mansion at this time.

Benefactor: I have the perfect place.

President: Thank you. We can discuss some stricter security measures for the future.

14

THE SECOND BRIEFING

Washington, D.C.

Dane casually adjusted his tie with the help of his reflection on the hotel's glass front doors. Charles had requested a different venue for this evening's meeting. After a quick internet search of the popular rooftop restaurant on 15th Street Northwest, he opted for a sports coat and tie. The venue was fancier than most places he frequented. He didn't want to stand out, but he was not going as far as a full-blown suit. He wore enough of those in the various embassies he worked at over the years. The more casual attire just fit better.

He also hoped Charles was covering the bill. He was being promoted soon to sergeant major. The pay hike was nice, but this area was not getting any cheaper. And with inflation, the raise would be barely noticeable. This is not the sort of place he would normally select, at least not without a special occasion.

Jack waited for him in the lobby. The elevator was open and empty. A quick push of the top floor button sent them on their way.

"Glad you could make it, Dane."

"Thanks, Jack. I am curious why Charles requested this meeting, especially since I have some troubling news of my own that I wanted to discuss with him."

"We know."

Nothing else was said during the ride to the top floor. Dane pondered the ominous choice of words. The elevator dinged, and Jack led Dane into the open-air restaurant.

The view caused his breath to catch. The sun was just setting in the West, but not before lighting D.C. ablaze in oranges and reds. The

Washington Memorial stood firmly to the south. The White House to the west felt so close, like he could touch it. But the view was a temporary distraction.

Dane's senses immediately picked up on the unnatural setup. Lights were dimmed to nearly nonexistent throughout the restaurant, save one illuminated table in the far corner. Soft music played at a barely audible level. And of course, the most telling feature was the complete absence of any patrons. The hottest place in D.C. for rooftop dining was completely empty.

"I guess I shouldn't be surprised by anything at this point."

Jack chuckled. "It is still fun to surprise you. Let's join our guests."

They approached the small table set for five. Dane recognized Charles, but could not quite make out the woman sitting across from him. Her back was toward him, but something was oddly familiar.

"Welcome, Dane. Won't you join us?"

The woman turned as Dane reached his seat. *What the hell?* he thought.

"I believe you know Ms. Blackburn."

Nicky appeared just as shocked to see Dane make an appearance.

"Surprise number two," Jack said as he found his own seat.

"Well, then I guess this is surprise number three," a man said as he entered the room from a nearby kitchen entrance. He dried his hands on a dish towel as he approached, then extended his right hand to Dane.

Quite the night for surprises, Dane thought, instantly recognizing the eccentric billionaire. *Or do you just pretend to be eccentric so nobody looks too close at what you are doing?*

"Jackson Lentz. I have been looking forward to meeting you."

"Dane Cooper. Nice to finally put a face to the financier behind this whole operation. I believe it is you I have to thank for all the support."

"You flatter me, Mr. Cooper, but I hope I can contribute more than just a plane ride. I am appreciative of all that you and your team did down there."

Everyone took their seats.

"Thank you all for coming," Charles offered. "We have quite a bit to discuss. It is unusual to have all of us together, so we decided on a more private setting away from my home."

"This is certainly private. You rented out an entire restaurant?" Dane replied.

It was Jackson who answered. "I own the restaurant and this hotel. The restaurant is closed for necessary repairs."

Dane smirked and looked around the pristine restaurant. "Now I get it. And now I know who to thank for addressing my transportation issues. I cannot thank you enough for the, uh, accommodation. It made our task that much easier."

Nicky looked confused. "What issues are we talking about here?"

"New York, Savannah, and others, Ms. Blackburn. Dane has very detailed travel requirements, which I do appreciate. Risk aversion and all."

She turned to Dane. "New York? Savannah? That was you?"

Jack answered for Dane. "It was your intel he actioned. It was your efforts that led to locating Henry Galfini and his associate, Tony Mazzo."

"Impressive," Nicky answered. "The world is better off without those scum. But throwing them in front of a train . . . kinda gross."

"Thank you, Nicky. My pleasure. And although it may seem excessive and gross, I really needed to conceal any possible evidence from the authorities."

Dane turned to Charles and Jack. "So, are we ready to discuss why we are here, or do we have more surprises?"

Charles smiled. "I appreciate your frustration. Let me assure you that was not my intent. Jackson can sometimes have a flair for the dramatic. I had no subtle way to introduce you to Ms. Blackburn. I mean, officially, as a member of The Cabal."

"Is that what you are calling it now? How about we talk about our real mission to the Horn of Africa? What strings did you both pull?"

Nicky and Dane looked to Charles, then turned their attention to Jackson.

"Yes, it has always been The Cabal. Unofficially of course. We hardly post ads at the YMCA. Charles and I began this journey a long time ago."

Jackson paused as a waiter from the nearby kitchen arrived to take their orders. Sensing the seriousness of his guests, the man was to the point, leaving the group with water and wine before departing as quickly as he had arrived.

Jackson took a heavy sip of wine. "Nicky. Dane. I did pull some strings for this mission. It is very important, and I believe by combining your talents as a team, you will be unstoppable."

"Not a complete answer. What does The Cabal want of us in Somaliland?"

Jack slid a thin manila envelope to each of them. Nicky and Dane began to read.

"As you can see, your ultimate target is Ibrahim Mohamad Mahmud," said Charles. "He is a human trafficker for a very powerful terrorist organization. His activities finance most of their operations."

"Does this have anything to do with Savannah?" Dane asked.

"Yes," answered Jackson. "Savannah was the lynchpin in the overall operation to eliminate Ibrahim. Your team's work there dealt a huge blow to their organization. So big, in fact, it has caused Ibrahim to emerge from the shadows so to speak, to repair his network. It is a real opportunity to cut the head off the snake. He has been in hiding for quite some time now. He hasn't been seen for years. This is the rarest of opportunities."

"Won't someone else just take his place?" Nicky asked.

"Not likely," answered Jack. "I have encountered this organization before. Think of them as a terror broker. Although they have ideals and demands and all that rhetoric, they have no operational wing. They fund like-minded organizations and let them take all the risk."

"Oh, like the United Nations," Dane stated, which earned a few chuckles around the table.

"They have a small core cadre. Very centralized and incestual. They do not embrace new members quickly, and paranoia runs rampant. You kill Ibrahim. That will set them back years."

"And with further insight into their operations, we can prevent them from rebuilding the network," Charles added. "Since Savannah, the chatter amongst these organizations has doubled. It has become an intelligence boon. The community has been slowly putting together myriad target packages. Some for the U.S., some for partners and allies."

"I can verify that, Dane. The NSA noted this increase the morning the Savannah incident became public. Lots of folks in the Middle East and Africa are scared. They're communicating, and we are listening."

Dane closed the file on Ibrahim Mohamed Mahmud, sliding the contents back to Jack. He turned his attention to Jackson and Charles. "I appreciate what you are trying to accomplish, I really do. But assign this to someone else. I have work to do here in the States."

"Mr. Cooper, we—"

"I don't want to hear it." Dane grew agitated. "I did the Savannah job like you asked. I took my eye off the ball to solve your big problem, and it's done. I need to focus on the Keeper. My work is here!"

"We have others working on the Keeper," offered Charles.

Dane stood to leave. "Whatever strings you pulled to have me deploy, undo it. Sorry, Nicky but the unit will give you a solid partner. I will give them all the work I have done so far. I will make sure you have a successful mission. I just can't take any more time away from looking for—"

Jack stood. "Dane, a word?" He nodded to the empty bar on the far side of the restaurant.

The pair crossed the restaurant to the ornate bar, Dane sat on a stool while Jack walked around to the far side. He pulled down two rocks glasses and studied the selection of spirits. Once satisfied, he retrieved a bottle of Copper Fox Rye Whiskey, poured a healthy serving into each glass, and placed the bottle on the bar.

"I have wanted to try this since I saw the distillery by Old Rag Mountain."

"One. Make it light. I am not staying."

"I get it Dane. I really do. And I can promise you we will not drop the ball with the Keeper."

"Jack, just stop. I know we are all trying to be good little soldiers here, but there is a possible link to my daughter. We need to analyze everything from that whack job Basker. Combine it with everything we have from Simmons. There must be a connection. We are just not looking hard enough. Those two can have someone else take out Ibrahim. I don't trust them to get to the Keeper."

"Well, trust is a funny thing, and I am asking you to trust me now. This mission is more important than you know. I can give you more details when it is over. But this organization has plagued our colleagues for over a decade. Secondly, I am assigning Sam exclusively to investigate the Keeper."

Dane sipped his glass. "So, the one person I actually do trust besides you."

"Yes. We have had some developments in the cyber world. Suffice it to say, it involves decryption and a lot of ones and zeros. I don't understand most of it, and it will take some time. Go to Somaliland. Finish the assignment. Once you are back, I hope to have further leads that we all can follow until it is over."

Dane drained his glass in one final gulp. "I'm holding you to that."

Nicky arrived at the bar as Dane set down his empty glass near the drink rail. "Can I borrow our guy?"

"Be my guest."

"Let's take a walk, Mr. Cooper. Show a country girl your big city."

"Hilarious," he responded sarcastically. "Don't you live in Baltimore?"

The pair exited the building and heading south for the National Mall. The White House, to their right, was illuminated for Christmas. The national Christmas tree had been lit last month with the surrounding area displaying trees from all fifty states.

"I had never made it into the city for the state trees. Can we walk through?"

"We can. Let's grab some cocoa. It is only going to get colder the longer we stay out here."

"We don't have to stay long. I just want to see Oklahoma's tree."

Dan pointed to the open field beyond the line of Christmas trees. "I think I see some tumbleweed over there."

"Ass!" she responded as she punched him in the arm.

It had been a while since he had come down for the Christmas festivities. Angela asked to come here every year. She would check the internet for details on all the events and celebrations. He often worked late, promising they would take a special trip into the city on the weekend. Sometimes, they did. But sometimes, they didn't. He regretted not taking her every single time she asked.

"Hello? Are you with me?" Nicky asked.

"Sorry, lost in thought, I guess. What were you asking?"

"Let's head over to the reflecting pool. I want to look up a name at the Vietnam Memorial, and I've heard Lincoln looks incredible at night."

"Let's do it."

They continued walking, mostly in silence. The air was cold, but not in a painful way. It stung in the way a tattoo needle pierced the skin, a pain to remind you of life, to knock you off autopilot. It stung, but was then immediately followed by relief. A never-ending cycle. When they passed by the Constitution Gardens, he paused.

"It was here, you know."

"What was here?" Nicky asked.

"This is where the recruiter bumped me and asked me to meet with Charles. That bench right there."

"Let's rest for a second."

"Hard to believe it has been that long since I have been around here. I live just a few miles away."

"You want to talk about what happened back there with Mr. Lentz and Charles?"

"Sorry about that. Believe me, it has nothing to do with you and everything to do with them."

"It's this Keeper, right? I was one of the analysts trying to crack Simmons' computers."

"I am frustrated, yes. But it is not that we don't have a solid lead yet. It is that they paused on that thread and sprung us up for Savannah. I know how important it was to destroy that ring, but that took time. Time to plan. Time to train. Time away from the Keeper and possibly Angela."

"But, people are working on the Keeper and your case. Maybe not on the streets, but work is being done. And from what I am hearing, they should be able to crack the encryption of the cloud data storage space the group may be using. Combine that with what Sam recovered from Basker's house, and we may have a game-changer."

"I know all of this, yet I feel useless. And now Somaliland. I should be here in case something breaks on the case."

"I am sure they will keep us in the loop. Shit, Mr. Lentz has a plane at his disposal. If something comes up, make sure Sam sends the plane. Hell, I want to come, too. I thought the train thing in New York was crazy, but a firefight along the Savannah River? Pretty hot, Mr. Cooper."

Nicky smiled at Dane. She was beautiful. Her personality was a perfect fit with his. They shared the same career goals. Shit, they shared the same hobbies with The Cabal. Illegal hobbies, but that was not important. On the surface, they appeared to be a perfect match.

"Thanks for the therapy, Nicky. Let's get this mission done so we can get back to work here. I will call you an Uber."

THERE WAS NO SCHOOL TODAY. WENT TO THE SHOWER AND BACK IN MY ROOM. THE TV WAS NOT ON. I HAD MY BREAKFAST. I DID NOT GET ANY OTHER FOOD UNTIL LATER. I THINK THE MAN MUST HAVE GONE AWAY. I READ MY BOOK INSTEAD. I HAVE A SHELF WITH ALL MY FAVORITES. I AM READING HARRY POTTER AGAIN.

15

THE COLLABORATION

Washington, D.C.

Devotee: We may have a problem concerning Zealot.

Keeper: What is the problem?

Devotee: There was a man searching the house when I got there. Once he left, I had no time to remove things. Police arrived.

Keeper: It is one of them. Visit the man the woman spoke of. Be vigilant. They may be suspicious.

The Thomas Jefferson Memorial came into view as they crossed the Potomac River along the 14th Street Bridge. Roger hated driving into the city, but had to admit it afforded travelers a majestic entrance. The river waters churned as boats drifted along, touring by water. The Washington Monument stood proud over all others, a beacon for every resident and visitor.

He had once enjoyed exploring the nation's capital, visiting the museums, walking along the National Mall, or even catching a Washington Nationals game. But the city had changed. The buildings remained. The monuments held true. It was the people. Anger. Violence. Intolerance. *I wonder if this city will ever heal,* he thought.

Roger and Pat turned north on 10th Street Northwest as they approached the J. Edgar Hoover Building, the FBI mothership. Carl had invited them to get a feel for the task force and meet the other members. They also needed to discuss the murders surrounding these cases. First, the reverend and then Johnathon Busker—in police custody no less. And now a third: Jill Clark, a parishioner at the reverend's church. She was found in her apartment after neighbors called the police for a welfare check. She had suffered torture equal to that of the reverend.

Roger eased the car to a stop entrance to visitor parking. He and Pat presented their badges. "Special Agents Roger Patterson and Patricia Stills. Here to see Special Agent Carl Blanchard."

"I have you both on my list. I presume you are both armed."

"We are," Roger answered.

"You are cleared to retain your weapons. Here are your visitor badges. They must be visible above the waist. You can park anywhere you want. Elevators on the west wall will bring you to the lobby."

"Thank you."

Once parked, he and Pat found their way upstairs.

"Special Agents Patterson and Stills?" a man asked as he approached the pair.

"Roger."

"Pat."

The three all shock hands. "Ken Sanders, special assistant to Agent Blanchard. If you follow me, I will take you to the task force conference room."

They rode another set of elevators to the fifth floor. Ken led through a series of hallways until they arrived at a glass conference room with sweeping views of the capital. Several people were already seated at the large table, with Carl at the head. He rose as they entered.

"Thank you for coming." He gestured to the two seats directly adjacent to his own. "Everyone, this is Special Agent Roger Patterson and Special Agent Patricia Stills of the VBI. Maybe go around the table for introductions."

"I am Dan Peters. Homeland Security. Center for Countering Human Trafficking."

"Morning. Nancy Foster. Homeland. I also work at the center with Dan."

"Shelly Jones. FBI. Analyst. Violent Crime."

"Henry Kirkland. FBI. Special investigator for the task force with Shelly."

"Andrew Parsons. FBI. I am a profiler for the Behavioral Analysis Unit, or BAU for short."

"John Oakes. U.S. Marshals. Fugitive investigations."

"Mark Smith. CIA. Analyst. Office of Middle East and North Africa."

"Ken Sanders. FBI. I work exclusively with Carl."

Carl clasped his hands on the table. "As you can see, we have a diverse group. My intent on bringing everyone together was twofold. Introductions, so everyone knows who is who, and to catch everyone up on five leads we are following."

"What are the five leads?" asked Oakes. "I am not tracking any of them at this point. At least, no fugitives we are looking for."

"*Yet*, John. Marshals were brought in because you are hunters. We want you in the game early as we develop our prey."

Roger rolled his eyes and mouthed the words drama queen at Carl.

"So, as I was saying, the fire leads are the discovery of Holly Jones and Jon Parker at Humane Hands, the later torture and murder of Reverend Anderson from that church, the torture and murder of Jonathon Basker, the Savannah port shooting, and finally the death of Ms. Jill Clark. She was found last night in her apartment in Pentagon City. You all have briefing packets on the reverend and Basker. I will let our colleagues from Virginia update us all on Clark."

"Let's not forget Dana Chase." Stills cleared her throat as she pushed packets to everyone around the table. "Ms. Jill Clark. Age fifty-eight. Retired teacher. She was found bound and tortured, just like our first two victims. She had no connection to Basker, but was a member of the reverend's church."

"Was the same device used?" Shelly looked through the other packets. "Some sort of drill?"

"Yes," Roger answered. "Similar wounds to the reverend. Cuts and stab wounds on the front of her torso and what appears to be drill holes into her spine."

"Did Basker have these marks?" asked Henry. "And if so, how did people in the hospital not hear his screams?"

"Because his mouth was wired shut," Pat answered. "Perp put fentanyl into his IV bag, then pulled the wires tight around Basker's mouth. This incident did not involve torture. This was a quick in and out to silence Basker. Drill to the spine and the drug overdose to ensure he couldn't be revived. We believe he used the fentanyl in case the doctors tried to start working on his injuries with no idea the drugs were in his system. Guaranteed kill."

"Theories?" Ken asked as he flipped through the briefing packet.

"Yes, Pat and I believe that there is a network of these child abductors, and Basker was a member who needed silencing. And as to Carl's theory about some sort of club taking these guys out, we believe the abductors are fighting back. We are working on figuring out where the reverend and Ms. Clark fit in all this."

Carl cleared his throat. "So, we need to dig into Reverend Anderson and Ms. Clark's lives. If they were both members of this club, they must have links to others. I know VBI and D.C. Metro Police are looking into this, but I would like Shelley and Henry to focus their efforts here."

Both agents nodded. "Next is Basker. Andrew, that's right up your alley. Full profile workup. Whatever we get, we will of course share with our Virginia friends for their investigation."

"Got it."

"And lastly, there is Savannah. Ken and I went down there the other week. Real shit show. Whoever did this was thorough and professional. Savannah PD, Staties, and Port Authority are baffled. Dan and Nancy, this will be your focus area."

"Already on it. Our office has been scouring big data for whatever insights we can get. Dan has already been down there once."

"I guess this is where I come in," said Mark.

"Yes, Mark. I need everything we can get on that ship, its crew, and its destination. Those girls were being sold to someone. I want to know the buyer and the broker. One of these parties may be a link to this club."

"That leaves the kidnappings to us. Roger and I are cross-checking data from Jon and Dana Chase. Pennsylvania has shared everything they have on Holly. We even took a trip up there shortly after the children were recovered to meet the investigators."

After the task force meeting had adjourned, Carl invited Roger and Pat back to his office. "Can we speak privately?"

With Ken trailing behind, they once again negotiated the sterile hallways. It was a path Roger hoped he could recreate upon departure, dreading the age-old shame of a man asking for directions.

The corner office commanded incredible views of the city, reminding them both of the powerful position Carl held. The office was spacious, with a large mahogany desk and a conference table. There was a more intimate seating area alongside the window not housing the desk. Carl led them to the area—two couches and a leather chair configured in three sides of a square to promote discussion. A freshly brewed pot of coffee, gently steaming, sat on the coffee table. They made themselves comfortable.

"I really appreciate you both coming down today."

"Like we had a choice, Carl," Roger answered.

"Listen, I get it. I know you have a lot on your plates. Virginia is a large area to cover with plenty of crime to keep your office busy. However, I believe that this task force could really do some good—provide answers to a lot of unsolved crimes and hopefully prevent future ones."

"We all share the same view," Roger continued, "but we can't run up to D.C. every time you want to have a pow-wow."

"I have no jurisdiction over the Virginia Bureau of Investigation. The only power I have is to step in if we believe that these cases are a federal issue better handled with our resources."

Roger's face began to emanate a light shade of red. "Listen here—"

Pat intercepted with a calming gesture, placing her hand on her partner's forearm. "Gentlemen, cool it. We are on the same team. And Carl"—she gave him that admonishing look—"Subtle threats are not conducive to teamwork. What is conducive is calling us. Give us a heads-up on what you need from us. Don't call our captain."

Carl raised his hands in a gesture of surrender. "You both are right. My apologies. I intended no threats, and I will try and do a better job of reaching out to you both. I understand you have a full caseload."

"Where is this coming from Carl?" Roger asked." You have always been kind of an ass, but you seem to be going a little overboard."

"Now Roger, this—"

"It's okay, Pat. I *have* been a little harsh with you both. I have spent the last year chasing these ghosts, this club, without any real interest from upstairs."

"Let me guess: Savannah?" Roger asked.

"Yes. This club was taking out some low-level assholes—like Arthur Camp—who were not really spiking on anybody's radar. Then, a few ripples with Henry Galfini, but still viewed as an accident. But Savannah was huge. Media is still covering it from coast to coast. That gave everybody a black eye. Authorities in Florida, Department of Homeland Security, and us."

"Follow the money," Pat chimed in. "Nobody put forth much effort until purses were hit."

"That's a little pessimistic, but not entirely inaccurate. The problem is speculation. The world thinks some privately funded mercenary squad attacked this port and we, the authorities, were unable to stop them."

"Leads to a perception problem," Roger added. "And with everything else going on in the world, whether it's the FBI's fault or not, you guys are taking the hit. That means your bosses probably spend more time on the hill answering to those jackals in Congress than in their plush corner offices."

Carl smirked. "Oh, and I am the ass? We are getting blamed for everything from the border crisis to the war in Ukraine and to the Chinese landing on the dark side of the moon."

"Real tearjerker. How about we focus on what we can affect?"

Pat had enough. "You really are an ass, Roger. Let's change the subject. What did you want to talk about, Carl?"

"Money. Like you said, Pat, follow the money."

"I am not sure what you are getting at. I meant when big business suffers, the authorities notice," she answered.

"What Carl means is follow the money that is funding this group. It can't be cheap, especially with the firepower they had in Savannah."

"And it's not just that, guys. There's all the secrecy. All the cloak and dagger crap. I feel it in my gut that Turner is involved. When shit goes down, he is nowhere to be found. His car is at his house. No travel records."

"And ambiguous technical surveillance?" Pat asked. "Nothing?"

"We have scoured CCTV cameras. Public cameras, business cameras, even ATMs. His credit cards have been active, but in areas nowhere near crime scenes. I know he was in Savannah. I know it in my bones, but he made a credit card purchase three hours before Savannah went down. In Fairfax, damn it."

"How about his phone?"

"Same. Fuckin' thing was hitting off a tower near the place he used the credit card."

"Okay. So, if you are right about Turner, then the only logical solution is that someone else is assuming his digital identity. Was there no camera footage from the place the card was used?" Roger asked.

"Of course not. Small deli off of University. Cameras have been broken for years. They never needed to have it fixed."

"Photo ID?"

"Negative. Nobody in the shop recognized a pic of Turner. Doesn't really help proving a negative. Place was packed. Tons of people pass through, so it is not inconceivable that nobody would remember him."

"You sure are hell-bent on Turner. Even if he is involved, he didn't take on the whole Savannah crew on his own. Any other suspects?" Pat asked.

"I think Dane Cooper is good for this as well. He certainly has the skills, plus the motivation. Ken has several packets of potential suspects."

"Twenty-six at the moment," Ken offered, speaking for the first time. "That includes Turner and Cooper."

"I have a colleague down at Quantico. He teaches an intel analysis course. Advanced course for senior analysts. They do a capstone project for a final exercise. He agreed to have them dive deep into our packets. We should have something in a week or so."

"I still think it is a pretty big leap to think these guys are rescuing a few children in this area and then decided to wipe out a large terrorist smuggling operation in Savannah," Pat said.

"I tend to agree with that, Carl. But I defer to your investigation. Let's table that for now and circle back to what you and Pat brought up: The money."

Carl nodded toward Ken. "This has been extremely challenging since there simply is no money to follow. We have talked with our Financial Crime Unit and the folks over at FinCEN since this may be a case of reverse money laundering so to speak."

"FinCen?" Pat asked.

"Department of Treasury folks. They monitor financial transactions. Big data pulls. Basically, think of them as financial analysts on a global scale. Money laundering is their specialty. I can't remember every act or code, but they have authorities on what is referred to as the Bank Secrecy Act. Its primary focus is to deny terrorist funding."

"So, this sounds like a needle in a haystack. Good luck with that."

"Funny, Roger. They do have methods to look for legitimate funds going for illicit means, but we need a starting point. If we identify a suspect, we could tear into their financial records to make a case. We just need that name first."

Roger stood to leave, with Pat following his lead. "Good luck combing through those records. You may be onto something. On the other hand, this group may just be pulling their resources together to get the job done. There may not be a Ross Perot."

Ken turned to Carl after the Virginia agents departed. "Ross Perot? The guy that ran for president against Bush senior in the nineties?"

"Read Ken Follett's book *On Wings of Eagles*. There was more to Perot than just a successful business. It's the reason a lot of folks voted for him."

16

THE TDY

Pellston, Michigan

The small plane touched down smoothly at the Pellston Regional Airport. Located a few miles north of Petosky, Michigan, the small airfield was the closest runway to their destination. Before their deployment, Dane had found a training facility up in the mountains near Dodge City. The city's name was oddly appropriate for the skills they needed to practice. The site offered training on marksmanship, off-road dirt bike navigation, and emergency medical care. And above all else, it guaranteed privacy.

Dane and Nicky unloaded their Pelican cases of weapons and their accompanying kit. They kept their loads light, since they needed to move quickly through the hazardous terrain of Somaliland to reach Berbera. A rifle and a sidearm were all they would need.

The intent was to avoid contact. If they encountered any, the fast KTM 350 four-stroke motorcycle engines should easily outpace any enemy vehicles. And since Somaliland had no functional air force, Dane was not concerned about air assets being used against them. Dane had selected these specific bikes for maximum fuel efficiency. The older models had three-gallon tanks, too. They would still need to carry fuel for the nearly four-hundred-mile trek, but smaller amounts than if they went with newer models.

A multitude of private training facilities can be found throughout the country, but Dane wanted this site in the upper peninsula of Michigan for another important training objective it offered: Maritime navigation and general boatmanship. There was no greater teacher than Lake Superior. Just listen to the lyrics of *The Wreck of the Edmund Fitzgerald*, he thought.

Dane was comfortable with boats, and had been his whole life. He had also designed and operated the exact boat, the Safia, they would use in the Gulf of Aden. The Safia had come to life on an old Panasonic Toughbook, where he used an auto-sketch program for some of the design basics. The rudimentary sketches were given to a local boat builder, and the powerful engine was ordered from the Philippines. The craft was intended to carry a platoon of soldiers to conduct beach landing operations under the cover of darkness. The Safia was light, fast, and quite maneuverable despite its steering apparatus of a Nissan car steering wheel connected to a large wooden rudder via hemp rope. He never got to use the boat for the intended mission, but had plenty of memories training aboard.

He wanted to brush up on his skills, but more importantly ensure Nicky was trained if something happened to him. Wounded or killed, he owed her the training to survive on her own. *She is wicked smart,* he thought. *She'll pick it up quickly.*

Once their rental truck was loaded, they began their four-hour drive to the site. They hadn't spoken much during the flight due to the noise of the aircraft and the voluminous amount of intel reports they needed to read, both from work and The Cabal. Both targets required intense scrutiny. The files from The Cabal were on a secure tablet that could be accessed with either of their biometrics. Virtual Machine software was hidden in a benign application on the otherwise normally functioning tablet. Utilizing an ultra-secure password, they could open a virtual machine and look at the information regarding Ibrahim.

There was not as much there as Dane had hoped, but the man had been a ghost for quite some time. Their military target was more fluid, since it entailed the static location of the meat-processing warehouse along with the moving target of the virus smugglers. It was the best way Dane could think of to categorize them. He and Nicky had finalized most of their mission planning before they left the D.C area, but still needed to work out the final touches and the physical integration of the two missions.

Dane was in charge of setting up this training, but CSM Reynolds had given a little pushback. He eventually relented, but not before bitching at Dane. "Are you telling me that in preparation for a mission in Somaliland, you know the hot place with deserts and rocks and mountains, you choose northern Michigan as an ideal training environment?"

"Actually, the location is in the upper peninsula. We land in northern Michigan, or Up North and drive from there. The upper peninsula is *Really* Up North," Dane said.

"I really hate you sometimes, Dane."

"Listen, CSM, the training camp is perfect. It's run by a couple of old SEALs. They have some special boat team guys, and two retired corpsmen for our live tissue training."

"Hell of a bill to get those goats for training."

"We need it. Nicky and I will be out there by ourselves. We need to ensure our medical skills are up to date. It's expensive because we have to have a veterinarian on site at all times to ensure the animals don't suffer."

"I know, I know. Just seems like Nevada or Utah would be a better place to train on bikes with all the desert mountains."

"Mountains are mountains. As long as we can maneuver among obstacles, the type of mountainous terrain doesn't matter. Plus, there should be snow on the ground. Different traction than sand, but it will require the same techniques to avoid crashing into boulders. The main selling point is Lake Superior. Probably the harshest maritime environment we can train in. The name of the town itself should instill confidence that I have chosen the perfect training venue."

"What's that?"

"Dodge City. What could be better for gunslingers?"

"I get it. Still hate you. Just make sure you two are ready to go."

"Will do."

"And Dane?"

"Yes?"

"Don't fuck this up."

Dane smiled to himself and snapped back into the present when the surface of Interstate 75 changed. The rhythm of the tires crossing the metal plate every second or so indicated they were crossing the Mackinac Bridge. Some called it the Mighty Mac, but whatever name you used was insufficient to capture its enormity. Just shy of five miles long, the suspension bridge connected the upper and lower peninsula of Michigan. Or as Dane had heard from some, connecting Michiganders and the Yoopers, Michigan's famed residents of the north.

Dane was always in awe when he crossed, and always mindful to be in a solid vehicle that could withstand the heavy winds between Lake Michigan and Lake Huron. The last thing you wanted to do was try and cross in some sort of Mini Cooper.

Nicky looked up from her reports and stared out the passenger window upon feeling the change, too. "It is beautiful here. Look at that water. I have never seen bluer. Where are all those boats going? And why are they shooting water into the air?"

Dane squinted. "Those are ferry boats heading to Mackinac Island. And the water is a rooster tail from the hydrojet engines. Looks like that is a Star Line ferry. There are a bunch of different companies traveling from Mackinaw City and St. Ignace. St Ignace is on the other side of the bridge."

"Wow. Pretty cool. What's on the island?"

"It is a cool place. First off, no cars. Everyone gets around by horse carriage or bicycle. Well, except for the firetruck. And I am pretty sure there is a cop car or two for emergencies. Fort Mackinac sits right above the town. They do reenactments and everything. Tons of things to see and do. One of the best places to vacation unless you want tropical beaches. The water is damn cold."

"Wait, wasn't that Jane Seymour movie filmed there? Mackinac is familiar-sounding."

"Yup, *Somewhere in Time*. Christopher Reeve was in it. Superman."

"Oh yeah. That hotel was amazing."

"The Grand Hotel. Super famous. I've walked through it, but the rooms are a little pricey on my paycheck."

"I'd love to see it if we have the time. Maybe we can save up for one of those rooms. We should get all that hazardous duty pay from this mission. Ha."

"We can try. I have an old college buddy who lives there. Fire chief. Family goes way back on the island. He could hook us up with some tours. Maybe get reduced rates at the hotel."

"I would love to see that hotel. Looked cool in the movie."

"Well, another fun fact if you like history. Rumor has it that Roosevelt met in secret at the hotel with other Allied leaders during World War II. And at some point, Roosevelt took a secret fishing trip to, I think, Lake Huron. I can't remember exactly."

"You sure seem to know a lot about this area."

"My mom is from around here. She grew up in a little town called Charlevoix, not far away. We can swing through there when we are done if you want. You will like the town."

"Wait a minute. That sign says Mackinac with a c for this bridge. But the signs on the other side of the bridge where we got on said Mackinaw City with a w. Why the difference?"

"Mackinac with a c is how the French spelled it, but it sounded like a w at the end. British controlled it next and spelled it like is sounded. It is crazy. Over time, the island and stuff kept the c at the end, while the city retained the British spelling with a w."

They continued chatting as they drove across the upper peninsula. The conversation flowed, and Dane realized how much he missed having someone to talk to. He had gotten to know Nicky over the last several weeks as they plowed through intel and imagery, and she trained him on the equipment she was bringing. They also spent time down at Dane's unit to train in the maze.

They visited the Africa room and worked on every conceivable lock they could encounter in Somaliland. The locks were fairly simple and soon Nicky could open just about all of them. People in the Horn of Africa tended to guard their valuables with rifles instead of quality locks, though.

Dane signed out several small cameras and listening devices along with some tracker tags. The hope was to install some of the tracking devices on boats containing the viruses to determine their final destination. After duty hours was when they got their real work done. It was hardly candlelit dinners but rather Thai takeout in Nicky's studio apartment. It was in those moments that he really got to see the real her.

"If you don't mind me asking, how did you become part of the club?"

"I guess it's only fair since I got to read the horrible packet about your daughter, Angela."

"Oh, I'm sorry. Didn't mean to pry."

"No Dane. Sorry, that sounded bitchy. It's quite all right. My son, Daniel, was taken when he was eight years old. Just grabbed while walking home from school in our neighborhood. The police did everything they could. Press conferences. Television ads. Posters everywhere. But nothing. And then three weeks later, a shallow grave was discovered by some hunters. It was Daniel."

"Did they catch the guy?"

"Yes, with my help. I had been at the NSA for over a year at that point. I was getting good at using all the systems and merging the data."

"I kinda understand," Dane said, with a little skepticism in his voice.

"Think of it this way: Law enforcement databases, at least at the time, were linear. Fingerprint database. Vehicle database. And so on. Our databases can converge at a much more rapid pace than a team of detectives. The investigators would have gotten to the piece of shit eventually, but I was impatient. Anonymous tip, and the guy was in cuffs the next day."

"I have been impressed with your work."

She laughed. "I am better at covering my tracks now. My supervisor caught my digital trail in the system. He was sympathetic. Let me go with a warning. I am a lot more careful now. . . . Okay, your turn, since we're opening up. What is the significance of that pendant in your shirt pocket that you take out and hold several times a day?"

"It was something I had made for Angela during my last mission."

"And you never got to give it to her. I kinda thought it would be something like that, but I was afraid to ask." Nicky sighed. She then opened her purse and pulled out a small stack of baseball cards. "I understand completely. Daniel was obsessed with baseball. I never leave home without these."

Dane had also met up with Sam before he left, knowing he had little time before heading overseas. They had dinner at an off-the-beaten-path place off Tackett's Mill Drive called Hector's of Lake Ridge. Dane was in the mood for Mexican food, and he didn't expect to run into that FBI agent or the two detectives from the Virginia Bureau of Investigation. He also knew the food was amazing and the portions enormous. He stuck to only one margarita, since they poured them strong.

Dane was still frustrated about leaving, but it made him feel better that Sam was still on the job.

"I am sympathetic, man," Sam told him. "I know you want to keep searching for Angela."

"I feel like I am taking my eye off the ball."

"I promise not to let up while you are gone, and Jed's back up from the bench."

"I just don't want to lose momentum."

"You won't. We won't. I will follow up on whatever leads we can generate. Once you get back, we will go eliminate this piece of shit together."

Dane was drawn back to the here and now. They were getting close. They had been traveling along the northern edge of Lake Michigan through small towns one after another along Route 2 before turning sharply north on 41 toward Marquette. The terrain became more mountainous as they headed west and north to the mountains outside Dodge City.

Dane was reminded of Camp Merrill in Dahlonega, Georgia, from his early days in the Rangers. The winding dirt road led into the center of the site. The camp itself was comprised of log structures nestled in a bowl within the mountains and rising on all sides. The woods were thick, but he could identify breaks in the tree line denoting hiking trails.

Dane shivered as he remembered Mountain Phase in Ranger School. The terrain was unrelenting. His back hurt just remembering the weight of the rucks and weapons. Even worse if it was your turn to carry the heavy machine gun, the pig. And, of course, the instructors gleefully threw flash bangs, telling their herd of Ranger students that it was incoming artillery, requiring the tired men to sprint up the mountain. *Assholes.*

Dane and Nicky stepped from the vehicle.

"It is beautiful here," she exclaimed.

"It is. Great place to polish up on some additional training."

The front door to what appeared to be main building opened. Dane had parked in the front, the American flag snapping in the wind on a twenty-foot pole, a dead giveaway.

"Marcus Baker. Welcome."

"Dane Cooper. This is my partner, Nicky Blackburn."

Hands were shaken all around.

"Let's secure your weapons in our armory and then I'll show you to your hooch. Let you settle in. Apologies in advance since our lodging is one large open bay floor plan. Forty bunk beds, but there are bathrooms on each end so you guys can have some privacy."

"This place looks similar to Camp Merrill. You guys pass through?"

"Yup. Bob and I both went through. 5-96."

"No shit. 4-98."

"Are you boys done? I may throw up if you start fist-bumping or high-fiving."

Both men laughed.

"We even have a dirty name on our obstacle course."

"Shit," Dane responded. "I hated that thing. Do you at least have blueberry pancakes?"

TODAY WAS SCARY. I HEARD A LOT OF GUNS. THEY WERE NOT REAL CLOSE BUT STILL LOUD. SOME WENT REALLY FAST WHILE OTHERS JUST POP-POPPED. MAYBE THEY WERE HUNTERS. MAYBE SHOOTING FOR FUN. I REMEMBER GETTING TO SHOOT WITH MY DAD. HIS BEST ARMY FRIEND TAUGHT ME TO SHOOT A RIFLE. DAD SAID IT WAS BETTER IF HIS FRIEND TAUGHT ME SINCE I WOULD LISTEN BETTER. WE ARE WAITING UNTIL I AM A LITTLE OLDER TO SHOOT DAD'S HANDGUN. IT IS BIG. HE LET ME SHOOT ONE HANDGUN. HE SAID IT WAS A 22 JUST LIKE MY RIFLE. IT DIDN'T HURT MY HAND.

17

THE PREPARATION

Arlington, Virginia

```
Devotee: The man she told me about is being watched. Protected by them.

Keeper: Can you tell how many of them there are?

Devotee: I know at least two. I don't want to do it like the hospital. I need time with him, like the reverend.

Keeper: Be patient. I am sure you will find a window of opportunity. We have time. They don't.
```

"I am going to have to use the old honey trap method and do this thing in one of the big fancy hotels downtown. Only way to get him alone. It is really the only choice I have."

Sam and Jack stood around a large table in a room off the mansion's main hall to discuss Sam's next operation, which required him to be a complete ghost. The table was covered with various photos of one of the largest hotels in D.C. Sam had acquired pictures of every conceivable entrance and exit point. He knew the location of all security personnel and every camera.

Analysts were still working through possible links between the two know members of this kidnapping group, Simmons and Basker. Originally thought lost, some encrypted data from Simmons' laptop was recovered from the cloud. Decryption algorithms were running around the clock to crack the code and compare it with the data Sam retrieved from Basker's electronics. Fortunately, Basker had been detained by the police and Sam had a head start on searching the man's home. It had been just as he expected: A nightmare befitting a stalker and kidnapper. He cloned all of Basker's electronics and photographed the entire dwelling, right down to the bizarre photos and clippings adorning the basement walls. He definitely needed a shower once he got home.

The team pored through every record available in search of any place where Simmons and Basker may have crossed paths. In the meantime, Sam wanted to remain busy. They were never short of targets requiring attention.

Babak Ahmadi was up next. Several pictures of him from all angles adorned the table. He pretended to work at the Pakistani Embassy in Washington D.C. as an economic advisor, but the FBI and several other three-letter agencies knew differently. Ahmadi was an Iranian military intelligence officer working in the Interests Section of the Islamic Republic of Iran, nestled inside the Pakistani compound. The Iranians had no embassy of their own, so they used a sympathetic neighbor to assist with their diplomatic and, of course, intelligence needs.

Iran's choice of Babak was a bad one. He was a crappy spy, a drug addict, and a probable pedophile. The FBI casually overlooked some of those proclivities since he was a wealth of information. His poor tradecraft was practiced across the Military District of Washington Area, exposing networks of spies, terrorists, and other agitators. He was a treasure trove for the FBI. Babak exposed foreign national collectors and terrorist networks, making them ripe for the picking. The Cabal, however, was not inclined to overlook his actions.

The initial tip actually came from one of Sam's friends, Daniel, a diplomatic security special agent assigned to the State Department's Protective Liaison Division. The two men bitched about the people they had to protect over a few beers a couple months back. Between gulps of beer and mouthfuls of onion rings, they one-upped each other with regard to the scum they interacted with. A delegation from the

Pakistani Embassy had visited the State Department a few months early, and Daniel received an intelligence briefing for his team from the FBI. It was standard practice for Diplomatic Services to be aware of suspicious foreigners entering the building.

The packet on Babak had been extensive. Daniel told Sam about Babak's red flags, especially the one where he seemed to have an endless supply of young nieces and nephews constantly visiting and traveling with the diplomat. It was impossible for him to have that many relatives all around the ages of ten to twelve.

Sam ran with that information. It didn't take too much digging to discover that Babak had a unique supplier that would fulfill his disgusting demands. Babak would periodically arrange for special evening events in swanky hotels scattered about the capital. He changed hotels to keep the establishments unaware of his activities. He also thought he was exercising his work clandestinely, which was never the case. The FBI would follow him on all these occasions setting up camp outside the chosen hotel. They occasionally entered the hotel, but that was normally just to use the restroom.

Babak wasn't fooling anyone. They knew he was in a hotel room fulfilling some demented fantasy. The agents didn't want to know anything further. They wanted to turn a blind eye as ordered and make it through these horrible shifts. Babak was a worm on a hook, allowed to exist so others could be brought to justice.

This upcoming weekend, Babak had planned a celebration for his birthday. He had already contacted his supplier to make all the arrangements. That supplier had been a wealth of information for The Cabal. He served a very private clientele, so his little enterprise was compartmentalized. That was actually more convenient for The Cabal.

Since none of the clients knew one another, each other's passing went unnoticed. Sam and Phil had eliminated the supplier several weeks ago, but were still impersonating him online to set up events for his clients. They were systematically reducing his book of business to dust. Tomorrow night was Babak's turn.

"Does it have to be in public?" Jack asked. "I just worry about drawing too much attention. Hell, if it happened on Pakistani property, they probably wouldn't even report . . . just quietly ship the body home."

"I checked out the embassy. No way I can get to him there."

"What about the residence? It would still be on Pakistani property."

"It is not separated. It is on embassy grounds, so that is out. Plus, the Israeli embassy is across the street. It is a law enforcement nightmare at the moment. Protesters and rioters everywhere. And, of course, eyes. Every camera in the capital is pointed at that area."

"I concur with your honey trap plan in the hotel, then. Just wanted to make sure we covered all options."

"This is our best option. This will be a high-profile death and certainly come to the forefront of the FBI's attention. Especially that asshole Blanchard."

"How about our FBI friends? I assume they will be watching him."

"I am certain they will be along for the ride. Tony is going to run lookout for me. He will Metro up from Virginia and mull around with the other unnoticeables in the city."

"You comfortable with Tony watching your six?"

"Yeah. No gunplay or combat tactics. This should be a simple job. He will be good."

"Okay. Your call. I know Dane and you were not happy with Savannah and wanted to get him a little more training."

"I do, but I think Dane was a little hard on him. He does need more training, but he also needs confidence."

"He seems all swagger to me, Sam."

"That is just it. It is a show. When we talked with him during the after-action review, he could not take any criticism. Tony got defensive and combative at first. He wasn't in units like we were that had that sort of blunt report after any action, real or training."

"Yeah, I can see that. So, is that what tonight is about?"

"It is. I haven't had time to get him out to my place yet. I am sure his confidence is in the toilet. A quick win tonight will help keep him on track."

"Your call. It is your ass that he will be covering. What's the play with Babak?"

"He thinks he is meeting his usual guy, his pimp. He may be slightly surprised."

"Ha, I bet. Are you guys almost done with this perverted client list?"

"Nearly done. Babak is one of the last. A few have fallen off the radar. They were older clients and seemed to have left the area. Phil is tracking them down. We may need that sweet ride we used for the Savannah job."

"Never hurts to ask, Sam."

"Never hurts. Is Babak going to overdose this evening?"

"Yup. He is definitely playing with fire tonight, and it will cost him. I'd rather beat him to a pulp. Injecting him with drugs seems kinda unsportsmanlike."

"But you know why you can't."

"I know, I know." Sam raised his hands in defense. "Just kidding. Drug overdose it is. You good with the op, Jack?"

"It's a go."

"Cool. So, back to the Keeper. I know the team is looking into our two assholes' past to see if they overlap, but are we making any progress on the fentanyl citrate?"

"We cannot find any records of the drug missing from hospitals or clinics. Rather, any record where it wasn't later recovered from either some junkie on the street or a doctor about to lose his license for dabbling in products from work. Either this guy is stealing it under the radar or getting the components through illicit channels and making it himself."

"Have you looked into vets? Specifically large-animal vets." Sam paused. "Well, actually all vets. I think they use it on smaller animals as well."

Jack shook his head. "I hadn't thought of that. Can they use this stuff on animals?"

"I don't think they do as much on small animals like cats and dogs, but I could be wrong. I would check them all out. But I am pretty sure they use it for surgery on horses and stuff. I would also check out large horse farms. Hell, maybe even cattle farms. I don't know exactly, but the sickos are getting it from somewhere. If it isn't from human clinics, well . . ."

"I will have the team look into it. Good catch."

"Look into what?" Charles asked as he entered the room.

"Sam reminded me that our killer and any of the Keeper's associates could be getting the fentanyl citrate from veterinarians. I will add that to the list of our inquiries."

"Excellent. Are you ready for your visit with Ahmadi, Mr. Turner?"

"Yes, we just finalized the details."

"Good. Jack, I'd like to talk about Jill."

"I have gone through the case file from our friend, the Cop. It was gruesome. Jill was tortured for quite some time. Same as the others. She was gagged and bound to one of her dining room chairs. She had lacerations from her neck to her waist and several holes in her back into her spine. Consistent with the reverend and Basker."

"Are the authorities working any particular leads that appear fruitful?"

"Very little trace evidence. No fingerprints outside of Jill's. They did find evidence that he gave her an IV. Probably used to keep her hydrated and administer drugs necessary to keep her conscious."

"These monsters are sick. Do you need help from me on this?" Sam asked. "My dance card won't be full after Babak unless the team spits out some connecting Basker and Simmons."

"Thank you, Mr. Turner. For now, Jack can run down these leads. Phil will assist. Once you are done with Ahmadi, I would like you and Jed back on the Keeper. I will link you with our digital forensic team, since you may have some insight into possible attack vectors. You bring a unique investigative mind, similar to Mr. Cooper's, that will help the team with figuring out new links. Jack will investigate from the murder angle, and you can follow up any leads once we crack Simmons' data from the cloud."

"Is that realistic?"

"Our analyst assures me he has a high level of confidence. The dark web uses onion routing to protect users. Once he cracks those encrypted paths and servers, he may provide some valuable internet mapping data."

Jack smirked. "Did you say onion routing?"

"I did, Jack. I don't thoroughly understand it myself."

"I do," Sam piped up. "It is really called onion routing. It was originally used by the DoD for communication. They use TOR, The Onion Router, to stay hidden and hide their online activity. A seeker would have to peel back the layers like an onion to find someone. I don't fully understand the tech for our communication system, but I suppose it is very similar."

Jack laughed. "I will never understand the internet."

Charles joined him. "Neither will I."

"Well, gentlemen, I know just enough to be dangerous. So, hopefully your tech genius knows a lot more. I do know that dark web internet traffic goes through relay nodes. It can be servers or even other people's computers. Probably can't see every node, but if he can isolate entry and exit points, that may help with our search."

"Well, then I am glad you are working this. Jack, how are we on reaching out to our network?"

"I sent a general warning out to the group. Most of them are on the peripheral. They have never had any contact with our Scout, Jill. The only direct contact has been me, you, our recruiter Andrew, and a few others."

"What do you suggest?"

"I suggest you temporarily limit your exposure, sir. Have you ever met Jill here?"

"No, we rarely met. And when we did, it was often at various coffee shops throughout Arlington and Alexandria. I did take her once to the club on King Street for a more private conversation. We were always discreet, but I was never truly concerned since she was in a distal support position. Her actions were not observable as illegal in any manner, nor would they lead anyone to The Cabal."

"Okay, that's good. I still recommend you lay low for the time being."

"How about you and Mr. Andrew?"

"Are you sure you don't want me on this first?" Sam asked.

"I got this. I will watch my back, Charles. I always do. And I will be keeping an eye on Andrew."

"Where are we hiding Mr. Andrew?" Charles inquired.

"We are not," Jack answered. "He wants to maintain his normal routine. We will just have someone with him every second of the day."

"Sounds like Andrew is being used for bait," Sam offered.

"In a way, he is. He is obviously scared. Terrified of what happened to Jill and the reverend, but he knows he can't hide forever. He said he would feel better if I watched his back and took this guy out before he struck."

Charles rose to leave. "It appears we have two solid plans. I will leave them in your capable hands."

18

THE TRAIN-UP

Upper Peninsula, Michigan

The beauty of setting up your own training was that you could control time itself. Dane always hated it when he had to get up at the crack of dawn with the Rangers. Hunter Army Airfield did not have rifle ranges necessary to train on and qualify, so the platoon or company would show up in the dark to draw and load equipment. The Rangers would pile into several five-ton trucks for the hourlong journey to Fort Stewart.

The privates sat near the front of the truck, singing vulgar Ranger songs, and telling outrageous stories and lies. The senior NCOs would sit at the back of the truck, normally with the cargo flap rolled to the top. This configuration allowed fresh air in and tobacco juice from tightly packed lips out. There were times they would be settled on the range, magazines full, simply waiting for the sun to rise.

Dane smiled at the memory. *Ridiculous. They could have completely slept in and still had plenty of time at the range.*

Dane wasn't doing that silliness any longer. That's why he told Marcus, the site owner, that he would head to the cafeteria at eight and be ready for the range at nine. Plenty of time.

Dane exited the bathroom with nothing but a towel around his waist. He was startled to see Nicky at the other end of the long room, momentarily forgetting that he did not have the privacy of his own accommodations. There were plenty of beds to choose from in the open barracks bay, but it had made more sense for them to each select the ones closest to their individual bathrooms.

It seemed a lot farther away last night then it did now. Dane couldn't avert his eyes. Wearing a terrycloth robe with a towel around her wet hair, Nicky smiled as she walked behind the door of her wall locker. He was mesmerized as he saw the robe drop to the floor. *Stupid door,* he thought.

He began to change behind his wall locker, chastising himself for his unprofessional thoughts. This was his partner for the mission. He had to remember that. Any romantic entanglement could compromise the objective. They needed to be laser-focused.

Dane had never had this issue before. For one thing, he had always been a married man. For another, he realized he had never deployed with a female partner. He had trained with women and interacted with women at bases and embassies, but he had never had a female partner for a mission. This would be a first. *Hell,* he thought, *I rarely even had any partner.*

"You ready?" Nicky's voice startled him as he pulled on his T-shirt. She had silently approached and leaned against his bunk.

"Damn, you scared me. What if I hadn't changed yet? I could have been stark naked."

"Even better for me then." She winked. "Come on, I'm starving."

They crossed the quad and entered the building Marcus had identified last night as the chow hall. Dane could practically taste the bacon as he walked through the door, with the coffee's aroma lingering, too. The large buffet against the far wall offered everything he craved. After filling their plates, the partners found a small table near the fireplace at the far end of the hall. It was not necessarily cold enough outdoors to require the heat it provided, but it was not necessarily warm either. It was one of those damp, overcast Northern Michigan days, with the Great Lakes providing just enough fog to block out the sun, but not enough for the haze to ruin your day. It was perfect for training.

"I know you told me already, but what is our game plan here? Five days, right?"

"Yup," Dane answered between mouthfuls. "Pretty sure we can get everything done in that time. If we need to stay longer, we can."

"Has anyone ever told you that you are a very fast eater?"

"Gotta fuel the combat chassis," Dane laughed. "I hear it all the time.

I guess I learned to eat fast in basic training. We were given almost no time to eat. Minutes at best. You ate fast or you starved."

"I know. I went through it as well, but then I grew up after graduation and began to eat like a human again. I learned to use utensils and everything."

"Some habits stick, I guess."

"Would you like a spoon to shovel that food in your mouth? It would be a lot faster and more efficient. You are dropping quite a bit off your fork as you stuff your face."

"Very funny. Noted. Are you going to bust my balls the entire time?"

"Depends on my fear of losing one of my fingers at a dinner table with you."

Dane raised his hands. "I surrender. Nice and slow. I don't want the loss of your finger on my conscience."

"Thank you. The agenda?"

"Well, today I figured we would take our time on the range this morning. Zero our optics. Work out the kinks in our kit, then go through some drills."

"What do we need for the range?"

"They have UTVs here. Let's throw our kit and armor in with our weapons and ammo. We can start stripped down and put on stuff as we move on to other drills."

"Stripped down, huh? What is it with you, Cooper? Always trying to get our clothes off."

Dane gave her a deadpan look.

It was Nicky's turn to surrender. "Okay, okay, I will be serious."

Dane continued. "After lunch, we are going to meet a few of the guys in the camp's garage. It's that huge hanger we passed on the way in yesterday. They store everything with a motor in there. It's also where the mechanics will fix the stuff we will inevitably break throughout our training. They call it The Thunderdome."

"Like the *Mad Max* movie?"

"I guess so."

"Do you anticipate us breaking a lot of stuff while we are here?"

"I am sure we will crash the bikes plenty. We need to know the basics of how to fix them while on mission, along with the boat motor."

"I am assuming you got an engine similar to the one we are going to use over there?"

"As a matter of fact, the exact same engine. When we bought the original for the boat years ago, we purchased several. We use the spare engines to train on back at our compound before guys deploy and use it for urgent spare parts needed by our teams overseas. Hard to get mechanical components in that part of the world. Well, reliable ones anyway. Easier for us to ship a part to them from one of our training motors and then order the part to be shipped stateside."

"Huh. I wouldn't have thought of that."

"Just want to be prepared. If we have engine problems, hopefully we can troubleshoot. If not, we will just have to find an alternative."

"You going to bring a paddle so you can bring us safely to shore?"

"I will bring two. I wouldn't want you to accuse me of misogyny."

"And after we play grease monkey?"

"Figured we would check out the bikes. Do a familiarization run today. Learn the area. There are a lot of trails—couple thousand acres of mountains here. Let's learn the main trails by day, and then do some runs with night vision goggles once we have mastered them. The depth perception can be brutal. I want to take this part of the training in baby steps since we don't need any catastrophic injuries at this point."

"Concur. I can ride, but it has been a while. I am fairly certain I will bust my ass a time or two."

"No worries. We both will. We will have plenty of time, and, like I said earlier, we can always stay a few extra days if necessary."

"When is the goat lab?"

"Tomorrow. I think we have ten animals. Have you ever done one? The live tissue lab?"

"No, and I am not going to lie. I am not looking forward to it. Seems cruel. I don't see why we can't just practice on mannequins. I don't want to cut on some poor helpless goat."

"First off, it is necessary. When we are out there alone, it's just you and me. Riding the bikes can be dangerous. Broken bones, crushed lungs, the works. Plus, we have an enemy that may not be too happy if they find us in their territory. I don't plan on getting shot. Nobody does. But I need you prepared to treat me and vice versa. We can't get that kind of experience on a rubber mannequin. We need to clamp real arteries. Sew real flesh. All of it."

"But the suffering."

"We keep it to a bare minimum. The veterinarian will be on-site the whole time. They keep the animal heavily sedated, and they monitor for pain responses. They will put the animal down before they let it suffer. I don't like killing them any more than you do, but if it helps one of us stay alive, the ends justify the means on this one."

Nicky's shuddered, then nodded.

"And boating. We will have five days and four nights to train on navigation. We don't have the same boat but that shouldn't make a difference for this and the final exercise. Navigation is navigation. I want to ensure we can both work the map and compass rose manually in the event of electronic failures."

"Did you say final exercise?"

"Yup. On our last day, we are going to run a modified full mission rehearsal. We will do an overland movement on the bikes during the day and into the evening. We will hunker down in a hide site for an hour and go over mission planning for the meat-packing warehouse intrusion. After that, we load the boat and then head to Copper Harbor."

"How far is that?"

"Should be about sixty nautical miles, close to the distance we will have to travel from Berbera to Djibouti. But don't worry about that now. We will build up to that."

Dane smiled as he thought back to that first discussion. It had been a grueling five days. Nicky had proven herself with her rifle and pistol. He was confident that she would have his back. Her rifle abilities were decent, but it was her pistol work where she shined. Nicky was quick on the draw, getting off her first shot with speed and accuracy. Dane knew that any fights would probably be at close range, so he was pleased. He could work distance shots, if necessary, with his rifle setup.

She may have been initially squeamish working on the goats, but now she was inserting chest tubes like a natural. They worked on eight goats, plus two pigs the training crew had brought. By the end, it was clear that they could keep one another alive under most conditions for twenty-four hours or until the next period of darkness. Enough time for a nighttime emergency evacuation.

And she was a natural on the water. It was the dirt bikes that were kicking her ass. She knew how to ride, but did not come by it naturally. Having a couple of wipeouts was understandable during training. They were getting the feel of their bikes, how they handled, how they accelerated, all that. But she didn't trust herself or her ability to keep her balance. Nicky kept putting a foot down when making turns. She needed to shift her body weight when maneuvering, not push off with a foot. Not in mountainous terrain. That is a sure way to break an ankle. Their mission movement in Somaliland would take place primarily during the day, but they needed to be prepared for night runs.

Nicky pulled up alongside Dane, the light green glow of the night-vision goggles reflecting off her face.

"You good?"

She fought to catch her breath. "I'm good. Couple of those rocks back there are chipped, and I have a few more dents in the bike, but good otherwise."

Dane laughed. They both wore padding to protect the shins, forearms, and joints. This was complemented by a lightweight chest plate to cushion any blows from a fall or brushing against something like a tree or boulder. Their actual body armor was strapped to their small backpacks, tied down behind each rider. Two gas cans apiece was the final addition to their load. This additional weight didn't help the handling of the sporty dirt bike, but they didn't have a choice.

"You gotta stop putting that foot down, Nicky."

"I know, I know. It is hard with the NODs. My depth perception is wrecked."

"If you have to slow down even more, do it. It is not a race. You can also peek out the bottom of your goggles and see the ground with one naked eye. It may help with the balance."

"Will do, boss."

"Smartass. Let's set up our hide site here."

They stashed their bikes in an outcropping of boulders and scrub brush. They concealed themselves with surrounding brush and hunkered down to go through photos and intel they had about the port and the portion of the site where they would hopefully find the biologics.

The partners also went over the packet on Ibrahim Mohamed Mahmud. The plan was to capture the virus samples first and prepare the boat for exfil. Only then would they move on Ibrahim. Dane had brought subsonic rounds and a suppressor for his rifle. He was hoping for some stand-off for the shot.

Once satisfied with their planning, they headed down to the boat. They reached the dock, but skipped loading the bikes since they would be using a different craft overseas and cramming them on this boat would achieve no valuable training. Folks from the camp would drive the trailer down to the lake and retrieve them both.

As planned, Nicky assumed the captain's chair while Dane attended to the lines. They had agreed that since Dane was more proficient with the rifle, he would provide security as Nicky navigated into open water. The port was the most vulnerable part of the operation. They would be out in the open. Exposed. But once they were on the water, there was no way for a potential adversary to follow. The boat engine they would be using was not any ordinary Somali design. The boat looked like a typical dhow, but its guts screamed performance. No craft other than a U.S. Navy interceptor could catch them.

The small training craft motored out onto Lake Superior, Nicky keeping a generally north heading. They both had a GPS with maritime software, but they also practiced with paper charts emblazoned with the compass rose and a sliding ruler. Hopefully, it wouldn't come to that.

I THINK RECESS IS MY FAVORITE. THE MAN LETS ME PLAY IN THE YARD FOR A WHILE. I DON'T KNOW HOW LONG. I DON'T HAVE A CLOCK. IT SEEMS LONG. SOMETIMES, I LAY IN THE GRASS AND WATCH THE AIRPLANES THAT I CAN SEE. I COUNT THEM ALL GO BY AND DREAM OF FLYING ON ONE OF THEM FOR A TRIP WITH MY MOM AND DAD.

19

THE HOTEL

Washington, D.C.

Sam adjusted his earpiece and checked his watch. Everything was going as planned so far, and his guest should arrive shortly. Tony was positioned out front of the hotel and would alert him when Babak Ahmadi appeared.

Believing that he was meeting up with his usual supplier, Babak would be severely disappointed. His pimp had promised a night to remember with several young children to sample, but it would be Sam's blade that would make the night memorable. The pimp had been disposed of weeks ago.

That, Sam remembered, had been satisfying. The poor man couldn't stand what he had become. He was sick. He couldn't be cured of his penchant for underage children, and he was tired of sharing that dirty secret with other horrible men. He couldn't live with himself. At least, that was what the note in his pocket said when he was found at the bottom of the bridge. A gentle push was all it had taken.

Sam depressed the talk button on a tiny Motorola radio. "How we looking out front, Tango ? We have any company yet?"

"In position, Sierra," Tony answered. "I have a good view of the front entrance. Embassy limo should be arriving shortly. No visual at this time."

"Good copy. Keep eyes out for any of his minders. They won't be far behind."

"Roger. Wilco. Out."

Sam knew that Babak would drag an FBI surveillance team to the hotel. They watched him daily. But with limited resources, the team would be light tonight. Probably a single car with two agents—one to drive and one to go foot, if necessary.

Babak was a notoriously inept spy, so heavy coverage wasn't necessary, which was convenient for tonight's Cabal operation. Taking him out was tricky enough without the prying eyes of law enforcement. Hopefully, since Babak rarely conducted operations in the evenings, the bureau would place junior and less-experienced agents with him.

Tony lurked along the streets, blending in with the city's homeless population. His baggy clothing and the hoodie pulled tight over his head masked his features. His limp strengthened his disguise, since many of those on the streets sustained injuries and rarely sought treatment. The vagrants slept in doorways, rustled through trash cans, and hobbled aimlessly through the city. Tents were scattered throughout the city, covering sidewalks, filling parks, and commandeering every underpass.

Tony's limp, however, was from a large caliber bullet that tore through his thigh. His physical recovery was progressing well. His mental was somewhat lacking.

Sam and Dane had been understandably angry with Tony for his rash behavior in Savannah. His actions almost cost them the mission. Almost cost them their lives and the lives of those girls. It was only because of Dane's calmness and quick thinking that the rescued girls got away clean. Almost. So far. The port became a media circus. The entire operation was exposed and that is where mistakes would, if any, be revealed. Evidence still could be found. Eyewitnesses debriefed. The plan was to swiftly rescue the girls from the dock. The ship would eventually have sailed, thinking the cargo must have been delayed or lost. Then once in the middle of the Atlantic, Sam would send the electronic signal detonating the explosive in the engine compartment. The ship would have been at the bottom of the ocean before anyone ever came looking for it. But that had not come to pass.

Sam brought Tony tonight to rebuild that mental confidence. Just like any Special Operations team around the world, the three of them conducted their hotwash afterward back on the plane to D.C. It was not to point fingers or cast blame, but to honestly evaluate each other's actions and find improvement. Tony had not been used to that kind of brutal honesty from his peers.

"I know I messed up. I said I wouldn't do it again."

"That's not the point, Tony," Dane said. "You have to walk us through what you were thinking, why you did what you did, and then we can work through other actions for the future."

"Fine. I wasn't expecting so many guys. I panicked."

"You stepped out too early," answered Sam. "By stepping early, you exposed yourself. They were right on top of you."

"You gave up your decision space," Dane continued. "Your options became extremely limited. You were committed at that point. You had no cover. Here is where you made your second poor decision."

"Great, let's just beat up on Tony."

"No, that's not it. We need to get you out to Sam's place for some more training."

"Once you heal up, I'll get you out to my range a couple of weekends to work transition drills and close contact engagements. I saw you holster your pistol and pull up your rifle. That wasted precious time."

"Time that you could have used. Sam was in a cover position if shit went bad, and he eventually got two. Initially, he couldn't shoot for fear of hitting you. You got too close. Your Glock has fifteen rounds. Those boys on your side weren't ready. Pistol would have been enough."

"Okay, got it. Thanks, I guess. I will take you up on that offer, Sam."

"Did you notice the armor, Tony?" Dane asked.

He nodded. "First thing I saw. Probably why my initial instinct was to go for heavier firepower."

"That's fair. I didn't notice it right away. I wasted a few bullets. Your cop brain probably took in the scene better, I need to work on that. I just saw the gun in hand and went for center mass of the torso, not even considering these guys may have armor plates."

"I saw the armor, but it was already too late. Guess I still could have called it out," Sam said. "I also don't think I had the greatest spot. Not a lot of choices, but behind and oblique to the target wasn't good coverage for contingencies. In front would have been better."

"That would have put you on the ship," Dane answered.

"Maybe I should have been. Probably could have found a nice high spot among the cargo where the crew would not have come snooping."

"We can keep that in mind next time we have to assault a cargo ship."

The men laughed, breaking the lingering tension.

Sam and Dane had talked later and consulted with Jack. They all agreed that Tony could become a valuable member of the team with a little more training. They needed to toughen his skin. In the meantime, he would fulfill smaller roles. They would build his skills and, more importantly, build back his confidence. Hopefully, that would happen tonight.

"First catch of the day."

Sam heard the call from Tony announcing Babak's arrival. He got the Empire Strikes Back joke, a reference to the rebels' escape from the ice planet Hoth. Tony might be green, but he was funny as hell and a complete Star Wars nerd. Sam could relate.

"I'll inform the emperor."

Although he carried his favorite knife and a clean pistol, Sam knew he would not be using either this evening unless absolutely necessary. No matter how badly he wanted to carve off pieces of the man, he needed it to look like an accident. The club had enough pressure on them as of late. Sam and Dane had been briefed about the FBI crew and the officers from the Virginia Bureau of Investigation. Charles had even mentioned that their old friend Carl Blanchard had formed his very own little task force to catch them all.

Sam remembered the smug look on the FBI agent's face when he sat across from him last summer in that interrogation room. The whole police crew were straining every arm muscle patting themselves on the back.

It was Sam who eventually wound up smiling. The lawyer Charles had sent made quick work of the detectives' case. Sam's items were returned and out-processing paperwork completed before his lousy cup of police station coffee even got cold. The look on their faces was precious.

The best part was that they were one hundred percent correct. He had played janitor for nearly three weeks. He did stalk that creep Arthur Camp. And he killed that bastard in the park with his own exhaust fumes from his car. But Charles had suggested something when planning the mission that kept his feet from the fire.

"Sam, I have been thinking. I want you to go to that school in your true business persona."

"How do you mean, Charles? And why?"

"We don't know how long it is going to take you to complete this operation. That means you may be spending quite some time at that school. The more time you spend there, the greater the probability of you leaving behind trace evidence."

"I see, kinda like create my own alibi. Well, not an alibi, but you know what I mean."

"Exactly."

"The state did start that new program to look into private security for all the schools. They don't think the school safety officer programs are working. They are looking for security contractors with combat experience, and they are really pushing for veterans. Fairfax County is going to host the pilot program. How about I head over to the county offices and see about offering them a security consult?"

It had worked and that prior visit to that elementary school had afforded Sam his freedom that day. He had gone over that place with a fine-tooth comb, guaranteeing he left fingerprints on at least several surfaces for the long-term. However, he knew that he was still on law enforcement's radar. So, that meant overdose or suicide tonight for Babak.

Everyone who knew the hapless spy recognized an arrogance about him, defying the Earth to rotate without his presence. It was impossible to believe Babak the international agent would take his own life. Suicide could not be the option. It would have to be an overdose. *Boring,* Sam thought. But at least he could have a little fun while killing him.

Getting into Babak's room had been simple and boring. The Cabal had selected this hotel due to its manager being a member. Gus had proven useful in providing safe houses, loiter points, or simply places to stage in the city when conducting local operations. He controlled the cameras. He controlled access. He controlled everything. So, tonight continued to be boring. Sam didn't need any fancy gadgets or electronic card reader. No subterfuge or the picking of pockets. Sam didn't even bring his rare earth magnet that was known to open several electronic locks. Gus had simply given Sam a key.

There was a note for Babak at the front desk stating that his guest was running late, but that he should enjoy fresh champagne in the room. Sam was waiting in a chair across the room obscured by the bathroom wall. The electronic beep of the door alerted him to his target's arrival. He pulled the ski mask over his head as Babak turned on the entry light.

Sam moved swiftly before Babak could turn on any more lights and adjust to the room. He grabbed the man roughly and pushed him toward the bed, pistol out and in Babak's face.

"Do what I say and don't try anything stupid." Sam pushed him to a seated position. "Sit down. Take off your shoes and socks."

Babak was terrified. He trembled as he followed orders. His hands shook as terror lit from his eyes. I *hope he doesn't wet himself,* Sam thought. *He is just a big coward and a bully.*

"Okay, take these." Sam tossed two needles on the bed. "Shoot up."

"But—"

"But nothing. You do it all the time, Babak. Everybody knows you are a closet junkie. Shoot between your toes like normal. This won't kill you. It'll just make it easier for us to talk."

Sam relaxed his posture and lowered the gun slightly to help sell his lie. It worked. Babak inserted both needles. The dose he took looked normal, but would be fatal. Sam had mixed it with some other chemicals, including fentanyl. He figured he had maybe fifteen or twenty minutes for a little Q&A.

"Landslide. I repeat, Landslide. Hostage rescue team is crashing the party. Can't be a coincidence."

Shit, Sam thought. He had to get out now. No time for questions, and no time to wait out the overdose. He had to hope the drugs traveled quickly throughout Babak's bloodstream.

He left through the room's front door and headed down the hall to the conference rooms. He had Gus put Babak on this floor due to its multiple exits and staff areas. There were several meeting rooms, complete with individual kitchens and serving stations. Sam did not anticipate a raid, but he always planned for the worst. This floor was a virtual maze and would slow down any tactical team assaulting the room or pursuing a target.

Sam opened a locker in the maintenance corridor behind one of the larger conference rooms. From there, he accessed the service entrance for the building's utilities. He gently closed the panel behind him. He could hear the subdued movement of combat boots moving down the corridor on the opposite side of the wall. A slim ladder delivered him to the basement and into the underground disposal area. It was an open garage filled with dumpsters and grease catches. Deliveries also entered through this space, evidenced by the mountains of wooden pallets scattered about.

The boys from Quantico obviously studied their objective, and a team was moving swiftly through the garage looking for threats before ultimately making their way to the belly of the hotel to join in the pursuit. They found nothing but normalcy in the garage as food trucks were unloaded, trash thrown away, and bed sheets and towels washed and folded. The team moved past and never noticed Sam Turner. He was dressed in a green jumpsuit, complete with the requisite reflective vest to ensure his safety, and casually jumped onto the forklift to return the large garbage bin to the outside curb. After all, tomorrow was trash day.

Benefactor: Are there any updates on the threat to our group?

President: We have men with the Recruiter around the clock.

Benefactor: Okay. Please let me know if anything changes. Have our colleagues left the States yet?

President: They will in the next several days. I will keep you informed.

20

THE RAID

Richmond, Virginia

Acolyte: What did you need to talk to me about? I am on track and on final.

Keeper: I know you are on track. I did not contact you. Why have you broken protocol?

Acolyte: You pinged my account. Probed exactly twenty-four hours ago. That is contact signal.

Keeper: Drop that account immediately! Go to alternate. Wait for my signal. Do not act! Do not collect.

The decision had been made to use the canine. They had debated at the command post several blocks away while waiting for the animal and handler to arrive. The post was a mobile RV of sorts with enough communication equipment to talk to the international space station. It currently held Roger, Pat, a communications specialist, and the Richmond SWAT commander, Lt. Curry.

The delay on the no-knock entry by the SWAT team was Roger's call as the on-scene commander. This was his bust. Curry was not happy waiting. His men were ready to go, and he was confident they would be successfully without the dog. Roger was sympathetic. Horrible visions were running through his mind as well, but the suspect was armed. Was violent. Was dangerous.

The home was small. It was one of those old brick homes built after the war to house the thousands of returning U.S. soldiers. Soldiers who would transition into a new all-power manufacturing workforce. The small homes meant tight corners and hallways, and doorways were not built in those days to accommodate men in full SWAT gear. This had to be done right. The canine was the nimblest of choices.

Ben Sebastian was about to have a visit from Richmond County Sheriff's Office and the Virginia Bureau of Investigation. An Amber Alert went out several days ago, notifying the public that Stacy Peters, age ten, had been abducted while walking home from school. Descriptions of the abductor were vague and varied from witness to witness. There was very little for law enforcement to pursue at first. Witnesses did generally agree on the involvement of a brown van seen speeding away from the area after a young man scooped Stacy off the sidewalk.

Those witness statements were not enough but, combined with the anonymous police hotline tip about Ben, Roger and Pat built a case strong enough for a judge to sign a warrant. Sebastian had a history of violence and previous brushes with the police regarding inappropriate relations with a minor. He had been a guest of the state as both a youth offender gracing the halls of juvenile detention and as an adult convicted of assault with a deadly weapon, possession of stolen property, rape, and attempted murder. He also owned a brown van.

It was the history of violence that gave Roger pause on immediately crashing the scene. *How come this piece of shit was not in prison with a rap sheet like his?*

Roger had confidence in the SWAT team, but the fur missiles, as he liked to call them, had never failed. Time and time again, he had watched as these incredible animals deftly maneuvered around obstacles, distractions, and dangers with pinpoint accuracy to bring down their suspect. He was confident today would be no different. He did not want to give Sebastian a fighting chance.

They team quickly stacked outside Sebastian's door once the canine officer arrived, with Richmond SWAT in the lead with Roger and Pat pulling up the rear. A young officer approached the door with his breaching tool as the dog handler took up position on the opposite side. The ding-dong tool was nothing more than a modified sledgehammer capable of battering in a door with the hammer end or prying said door open with the curved end. The officer lined the hammer up with the locking mechanism and awaited the signal. With a nod from the team lead, he smashed the space between the doorknob and the door frame to propel the door open. The fur missile launched.

The team followed closely behind the dog, initially into the front room of the house. The four SWAT members split two and two covering their corners, clearing the room. Roger and Pat trailed the team as they secured the small home. The screams from the back bedroom motivated the team to move quickly.

Sebastian was having a bad day. Cujo—Roger couldn't remember the dog's actual name—had locked onto their suspect's arm and thrashed him around the room. Ben tried to strike the animal with his free hand, but each attempt caused the dog to thrash harder. Blood from Ben's wounds painted to walls and the crumbled sheets on the bed. A small handgun on the floor was just out of Ben's reach.

The handler retrieved the canine, wresting it from its prey, while the rest of the team secured the suspect. They ignored Ben's wounds for the time being. He could afford a little blood loss. They needed to continue their search.

It was Roger and Pat who found the child. She was rolled up in a blanket in the hallway closet. Smothered. The emergency medical team rushed into the house when the all-clear was given but there was nothing they could do. Stacy Peters had been dead for some time. They were too late.

Roger went through the motions for the rest of the morning, the small house filling with analysts collecting and preserving evidence. Pat directed the team, ensuring the entire scene was catalogued.

He watched them scurry about. Emotionless. Drained. *Why bother?* he thought. *We know what happened.*

"I'm going step outside, Pat. Make a few calls."

Roger descended a few concrete steps into the backyard. He knew the commotion at the front of the house would be distracting. Additional law enforcement, the media, and the normal gathering of nosey neighbors massed in the front yard. Everybody wanted answers—

answers he didn't have.

Why did this happen? Because this world is full of monsters.

How could nobody know he was capable of this? Because we are no longer a community in this country. The neighborhood culture has become extinct. We are a nation of strangers. The residents of this community didn't even know a killer and a rapist lived among them.

Why didn't the police act sooner? Why didn't they stop him before he killed that little girl? Because we have rules. Monsters have rights. Laws must be followed. Due process played out. Even when the truth is known. But that wasn't the whole story. Roger knew that. *This country has gone soft. We make excuses for them. We sympathize with the criminals. We make them the victims. Victims of mental health. Victims of society. They can't be held fully accountable for their actions.*

Roger was still haunted by the scene later that afternoon while he and Pat worked on the crime scene boards.

"You guys have a moment?"

"Sure," Pat answered. "What's up, Captain?"

"Chief wants an update by close of business today. I was hoping you could bring me up to date on both lines of effort you have going. The murders and the kidnappings. Plus, any new Task Force developments."

Roger rolled his eyes. *Of course the chief wanted all these updates. I bet the governor's office is tearing him a new one daily. That was always passed down the food chain. Capt. Ivers was near the bottom. Probably didn't have any ass left to chew.*

"Sure, Captain. Here or your office?" Roger offered.

"Whatever you think is best."

Roger pulled over a chair from a neighboring cubicle. "Here ya go. Better to brief here off the boards."

Roger and Pat had reworked their boards to reflect both lines of investigation. The first board covered the abducted children. The second was filled with the murder victims. But there also stood a third. Very little information was on the board titled Task Force. When he and Pat found connections between one and two, those connections made their way onto the third board. It was scarce at the moment.

"I'll let Pat catch you up on the abductions."

Several names were written across the center of the dry-erase board with lines denoting possible and confirmed linkages. Angela Cooper. Dana Chase. Holly Jones. Jon Parker. Elliott Nobless. And finally, Stacy Peters. A thin black line gently crossed throughout her name, a fresh marking made by Roger only moments ago when they returned from the scene. Another one he had failed to save. Another one taken by an animal that should never have been allowed to see the light of day.

"Sir, we have two bins we are working. Bin one we believe contains the victims of a serial abductor or abductors. We have fairly substantive evidence linking these kidnappings."

"I know you were bouncing this theory around. Is this our official stance?" Capt. Ivers asked.

"Yes," Pat answered. "The attempt on Elliott Nobless last week solidified our theory. Him, Dana Chase, Holly Jones, Jon Parker. The methods are all too similar. Right out of the same playbook. Or rather, similar interpretations of that book."

"I notice you have Angela Cooper in parentheses off to the side."

It was Roger who answered. "It's because we don't have a body yet."

"Damn, Roger," Pat continued. "Sir, she is in parentheses since we do not have enough evidence from her case. We have interviews with her parents, neighbors, teachers, etcetera, but we don't have a crime scene. We have the entire park where she was last seen. It is very thin. However, we were able to examine the remains of Dana Chase. Additionally, through interviews with Holly Jones and Jon Parker, we are fairly certain she was held with them at the same location."

"Why again was she killed?" Captain Ivers asked.

"Our theory, sir, based on the conclusion provided by the medical examiner's office, is that she was not longer desirable due to seizures."

"What my partner is trying to say is that Dana Chase was broken in the mind of our abductor. Brain tumors were causing seizures. He killed her and dumped the body. We believe he went back on the prowl. He needed another toy. Jon Parker was his next victim."

"So, the consensus is some monster held Chase, Jones, and Parker at different points in time. Possibly Chase and Jones together. Then later, Jones and Parker after he killed Chase."

Roger and Pat nodded.

"Could this be the same sicko that tried to grab the Nobless kid?"

"Basker?" Roger shook his head no. "He did not seem as sophisticated as whoever grabbed the others. His abduction attempt was sloppy, ill-planned. It felt like it was his first attempt. Not the kind of planning that would scream experience. Plus, there is no evidence so far tying Chase, Jones, or Parker to his residence. And there were plenty of pictures of children and parks and houses, but nothing tying him to the other victims. He was probably new to the group."

"So still nothing on Angela Cooper?" Ivers asked. "When was the last time we updated the family?"

"No, sir. We have not been able to link her to any of these cases," Pat answered. "Hers, however, is similar to all of them. As for Angela's folks, we speak to her mom, Jenny, about once a month. She normally calls. Her father, Dane, has made it clear that he wants nothing to do with us unless we have an answer."

"Okay. So, if this group exists, we have one still missing, one murdered, one botched attempt, and two that miraculously escaped."

"As far as we know," Roger stated. "We have been digging for links or leads to other abductions."

"And no idea how Chase and Parker escaped, other than this mystery group of vigilantes?"

"Correct, sir. Which leads us to board number two." Roger directed the captain's attention to the next board. The murder victims were listed chronologically in the order of their murders: The reverend, Jill Clark, and Johnathon Tyler Basker. "We believe that the escape of Chase and Parker led to the development and planning of these murders."

"This is the focus of Carl's task force, right? Figuring out how these murders are linked to the vigilantes."

"Yes, sir. Any linkages will benefit our abduction cases. It is the same killer, and he is working for someone. Someone desperate enough to stop this vigilante group."

"We believe that not only did this vigilante group rescue Jones and Parker," Pat continued, "they also killed the abductor. This kidnapping ringleader knows it. He is scared, so he sent out an attack dog to eliminate his enemies. To stop them for good so he can go on with his abductions."

"Theories on our suspects? The ringleader and his merry band of perverts?" Ivers asked.

Roger paused momentarily before answering. "They may not intimately know each other. . . . Maybe a poor choice of words. We don't think they have routine in-person contact with one another."

"If they are truly working as a group, helping and teaching one another, you would figure that they would have to know each other."

"Not necessarily, Captain. I would not be surprised if most of them were complete strangers. They probably using some dark web B.S. to chat and share perverted stories and fantasies. It would also make more sense for security, especially if one of them gets caught. Like Basker."

"But you two think this so-called leader and the killer are chummy?"

"They at least know and trust one another," Pat offered. "These killings are important. It is for everyone's protection. If you are going to these lengths, you don't just hire a hit man from the yellow pages."

"But if they don't meet in person and only communicate online, why would they need to eliminate one of their own that was caught?" Ivers asked.

"No communication is completely secure," Pat said. "And maybe they are more vulnerable than we think. We just haven't found that Achilles' heel yet."

The phone at Roger's desk rang. "Patterson. Yup, he is right here. We were just wrapping up a briefing. Yeah, okay." Roger covered the phone with his hand. "It's Carl, Captain. He wants to know if we can come out on a field trip."

SCHOOL ISN'T TOO TERRIBLE. MOSTLY MATH, SCIENCE, AND ENGLISH. WE ALSO HAVE HISTORY CLASS EACH DAY. THE MAN TEACHES ABOUT AMERICA AND ALL THE HISTORY WITH WARS AND STUFF. HE ALSO TALKS ABOUT LAWS AND GOVERNMENT AND STUFF. HE SAYS THE CURRENT LAWS ARE UNJUST. HE SAID POLITICIANS ARE BAD. THEY FORGET THAT THE PEOPLE OF AMERICA ARE THE LAW.

21

THE INQUIRY

Arlington, Virginia

The conversation paused as the waitress topped off all three cups of coffee. She left behind the bill and several mint candies on a plastic tray. The coffee was the necessary fuel for the activities to come. It was six in the morning, and the team was readying for interviews, courtesy of Carl and some friends at the FBI.

The intent behind the early visit was to catch their first subject completely off-guard on his way to work. Nothing was more unsettling than rushing out to work with your first coffee of the day in hand only to find state and federal investigators on your front lawn with questions. It would ruin anyone's day.

Carl answered his phone. "Blanchard. Yep. Thanks, John." He returned his attention to Roger and Pat. "That was Oakes. U.S. Marshal. Not sure if you remember him from the other day at our introductory session downtown. Anyway, our target is home and ready for us to swoop in. Oakes will go find and babysit our second potential lead for this morning while we conduct the questioning."

"How did you come up with these names again?" Pat asked, trying desperately not to yawn.

"After Turner slipped through our fingers last summer, I decided to take a different approach."

"By slipped through your fingers, do you mean having the best alibi ever, since he was sitting in a jail cell while Jones and Parker were being rescued? That kind of slip through your fingers?"

"Very funny, Roger. But actually, that got Ken and me brainstorming on how this club may actually operate. Not as a team all the time, but rather on a case-by-case basis."

"What do you mean?" Pat asked.

"What I mean is they may very well work independently. They are assigned cases by whoever is in charge. Occasionally, they may work together or assist in some way. Take the elementary school and that creep Arthur Camp. Our suicide in the park. The exhaust fumes routed to the backseat. We thought Turner was the other janitor. His name was Bell or something. Figured Turner stalked Camp long enough to learn all his dirty little secrets and then finished him off when he had enough evidence."

"Well, *you* thought that, Carl. Pat and I were not entirely sold. We agreed the suicide did look suspicious. I had doubts, I will admit, but there just wasn't enough evidence to suggest anything other than a deranged man at the end of his rope who knew the police were closing in. It was just a matter of time. He probably did not want to go back to prison for child molestation. Those felons are treated particularly nasty by the other inmates. Even criminals have standards."

"Yeah, yeah. But Turner's prints were at the school. I just didn't know he did a security consultation there. But what if that consultation was reconnaissance? Turner goes in using his security consultant business as a cover. He checks the place out, identifies Camp, and then leaves. Someone else picks up from there. That other person gets hired and gathers evidence on Camp. Hell, there could even be a third person that did the kill in the park. Each member has a role to play. They probably don't even know each other. Almost like those terrorist cells where everyone knows only their job. They only know their piece without seeing the completed puzzle."

"I see where you are going with this. It is an interesting approach. It also would be the safest way to play it in the event one of them got caught. That person would only know so much, and the gamble would be that hopefully it wasn't enough to bring down the rest of the team or the head honcho himself. So, how did we land on Tony Carter for this morning? What role do you think he is playing?"

"Remember, I have a friend down at Quantico that teaches an advanced intelligence analysis course for our senior folks?"

Roger smirked.

"Screw you, Roger. I have friends."

"Right."

"Boys, stop. Carl, if you would please."

"Not sure how you put up with him, Pat. Anyway, Ken researched unsolved cases and/or what we are calling *anomalies*."

"Let me guess. Questionable rulings on cause of death. Suspicious suicides or accidents?" Roger asked.

"Exactly. Twenty-six to start. There have been more than expected over the last several years, but these were our most promising. Plus, twenty-six students in the intel analysis class."

"Are all the cases in the greater metropolitan D.C. area?" Pat asked.

"All but four. We threw in two from West Virginia, one from Pennsylvania, and one from North Carolina. The rest are from northern Virginia, D.C., and Maryland."

"Interesting." Roger slid his cup to the edge of the table.

Carl and Pat declined a refill from the waitress.

Carl continued once she left. "For their final project, the students are each assigned a case study. Then they are given a list of ten subjects. In this case, it was the list we previously created with a few minor adjustments. Turner and Cooper are still on it. We had initially dropped an ex-cop named Ferguson from the list since he was under surveillance when the children were recovered at the church. But using our new theory about how this group operates, we added him back. The students then conducted an exhaustive search on the suspects and any relation to their assigned crime. Nothing is off-limits. Well, everything needs to remain within legal bounds, of course."

"Does that sound a little suspect to you, Pat?"

"Sure does. Sounds like some FBI big brother shit."

Carl rolled his eyes. "I expect it from him, but now you, too? Thanks. This is all perfectly legal. The analysts can search any public or law enforcement database. They scour the internet as all sources of open-source intelligence. You would be surprised how much is out there on everybody. Our digital footprints are larger than you can fathom. The students then developed a packet on each subject and assigned them a probability score. It was a percentage indicating the likeliness that the suspect had any involvement in the crime."

"So, your analysts developed a pattern of life, so to speak, for each subject and then compared it to the crimes? Okay, consider Pat and I impressed. Especially with how you found the manpower. Pretty sneaky, Mr. FBI Man. How was Mr. Carter's score?"

"He scored high in six cases. Over seventy percent in each, based on his background, his temperament, and his pattern of life. He has a military background, and he works at the ATF. He has tried out for their special teams but was unsuccessful. His files indicated that he volunteered again to take the assessment, but then withdrew after his wife and child were murdered."

"What happened?" Pat asked.

"Robbery. Some strung-out piece of crap was holding up a local mom-and-pop place. Tony's wife and four-year-old child stopped in the store at the wrong time. Both were killed at the scene."

"Sounds like motivation to me," Roger added. "But his child was murdered, not kidnapped."

"You make a good point, but that is where we made some adjustments to our suspect list. Instead of only kidnappings, we also looked at all violence against children. We needed to identify a motivator for these guys. The abduction of a child would certainly be a good motivator. If your child was murdered, wouldn't you want to take revenge on others that prey on children?"

Roger nodded. "That is a pretty interesting way of looking at this."

"I think those are pretty good odds for Mr. Carter. How are we playing this? Are Roger and I good cops to your bad cop?"

"Let's all be bad cop today."

They drove the short distance to Tony's house in Carl's vehicle. Roger was clearly unhappy sitting in the passenger seat, while Pat smiled away in the back, enjoying her partner's slight discomfort. Carl pulled into the driveway, parking directly behind a Toyota Tacoma pickup truck. Tony was just coming out the front door.

"Excuse me, can I help you?" he asked. Although there was not instantaneous cause for concern, Tony was still a federal agent and clearly had his guard up. The three people in his driveway did not yet pose an immediate threat. His hand wasn't near his weapon, but it wasn't not near it, either.

Carl was already out of the vehicle and approaching Tony with his badge in his outstretched palm. "FBI, Mr. Carter. Sorry to disturb you this early in the morning, and we certainly did not mean to startle you."

You one hundred percent wanted to startle him, Roger thought.

"These are two colleagues of mine from the Virginia Bureau of Investigation. We need to ask you a few questions about some ongoing investigations."

"I wish you would have called ahead. I am on my way into the office right now. You are more than welcome to follow me over and I can get you linked up with the appropriate ATF agent for your case."

"Sorry for the confusion. It is you we need to speak with."

"Okay, I just hope this doesn't take too long. It would still probably be better to head to the office. I don't keep case files here."

"I think we can accomplish everything we need here, if that is all right with you," Carl answered.

"Come on in." Tony turned and entered the house, leaving the door open for the team to follow. They all noticed Tony's slight limp as he led them into a small living room. He was trying to hide the injury, but it was obvious he was favoring his right leg. The left was injured. Once everyone was settled, Roger began the questioning.

"How did you hurt your leg?" he asked.

"Overdid it in the gym the other day squatting. Strained my quad pretty bad. Doctors think I have several microtears."

"Ugh, that must be painful. How long have you been with the ATF?"

"About ten years now."

"You like it?"

"It's okay."

"And before that? You served in the Air Force, right?"

"I was with the Special Police for six years. Are you going to tell me what this is all about?"

Pat's turn was next. "Have you ever worked for the Fairfax County Schools?"

"No, why?"

"Never worked in an elementary school as a janitor for a short stint? Maybe while you were in between jobs or for a little side hustle."

"No. That is ridiculous."

"Why? There is nothing wrong with working as a janitor. When you were an SP, did you ever have any issues? Did you have any complaints against you? I assume your discharge was honorable after eight years."

"Nothing wrong with being a janitor. I just meant to say that I would have had no time to do that type of work. I left the service and went right to the ATF. I did six years as an SP, and then I got out. And yes, it was honorable."

Pat could see the irritation building. "You ever vacation in New York City?"

"I have been there occasionally for work, but what is this all about? These are the most random questions and make very little sense."

"It's about murder, Mr. Carter.," Carl answered. "I hope you may have some answers for us."

"What does a murder have to do with my military service or the possibility that I moonlight in the custodial arts?"

"Murders actually. Plural," Carl continued. "We are hoping you may be able to fill in the blanks for us."

Carl placed several photos from the New York train yard on the table. The gory photos showed what was left of Henry Galfini and associate Tony Mazzo.

Tony grimaced. "All right, I think I have had about enough of this. I also think you should show a little more professional courtesy instead of looking down at me from your high FBI perch."

"We are just lowly Staties," Pat offered. "We don't get to look down on anybody really. Well, maybe the traffic cops."

She looked to Roger. "Can we make fun of them?"

"Absolutely," Roger answered.

Tony readied himself to stand. "Enough, get—"

"You ever seen this man?" Carl slid a full-size photo of Sam Turner across the coffee table.

Tony looked like he had seen a ghost.

"How about a trip to Savannah?" Carl prodded. "You been there recently?"

More photos were spread across the table. Close-up shots of the dead traffickers, their bullet-ridden corpses laying around the port.

Roger and Pat closely watched Tony as Carl continued with the slide show. They could make out faint expressions on Tony's face. Whatever his involvement might or might not be, he was clearly hiding something, and the entire discussion was making Mr. Carter uncomfortable.

"Get out of my house. If you want a proper discussion, I can be contacted at my office. If you suspect me of something, then we can go through the lawyers. But this isn't happening, Mr. Blanchard. I will be filing an official complaint with your department later this morning after consultation with my superiors." Tony looked at Roger and Pat. "I don't know if we will bother with you two. You are obviously just doing the bidding of the FBI here."

Roger and Pat didn't even give Tony the courtesy of acknowledging his offense. Neither of them cared.

"Okay, Mr. Carter." Carl deposited one of his cards on the coffee table as they all stood to leave. "In case you change your mind or have a sudden epiphany. The pieces are coming together, with or without your help. And you know what I am talking about. DNA from blood never lies."

"Well, that was fun," Pat said as they pulled out of the driveway. "He really is not a fan of any of us."

"Yeah," added Roger. "We are not worthy of his loathing. Only Carl here, the big shot from the FBI."

"I am terrified of his wrath," joked Carl. "Pretty sure my bosses won't even answer the phone for a complaint from him."

"You thinking gunshot wound for that leg, Carl?" asked Roger.

"I am. We think one of them got hit during the Savannah operation. We may have inadvertently stumbled onto a break with our first shot here, and we still have several to go. Tony may know a lot more than he is letting on."

"And he definitely knows Sam Turner."

"You're right, Pat. I thought he was going to jump out of his skin when I laid down that photo. This guy is ripe. Maybe I need to apply a little pressure. He is the most promising so far. We have a few more at sixty percent, and you know those two. Sam Turner and Dane Cooper. The rest are in the fifties."

"What are we waiting for?" Pat asked. "Let's get moving onto our next subject."

Carl's phone buzzed. "Yeah. Hey, John. Okay."

He ended the call. "All right guys, our next one is ready."

President: Our team has departed and should be settled in the next day or so.

Benefactor: Thank you for the news. Will we be getting regular updates on their progress?

President: Yes. I spoke with the General. He will keep me informed. Once he knows something, I will.

Benefactor: Excellent. I believe this operation will be a great success.

22

THE DEPLOYMENT

Nairobi, Kenya

The plane touched down in Nairobi, Kenya, after eight exhausting hours. That, coupled with the previous eight-hour flight from Washington Dulles to Amsterdam, had wiped out the weary travelers.

Dane had tried everything he could, but he and Nicky had to ride coach for the entire trip. State Department folks were probably up in first class, but the Department of Defense would not hear of such luxurious nonsense. That was a waste of taxpayers' dollars. You had to follow the Joint Traveler Regulation. Since the trip was over eight hours, though, they were authorized to stay overnight and rest in Amsterdam before continuing on the next day. The additional cost of hotel rooms was more than the first-class ticket.

There was no sense trying to determine the logic, if any existed. The Department of Defense was nitpicky when it came to travel. *DoD has more to worry about than a couple of airline upgrades,* he thought.

He and Nicky entered the small airport and headed directly to the single baggage claim belt. The stale air and oppressive heat worsened their already declining moods, and Dane knew it would be a while before the bags were unloaded. Although he loved the country and its people, they tended to move a little slower than he would have preferred at the Jomo Kenyatta International Airport. And it was neat and clean, but a far cry from international airport standards. A few flights a day left the continent, while a majority of flights were between neighboring countries.

Over an hour later with bags in tow, they breezed through customs with barely a glance. The embassy had sent an expeditor to ensure the arriving Americans were not delayed any further. He whisked them through security, barely showing their passports to the Kenyan officials before heading out to a waiting Land Cruiser. The final leg of their journey began north along the Nairobi Expressway.

Despite the dark and the years since he had driven these roads, familiar sights were coming back to Dane. They passed a large office building that he remembered housed an ice skating rink, of all things. A sign with an arrow pointing down a side road advertised The Carnivore Restaurant. When Dane had told Nicky about the place and his desire to take her there, he compared it to a Texas De Brazil in the States. Servers walked around with different grilled meats to sample. You had a little card on your table with a green side and a red side. If it was green, servers would offer you generous portions of meat. The only difference is that several of those meats had been walking below the elevated dining platforms moments earlier. Alligators, chickens, and other creatures roamed, pranced, and squawked as they patiently waited their turn.

Dane went to nudge Nicky and point the place out, but she was sound asleep. He would have to enjoy this trip down memory lane alone. Once in the heart of the city they turned east on the Embu Nairobi Highway. This was the Westlands area where Dane had lived before. Terrorists rocked the area back in 2013 with an attack the Westgate Shopping Mall. He couldn't remember the reason for the siege. *Damn,* he thought, *I used to go there all the time to get food at the basement grocery store, Nakumatt. Or to head over to the food court for a taste of home, or more like to see how KFC tasted different in Africa.*

The driver left the highway and weaved north along Limura Road. The city gave way to more of the lush forest Dane remembered as the vehicle climbed toward the more rural areas. They passed Java House Coffee and the United Nations Avenue that led to the U.S. Embassy and the UN. They would head there tomorrow.

Their final destination was only a short ways ahead. The driver turned right and slowed at the Two River security checkpoint. The embassy badge around his neck guaranteed swift passage for him and his passengers. From there, the City Lodge Hotel was simply another block ahead. The hotel was one of the nicest in the area. Dane was looking forward to relaxing after such a long journey.

The next morning, Dane jolted awake and took in the strange surroundings. After traveling halfway around the world, he was understandably groggy. His chirping alarm harnessed his senses, and he relaxed back onto the bed. Ah, Nairobi. He could hear church bells in the distance, recalling that this part of Africa was predominately Christian. Kenya and Ethiopia had strong roots in the religion, with many coming to believe that Ethiopian Monks were entrusted with guarding the secrets of the Ark of the Covenant.

He barely remembered checking into their room and then practically dragging Nicky to her bed next door. He ensured she set an alarm before passing out, but she didn't even remove her shoes. They had booked a two-bedroom suite with a shared living room and kitchen. It seemed the most practical and, although Kenya was generally a safe country, they were still foreigners in a foreign land. They needed to stick together.

Dane quickly showered and dressed, throwing on slacks and a long-sleeve collared shirt. Most embassies in Africa maintained a relaxed dress code due to the oppressive heat. Diplomats in Paris or London would wear heavy tweed jackets or neatly tailored suits. In Africa, common sense prevailed. The looser fitting the clothing, the better to take advantage of any available movement of air. Dane didn't bring any semblance of a suit, but he did throw on a tie for good measure.

They were meeting the ambassador before hopping a private flight over to Djibouti. They didn't need to return to Jomo. Their flight would take off from the less-traveled Wilson Airport. Fewer prying eyes. Although there was nothing secretive about this portion of the mission, it still never hurt to obscure as many operational movements as possible.

Dane left his room and entered the shared spaces. There was a fresh pot of coffee next to a travel mug and a note: *After everything you did last night, I can at least buy you breakfast. In the lobby – Nicky.* Dane poured a healthy amount in a Styrofoam cup and headed out. Although elevators were available, the glass stairwells offered amazing views of the foliage throughout the lobby. Once there, he spied Nicky in the restaurant.

"Wow, you're alive?"

"No kidding. I was pooped last night. Thanks for getting us settled. I am sure I was no help."

"For a small woman, you sure are heavy as dead weight."

Nicky smacked him on the arm as she stood up. "Grab a plate, smartass. I ordered us each the buffet. I figured you would be starving since you always seem to be eating."

With full plates, they returned to their table. Fresh water and coffee awaited them. "I still don't understand why we are spending a day at the embassy. We are working out of Djibouti, not Kenya."

"It gets tricky whenever you talk anything Somalia. Everyone—and no one—wants to own it," Dane answered. "Since there is no embassy in Somaliland territory, Kenyan, Ethiopian, and Djiboutian ambassadors share state department duties. Meeting the ambassador here is a courtesy and a way to make sure he doesn't have any objections that could disrupt our work."

"And we are skipping Ethiopia? That ambassador is not even in country, right?"

"Yup," Dane answered between mouthfuls. "But that ambassador rarely has any interest in Somaliland. I have actually never met with the COM in Addis."

"COM?"

"Sorry, chief of mission. Ambassador. Normally, they have a deputy as well."

"Okay, cool. So, after today, we fly out to the base. No COM meeting in Djibouti?"

"Nope. They don't have one at the moment. And even if they did, it gets complicated since these are active war zones. States Department is kinda in charge but really the military commander of the base is head honcho over here. He is the one we have to brief."

"Well, you just let me know what part to play. You say all the cool operational jargon, and I will dazzle them with my technical knowledge and charming wit."

"Charm away, Nicky. Anything will help at this point. They often roll their eyes when we come into town. It normally means their usual way of doing things is going to be disrupted, and they don't like that."

"Ha. I just can't envision you and your merry band of pirates causing headaches for commanders over here throughout the years. You all seem so innocent."

Dane smirked. "I will admit that we have been less than cordial at times. But it was with the best of intentions."

"Sure. Are we taking a little puddle jumper over to Djibouti? I love saying that, by the way. Dji . . . *bouti*," she said.

"I am glad you are having fun being childish." Dane smiled. "Yes, it will be a small charter plane this afternoon. We will land at the airfield and literally taxi onto the Marine base. SOCOM has some sleeping quarters, but I booked us off-base at the Sheraton. It's right on the beach, and it has a nice bar. Beats staying on a dry post."

"I thought there was an embassy now in Somalia. So how does that work?"

"That is the embassy in Mogadishu, the capital of the Federal Republic of Somalia. It is fairly new. Somaliland refuses to be part of the country, though. It declared its independence in the nineties or something. They don't recognize the authority of the Somali government, which, to be fair to them, has changed a lot over the years and normally was less effective than not. Plus, soldiers from several other African and UN nations have had to send in military forces to keep the peace. Somaliland wants no part of it."

"Crap, don't tell me we have to see another ambassador."

"Nope. Nobody recognizes them as a country. And Somalia just leaves them alone. Nothing really worth fighting over."

"Wow, you really take a girl to all the nicest places."

"Don't look at me. Look at our bosses and, of course, Charles."

Nicky looked around before answering. They were clearly alone. "So how do you think our other mission is going to play out here? Somehow, I don't see our bosses being too pleased that while we were here, a major terrorist just happened to lose his life."

"Yeah, I am still working on that. The only really solid way is to make it look like it was some interclan rivalry or revenge."

"How are you going to pull that off?"

"Basically, by not getting caught. If it was a drone hit or a warhead on forehead, the U.S. would have a hard time denying involvement. But if a terrorist is shot and there are no Americans in sight, then the obvious conclusion is one of their own killed him. It happens all the time. I am confident there is some outstanding feud here that the locals will pin this on. As long as nobody sees us and can point a finger at the United States, it will all blow over."

"How about on the international scene?"

"Yeah, that is a different story."

"It will send a different kind of message, Dane. The locals here are probably not aware of all of Ibrahim's activities, but just know that he is a bad and powerful man. Those in the community will know that he was lured out of hiding and then eliminated."

"It is going to shake up some folks for sure. And you would know better than me coming from your world. We just have to stay on mission, complete the tasks, and get the hell out of Dodge. Let Charles and the others worry about international blowback."

They finished their breakfast and headed outside to meet their driver. Although Dane had driven here before and was more than capable, it made more sense to use the embassy-provided drivers for this short of a visit. Additionally, the driver was cleared to drive through the security checkpoint onto embassy grounds. Dane would have had to park in the visitors lot and traverse layers of security. The embassy car would be capable of dropping them right at Post One.

A short while later, they maneuvered through the streets with the embassy driver. The morning commuters seemed to drive with a sense of urgency bordering on demonic possession. Rubbing was racing in Nairobi, the vehicles full of dents, and the roadways were clogged after a sprinkling of matatus and motos joined the mix. The madness spiraled out of control. To Dane, it felt like something out of an action movie.

The matatus were small buses overloaded with people, luggage, and animals. Goats would be tied to the roofs while people hung onto the outside, gripping windows and door frames for dear life. The tiny motorcycles, or motos, danced in and out of traffic with no regard to any laws. Instead of traffic lights, most intersections had roundabouts. This no-holds-barred cage matches would suck traffic in one side and spit them out the other.

Dane did not miss driving here.

Security waved them through the embassy's gated entrance. Many embassies around the world were actually compounds with several buildings: The embassy itself, quite often a USAID building, and sometimes even housing for the ambassador or staff. The exterior of the compound would normally be secured by local security forces, overseen by the regional security officer, or RSO. Also under that office's purview were the contingent of Marines assigned to the post. They controlled access to the main building. Post One was the front door, Post Two the back.

Dane always befriended whatever contingent of Marines he found. He didn't always visit the nicest places, so it didn't hurt to have some Marines backing you up. Plus, they have the pulse of every embassy. They move unnoticed in the shadows, mostly ignored by the predominantly State Department staff. They have all the good dirt. And lastly, they were generally good people. They would look up to senior military folks like Dane and ask for guidance. They were usually happy to find camaraderie in foreign lands.

Dane didn't get a chance to meet any Marines today. He and Nicky were in and out of the embassy quickly. They had a brief discussion with the ambassador, revealing a sliver of the real mission. If she knew exactly what they were planning, she would have shut them down immediately.

Afterward, they were invited to the chief of station's office. The CIA man was not as clueless as the ambassador. He generally supported the operation. He opined a little and vaguely offered support without a concrete committal. Typical. Dane had been down this path before. If the team was successful, the chief would take some credit. If it failed, he would wash his hands of them. Some things never change.

I WENT OUTSIDE FOR RECESS TODAY, BUT THE MAN DIDN'T LET ME STAY OUT LONG. THERE WERE LOUD NOISES AND BANGING. I HEARD PEOPLE SHOUTING. NOT SURE WHAT THEY WERE SAYING. OUTSIDE SMELLED LIKE THE FREEWAY WHEN WE WOULD DRIVE TO FLORIDA. I WOULD PUT MY ARM OUT THE WINDOW. MY BROTHER JOKED THAT IT WOULD BE CUT OFF BY A TRUCKER. THE MAN TOLD ME OVER THE SPEAKER TO COME INSIDE.

23

THE FRIEND

Occoquan, Virginia

Devotee: I found a way to get to him. It will be risky, but I can do it right under their noses.

Keeper: Good. I need you to take care of this. We must not let them get any closer.

Devotee: Soon. Very soon. Can I then start collecting?

Keeper: Yes. You can then begin your journey. Be careful.

Jack sat idle in the left lane, waiting for the red light to change. He was on the final leg of his surveillance detection route. He was meeting a former mate from the teams. And although it was perfectly reasonable that two old colleagues meet for lunch, they wanted to keep this meeting away from the prying eyes of D.C.

Operational secrecy was a must in this town of brigands, spies, and scoundrels. Secrets would be passed today. No reason to advertise it to the world.

Dane had told Jack about this small riverside town called Occoquan. It was off the beaten path, and you would rarely just stumble across it. You needed to be heading that way. It was busy, but not busy enough for a tail to hide for very long. The quaint town had several shops and restaurants, but really only one main boulevard. Jack would know if he or his friend brought company.

The light changed, and he drove down the ramp from the Franconia Springfield Parkway onto the south bound, I-95 HOV. Only seven cars took the turn with him. And after several miles only one of those seven exited at the Occoquan sign. Jack stayed in the right-hand lane on Ox Road while that traveler moved to the far left lane for a turn onto Old Bridge Road. He was clean.

A quick right on Riverview followed by a left at the bottom of the hill brought Jack into town. Huge, majestic homes bordered the Occoquan River until the road crossed under the 123 Bridge giving way to the city. Jack parked under the bridge and walked along the boardwalk to Madigan's Waterside Grille. Dane said it was a great place to have a meal and enjoy the river. He was right.

Connor was already seated at an outside table, away from any revelers. It was midafternoon on a weekday, so the crowds were not large. The usual town locals could be seen starting their evening off early, but they normally planted themselves at the western edge of the deck at the tiki bar. Connor already had two pints on the table.

"Jack, old boy! Good to see you."

"You too, Connor. I really appreciate the help."

The men shook hands and settled into their seats. They chatted while checking out the menus and placing their orders. Once the waitress departed, the conversation became more serious.

"So, how is the spy life at MI5 treating you?"

"It's got its ups and downs, Jacky." Connor and a few others were the only ones allowed to call him that. "I have a cushy little office over at Langley. Doing the liaison thing for a bit. Looking out for domestic threats against both our nations. I have been watching the news lately. . . . Sounds like you and your boys have been busy. Probably making some very powerful people unhappy. And costing the good taxpayers a nickel or two."

Jack trusted Connor with his life. He couldn't count the number of times the man had literally saved him. Charles concurred, so Connor was occasionally consulted on high-level matters where accesses had to be delicate. He also always offered his combat services, if necessary. He knew that Jack wanted to shield him from this world, but certain debts were owed. If called upon, he was more than willing to lend his gun to the cause. Jack had thanked him, then assured him it was unnecessary while promising to call if it wasn't.

"We have," Jack said. "However, we are trying to not outpace ourselves, and this current problem has become catastrophic."

Connor grimaced. "How many have you lost?"

"Two so far. It was not pretty. They suffered. Jill was our spotter. She conducted most of our initial bumps for new recruits. She interacted with them. Gave us a solid first impression and recommendation on whether to proceed with recruitment. The reverend, on the other hand, was an unwitting member when I dropped off those two children at his church last summer. My actions placed a death sentence upon him."

"Not your fault—you were doing the right thing. The animal doing these killings is at fault. I never did get to follow up about that one. What happened there with those kids?"

"My associate neutralized the perpetrator in question. That is one body that will never be found. I scooped up the children while he finalized business. Jill had a key to the church and let me in. Best we could do in a pinch."

"Your associate? That's rich, Jacky. You mean your boy Dane. The one in the Horn of Africa right now?"

Jack tried to hide the surprise on his face. He had never told Connor about anyone else in the club.

"Relax. I only put it together because I know about you and what you guys do. Some FBI putz was asking about Dane and a couple of other guys a few months back, wanting to know if they worked in the community and all that. They hit our offices, then the folks down at Fort Bragg. I think they even bugged SOCOM in Tampa."

"Isn't it Fort Liberty now?"

"Still Fort Bragg to me no matter how much money they waste trying to tell me otherwise. First place I got to do some serious training with the Yanks."

"Me too." The two men clinked their beer mugs. "What did you guys tell him?"

"Well, I knew nothing about the guy, so I was quiet. My compatriots at the agency knew the guy, but also said nothing. Once the fed left, I asked the guys. They told me Dane was top notch, but had fallen off his game after his kid was nicked. They did hear that he had hit rock bottom and was trying to crawl his way out. He had friends in high places that were giving him another chance. Whatever the FBI wanted with him must be serious if they are digging this deep. Dane must have snapped or something. Losing a kid will do that."

Jack nodded. "Got it. I didn't realize Carl and the FBI were digging like that on Dane. We knew there was a formal inquiry into another associate, even going so far as arresting him, but that didn't work out well for the Feds."

Connor snapped his fingers. "Carl! That's the fed. Kind of a prick. Acted like he was some big shot."

"Well, he has built a task force to find us, so someone must think he is important. Between his guys and this killer, we are getting squeezed. Do you guys have a play in the Africa mission?"

"Nope. Agency is keeping tabs but that is it. Chief over there got a briefing, and I am sure he gave them the standard disclosure about agency involvement. They don't like the mission, but their hands are tied. They are afraid it will disrupt things in that region. They are standing by to place blame or take credit. You know how they operate."

"I never realized how smoothly things were going over there at Langley. Sounds like a well-oiled machine."

Both men had a good chuckle. The waitress arrived with their food and drink refills. They thanked her as she left.

"So, I researched what you asked for, Jacky, and it is not pretty. The messenger bag at your feet has all the information you and your team will need. It is fairly detailed. You can enjoy a little nighttime reading later. I will give you the Cliff's Notes version. It all started in Afghanistan around 2003. I am sure you remember it. Quite brutal in those early days."

"Wish I could forget. I did two tours over there before heading to Iraq. You and I were together the for the last time in '02. Islamabad, if I remember correctly. Chasing those shitheads all over the mountains.

I switched squadrons after that and spent most of my remaining time in Iraq."

"Well, I'll tell you things got brutal. Remember the beheading of that journalist?"

"I do, but wasn't that in Pakistan? Karachi, right?"

"It was. Islamic extremists. Not al-Qaeda, but supporters. But remember what effect that had not just on the soldiers, but the world. You read about those kinds of acts in history books, early pre-modern fighting that was gruesome Genghis Khan-type shit. But not on the elegant battlefield of today."

"I remember, Connor. They sent out videos. It was disgusting."

"Exactly, and that's what they wanted. Shock. Awe. Fear. That marked a turning point in what can only be described as an all-out war against Western society. Many in the intel community believe that we witnessed the rise of ISIS, the rise of the caliphate, as early as 2002. Possibly earlier."

"So, groups like al-Qaeda, al-Shabab? Where did or where do they fit in?"

"Puppets. Surrogates. Useful tools in the war against the West. We, the collective Western allies, were not prepared for the brutality of the extremists. We knew of cruelty in warfare, but not like this. Sure, there were atrocities in the big wars, Korea, Vietnam. Of course, people colored outside the lines, but they were isolated. There are rules. And one of the big ones is you don't cut off an enemy's head."

"I know. We tried to keep some mythical moral high ground that didn't exactly serve us well. I don't think we needed to start taking heads, but maybe find some middle ground."

"Not all of us, Jacky. That is where I believe your boy here fits in. There were some that believed we should fight fire with fire. An eye for an eye kind of justice."

"Connor, are you telling me we had teams going around Afghanistan cutting off terrorists' heads?"

"Not exactly heads, but we did field teams to inflict terror on them. Torture squads to show the enemy that we would not be intimidated. Adapt their tactics and use them against them. We were essentially becoming the terrorists."

"I heard rumors. So, you are telling me those rumors were true."

"Yes. A small group was formed. CIA led of course with a smattering of contactors and soldiers. They pulled from some of the Psyop units. Special Forces. Fighters. Not just people that hid behind those Hesco walls and celebrated Taco Tuesday or some shit, but the ones that were out there mixing it up and getting to understand the Afghani people. They had language skills and knew people. Knew what they feared."

"I can't believe this was sanctioned or that some general rotating into theater didn't put a stop to it."

"That is eventually what happened, mate. The wrong general found out, and the program was shut down. It had to go underground."

"So, you are telling me it went purely contractor?"

Connor snapped his fingers. "Exactly. They weren't going to let this go. The Daesh were getting stronger. Their tentacles extending their reach. The Middle East. Africa. Eastern Asia. Even in small pockets throughout Europe and South America. So, the teams went global. In steps DSS."

"DSS? Never heard of them."

"Dynamic Solutions Services. Very small, niche company. They stayed off the public's radar. They did Uncle Sam's dirty work. Real group of psychos from what I heard. Retired military. Mercenaries, criminals—all with a certain moral flexibility."

"I find all of this hard to believe, Connor."

"Remember the world back then and the rise of ISIS. Osama bin Laden was killed in 2011. It looked like the West had won in both Iraq and Afghanistan. We were training the locals to take over so we could finally go home and bam! Here comes ISIS. And they are killing it. Taking huge swaths of land. Beheading Western journalists. Burning Jordanians and Kurds in metal cages. They just suddenly appeared, and they dominated. And nobody could seem to stop them."

"I do remember that. One second, we have the Taliban, Al-Qaeda, Al Shabab, Al everyone back on their heels, and then ISIS comes along."

"Yup. But Jacky, they were there all along. Like I said, pulling the strings in the background. We just never saw them. But they were losing—globally losing—so they had to emerge. And they showed their true colors. They showed the true violence they were capable of for their cause. We had to respond."

"So DSS stepped in."

Connor nodded. "DSS swept in. They got more funding and support than ever. Black ops money of course. Traceable to no one. They were unleashed on Daesh. Nothing was off the table. Stop them and save our way of life, no matter what."

"Which brings us to today. Are they still active?"

"No. At least not as DSS. They lost their funding in late 2019. The war against ISIS appeared won. The United States declared victory. The funds for DSS were needed for other secret wars. The company survived. They picked up other scraps from the bigger companies. Small contracts here and there. Enough to keep the lights on, but not enough to retain all their people. They have had huge turnover over the last several years. They are a remnant of what once was, but I wouldn't be surprised to find a few of them still around practicing their craft on behalf of somebody."

"So, you think my killers are connected how? You think they have become their own masters?"

"The holes in the bodies. It was a fairly common technique used by those teams. Those holes are from handheld drills, both battery-powered and manual crank."

"Holy shit." Jack nodded toward the briefcase. "Did you find files on possible suspects?"

"No. A majority of these, um, operational details were not captured for posterity. Nor were the actors given credit for their deeds. What I was able to find are pieces to the puzzle. Redacted documents, purchase orders, finances. Plus, a few dossiers on key staff personnel in DSS. These people may know who you are looking for."

"Do you really think anyone would want to dig up dirt on the company that may give it a black eye or hurt their current business?"

"From the little I know about your little club, it sounds like your fellas can be quite convincing when needed."

Cyber Tech: We have made progress with their messaging board. We have it partially mapped.

President: That is great news. When do you think you can crack their whole network?

Cyber Tech: It is not quite that simple. We have been conducting intrusions. They may notice slight disruptions. They may not.

President: I trust you will proceed with the appropriate balance of caution and conviction.

24

THE STAGING

Djibouti, Djibouti

"Wow, is the admiral always that grumpy?" Nicky asked. "First time meeting that one, but he didn't seem to like supporting us."

"He doesn't have to do anything. His troops just need to be on alert in case we get in trouble in Somaliland."

"I know, yet I have never met a base commander that approved of our operations in the Horn of Africa. They think all Special Operations folks are just a bunch of cowboys running off at the mouth and going off half-cocked."

"Wait, is that not the case? That is the only reason I was going along with all this. I figured I would have a front row seat to some cool masculine shit."

"Quite the comedian. Our timeline still good with the viruses moving toward Berbera?"

"Yup. I checked in before that ass-chewing. My folks were much nicer than the ones here. Shipment is expected to arrive three to five days from now.

"Perfect. That gives us plenty of time."

Dane and Nicky walked across Camp Lemonnier in Djibouti. The base commander's Special Forces teams were asked to be the quick reaction forces, or QRF, while the pair deployed to Berbera. The troops would be on alert, ready at a moment's notice, to board V-22 Ospreys and respond to a crisis. That crisis would be any incident the pair had while in Somaliland.

The troops were not concerned. They were excited for the possibility of action. Being stationed at the camp was hardly glamorous or exciting. It was much better to race away in some Ospreys on a secret mission than to sit around playing pickup basketball between guard shifts.

The admiral wasn't happy because the request probably came at the last minute, and the base commander was told to have forces on standby, not asked. Base commanders did not like to be told what to do. They also did not like to be left out of mission planning. They were often treated as a simple custodian of the base, and that could grate on the ego.

Dane did his best to soften the blow during the brief, letting the commander make suggestions about pickup and rendezvous points. He also had strong opinions about the conduct of the operation. Nothing Dane could do about it except be on the receiving end of the commander's angst. The plan was approved as-is well above either of their paygrades.

Dane was amazed at how the base had grown over the years. The only modern indulgences back in the day had been the Green Beans coffee place. Now, there were plenty of restaurants, modern housing, and even a pool. Dane had lived in containerized housing units, lovingly referred to as CHUs. They would be stacked all around the Special Operations compound, and housed two soldiers apiece. The twenty-foot shipping containers had bedrooms on each end with a shared bathroom in the middle. They were not exactly roomy. They were also stacked one upon another with a makeshift railing system that resembled faulty scaffolding. One push against those rails, and a normal human would plummet to the ground. Most of the CHUs were used for housing, with some set aside for office spaces. They would be scattered around a cement area with little signs designating their occupants.

However, modern buildings across the compound had interrupted Dane's trip down memory lane. *It is too soft here,* he thought. *Soldiers don't need to suffer, but they don't need to be pampered, either. They forget they are on deployment to rain down hell upon the enemy if called. Not to celebrate Taco Tuesday or whatever the hell they did nightly to make everything feel like a party. War is not a party.*

He and Nicky had flown in earlier that day, with the private plane from Kenya ignoring the tower calls from the Djibouti-Ambouli International Airport's control tower upon landing. They taxied over to a set of Camp Lemonnier gates, which opened and let the aircraft roll right through to a tarmac. The pilots would deal with customs later.

Djiboutian officials did not need to know the identity of everyone who transited the base. They would complain, but the military knew how much money the base generated for the tiny country to supplement its weak economy. The country's port was the only other real economic powerhouse in the region. The port had a strategic location at the opening of the Red Sea, which was fortunate since Djibouti needed to import nearly everything.

Dane and Nicky spent the morning checking all the equipment that had been shipped, with the help of one of Dane's colleagues sent over to assist. Mac was a jack of all trades. He was a logistician, a mechanic, and even a qualified armorer. The configuration of the KTM motorcycles was the most crucial aspect of the whole operation. The trio ensured all fluids were topped off, tires properly inflated, and equipment secured to the dirt bike frames.

They loaded the bikes into the back of a small Mercedes panel van using ratchet straps to keep them upright. Ramps for each bike were also placed inside with the rest of the team's gear. Once they began the mission, they needed smooth and rapid unloading so as not to draw unwanted attention.

The plan was for Mac to retain possession of the panel van while Dane and Nicky left the base in a local car. They had reservations at the Sheraton and would enjoy their last night in comfort.

After conducting an all-day surveillance detection route starting the following morning, they would meet Mac at dusk to switch vehicles. Dane and Nicky would drive the van as far as they could before the mountainous terrain necessitated motorcycle travel, then they would ditch the van. Someone would either retrieve it later or, more than likely, it would be stolen within hours, never to be seen again. It was considered expendable for this operation. But that was tomorrow. Tonight, they could relax one final time.

Dane and Nicky loaded up their car and drove north out of the camp.

"Those Marines look miserable," Nicky said about the gate guards they passed.

"Well, it is a thousand degrees out, and they are in full battle rattle out in the sun."

"Battle rattle?"

"All their shit. Helmet, armor, all of it. This is still designated as a combat zone."

"At least they are not paying taxes at the moment."

"Nope, and neither are we. Plus, all of us are getting hazardous duty pay."

"Is that how you become rich in Special Operations? Isn't it like a hundred bucks a month extra or something?"

Dane laughed. "Yup. And I have been amassing my fortune one small trip around the world at a time."

It was Nicky's turn to laugh. "So why the Sheraton? I understand that we want to disassociate from the camp, but won't we stand out?"

"The Sheraton is a popular place for Western tourists and businessmen. We will blend in. It will be easier to start our surveillance detection route from there, rather than the front gate of a military base. We can scope things out before we leave. Plenty of vantage points to see if someone has set up a surveillance bubble for us. Hard to do with a single-entry point base. Plus, it has a nice pool, a good restaurant, and a small beach on-site."

"I have heard about all the shark attacks in this part of the world."

"So, you don't want to go swimming with whale sharks later?" Dane asked. "I can get us a tour. You just jump right in with those suckers. They don't bite."

"Hell no! But what are we going to do tomorrow for our detection route?"

"We are going to do some tourist stuff."

"And what pray tell will that consist of?"

"Well, we will head out to Shark Pit."

"What part of no sharks did you not understand?"

"Ha. It's a beach area with amazing colors. And it's near Lake Assal."

"No sharks in the lake? I don't want to find out about some prehistoric predator that has somehow survived in this lake. I know they aren't supposed to be in fresh water, but I have seen Shark Week and know some can survive there. Bull sharks in particular. And they are nasty. Better not be any in Assal."

"No sharks, but it is a saltwater lake. I think it is the lowest point in Africa since it is way below sea level. They mine salt from the area. Supposed to have beautiful views."

"We are shopping at some point, right?" Nicky asked.

"Of course. I anchored the route with several small towns where you can check out local arts and crafts."

They pulled into the Sheraton parking lot.

"I meant to ask you something, Dane, before we head inside. I don't want someone to overhear us."

"What's up?"

"The use of our rifles has been bothering me. Or, more specifically, the use of our ammo. We probably won't exactly have time to pick up all the brass if something goes wrong, or when you pop Ibrahim Mohamad Mahmud."

"It shouldn't be a problem. Western-style weapons and ammunition have proliferated all over the world. Lots of them found their way to Africa. You would be surprised how many militias and gangs carry M4-style weapons over here. Same with our handguns. You won't see a lot of Glocks, but all the handguns here shoot 9mm. All of them. Last time I was here, I shot my Colt .45 at the range. The size of the bullet rocked their world."

"Okay, that makes sense. I just kept forgetting to ask."

They retrieved their small personal bags from the trunk of the sedan. Mac had their mission bags in the panel van with the bikes. When they did the exchange, Dane and Nicky would leave their personal bags with him. They entered the gaudy lobby and found their way over to the reception desk. Just as Dane had said, the area was filled with mostly westerners. Nicky noticed a group of Turkish Airlines flight attendants heading toward the elevator with their small rolling bags. As the elevators opened, out poured another group of women, dressed this time in beach clothes and carrying towels.

"Is there another reason we are staying here?" Nicky asked.

Dane paused while filling out the paperwork for their rooms. "What do you mean?"

"There seems to be an abundance of young attractive women moving about the lobby."

"Huh. Never thought of that. I guess all the airlines do house their flight attendants here for overnight stays."

Nicky punched Dane in the arm. "Pervert."

"Hey, not my fault. Here is your room key. Did you want to freshen up or just head out to the pool and beach?"

"I guess I can unpack later. Let's head out and get to that sunshine."

The elevator doors opened. Dane stepped inside and pressed the number for their floor. "Good. If we hurry, we can catch the ladies."

Nicky punched him again as the doors closed.

A short time later, they met on the gravel path to the pool. Dane wore trunks and a T-shirt, along with the obligatory flip-flops. He looked like an average guy going to the pool. Nicky, on the other hand, had gone all out.

Her white beach coverup was thick enough to be modest, but did not have quite enough opacity to hide her bikini underneath. The bronze two-piece suit cling to her every curve, and the color complemented her complexion. Her perfectly manicured toenails poked out from braided sandals upon which she seemed to float across the footpath.

Dane was stunned, and she knew it. She gave him a wink as she passed him on the way to the kidney-shaped pool. Lounge chairs surrounded the tiny peninsula deck mostly occupied by the flight attendants from the lobby. It jutted out into the ocean, surrounded on three sides by water. Dane peered out past the scattering of tiki huts to watch the enormous cargo liners push on past for the port of Djibouti to their north.

They found two loungers and settled in to relax. Nicky removed her coverup and spread lotion across her chest, arms, and legs. Once finished, she laid down on her stomach and passed the bottle to Dane.

"You mind?"

Dane rubbed the bronzer lotion onto her back. She cracked the pages of her book.

"Don't forget my arms and legs, please. I don't want to burn before the big trip."

Dane hesitated, but rubbed the lotion across her thighs and calves. *This was a very bad idea,* he thought. *I need to stay mission-focused.*

"Thanks." Nicky winked before staring back at her novel.

Dane put on his own sunscreen, preferring to sit up while he tried to read his book. It was the new release by William R. Forstchen, *Five Years After*. Dane had thoroughly enjoyed the first three books in the John Matherson series, but was having a hard time concentrating now. The attendants did not interest him at all. He kept sneaking glances at Nicky as the sun bounced off her body.

I am in so much trouble.

They had only planned on spending about an hour by the pool, since they really didn't want to burn up in the hot African sun. They were not that far from the equator, and a bad burn could really complicate the mission. *Hell, my thoughts about her could mess this up as well.*

"I made reservations for us at the front desk to eat here tonight if that is okay with you."

Nicky paused and placed a bookmark in her novel. "What, you don't want to show me the Djibouti nightlife?"

"Well, there are a couple places, but the town can be a little rough after dark."

"So now I can't take care of myself?"

"Not what I meant. I just thought maybe we would eat here. There is a nice restaurant. After that, they have a poolside lounge that might be good for a cocktail." Dane said, pointing to a small outdoor bar over his shoulder.

"I am just messing with you. What time is dinner?"

"Does seven work?"

Nicky glanced at her embassy-issued cellphone. "Well, it's only four now. Whatever should we do with our free time?"

Dane hoped he wasn't blushing.

"Well, you seem more interested in looking at me than those flight attendants, so I will make the first move and leave the decision to you."

Nicky stood and gathered her belongings. "Your choice," she said as she placed her room key in Dane's hand. She rose and walked back toward the hotel entrance .

I WANT TO GO HOME. I WANT TO SEE MY MOM AND DAD. IT WAS RAINING TODAY, WHICH MAKES ME SAD. AFTER RECESS, THE MAN WAS GONE. NO SCHOOL, SO I READ MY BOOKS. I AM ON THE FOURTH HARRY POTTER BOOK. THE PRISONER OF AZKABAN. I AM NOT SURE HE HAS ALL THE BOOKS. I HOPE SO.

25

THE RECRUITER

Roosevelt Island, Washington D.C.

Devotee: I found a window of opportunity, so I took it.

Keeper: Did he talk about a leader? Other members?

Devotee: Two leaders and the people killing our friends. I have them all.

Keeper: No more torture. Quick, straight killings. Make sure to cut the head off the snake.

Jack eased the car from the George Washington Parkway into the Theodore Roosevelt Island parking lot. *Damn, these Yanks sure do love their ex-presidents,* he thought. As he found a space, he marveled at the beauty of the Memorial Park.

England certainly had its fair share of beautiful parks and gardens. The gardens of Kensington Palace and Hyde Park near the center of London always came to mind as an example. The lush foliage brought tourists from around the globe to wander from the royal grounds over to the adjacent park, feeding the ducks as they strolled along the serpentine shores.

But nothing compared to the volume and beauty of America's conservation efforts. Roosevelt Island—the eighty-eight-acre island designated to celebrate an iconic American president and its first true outdoorsman and conservationist—was just one example. Credited as the first true naturalist president, number twenty-six would go on to establish national parks, forests, and memorials. All that was an effort to preserve and protect U.S. national resources.

Jack had visited several national parks throughout the country, but it would take several lifetimes to visit them all. *Europeans can never truly understand the vastness of America without witnessing it firsthand,* he thought.

Jack exited his car and made his way to the footbridge. Without a boat, this was the only way to reach the island. The pathway crossed a small branch of the Potomac River to deliver visitors to the Swamp Trail. Jack took a right and then a quick left to head to the center of the park. He marveled at the beauty of the restored island, but then remembered he was here on business.

He quickened his pace until he arrived at the memorial courtyard. The ground quickly turned from gravel and dirt into neatly laid brick. He scanned the area until he spotted Charles tucked away in one of the wings, reading the paper and sipping coffee. Just a regular Washingtonian escaping the oppression of the nation's capital. Jack sat beside him.

"How did it go with your friend? I can never remember—is he MI5 or 6?"

"Connor is with MI5. Internal and domestic security."

"Then what is he doing over here at the CIA? Isn't that external work?"

"Well, yes and no. The last twenty-five years have really blurred the lines between the two. I look at it as offense and defense, sir. MI6 is running around the world trying to stop attacks while MI5 is gathering as much intel as possible to stop domestic attacks."

"Simplest way I have heard it explained, Jack."

"Well, it's the best I can do. Hell, I could be wrong about the whole thing. But whatever the case, Connor has good access and placement for our particular needs at the moment."

"What did he have for us?"

"Have you ever heard of Dynamic Solutions Services, or DSS?"

"Can't say that I have. What services do they offer?"

"Offered. The company appears defunct. But they had a good run. Their menu was quite large, running from brutal to downright sadistic and illegal. Apparently, some had a penchant for drills, both electric and mechanical, for enhanced interrogation techniques."

"I always heard rumors about US. sanctioned death squads but I never saw any proof. Are you telling me those ghost stories were real, Jack?"

Jack padded the soft leather satchel he was carrying. "I have plenty of evidence right here. Connor gathered what he could. I made a few copies for you. Figured additional sets of eyes may help figure this out. I briefly skimmed the dossier and made a short list of potential interviewees."

"Hmm," Charles said as he accepted the thick folder. "We need to develop a strategy here. We just can't start knocking on doors and asking folks if they participated in illegal torture by drilling holes in their victims."

"I agree, sir. I think now is the time to shift Sam's focus from the Keeper to this. He is the right person, and this thread may end up leading to the Keeper himself."

"How so?" Charles asked.

"Well, Sam has his security company. Would it be that far a reach for him to do some headhunting looking for some new recruits? Many of these guys have legitimate experience."

"You mean legal experience?"

Jack chuckled. "All of them have that on paper. They don't exactly advertise their time with illegal death squads. Sam could interview some of the operators from the field. I could contact some of the management purporting to represent overseas business interests requiring specialized security services."

"Well thought-out. I suppose you have broken out a list for Mr. Turner?"

"I have. But I am hoping he will go through the dossier and have thoughts of his own. I wish Dane was here to also take a look."

"Mr. Cooper should be home soon, and I am sure he would be eager to join this pursuit. In the meantime, I am confident in leaving this matter to you and Mr. Turner."

"Any word on how the mission is proceeding?" Jack asked.

"I am told he and Ms. Blackburn are ready and will be departing for their objective any time now. Now catch me up on the hotel operation and Babak."

"Good. We need them both back. If Sam can go through one of those intel packets, then we can keep narrowing down potential suspects."

"Speaking of Mr. Turner, what happened with our diplomat friend?"

"I have no idea, sir. I can't say that it was a setup, but the FBI Hostage Rescue Team was all over that place."

"I suspect that our friend Mr. Blanchard is trying to anticipate our moves and hedge bets against high-profile targets."

"It sure looks that way. Luckily, Tony spotted them coming in and gave Sam a few moments to escape."

"How did he manage to avoid capture? The FBI is very thorough when conducting raids."

Jack smirked. "You know Sam. He has always been an exceptional professional, but he seems to have finely adopted some more detailed contingency planning measures since working alongside Dane. He outdid himself at the hotel."

"How so?"

He literally walked out the back door right by the entry teams, pretending to be a maintenance worker. Well, he actually drove out the back door."

"Drove?"

"Yes, sir. He used a forklift to return a large trash dumpster to the curb. FBI team ran right by him."

"Very amusing. Unfortunately, it appears Mr. Ahmadi survived. He is heavily guarded at Sibley Memorial Hospital. I have heard through the grapevine that the State Department is pulling its hair out over an attack on a foreign diplomat."

"What can they really do? The Iranians can't say anything, since he is not supposed to be here in the States on their behalf. The Pakistanis might complain behind closed doors, but they know the game. Go along to get along. They need the US more than we need them. I think the FBI will have the most heads rolling not only for the botched raid, but if they had knowledge about Mr. Ahmadi's illicit activities and did nothing. The director is going to be before a congressional committee any time now."

"You are probably right. Let's focus on this nasty business with our people. Babak is going to be hospitalized for a little while, and then probably told to keep a low profile until this blows over. We have effectively put him out of commission."

"Temporarily."

"Once he is back on his feet, and assuming he is still in this country, we will finish what we started."

"Good." Jack checked his watch. "I need to head over to pick up Andrew at his office. It is my turn to stay with him tonight."

"Give him my best. And thank him for what he is doing."

A short while later, Jack pulled his car into the now-familiar downtown D.C. parking garage. It was several blocks from Andrew's office and the garage where he parked. That gave Jack the opportunity to scan for any anomalies and possibly catch an assailant off-guard. Everything appeared normal after circling the office block, so Jack headed inside.

The elevator dinged at the ninth floor. He nodded his head at the receptionist and headed to the company's lounge. There, he found Frank sitting at one of the small tables, a newspaper spread out before him. *All these papers. I didn't think they printed them anymore,* Jack thought.

"What's the word, Frank?"

"All's quiet. He had several back-to-back phone conferences, but he should be wrapping up soon."

Frank and a few others took over the duties of Andrew's former car service. Like many businessmen around the world, time was money, and time was better spent working during daily commutes and office visits. Andrew had an arsenal of phones and computers in the back of the limo. Car service employees were the perfect cover for guarding a man on the move during business hours. They used different tactics after-hours.

"Great. Toss me the keys. I checked out the garage. All clear for now."

Frank obliged and folded his newspaper. "Cool. I'll head down now and keep an eye out." He looked at his watch. "You have about five minutes until he is done. Text me when you are on your way down."

Jack helped himself to a cup of coffee before heading back out into the office foyer. Andrew was nothing if not punctual, and he would be ready to leave after his meetings. He probably has several more calls to make during the ride home.

"Hi, Sheila. He about wrapping up?"

"Hi, Jack." She looked at her computer screen. "Should be, and he needs to move. He has a call with another client at fifteen past the hour. Go on in. It will be a good two-minute warning for him. Just keep the noise down. He has been on speakerphone, and I could hear them talking for most of the meeting. Hushed tones, but still annoying at times."

Jack winked. "Will do. Thanks."

He pushed open the door, then stopped in shock as his coffee splashed to the hardwood floor. "Sheila, call 911! Andrew has been attacked."

Jack stepped carefully into the crime scene. Andrew was clearly dead. Paramedics could do nothing for him now. And neither could Jack, but he knew that he had precious moments to investigate the scene before the authorities arrived. He moved gingerly along the edge of the room like he was walking on a freshly mopped floor. He did not want to disturb any evidence, but that was secondary to seeing Andrew up close. But, even from this distance, it was clear that he had died in a manner similar to the reverend and Jill.

It was a large, long room with Andrew's desk just in front of the back wall. Jack needed to move quickly to cover the distance.

Andrew Stevenson, The Recruiter, had been duct-taped to his office chair. The assailant had also covered his mouth. The noise Sheila had heard was not Andrew talking loudly on a conference call. It had been the TV in the corner tuned to the Consumer News Business Channel. Nonstop discussions about the market, trading, and economic results were the only noise in the room. The killer had been clever. The volume was loud enough to suppress any noises from a struggle, but not enough for clear, intelligible words to travel beyond the closed office door.

Jack approached carefully to avoid the drops of blood scattered around the soft leather chair. Andrew's head was slumped against his chest, his hair matted with blood. His chest and abdomen were bare. The killer had cut open Andrew's dress shirt and undershirt, giving him a clean canvas for his work. Using his cellphone flashlight, Jack examined the wounds. The recruiter suffered occasionally from migraines and kept the office lights dim, lest they trigger an attack.

Several small holes pierced Andrew's body. *That damn drill,* Jack thought. There were also several slashes, indicating that a hunting-style blade had been used to make the man talk. Jack also noticed that a portion of Andrew's right ear was missing. It was cleaved off at the top about a third of the way down. The other piece was pressed against the man's chest. Jack didn't need to disturb the body to guess that the other ear had suffered the same fate.

Jack moved around to the rear of the chair. Two clean holes had been drilled into the chair. The agony Andrew endured was unthinkable. He would have heard the drill bit chewing through the chair, wondering when it would burrow into his back and spine. Those two holes were definitely the final cause of death and responsible for the large pooling of blood behind the body.

Jack heard commotion out in the lobby. The police were here. His time had run out. He quickly shut down his flashlight on the phone. He pulled up the encrypted app and sent a message to Charles. His final act was to step over to Andrew and check for a pulse. He knew there would be none, but he needed this ruse of checking for signs of life to explain why he was in the room.

The first officer arrived in the room. "You. Stop right there."

"Yes, yes." Jack responded with his hands raised and out to the front, showing that he had no ill intentions. "This is horrible. Just, just checking for a pulse. I think he is dead."

"Move away slowly."

The officer had his service pistol in his hand, but had not yet raised it toward Jack. He clearly didn't know if this was a good Samaritan or the killer. Until that was determined, he never took his eyes off him as Jack slowly retreated from the room along the path he took to enter.

Jack reached the door as other officers arrived. They moved cautiously into the room. The brutality of the scene was not something many of them had even thought of in their lives. Two officers remained with Jack and escorted him out into the hallway. A large crowd had gathered. Sheila was crying uncontrollably. After a quick search of his person, Jack was directed to the waiting room sofa, accompanied by one officer to keep an eye on him.

Jack pulled out his cellphone and finished his conversation with Charles.

Chief: He got to The Recruiter. I had no idea he would be this bold.

President: That is terrible. Are you being questioned?

Chief: I am. I can't leave right now. Broke away to inform you. Will be back as soon as possible.

President: I will notify everyone. We are all targets now if we were not already.

26

THE INFIL

Mountains outside of Woqooyi Galbeed, Somaliland

The sun had already set, ushering in a darkness few would ever experience. The western desert and mountains had almost no inhabitants, save a few roaming bands of nomads. Their camels were laden with goods and wares destined for larger cities along the coast. They traveled ancient routes used by their forefathers and theirs before.

The routes rarely took a straight-line path due to the mountain, but more importantly, due to the watering holes. It was those holes that sustained both travelers and their mounts. The ambient light found in western society was absent.

Dane and Nicky were in absolute darkness, their NODS scarcely able to pick out the narrow trail they followed. Dane was in the lead, restraining the power of the motorcycle, lest he create too fast a pace for either of him. It had already been a long day, and he knew they needed to stop and rest soon.

Dane had awoken early on that previous morning. He always did that before any mission. Nervous energy. He slipped out of bed and dressed quickly. The covers had partially fallen off the bed, so he gently pulled them up to cover Nicky. She still had another hour to sleep, and he didn't want to wake her. He couldn't remember what time they finally drifted off to sleep.

He shook his head to clear the fog from his brain. *I hope this wasn't a bad idea,* he thought. Once the coffee pot was prepped, he left her a quick note and headed back to his room.

They met for breakfast later that morning. Dane anticipated a certain level of awkwardness, but found none. Nicky was bubbly and energetic, eager to begin the mission. They didn't even speak about the night before and what had transpired between them. *Probably for the best,* he thought. *We have enough on our minds right now. We can certainly figure this out when we are home safely stateside.*

They both ate as if it was their last meal.

"Do you have your pendant?"

"Yup. Your cards?"

Nicky nodded and patted a small pack on her left hip.

As they prepared to leave, Dane guided Nicky to several spots around the hotel that had vantage points for clear views of the outside streets and parking lot. Two spots in particular interested him. One was a large bay window overlooking the front of the hotel and the guest parking lot. The other was just outside the dining room, offering broad views down the single road leading to the Sheraton.

"You see those spots there and there?" He asked Nicky as he pointed toward two separate side streets with parking space. "If we have any company today, those would be good spots to start a follow. We need to keep an eye out for Ethiopian surveillance."

"What do you need me to do, Mr. Spymaster?"

Dane smirked at her. "I will spot using the mirrors as much as possible. I will call out the makes and models I see along with a general description. Plates will be very difficult since they all say Somaliland in English but the numbers and letters below are all in Arabic.

"I will not remember those. I can't read Arabic anyway."

"Me neither. Hopefully descriptions of the vehicle and driver will be enough."

And sure enough, when they had departed the Sheraton, two vehicles decided to join their sightseeing trip. The first was an older Toyota sedan. It was tan, with distinct markings due to what appeared to be several collisions. *It should be easy to pick out of a crowd,* Dane thought. The second was a medium-sized motorcycle, black and brown with obvious rust. The motorcycle was slightly larger than the motors typically swarming these roads. It was probably selected for the larger gas tank, offering increased mileage for surveillance purposes.

In either case, the Ethiopians lost interest after their first stop. All that preparation for nothing. The area they stopped to see—the shark pit and Lake Ghoubbet—was barren with only a few small huts selling food and trinkets.

Dane quickly identified the men from the motorcycle and sedan. Standing out like sore thumbs, the surveillants watched Dane and Nicky explore the shoreline, take some pictures, and barter with merchants hoping to profit from Western tourists. After twenty minutes the men determined that Dane and Nicky were no threat to the Ethiopian government and promptly left. *Good,* Dane thought. *Let's hope they don't come back.*

"It looks like our friends are leaving."

"Does that mean we can goof off now before the mission?"

"No. We could pick up others later by purpose or accident. We stick to the route."

The surveillance on the two was absent for the remainder of their route. Dane and Nicky bounced from town to town, acting the part of tourists. They traveled south and east, eventually arriving at the rendezvous at dusk. Mac was exactly where he said he would be. The panel van was covered in dust from traveling around the city. It blended in with the locals quite well.

They quickly swapped vehicles. Mac headed back to Camp Lemonnier, while Dane and Nicky drove further east to the crossing point. The town they had chosen was deserted, so nobody witnessed them cross over the imaginary line in the desert separating Somaliland from Djibouti. Dane was pleasantly surprised at the durability of the van and the amount of distance they were able to travel before switching to motorcycles. They were definitely ahead of schedule. They would be able to rest a little while longer this evening, which was a blessing. The terrain was rough, and they each felt every bump and jolt, regardless of how much abuse the sophisticated shocks of the KTM motorcycles absorbed.

Dane called a halt, observing an outcropping of rocks perfect for an overnight hide site. It was unlikely that anyone would stumble upon them. Nonetheless, Dane placed motion sensors along the trail in the event some nomad or shepherd happened along the path. They were both too exhausted to stand guard. Nicky had already pulled some Woobies from their packs, creating a makeshift bed. They naturally fell into each other's arms, like a habit from years in the making. Dane and Nicky were instantly asleep.

The next morning, Dane climbed to the peak of the mountain for a view of what lay ahead. They had decided to use the terrain to mask their travel by skirting Hargeisa to the north. The mountains north of the capital city concealed their movement from any interest the city may offer. Dane observed the mountaintop city due south of their location. They were only about fifty miles from their destination. It would be a rough ride, but, absent any issues, they should arrive in Berbera at sundown.

Nicky had already broken down camp and brewed two cups of coffee by the time Dane returned. It was no Dunkin Donuts, but Dane appreciated the hot, instant coffee concoction. Best cup of coffee he ever had.

"Well, someone has a big shit-eating grin. What has gotten into you? "Nicky asked.

"Just enjoying the morning," Dane replied.

"You are loving this shit, aren't you? Sleeping on the ground. Peeing outside. I would rather be back at the Sheraton. That bed was soft." Nicky moved closer and wrapped Dane in a hug. "And I had great company."

"You had company last night also, and you stole the covers again."

Nicky laughed. "It was to make you move closer. And the ground was not soft in the least."

"You are right about that. Takes getting used to. I guess I just forgot how much I loved deploying at times. Being in a foreign country. Trying new food. I mean, look at this view."

"Yeah, it's neat and all, but remember this little vacation could turn stormy if we are found by the wrong people. And I really don't plan on sampling any of the local fare. I didn't bring enough Cipro."

"I know, Nicky. I enjoy the little moments. I might be able to raise you up some baby goat. It is a delicacy here."

"I will pass. Is it as gross as it sounds?"

"Worse. Not enough Cipro in the world would fix that stomachache."

"Let's stick with the packaged food we brought."

"Agreed. So, when we get settled in the safe house, I want to check out the boat, the slaughterhouses, and Ibrahim's digs. Do you need to put sensors out tonight for the bio agents?"

"We can if we have time. If not, tomorrow night will be fine. We still have a large enough window to get them emplaced. Shipment should arrive in about three days, give or take."

They finished the trip across the mountains and down into lower terrain along the coast of the Gulf of Aden. The sun had set hours before and the moon cast an eerie glow across the water's surface. That black water was motionless. An early wind had died down with nightfall, so instead of the howling wind, they could hear the noises of civilization coming from the urban center of Berbera.

They killed the motorcycles and pushed the bikes through the light sand. Dane did not want to announce their arrival and draw a curious crowd to observe new visitors to the city. The safehouse was located on the eastern edge. They had traveled almost exclusively through the mountain, only chancing observation when they had to cross the two major roads leading into the city. They circled Berbera to the south and approached from the east. The safehouse was close to both the port and the slaughterhouses. Ibrahim's location would be a little harder to get to on foot, but Dane would worry about that later.

Dane eased open the courtyard gate to their new home. The hinges had been recently oiled, negating any announcement of their presence. They rolled the bikes around to the back of main structure, then covered them with a tarp. It was best to keep them out of sight until they needed the powerful machines. The compound had a back gate as well, which they could use if they needed to leave in a hurry.

Dane and Nicky inspected the compound before entering the main building. Ten-foot walls surrounded the entire compound. They were topped with broken glass, glued in place to prevent intruders from climbing inside. There were several small sheds scattered about, along with a well in the corner of the courtyard.

"I am not drinking from that," Nicky whispered as she pointed to the well.

"Neither of us are. There is supposed to be fresh supplies inside, which will include bottled water. Except for an angry government, uninformed about our mission here, sickness is our worst enemy."

The compound also had a mechanics bay filled with discarded parts and equipment. Dane risked a narrow beam of light from his flashlight to ensure no surprise awaited them in the shed. It was devoid of human life.

They finally went to the back door of the main dwelling and entered. It was a fairly large two-story building. They maintained light and noise discipline as they moved from room to room. The first floor had a large kitchen and two meeting rooms. Old conference tables dominated the center of each, with tattered chairs scattered about. The final room on the floor was the first of several bedrooms and a neglected bathroom.

Nicky peered inside. "They don't even have a shower curtain. I may pass on showering."

"You may reconsider in a few days. Or, I may have to kick you out of the house if the stench becomes too much."

Nicky gently punched Dane's shoulder. "But this is disgusting. I think I would get dirtier if I used this one."

"The ones upstairs are probably better. This seems like an old mission planning safehouse. The senior folks staying here probably used the upstairs shower and kept them in better condition. This bathroom was probably only used as a common toilet for all when they had to brief their soldiers or something."

They climbed the narrow marble staircase to the second floor to find Dane had been correct. The floor had six bedrooms, three on each side, and two bathrooms in much better condition than the downstairs. The rooms were sparse, but they only needed a bed, which each room had.

"Let's use the bedroom in the back right corner. Less likely to be seen by someone in the city, but we still need to be careful about lights."

"I saw a whole bunch of sheets in the first rooms. We can grab them and cover the windows."

Dane and Nicky spent the next several hours making the house as livable as possible. Floors were swept, and one of the bathrooms was clean enough that Nicky agreed to eventually shower. They found fresh food and supplies in the kitchen, along with the promised bottles of water. They kept the light to a minimum, and Dane pan-fried them up some steaks. At least, he hoped it was steak. They took their meals into one of the conference rooms to eat.

"Place your rifle on the floor outside the room, Nicky. Just keep your pistol."

"You told me to keep my weapons near me at all times."

"Yes, but it will still be close. Just outside the door. Did you notice the temperature in this house?"

"Actually, I did. I noticed that each room has an individual air conditioning unit, but the hallways and bathrooms are hot."

"Yup. They don't have enough power to cool the whole house. They only make the bedrooms and conference rooms comfortable. The A/C will mess up the glass on your weapon's sights."

"How so?"

"If the glass is cooled in one of the rooms, it will fog over in the heat in the hallways and outside."

"Ah, like my sunglasses fogging up when I get out of a cold car in the summer."

"Exactly like that. We want to keep the glass warm in case we need to use our sights quickly in a battle. Now let's finish up eating. I still want to check out the roof before we head out to do a little reconnaissance. I want to make sure we can fight from it in case of an emergency."

Nicky quietly chewed her steak. "You really do try and think of everything."

Closer: I know you are still on mission and not up on comms.

Closer: Things are getting bad. I am not worried about these guys getting to me, but I want to take every precaution in case something does happen to me or the chief.

Closer: Let me first apologize about breaking into your storage, which needs a good cleaning by the way.

Closer: One of the Chief's buddies put together a packet on a company named DSS. I put a copy in your cabinet on the back wall.

I HID A NOTE THE OTHER DAY IN THE BATHROOM TO SEE IF I CAN MAKE A FRIEND. I HID IT BEHIND THE TOILET, HOPING SOMEONE WOULD FIND IT. I DON'T THINK THE MAN HAS A CAMERA IN THE BATHROOM. I KNOW THERE IS ONE IN MY ROOM, BUT I HAVE A TALL STANDING THING TO GIVE ME PRIVACY. HE TELLS ME TO CHANGE BEHIND THERE. THE NOTE WAS GONE.

27

THE SNITCH

Washington metropolitan area

Tony's voice shook as he spoke. "Hello. Can I speak to Mr. Carl Blanchard?"

"Yes, this is him," the agent replied.

"This is Tony. Tony Carter. We spoke the other day."

"Well, Mr. Carter, I certainly do remember our little conversation. What can I do for you?"

"I am ready to talk. Talk about Sam Turner. About Savannah and the diplomat."

Eric: And now we go over live to Carlson Newton on the scene of another horrible tragedy in the city.

Carlson: Thank you, Eric and Joyce. It is a grim scene here in what has been described as a horrific murder in this downtown office complex, the Scottsdale Building. Andrew Stevenson, founder of this very successful headhunter firm providing professional recruitment for many large firms both nationally and internationally, was found tortured and murdered in his very office. This brazen crime was conducted while staff and others were right outside his door, unaware that their boss was suffering just feet away. So far, the police have provided very few details as they investigate the scene. What we can tell you is several investigators believe this murder is connected to three others in the metro D.C. area.

Joyce: Would that be the Reverend John Anderson, Ms. Jill Clark, and Jonathan Basker?

Carlson: That is correct, Joyce. Reverend Anderson was murdered and tortured last month in his Humane Hands church. The police initially believed robbery was the motive. However, as other crimes appeared, they came to believe they had a serial killer on their hands. Ms. Jill Clark was murdered in her Pentagon City apartment. That case is still open, and we have had no leads about her connection to the reverend, other than she was one of his parishioners.

Eric: And Basker?

Carlson: Yes, Eric. This daring crime here today is eerily similar to the death of Jonathan Basker, who was killed right under the authorities' noses. He was arrested for the attempted abduction of a child and injured by bystanders during the attempt. He was being treated for his injuries when he was murdered in his hospital bed under police watch last week.

Joyce: So, a total of four similar murders?

Carlson: Yes, and the police are baffled. They are being aided by the Virginia Bureau of Investigation as well as federal authorities from in and around the capital. Earlier, we were on the streets, and the good people of Washington D.C. are nervous. Nervous that a vicious serial killer is loose and at large. His targets appear random. These four victims come from all walks of life and from different locales around D.C.

Eric: What a terrible tragedy. This has been a violent month for the nation's capital.

Carlson: Yes it has, guys. Where I am standing now is only a few blocks away from where a diplomat from the Pakistani embassy was brutally ambushed and drugged in his hotel room. Police still have no leads, and the Pakistani government is threatening departure from the United States if the assailant is not apprehended. The Pakistani ambassador is set to speak before the United Nations General Assembly this afternoon.

Joyce: Thank you for staying—

CLICK.

Roger turned off the television. He had heard enough about these vicious crimes in the last few weeks. It wasn't even worth turning on the TV anymore. He turned his attention back to Pat and Carl. They were speaking to Andrew Stevenson's driver, who also happened to be the one who discovered the body.

"Can you state your full name?" Carl asked.

"Jack. Jack Davies."

"I noticed the slight accent. How long have you been in the state, Mr. Davies?"

"It's been quite some time now. I have been a naturalized citizen for over a decade."

"And you were employed by the late Mr. Stevenson?"

"That is correct."

"In what capacity?" Carl continued as he took notes on a pocket-sized pad.

"Secure transportation. We provided Mr. Stevenson driving services to and from his residence daily and on certain circumstantial occasions. We ensured his safety during those commutes."

"Could you elaborate?" Pat asked, speaking for the first time. Although she and Roger had no jurisdiction in the city, Carl had brought them in under the auspices of the task force granting them temporary federal authority to investigate this case.

"Well," Jack answered. "For instance, last week, Mr. Stevenson had meetings in New York. He doesn't like to fly or take the train. We drove him up early in the morning and back home that evening. He said he also prefers the limo so he can work in the back. He has a whole office suite back there."

"Do your services extend outside of Mr. Stevenson's travel requirements? Do you provide protection at his residence?" Carl asked.

"We do not. Our company has another division that can provide those services, but Mr. Stevenson only requested secure transportation."

"Don't you find that a little odd?" Pat added.

"Not particularly. Maybe he had a great security system. Maybe he has large dogs. Lots of people pick our service because they feel safe in their home, but not always in public. He also likes to be driven, so maybe the extra cost was worth it for him. I can't be exactly sure, ma'am."

"Can you walk us through your discovery of Mr. Stevenson?" asked Roger.

"Sure. I arrived around three-thirty, I did a cursory search of the limo in the garage to make sure the vehicle hadn't been tampered with. I checked the doors, the boot . . . sorry, trunk. I made sure all the tire pressures looked good. I started the vehicle also to make sure there were no mechanical issues. Standard procedure."

"Had it?" Carl asked. "Been tampered with?"

"No. I then came up here to the suite to relieve Frank."

"That would be Frank Richards?" Carl continued. "We will be speaking with him also."

"Yes. Frank said all was good. He then left and went down to secure the limo for our arrival. Standard procedure is for him to start the vehicle, conduct a similar check, and then stand by for our arrival. I would bring the principal down and, once we departed, he would be free to go. I had a few more minutes, so I grabbed a cup of coffee. By that time, it was almost four. Sheila told me to go right in. He would be wrapping up any second. He needed to head down to the car since he had a four-fifteen call on the way home."

"Did Mr. Stevenson have any enemies that you knew of? Any specific threats against him that prompted him to have private secure transportation?" Roger asked.

"Not that I am aware of. He always used a private car service in the past. He said the world was getting crazy and he might as well have protection while on the road. Like I said earlier, he was not an unusual client."

Roger continued. "Did you ever have any incidents while transporting Mr. Stevenson?"

"Nothing other than the usual. Crazies running up and pounding on the hood while stopped at lights or throwing something. We recorded every incident, but I never saw anything outrageous."

"I assume you're armed, Mr. Davies?" Pat asked.

"No, ma'am. I was. I informed the first officers on the scene that I was carrying a licensed firearm authorized based on my profession. They took possession and said I could retrieve it when I leave."

"One last question," said Carl. "Why did you enter the room farther?"

"I wanted to check for signs of life. I knew from the look of things it was improbable, but we are trained in life-saving techniques. I wanted to try and save him if possible."

"Thank you, Mr. Davies. We will be in touch if we have any further questions."

Jack stood and exited the room. As he did, Ken entered the room quickly.

"Boss, just got word from John Oakes. He went to pick up Tony, but police were already there. Tony was shot and killed."

Carl turned to Roger and Pat. "I hadn't had time to tell you guys yet. Tony contacted me and said he was ready to talk about Sam Turner. He mentioned Savannah and the diplomat."

"Holy shit!" exclaimed Pat.

"Guys, I think it's time to arrest Mr. Turner again," Carl said, taking out his cellphone.

Roger removed his own phone from his coat pocket. "Agreed. I will call it in with my folks."

Sam pulled out of the farmhouse's gravel driveway onto the main county road to begin the drive home to Winchester. It was a short thirty-minute ride from Strasburg, but it had been a long day. Plus, one never knew what could happen on interstate 81. The two-lane highway was notorious for traffic backups from the tractor-trailer convoys ebbing and flowing north and south. The freeway was a major conduit for the exchange of goods across the country. Sam could appreciate these long-haulers and the services they provided. *But couldn't they just stay in the right lane instead of passing each other at a snail's pace?* he thought. *The left lane is for speed. For crime.*

Sam had gotten an early start on the list of interviewees suggested by Jack. Charles gave Sam a packet containing former associates of DSS, but warned him to be careful. One of these potential suspects could be the one killing their members. Sam had been cautions and dutiful in his work. He texted Jack before and after each interview, in case something went horribly wrong. He also did it to prevent duplication. It would be a waste of effort if some other members contacted the same person. It would also look suspicious as hell.

His purported reason for his visits to former members of the company was to inquire about possible employment. Sam's story was that several former security contractors were looking at forming a small firm and they needed subcontractors on file. If these subcontractors were interested in possible work, Sam and his partners would use those resumes to bid on contracts.

It was a very lucrative business, but one that required top talent since the market was flooded with qualified individuals due to the drawdown of conflicts overseas. Retiring soldiers often desired to stay in the game, and private security firms were often a natural fit. In his experience, Sam actually found that not to be the case. It was true that his firm and others did use primarily veterans, but the art was finding the right veteran.

Some thought they had marketable skills due to military service alone, but that wasn't always true. A soldier or sailor might have been a great mechanic or tank gunner, but they did not have the skills necessary for protective services. And even those who did were often burnt out, living in the bottom of a bottle, or simply too injured to perform the duties. He didn't need guys to run five miles every day, but they might have to run flat-out for five minutes protecting an asset.

Jack hadn't had time to fully vet the former DSS associates. He had basic dossiers on several individuals, so Sam picked those located along his route home. He had been away from his Winchester home for a while and was looking forward to some relaxation. The team had been going pretty hard. He needed a good night's sleep and maybe some range time to knock off the cobwebs. Then, he would be ready to tackle the list head-on. He would just start with these few and pick up in the morning.

The first stop had been a small ranch house on the outskirts of Manassas. He sensed failure when he parked next to the wheelchair ramp leading to the front door. The man's wife had answered the door and invited him into his home after giving his two-minute elevator pitch. He found his target sitting by the back bay window, staring at the television. An old Green Bay Packers game dominated the screen.

He turned in his wheelchair, and Sam could see that he was missing both his legs from above the knee. He wasn't wearing any prosthetics, and none were visible in the room. Sam explained to the man the purpose of his visit, apologizing for not knowing his condition.

The man laughed it off. "Son, I lost my legs in Iraq. I would be pretty useless to protect anyone unless they were a mid . . . of extremely short stature. There isn't exactly a place on a resume to put my height."

They both had a good laugh.

The man continued. "However, I am intimately familiar with security operations. And even though I am not chasing down any threats, I could fill any sort of staffing role that your company might need. They don't call me Wheels just because of this chair. That was my nickname since once I start chasing something, I don't stop."

"Sir, I will definitely keep you in my rolodex for when we start filling out staff. I have a feeling you would find a way to run somebody down, regardless of your stature."

His second visit had not gone well, either, but for different reasons. The first man had been listed as a field operative with the company. His second stop was listed as upper management. And his role in the company must have been pretty high up, considering the elegance of his home. Sam pulled in through an ornate front gate and stopped in front of sweeping marble steps.

The man was out on his porch before Sam's feet hit the intricately stamped concrete driveway. He couldn't even give his two-minute pitch before he was shut down by the man. He stood on his steps, with a raised voice explaining to Sam that his lawyer has already been notified, and he would not be the subject of these vicious lies. He would sue Sam for slander.

Sam was stunned. He had told the man through the speaker box at the front gate that he represented a developing consortium of security specialists with the intent of forming a new company. Apparently, the man saw right through Sam's ruse, but not to his true purpose.

He ranted on about how the press was misrepresenting themselves in order to gain access to his property and spread lies about his past. The police were on their way, and he would gladly watch as Sam was hauled away in cuffs.

Sam highly doubted that would be the case, but he did not want any law enforcement encounters. He did not need the attention, so he left the man on his steps, screaming at the top of his lungs. That led him to his third and final stop.

The large farmhouse sat on a nice piece of property in Strasburg, Virginia, with the man had plenty of open land surrounded by thick woods. A large barn stood in the distance a couple of hundred meters behind the house, resting prominently on a slight rise.

The man sat on a rocking chair on the front porch, facing west, probably anticipating a spectacular sunset. Sam found the place amazing. The man was polite, articulate, and serenely calm. Sam silently wondered if he was stoned or on something else more powerful. Overall, though, Sam could sense a certain degree of silence. He noticed a neglected playset in the side yard, along with small bicycles alongside the house.

The man caught him looking and explained. This was his dream home, dream lifestyle for his wife and two small children. They would raise their family away from the filth of the big cities. The modern world was not for him—until the modern world took his family from him. His wife and children had been killed in a car accident along Interstate 66 traveling home from a school trip to the capital. His whole life ended. He withdrew from the world to live out his years, mourning and remembering what he once had. In peace.

It had been quite a day and Sam was happy to finally be off the freeway and ready to turn onto his long country road.

Ah, home, he thought. *Finally.*

Oh shit. Sam reached for his cellphone.

"Jack, it's Sam. I have a big problem."

"We have some pretty big ones here as well. You go first."

"This is real déjà vu. My house is surrounded by squad cars. Pretty sure I am going to be arrested again."

"Damnit. Okay. Hang tight. I will talk with Charles and get a lawyer out to you quickly."

"What was your bad news?"

"Somebody shot and killed Tony."

"Shit. Was he tortured like the others?"

"No. Single shot to the head."

"I hope that isn't what this is about."

"I think it is, Sam. Hold tight."

Chief: Sir, Tony was killed. I went to warn him since he has not been responsive lately.

President: This is terrible news. Have you been able to reach the others?

Chief: I have. They are all in hiding out of town. We have another problem.

President: I can't imagine things getting worse.

Chief: Sam Turner has been arrested for Tony's murder.

28

THE MISSION, PART I

Berbera, Somaliland

Devotee: I got one of them today. Simple shooting like you asked.

Keeper: Good work. Take as many as you can as quickly as you can.

Devotee: I will make a plan for the leaders. May do something more spectacular.

Keeper: Excellent. Just don't take large risks. Keep them confused and vulnerable.

Dane and Nicky were shrouded in darkness, their bodies threaded among a large pile of rubble. They used the concrete pieces to mask the outline of their bodies. The countryside with littered with collapsed buildings, abandoned structures, and scattered debris.

Dane never took his eyes off the road or the warehouse. He was pulling security to the front. Nicky faced the opposite direction, ensuring nobody approached from the rear. They had been in place for a few hours to get acclimated to the environment.

They could not have asked for better lighting. The waning crescent moon provided very little light for the naked eye, but the night vision devices they each wore gave them complete mastery of the dark. Contrary to popular belief, night vision devices need at a least a small amount of light. The devices were unable to create images in total darkness. It was always a balance between enough light for the goggles, but not enough so the enemy could see you coming.

When they had placed the sensors the night before, Dane and Nicky realized they had extra. They planned the mission through map and imagery reconnaissance, but the actual ground truth could not be captured from a satellite. Many of the roads leading in and out of the area were impassable, leaving only one decent route to the meatpacking facility. They placed the two planned sensors near the warehouse and two more along the road, then placed the spares even farther out to provide themselves some reaction time. Extra warning certainly couldn't hurt.

Nicky's TAMI device began to quietly vibrate.

"Our package has arrived," she whispered to Dane. "The two far sensors pinged. We have around five minutes."

"Can you tell what they have?" Dane asked, eyes glued to the road.

Nicky studied the device, shielding the small screen with her hand. "Looks like we have Ebola and Marburg. Both nasty and normally fatal."

"Okay. Time to move."

With Dane in the lead, they rose silently and made their way to the west side of the building. Animals awaiting slaughter were penned on the south side of the warehouse. Once the veterinarian gave them a clean bill of health, they were led inside for processing. Refrigeration in large quantities was rare in this part of the world. The animals would be packaged quickly and loaded aboard the appropriate vessel for speedy transport across the straits. Some of the boats had mild refrigeration, but not in adequate amounts necessary for the quantity they were slaughtering. Speed would be of the essence. They would have to move quickly to retrieve the samples once they were brought into the building.

They did have a stroke of luck at the port, which made the mission easier. After placing the sensors last night, they revisited the docks. They found the boat on their first evening in town and every night since to ensure it was not tampered with. It was fully fueled and ready to be put to sea.

Dane didn't dare start it up until they were ready to leave on their final night, but he did inspect the wires and cables. The only issue was the battery. They were notoriously awful in this part of the country. The boat had been delivered with several in the front bulkhead. Dane had them spread out connection wires ready to attach sequentially if necessary pending the find of a faulty battery. He realized that it may take one or two tries to get the motor started as he switched batteries. The tester said they were good, but in the end powering up the engine would be the only true test. They hadn't loaded the bikes yet. They would do that at the last minute in case the shit hit the fan and they needed alternate transportation.

One of the nights at the docks, they noticed that the place was deserted. Not even a single security guard. And this wasn't like the marinas they were used to back in the States. There were no live-above yachts or houseboats. These were mostly small fishing and transportation vessels whose crew would sleep in town for the night. On a whim, Dane broke into the dockmaster's office. It wasn't even locked. He found multiple shipping manifests, photographing each and every one. Back at the safe house he securely transmitted them back to the unit for translation.

The risk paid off. The intelligence analysts determined the exact ship destined to transport the deadly viruses. Sifting through dozens of shell companies, they identified the Chinese attempt at obfuscation for a visit the next evening. The ship was already dual-tagged, and its location was being tracked by the task force back home. The last thing left to do was to steal some vials of the deadliest viruses on the planet.

At the warehouse's back door, Dane knelt in the dirt. Nicky immediately took up a position pulling security, while Dane gripped a dull red-lens flashlight in his teeth and pulled out his pick set. He had come every evening to practice on the lock. It was a cheap three-pin tumbler deadbolt he had opened each time with ease. Tonight was no different. It was also fortunate that the warehouse did not operate every day. The place was mostly abandoned until enough shepherds brought their flocks in for sale. They would gather about four miles outside of town near a watering point at the base of the mountains. Once the slaughterhouse was ready to purchase the animals, a long caravan of beasts would parade down the main road on their way to a grisly end.

Dane and Nicky had debated on the best place to intercept the packages. Sneaking into the warehouse with all the activity and light would be tricky. The noise from the animals would cover their movements, but the risk of discovery was too great. Stealing the vials when they were driven to the docks was an option, but it would be hard to determine the right truck to rob. Nicky dismissed outright Dane's thought to ambush the vehicle on the road, then kill and bury the bodies. They *were* technically enemy combatants participating in biological warfare efforts.

"We can't do that, Dane."

"Why not? This is dangerous country. They wouldn't know it was us. Anybody could have ambushed them."

"I would rather not have a round pierce a container or vial, providing us all with a nice little virus that can't be cured."

"Okay, okay. I see your point."

They had settled on a hybrid of the first three options. They snuck into the warehouse and hid along the back wall. It was filled with junk and unused equipment. Nicky mounted an antenna on her TAMI device to increase its range as a detector. It helped with direction-finding, homing in on the exact pallet of meat containing the viruses. They couldn't see the loading of the trucks from that position, but she could identify the pallet in question when it was moved near the roll-up door for loading.

"I hope they hurry up," Nicky whispered.

"I know. It smells like hell in here, though. The whole country doesn't exactly have a pleasant odor."

"You take a girl to all the nice places."

The TAMI device began to softly vibrate, and Nicky could see the direction-finding arrow traveling through the warehouse and increasing in strength.

"Time to move," she whispered.

The pair snuck back out the door and moved closer to the loading bay. Once they were in a position with good eyes on the trucks they halted. There was a single light above the loading dock, but it was small enough to ensure the workers loading the meat could not see Nicky and Dane about thirty feet away. Dane handed Nicky his rifle and checked that he had all the rest of his equipment. They did a final commo check.

"Check, check," Nicky said softly, her throat mic transmitting her voice to both their earpieces. The earpieces were specifically molded to their ear canals and worked as a communication platform as well as cancelling loud noise. The throat mics wrapped around their necks with the transmitter resting firmly against their voice boxes. Dane had also used several types of mics over the years, and although these were not his favorite, they did keep a mouthpiece away from his face that might obscure close-in actions like lock-picking or operating TAMI.

"Lima Charlie. How me?" Dane replied.

"Licking Chicken. Get moving."

Dan laughed and then sprinted through the field, taking refuge behind a small, neglected structure to wait for Nicky's signal. He hated to split up, but it really was the only way. Nicky could take care of herself. They would meet back up at the predetermined location soon. He wouldn't be that far away if she ran into some locals.

"Look sharp. Package just loaded, Dane. Let the next truck pass. It will be the second one."

"Roger."

"Moving to the rendezvous point. Don't mess it up."

Dane smiled. Nicky was always busting his balls. When the second vehicle slowed for the turn, he stepped out and jumped on the back of the truck. He didn't like leaving the rifle with Nicky, but he remembered what happened in Savannah when he jumped aboard the ship. It had caused harm to both him and the weapon. The rifle had still worked, but this situation would be different. He was dealing with ordinary workers not looking to kill him. They would probably be terrified if they saw him in all his combat gear. Of course, the point was to avoid that at all costs. At least he still had his pistol.

A quick peek inside revealed that he was alone, as expected. He pulled the second TAMI device from his leg pouch. He was glad they brought two. He was nowhere near as proficient as she was in setting up and using the device, but he had mastered the basics before they deployed. Nicky had calibrated it for what he needed it to do tonight. He should be able to handle the rest.

He quickly unsealed the pallet and ran the scanner over the packages of meat. He estimated five minutes before the vehicle entered the port area and he would be caught. He didn't have time to waste. The meat was not individually wrapped, just loose in flimsy plastic garbage bags, causing his gloves to become slick with blood. It was hard to grab a piece and then find a spot to set it aside.

This is going to be harder than I thought. And messier.

DING. He found his first sample. TAMI told him it was Ebola. The meat went right into his dump pouch on the rear of his gun belt. *I will be throwing that bag out after this mission,* he thought.

DING, another. *Crap*, he thought, another Ebola. He needed one of each. Dane put the meat aside.

DING, Ebola.

DING, Ebola.

He was running out of time. Dane felt the truck accelerate. They reached the edge of civilization, where the roads were better. The city did not have many cement roads, save those leading into and around the port.

DING, Ebola.

DING, Ebola.

DING, Marburg. Dane jammed all the meat back into the plastic bags. They were all different cuts and sizes, which made reassembling the pallet challenging. The smells made him want to vomit. Finally packed, Dane closed the container, knowing that he had only seconds.

It was now or never. He opened the back flap and jumped blindly off the left side of the truck, landing hard against a donkey and knocking the load from its back. Dane crashed into the dirt.

The shepherd was shocked and stood staring at Dane. He rose to wobbly feet as the stars faded from his eyes. Dane ensured the packages of meat were secure in the pouch and that all his equipment was present. Nicky told him that the vials were strong and would be hard to break. He just hoped that was true and that he hadn't just infected himself and this innocent man. *Please be donkey-proof,* he thought.

He placed his hands together as if in prayer and nodded to the man in a gesture of apology. He then turned away and sprinted toward the rendezvous point, offering the shepherd another apology over his shoulder. "Waan Ka xumahay."

Dane moved silently among the still-sleeping masses. Call to prayer was still a few hours away. He was anxious to finish this mission and get home. He needed to touch base with Jack and Sam about the Keeper. He needed to get back into the hunt. It helped talking about things with Nicky, but it would never extinguish the fire in his belly to get Angela back. Nicky had lost her Daniel, but he still had a chance with Angela. He would get her back.

Dane cleared his head and focused on the task at hand. It only took a few moments to find Nicky huddling once again amongst a pile of forgotten rubble. She flashed her tiny red-lens flashlight three times toward Dane as he approached. He returned with two quick bursts. He settled in beside her.

"How did it go?" she asked.

"Good. I got one of each. This is gross. Dane pulled out the pieces of meat while Nicky opened two small containers. They gently pulled the glass vials from the animal flesh and placed them gently inside. They stood to leave, tossing the meat into the dirt. Nicky noticed Dane moving awkwardly.

"Are you okay?"

"Yeah, just sore. I collided with a donkey."

"Damn, Dane, you are weird."

"Let's go load the boat. That was the easy part."

THE MAN KEEPS PUTTING NEW THINGS IN THE YARD. THEY ARE EXERCISE THINGS. HE TOLD ME TO START DOING PUSHUPS AND SIT-UPS DURING RECESS. HE SAID WE WILL BE ADDING GYM CLASS TO SCHOOL SOON, SO I WILL GET TO GO OUTSIDE TWO TIMES A DAY. ONE FOR RECESS AND ONE TIME FOR GYM.

29

THE STALK

Across D.C. and northern Virginia

```
Devotee: They have become more cautious.

Keeper: They are probably starting to fully realize the danger they are in.

Devotee: I will be patient and careful. I will find a weakness in their defenses.

Keeper: We are almost done. Then you can begin collecting as promised.
```

Shooting the man had been boring. He wanted to have fun and play his games. They would pretend to be tough and resist his questions. He would have to find clever means to inflict the right amount of pain yet avoid his subject falling unconscious. Nobody could hold out forever. He was destined to win every time. But it was always fun. Never boring. No two were ever the same.

The reverend had played dumb. He was a tough old guy, but screamed nonetheless. He cried, he prayed, he denied knowledge of any club hunting them. He would never support vigilantes taking the law into their own hands. He had no idea how those children ended up in his church that night. Blah, blah, blah. Until he did. He had an idea all along. He just needed help finding it.

"Jill, did you get the key from the front office?"

"I did, Reverend. Thank you. We will be in early to set up the breakfast fundraiser, and I really hate disturbing you just to watch a bunch of us old

ladies preparing enough breakfast to feed an army."

"Absolutely no worries. I am not much of a late sleeper anyway. I may just come down and join you gals for some coffee."

"It will be hot and fresh waiting for you. I will return the key once the front office opens for the day."

And as the game came to a conclusion, the idea came to light. It wasn't me, he said, but maybe someone with a key. Who could that be, I had asked. He cried even more when he said her name. The game was now over. I won.

She, on the other hand, was a tough old bird. She shook. She struggled. She wanted a fight. But that was not her role in the game. I was in charge. I was the dungeon master, and she had to play by my rules. But she wouldn't. She resisted my every move. She claimed to know nothing of this group and, although she attended the reverend's church, it was silly to think she would have a key for some reason. She didn't work there. This tested my skills in keeping her alive. Skills I don't normally use. I was rusty, but I kept her among the living until I couldn't any longer.

But providence shone down upon me with a *DING* from her computer. It was a message from a close friend worried about what happened to the reverend. Worried for her safety. *But why are you worried?* I wondered. *Maybe I will have to find out. Another person for my game.*

This man would be harder to get to than the others. I see you guarding him. I see you driving him around the city. I see that fancy office building with views of Washington. But you can't be with him every moment. Lucky for me, I am prepared to get into difficult places. I belong to several temporary agencies doing the necessary jobs most people don't notice. Nobody ever gives the lawn maintenance crews a second thought. They are invisible. Janitors are needed almost everywhere. I used the service to interrogate that weakling who was caught and guarded at the hospital. I was just another orderly moving around patients and dirty linens. I emptied bedpans and retrieved wheelchairs for those discharging from the hospital. Fortunately, he convinced me quickly that he had said nothing. I didn't have much time with that one, so I had to finish the game quickly.

I had more time with the business bigwig. He told his secretary he would be tied up for about three hours and to hold his calls. He had no idea how tied up he would be. Here, I had to be clever once again. The game was always different. People were right outside the door. Entry was easy. Those old building had corridors for maintenance and large drop ceilings for the running of copper pipes and wires. I easily accessed the space like anyone would to repair a leaky pipe. I dropped down behind him. The television would only mute so much noise, so my favorite methods had to be altered. I couldn't have him screaming loudly. But once I found out he was right-handed, I simply loosened that restraint and gave him paper and a pen. The drill wasn't even necessary for him. I just did it for fun. My blade did most of the work, and he gave me plenty of names. The names of the men hunting us. The name of the one directing the hunt. The name of the one paying for it. More names to play with. But this time, the game had to change.

The Keeper told me to act before they could regroup. Take out the foot soldiers quickly and cut off the head of the snake. Hit them hard while they are confused, he told me. I wanted to play my games, but they would have to wait. I wanted the Keeper to be pleased. I wanted to learn a new game. His game. Collecting. It is time to remove the head of the snake. Time to choose.

"We are clear, sir. Time to leave."

Jack led Charles out of the mansion and opened the rear passenger door. Once Charles was settled, Jack took his spot behind the wheel. He pulled onto the connecting street, alert, eyes taking in every detail. A garbage truck moved away from them, which was normal since it was pickup day. A lawn maintenance crew trimmed bushes across the street. Simultaneously, large mowing machines traversed back and forth across the yard, creating a visually pleasing pattern in the freshly cut grass. Also normal. There were no suspicious vehicles or bystanders observing their departure. But Jack still remained on high alert and only began to relax once they reached the freeway, merging into the HOV lane toward D.C. They didn't have three or more people for free travel, but it was worth the twenty-dollar fee to avoid the traffic. Plus, the off-ramp led them straight to their first destination since the Pentagon traffic along I-95 was some of the most unpredictable in the world. Los Angeles claimed the title, but Jack thought otherwise, especially when he has been stuck for hours only trying to go three miles.

"Sir, I really think we should consider moving you out of the mansion today."

"Nonsense, Jack. We have privacy and state-of-the-art security. The structure is seated well away from the roads, and the thick frosted glass makes it nearly impossible to see through the windows at any distance. And don't forget all the outside sensors and lights. Plus, I have you."

"I appreciate your confidence, but I am only one person. Nothing is foolproof. If the killer is determined to get to you, it will be difficult to stop him. And I can't be at the mansion twenty-four-seven."

"And I appreciate your concern. Let's play it by ear. I know you are eager to pick up the search for this killer, especially with the arrest of Mr. Turner. I am sure babysitting me is not your ideal pastime. You could probably be doing better things with your free time."

Jack laughed. "And miss your amazing company? Never." He returned to serious. "Has there been any news from the legal team?"

"They have detained Mr. Turner in Winchester County. The legal team arrived, but was unable to see him. He was going through the booking process."

"That shouldn't take that long. Enough time has passed. What is the delay?"

"Procedures, Jack. Procedures. The state arrested him on a federal holder. He is in limbo until the feds transfer him. He will have to start the whole process all over again in their system. Then they will set a date to go before the magistrate. I assume somewhere in there the lawyers will meet with him."

"Sounds to me like they are stalling, sir," Jack said over his shoulder from the front seat.

"They are. I am certain they read Mr. Turner his rights, but they will do everything they can to get him to talk before the lawyers arrive."

"Sam knows to keep his mouth shut."

"Mr. Turner is smart. However, I assume he is using this time to cautiously poke around and find out what evidence they may have against him. I trust him to protect us and The Cabal while maybe getting a few tidbits from the authorities."

"Why Tony's murder? I realize Sam's prints are in the house because they met there before the diplomat hit to go over the plan. And I believe Tony needed some reassuring after Savannah."

"Well, my sources informed me that Mr. Carter was contacted by the FBI task force and decided to talk about Savannah and our diplomat friend, Mr. Ahmadi."

"What?! The FBI task force? The very one we have tried so hard to stay out of their crosshairs?"

"Yes. Specifically, our good friend Mr. Blanchard."

"This looks really bad for Sam. So they think he knew, and he tied up a loose end. Damn."

"They do and it does. The good news is that the evidence against Mr. Turner will be circumstantial. They have no hard evidence since we know he is innocent. We will just have to let this play out. Sam will be out of the fight for the foreseeable future."

They pulled through the security gates at the Pentagon, proceeding to the river parking lot. Somehow, Charles had procured Pentagon Facilities Alternative Credentials, or PFAC, cards for each of them, which were magically renewed every year. Jack was always amazed by the access and influence the man still had.

While Charles attended a few meetings, Jack made his way to the first-floor food court. Charles was arguably in the safest building in the world, and Jack needed more caffeine. He purchased a large black coffee from Dunkin Donuts and settled onto one of the many couches to catch up on the news. Monitors spread throughout the area broadcasted news on every screen, but Jack kept finding himself distracted by all the people walking through the area.

Jack remembered a duty assignment two decades ago. He was on a joint mission on behalf of the queen and the British Army. It was a different Pentagon back then. Men wore suits, and women wore dresses or modest skirts. Times had changed. Suits were almost nonexistent, skirts barely covered the swimsuit area, and hairstyles included every color of the rainbow. He laughed at himself. He was becoming a curmudgeon, and he needed to get with the times.

Charles finished his meeting, and they exited the Pentagon grounds. They headed over to southeast D.C. and Marion Barry Avenue. It was not the safest area, but they were not there to meet safe men. This was one meeting where Jack was most definitely in attendance. Not for Charles's safety meeting in the back room of the smoky club, but because the man they were there to meet was an ally, Alberto Ramirez.

Big Al, as everyone called him, was the owner and proprietor of this particular gentleman's club, along with several others throughout the city. He also happened to be a black market arms dealer specializing in handguns.

Big Al had also lost his teenage daughter, who went missing on a humanitarian trip to Haiti, never to be seen again. She and her friends had been trying to help the people and had paid for it with their lives. The Cabal needed to restock on firearms, and Big Al was always ready to help.

Their business concluded with a round of whiskey shots and firm handshakes, then Jack and Charles proceeded to their last destination, the Army Navy Country Club in Arlington, Virginia. Charles had been a member for as long as Jack could remember. They stopped in for supper several times a week, Charles ensuring his political and business networks remained intact and Jack filling his belly with the gourmet fare. This wasn't so bad. After this, it would be back to the mansion.

Jackson Lentz rose early and checked the overseas markets. He savored a steaming cup of coffee until he was finally satisfied with the necessary adjustments. He had business at the capital, but knew the politicians enjoyed later starts to their days. No need to rush, so he called up his helicopter pilot when his cup was empty.

Ever since 9/11, the federal government restricted the airspace over the Capitol except for police or medical emergencies. Jackson understood the logic, but was still annoyed with the inconvenience. At least he had a standing agreement with the helipad at National Harbor.

A private car would be waiting to whisk him into the city. It would make the journey longer, but there was nothing to be done about it.

A short while later, Jackson was airborne and heading east across the Potomac River. They had to stay at a low level crossing the river and then circle around to the east and approach the pad in a westerly heading. The Potomac River was the approach and departure path for planes serving the Ronald Reagan Washington National Airport, or DCA. The airspace was limited to avoid fatal collisions, and specific low-level corridors had to be used by the rotary wing craft. There couldn't be any inference with the commercial airline traffic.

The private limousine was waiting, ready to do battle with the relentless D.C. traffic. Jackson was glad he didn't have to worry about it. He could relax in comfort and prepare for his meetings on the Hill.

The first was with the House Energy Subcommittee on Communications and Technology. Jackson's company was working on a contract to shore up the emergency communication system for the region. Ever since the FBI director spoke to Congress about the vulnerability of the country's infrastructure, every politician was clamoring to jump on the bandwagon. What these jackals didn't understand was that they had neglected these systems for so long that the technological overhaul needed was a tremendous lift. And, of course, they wanted everything fixed now.

Next was a meeting with the gentlemen from the great state of Alabama. Jackson was constructing a new manufacturing facility, and the Environmental Protection Agency was giving him a hard time. The Defense Department wanted a ramping up of satellite and aircraft components. Jackson, however, could not speed up with the EPA slowing him down. He hoped pressure from the senators would break the gridlock.

Lastly was a White House reception with a Japanese delegation, including the prime minister. The Commerce Department was brokering a deal to increase the importation of Japanese industrial machinery. Jackson also had his fingers in that proverbial pie.

Jackson sighed as the Capitol came into view. It would be a long day. At least he knew the sushi would be good.

These snakes both travel in important circles. They move in and out of government buildings like old friends. Security there is overwhelming. The Pentagon. The Capitol. Even the White House. Too many eyes. Their homes are secured by state-of-the-art security. However, one is more vulnerable than the other. He lives a secluded life along the river. Alone. The other is in a more publicly accessible place, but he has some sort of man servant. Jack is his name. He is on my list, but he looks dangerous.

Of course, all these new players are dangerous. Except maybe the old men. Theirs will be a different game. Jack and Charles are not shut-ins. They don't stay hunkered down in their fortress. Those snakes do not hide. They travel the same transportation arteries that we do. They can bleed like we can. Maybe an arterial bleed is the right answer.

30

THE INTERROGATION

Fairfax, Virginia

Sam looked around the small holding cell. He had been in here for a few hours with nothing to do but stare at the walls. It was a ten-by-ten room with benches along the wall, save one corner with a small commode. He had resisted the urge to use it. *Well, at least they haven't dressed me in orange,* he thought. *That might be a positive sign.*

Sam heard movement and a commotion as a series of doors appeared to be locked and unlocked. He could see directly out the front of his cell, but it was hard to see left or right down the corridors. Shortly thereafter, an officer appeared at the cell door.

"Place your hands together through the bars."

Sam obliged. The guard cuffed him, motioning for Sam to step back from the door. Once he did, the cell was unlocked. *Let the adventure begin.*

Sam was led through a series of hallways, eventually stopping before Interrogation Room 2. A second guard was waiting there. *They are taking this seriously. I must be really dangerous,* Sam thought.

The escort guard gestured to a chain and metal loop at the center of the interrogation table. Once Sam sat, the man unlocked his cuffs and secured the handcuffs to the table. The other guard never took his eyes off Sam.

"I don't suppose I could have a cup of coffee and my phone?"

The guards turned wordlessly and left the room. Through the open door walked Special Agents Patterson and Stills, followed closely behind by Carl Blanchard.

"Great. Looks like the gang is all back together," said Sam.

The two agents sat opposite Sam. Carl took an end chair after closing the door. Roger began the conversation after opening the large case file he had placed on the table.

"This is no time for jokes, Mr. Turner. You are being charged with the murder of Mr. Tony Clark and the attempted Murder of Pakistani diplomat Babak Ahmadi."

"On top of that," Patricia added, "Georgia authorities are currently filing charges of murder related to the Savannah Port incident. I believe the count is up to twenty-one."

"That is a lot of murder," Sam replied.

"But it is your lucky day," Carl chimed in. "To make life simpler and hopefully save some taxpayer money, we are going to roll all these together under a federal indictment. We can save even more money if you simply confess and give us the names of your compatriots. Unless you did that port operation all by yourself. I highly doubt even you could pull that off. I guessed three. Savannah authorities believe five or more. We have a betting pool going."

"Can I get in on it?" Sam asked.

Carl scowled.

Sam's mind reeled despite his calm demeanor. He ran through every possible scenario, finally landing on the most probable. Tony had talked, or was going to talk before the Keeper's people got to him. Sam knew that he should wait for legal representation, but he needed to play along for now to see what they knew. The fact that they were trying to tie him to Babak and Savannah was troubling. Maybe Tony gave them a teaser. He needed to find out fast.

"I am sorry to disappoint, gentlemen and lady." Sam nodded toward Patricia. "I have no idea what any of you are talking about. I am not sure why I am even a person of interest in any of these crimes. Also, is the officer who just left grabbing me that coffee?"

"Is this a joke to you? "Carl asked as his anger surfaced. "The sheer volume of dead bodies around you is staggering."

Good, Sam thought. *Get angry. Make a mistake.*

Roger, on the other hand, kept his cool. He pulled three large photos from the file and pushed them in front of Sam.

"Let's talk about Tony Carter first. It appears entry was made using the back door. There was no alarm system in the house. No dog. Nothing to alert Tony that you were in the house. You must have completely taken him by surprise."

"Was he drinking?" Sam asked. "He must have been drinking if he wouldn't have noticed someone entering his home. Probably drunk."

Roger ignored the question and continued. "The next picture is the chair Mr. Carter was sitting in right before you shot him in the back of the head. And finally, here he is after falling out of that chair due to a single round you put into the back of his head. Were you alone or did you have help from other members of your little club?"

Sam studied the photos, looking for clues. He could see a rocks glass on the far-right end table containing what was probably whiskey. Although he couldn't see the TV, its glare was obvious in the photo. It was on, and Tony would have been staring right at it. Newer TVs had improved screens that would not reflect images like older TVs. Lots of those were practically mirrors, but not this brand. Tony was probably drowning his sorrows and didn't see or hear a thing.

Sam also looked at the wound. Single shot into the parietal bone. If he had all the time in the world, he would have chosen a different spot. He would have angled the head shot from the left or right to aim for the temporal bone by the ear. That would have switched Tony off immediately when the bullet hit the nerve center the bone was meant to protect. The back of the head can be finicky. People have survived gunshot wounds at that location.

On closer inspection, Sam also saw the powder burns surrounding the wound. It suggested that the gun was put against Tony's head. He knew it was coming. This was no surprise. His senses were dulled, and he was probably reeling in guilt. Deep down inside, he probably had lost his will to live anyway.

The killer probably spoke to him. Told him not to move and maybe explained why this was happening. Told Tony that they would all be dead soon. He was just one of the first to go. Sam also knew this was a rookie move. Blood and brain matter would splatter on the gun's barrel if it was placed in direct contact with the intended victim. It was a sure way to create physical evidence, tying the weapon and owner to the crime scene.

Sam would have created space. Create a standoff distance to avoid contamination of the weapon. A couple feet back would have at least minimized the contamination of the weapon. If this had been Sam, he never would have taken the chance. That weapon would have been untraceable and destroyed immediately after its use.

"Interesting theory, officer. First off, I didn't have help since I didn't do this. Secondly, I have no idea what club you are talking about. I'm not much of a joiner."

Patricia read from the notepad. "We have evidence that you were in the dwelling. We found partials and full prints in the kitchen and the bathroom. You prints were on doorknobs and faucet handles. I think they even got one off a dirty glass in the dishwasher. Had yourself a little drink, maybe? I wonder what sink you used to clean up afterwards."

"I actually used the bathroom sink after I peed. Washed my hands. I am not a heathen. And it was water. Tony is a very gracious host, and I was thirsty."

"So, you do admit to being in the house?" Pat confirmed.

"Yes. I have been there prior to this even for a different purpose. Business. Recruitment. You guys do know I own a security company, right? You should have remembered that from the last time you decided to make me your guest. I hope you wrote it all down, at least. It was kinda a key point of my case being tossed. However, I came across Tony's profile online. He was former military and currently with the ATF. I guess the job wasn't for him. Or maybe he wanted to contract and make more money. He didn't say—only that it was time for a change. So, I set up an appointment. It was a long drive, and I had a lot of coffee that day."

"Let's switch gears." Carl pulled an eight-by-ten glossy photo out of his briefcase. It was the official embassy photo of Babak Ahmadi. "Do you know this man?"

"No."

"Did you know that he was a suspected pedophile?"

"No. Should I? Or better yet, did you know? I would hope the FBI does not ignore these types of things."

"So, you are telling me you didn't play a role in ambushing and drugging him in a D.C. hotel room?"

"Nope."

Carl sat back in his chair. "What role did Tony play in this little vigilante scheme?"

"No idea. I wouldn't know since I was not there. You should have asked him."

"Oh, we did, Mr. Turner. We did. We know you needed help with that one."

No, you didn't, Sam thought. *You were going to talk to Tony, but someone got to him first. But he must have mentioned only me by name. They are not asking about anybody else. This is all circumstantial at this point. Me being in his house was legit. We concocted that little rendezvous in case we were discovered together without a good cover story. Tony had even posted his resume online. It's Savannah and this Babak idiot I am worried about. I wonder if I was a suspect for both of those before Tony even reached out to them.*

Silence permeated the room. Carl, Roger, and Pat just stared at him. It felt like hours. Sam broke the silence.

"Is that cop hurrying back with my coffee? I really don't like it cold."

Carl pulled more photos out of his briefcase. They were all shots of the Savannah port. Yellow tent cards marking evidence locations. Dead bodies outlined where they had fallen. The ship run aground in the Savannah River. *We really tore that place up,* Sam thought. *But did we leave behind any evidence? I don't think so. Only that idiot Tony, who jumped the gun and got shot. Wonder if they found his blood or something, and that's what they were holding over him.*

"Why don't you look through these photos of the Savannah port. See if any of these jog your memory."

The feds left the room. Sam knew they were going into the control room to talk behind the one-way glass window on the far wall. Sam knew behavioral specialists also were behind that wall, watching his every move and looking for that tic or pupil dilation indicating surprise or deception.

He had training throughout his military career on interrogations, but these were pros. He would have to tread lightly. He did heed the advice of an old CIA buddy who years ago told him to pop a tablet of Pregabalin or Lyrica before the questioning. Sam didn't fully understand the medical jargon, but his friend said it would suppress nervous tics in his face when pressed during interrogations. It can last up to eight hours. Any edge over the enemy is better than nothing at all. Sam kept a bottle in the truck's glove box. Who knows if it was working.

After several hours with nothing to do but stare at the Savannah photos, he heard the familiar sound of the door being unlocked. To his surprise, three guards entered the room, one holding leg cuffs. *I guess we are going for a ride.*

Sam offered no resistance as he was shackled and escorted out of the room. It was a short walk to a loading dock in the back of the station, where a van was waiting. Two of the men got up front and the third accompanied Sam in the backseat. With a squad car escort, they ran lights and sirens in the direction of the city. *Shit,* Sam thought. *I am headed to the DC Jail.*

The DC Central Detention Facility was built in the seventies and was not configured to hold convicted felons. It housed those charged mostly with misdemeanors or, in Sam's case, those awaiting trial. Sam knew that if he was convicted, he would become a guest of the Federal Bureau of Prisons. They could place him anywhere in the country. For now though, this should be his new home for the foreseeable future.

It was a short twenty-minute ride. And this time, he received the full works: Photos, fingerprints, sheets, a towel, and a baggy pair of orange prison scrubs with a white T-shirt. He was ordered to change on the spot, and his personal property was confiscated. After his wardrobe change, he was led to his cell, then ordered to deposit his items on the bunk inside. It was almost comical trying to walk with leg irons, but he tried to remain serious and focus. He was in a lot of trouble.

The guards took him back the way they had come through another series of hallways. Eventually, Sam found himself in another interrogation room. Once again, cuffed to the table.

The usual suspects were already present when he was led through the door.

"Now that you have had time to think, are you ready to talk?" Carl asked.

"I have pretty much explained that I had nothing to do with any of these murders. I am not certain why you three are so adamant that I was. We seem to be at an impasse."

"Mr. Turner," Carl continued. "We know you were involved in all three. We know that Tony was involved. And we know others are involved. It is only a matter of time until all the pieces fall into place. You sure you don't want to speed up that process?"

Sam looked at Roger and Patricia. "Is this my final destination?"

Both nodded.

"Excellent. I would now like to speak to my lawyer. We are done talking."

The three rose to leave the room.

"That is your right, Mr. Turner. Your lawyers have arrived and completed security. We will show them in shortly."

"Oh, and Carl?"

He paused at the door and looked back at Sam.

"Be a dear. Don't forget that coffee. Black, please."

I FOUND A NOTE TODAY. I WAS SO EXCITED. IT WAS FROM A KID NAMED LARRY. HE IS SCARED AND DOESN'T KNOW WHERE WE ARE. HE GETS RECESS AND GYM, TOO. MUST BE AT DIFFERENT TIMES. HE SAID THERE ARE CAMERAS OUTSIDE, SO WE SHOULD ONLY PASS NOTES IN BATHROOM. HE IS SCARED THAT THE MAN MIGHT FIND OUT. I WON'T SAY ANYTHING BAD IN NOTES, JUST IN CASE.

31

THE MISSION, PART II

Berbera, Somaliland

The easy part was done. Or, at least, the easier of the two. Dane and Nicky had secured the bikes and the biological samples on the boat without incident. Now it was time to end the life of Ibrahim Mohamed Mahmud and get out of Dodge.

They still had plenty of darkness as they headed east toward Ibrahim's compound. The town of Berbera was still asleep. The morning call to prayer was hours away. It was a nationwide alarm clock, but Dane and Nicky planned to be out on the Gulf of Aden, churning towards Djibouti, long before the city awoke.

If not, they would find the streets littered with worshippers who stop in their tracks no matter what they are doing and answer the call. They carry their small prayer mats everywhere. Dane did not want to be caught up when that happened, especially since they had to travel south toward the Burco Shiikh Central Mosque. Hundreds of worshippers would surround the landmark.

One added bonus contributing to stealth was the lack of dogs in this part of the world. The continent of Africa, minus a few countries, seemed to have a distain for the animals as pets. South Africa of course, loved the Rhodesian Ridgeback. Dane couldn't remember ever seeing a dog in East Africa. The Middle East was the same. There were some in the north with a scattering of strays around the southern cities, but that was about it. Iraqis and Africans had always been amazed by the working dogs of the U.S. Army. Scared, but amazed.

There was an abundance of goats, but they didn't warn of strangers quite like canines. As long as you didn't take away their food, the goats throughout the city just continued to chew on garbage. They roamed the streets freely, and Dane never did see any markings. He had no idea how someone told the goats apart. *How can you claim that a goat is yours without proof?* They must have a system here not known to him.

Plastic bags found throughout the city appeared to be the goats' favored meal. *Plastic bags must be the national flower for all the Somalia regions,* Dane thought. Small black and translucent green plastic bags littered the countryside. They were used for one of the most distributed items in the region, khat. Khat is a staple in nearly every Somali household.

The leafy plant was chewed by nearly the entire male population. Once ground up by the teeth, the consumer would then tuck the remains up into a cheek pocket, similar to chewing tobacco. Depending on the strength of the strain, users could experience anything from mild euphoria to grand hallucinations. Somali soldiers often used the substance to hype themselves for combat. Khat was bartered and traded throughout the country. It was better than currency sometimes. The small plastic bags, however, were carelessly discarded.

Dan and Nicky moved silently through the neighborhoods, avoiding the roads at all costs. This was hardly a busy metropolis, but there were a few vehicles on the road getting an early start to their day. When they were less than a kilometer out, Dane called a stop. Nicky moved in close so they could talk.

"Did you hear that?" Dane whispered.

"Hear what?"

"Gunshots, I think. Listen."

They remained absolutely still listening to the air.

POP . . . POP, POP, POP.

All hell broke loose with the sound of automatic weapons fire.

"Shit! That is coming from the direction of the compound."

"Should we move up and take a look?" Nicky asked.

"We have to. Stay low. Slow movements and stay close to cover."

They inched forward as the sounds of the battle intensified. Lights came on in the homes around them. People were not coming outside, though. That was good. They knew what the gunfire meant, and they were probably looking for places to take shelter. They would not dare step outside until the fight was long over.

On the last block before the compound, Dane and Nicky got a full view of the commotion. Several technical vehicles with about twenty of so fighters spread out along the compound's north and east sides, firing into its walls. Return fire from inside the compound appeared mostly ineffective.

Dane and Nicky laid in the prone position, watching the raging battle. The noise was overwhelming. There was no need to whisper at that point.

"What the hell is this?" Nicky asked.

"If I had to guess, some sort of power play. Or revenge. Maybe a clan is settling an old score now that Ibrahim has come out of hiding."

"Maybe they want his business."

"Very good possibility."

"Well, it is going to be pretty difficult with all of this to get in there and kill him."

"Maybe they will do it for us, Nicky. I think we should wait and see how this plays out. Plus, I don't think we have any other choice."

The battle continued will little progress made by either side. What concerned Dane was that Somaliland forces might be en route. They probably had a small outpost here in Berbera, but they would not engage without reinforcements from Hargeisa. It was a solid two-hour drive at best, but Dane certainly didn't want to be there when they arrived. He also didn't think it would last that long.

How could it? he thought. *They only have so many bullets. Plus, they are eventually going to get inside the compound or die outside.*

As if in response to his thoughts, there was movement on the west side of the compound. An SUV burst out of a back gate. It swerved and side-swiped a small dwelling and temporarily stalled. The driver frantically turned over the engine. Dane suspected the SUV was heavily armored and that was how the driver lost control trying to turn.

A technical—or rather, a Toyota Hilux with a machine in the back—disengaged from the fight at the walls and attempted to back onto the road. Its front tires caught on debris, and the small pickup rocked back and forth trying to break free.

Dane saw their chance. "Nicky. On me."

They sprung to their feet and raced toward the technical. It broke loose and slid onto the road. Without missing a beat, Dane shot the soldier manning the machine gun. He rotated slightly left and put a second round into the head of the driver. The vehicle rolled slowly to a stop. In the meantime, the SUV recovered and pulled out onto the same road.

Dane reached in the cab of the truck and pulled out the dead soldier.

"Gross!" exclaimed Nicky.

"I need you to drive. Hop in. Don't lose that SUV."

She jumped behind the wheel and Dane could feel the machine roar to life. The Toyota Hilux was arguably the most dependable vehicle in the world. They were little tanks that just didn't seem to know the word quit. Dane had used them several times over the years, and they never let him down. That was why third-world militias and armies depended upon them across the globe.

Dane remembered a meme he had seen on social media. It was titled "Hilux: The Evolution of Revolution." It showed how different models of the Hilux over the years could accommodate Soviet-era mounted weapons. It was pretty funny, but also true. The vehicle was rarely ever seen in the U.S due to the lack of any sort of emission controls. The cost to upgrade the vehicle to meet EPA standards was astronomical. American consumers were offered the Toyota Tacoma, and they were *not* the same thing.

With the engine roaring, Nicky took off after the SUV. Dane struggled in the back to get the DShK machine gun operational in the bed of the truck. Potholes and debris in the road bounced the tiny Hilux around considerably. The weapon's previous owner had loaded the belt of ammunition, but it had jammed. Dane knew that happened often in these parts of the world.

The soldiers knew how to perform maintenance on the weapon system, but they usually neglected the ammunition. It was stored in cold damp rooms, where it accumulated rust. That appeared to be the case here. The belt was jammed on the shuttle feed system.

Holding on for dear life with one hand, Dane reached into one of his side pouches. He normally kept emergency oil there, anticipating weapon malfunction when operating in sandy environments. Single-handedly, he poured the oil onto the left portion of the ammunition belt as it entered the tray. He reached under the gun and heaved on the charging handle.

It worked. The belt fed in smoothly, and he was in business. Despite what Hollywood movies depict, it is actually quite challenging to fire from a moving vehicle. That's especially true when traveling along these roads. The hood of the cab had a makeshift metal mount welded in place. Dane found that if he rested the weapon in that cradle, he could get off a well-placed shot. The problem was that made it a fixed weapon. He could only shoot straight ahead.

Dane leaned his head through the broken passenger window.

"Nicky!"

"What? I am driving."

"I need you to get close and keep him in front of us so I can shoot. If he turns, aim for the side of the vehicle for as long as possible so I can get off some shots."

"Okay!"

Dane stood back up and prepared to pull the butterfly trigger. They hit a short straightaway, and Nicky gunned the engine. With the SUV in his sights, Dane fired off a short burst. The rounds slammed into the back of the vehicle. They did not penetrate, but caused severe denting. Dane knew a single round might not get through, but several in the same place would have a chance. But the SUV drifted around a corner before he could get another shot. The vehicle then conducted several turns on the short streets, realizing what Dane was trying to do.

He lined up and prepared for his next shot. The SUV appeared likely to make a wide left turn. *Perfect,* he thought. *A side shot.*

"Keep on him as long as possible," Dane shouted toward the cab.

The SUV began the long sweeping turn, and Dane fired as soon as Nicky had lined the Hilux up with at the driver's window. This time he did not let go of the trigger. He put nearly a hundred rounds into the side of the SUV before the gun went dry. But that was enough. The vehicle lurched before crashing into the side of a building.

Nicky brought the Hilux to a sliding halt as Dane leapt from the bed.

"Stay here. Cover me."

She took up a position on the driver's side. The glass had blown out during their chase, and she used the door to protect as much of herself as possible. With her rifle homed in on the back driver's door, Dane attempted to open the front. The driver was injured, but had enough of his wits about him to keep hold of the door.

Dane hadn't brought along any demolition gear, but he did have a few grenades. He peered at the frame between the front and back doors and saw where several rounds had punched through. The glass was tinted, so he couldn't see if he hit anyone inside. Time to find out.

He removed a grenade from his pouch and pushed it as far as possible into the hole. He called Nicky on the radio and told her to take cover. He knew there might be an interior layer of armor in the vehicle, too, and that should take care of it. He pulled the pin and moved to the front of the vehicle behind the engine for cover. He also didn't want to cross Nicky's weapon's line of sight.

The explosion rocked the vehicle, but Dane wasted no time. He immediately inserted another grenade, but it was a smoke this time. He again called Nicky.

"I am moving to the front of the car. I will stay low. When the doors open from the smoke grenade, you shoot the ones on your side. I will cover the passenger side."

"Roger."

And he pulled the pin.

It took only seconds, but the doors flew open with smoke pouring out. Two people got out on Dane's side, and he quickly put several rounds in each. He could hear Nicky shooting on her side, so he pivoted around the engine to see whether she needed any assistance. She did not.

Two more were dead on her side. Dane pulled a photo from his breast pouch and compared it to each of the men. Ibrahim had been behind the passenger seat. He was very much dead.

Dane raced back to the Hilux. Nicky had already gotten back into the driver's seat. She had seen it, too. The remaining fighters from the compound had arrived. The Hilux accelerated back onto the road, fishtailing as it gained traction.

"Turn right here." Dane pointed. "We will have to get back to the boat before they catch up with us."

"This is going to be tight."

"I need you to make a series of left and right turns for the next several blocks. Once we hit the main east-west running road, take a right and don't stop until we are at the port."

Dane turned to the window.

"What are you going to do?"

"Slow them down, or at least make them think twice about following us."

Dane shifted his body partially out the window and took aim at their pursuers. He didn't want to blindly fire, since there were innocents in several of these homes. At the same time, he did not want a vehicle-mounted DShK getting a shot off at them.

The pursuing Hilux rounded the second corner, slowly since it was a tight turn. Dane fired off several shots, striking the soldier manning the heavy machine gun. After the next turn, he sent a nice burst into the driver's side of the windshield. The Hilux smashed into a pile of rubble.

"That's taken care of. Take me to my yacht, fair maiden."

"What the hell is wrong with you?"

LARRY AND I HAVE BEEN PASSING NOTES FOR A WHILE. LARRY SAID HE HAS BEEN SNEEZING A LOT. HE HAS ALLERGIES. THE MAN GIVES HIM MEDICINE, BUT SEEMS ANNOYED WITH HIM. LARRY SAYS HE SMELLS ANIMALS TOO, BUT DOESN'T HEAR THEM. HE HEARS A TRAIN WHEN HE IS AT RECESS, BUT DOESN'T KNOW WHERE THE SOUND COMES FROM. I DON'T HEAR A TRAIN. STRANGE.

32

THE HOMECOMING

Africa, Europe, and the United States

```
Devotee: Watch the news today. I have set a plan in motion.

Keeper: Remember, we want to move quick. No playing games.

Devotee: No games. I promise. But this one will be creative and should finish them.

Keeper: Excellent. I will never forget your accomplishments.
```

The vials were secured by the Explosive Ordinance Detachment back at Camp Lemonnier. They were not doctors or scientists used to handling deadly viruses, but they did know how to handle sensitive materials. Nicky helped them secure the vials in the secondary safety containers for their long shipment stateside. She closely followed the Centers for Disease Control and Prevention standards.

An agency plane was to handle the discreet delivery. Civilian and military aircraft did not have diplomatic immunity when traversing the globe. The team was fairly certain several countries would not appreciate the viruses traveling through their airspace.

The boat held together well for their journey west. It had taken several hours, but they arrived by daylight and met a Navy patrol boat. They had kept a westerly course remaining approximately two miles off the African coast. The patrol boat had met them at predetermined coordinates in the Gulf of Aden and guided them in. The tiny dhow looked ridiculous among the giant ships of the Navy. Service members crowded the deck to watch the tiny boat pass by. They had never seen a local vessel enter the highly guarded American port. This was something special to see. The dhow would be secured at the port until it was transported to its next location.

"I wonder if they are more surprised by the dhow or the hot chick coming into port," Dane mused. "They sure are staring at you."

She wrapped an arm around his waist. "Us. You never know. They could be looking at you."

The admiral had words for the pair once they returned to the base. They had been brought straight to his office, and he was fuming. Dane figured word of the firefight was get back to the base, but he had hoped they would be gone before it did.

"What did you two get into? There are reports of shooting throughout the city as rival clans traded gunfire throughout Berbera. You two better not have had something to do with it. You better not have lied to me and conducted some off-the-book ops in my backyard."

"Sir, I can assure you, we did not. We heard the fighting on the other side of town and went the opposite direction. We did not want to cause an incident."

The admiral stared at Dane for a moment, assessing whether the man in front of him was feeding him a line of horse shit. "I have no proof of your involvement. But believe me, if I find any, you and your little special operations buddies are going down. Now get the *hell* out of my office!"

Dane turned and left promptly in the event the admiral changed his mind. He doubted their paths would cross again.

Dane and Nicky departed for Kenya on the next possible flight, the first leg of what would be a long journey home. They arrived in Nairobi with enough time to check out with the Regional Security Office. He couldn't have cared less. They went up behind the hardline in the agency spaces for a quick VTC. Command back in Washington wanted the CliffsNotes version of the operations. A more formal debriefing would take place upon their return.

Dane just wanted to get to the hotel and shower. He felt disgusting, even though they had cleaned up and changed at the camp in Djibouti. He had burned his drop bag. The blood and animal smell would never wash out.

Two hotel rooms had been booked for them at the place they had stayed on the way over. They never even used the second one. No sense. They were not going to be separated. And at this point, they were walking zombies. They rinsed the filth from their bodies for a second time and collapsed naked into bed, both asleep within minutes.

They had a late morning flight the next day. One night's rest was not nearly enough, so they planned the route home for two legs. The first was an eight-hour direct flight to Amsterdam. It was painful being cramped up for that long, but Dane had booked a luxury hotel in downtown Amsterdam for the night. One room only.

He didn't care that the bean counters at home would notice them sharing a room when they submitted their travel vouchers. He was once again saving taxpayers' dollars. The second leg would begin the next day with the final eight-hour flight home. But that was tomorrow. They still had tonight.

Dane and Nicky checked into the enormous suite. It was well over the cost of per diem, but Dane didn't mind spending his own money. Champagne, chocolate-covered strawberries, and dinner awaited them. The metal trays were still hot.

The room was a luxury suite with a sweeping view of the city. The lights sparkled through the large bay window. They could see people scurrying about below. The main living space had a huge California king bed with a sectional couch, large desk, and modest dining room table. Fresh flowers were scattered among the various tables. Dane watched Nicky's eyes beam at the sight of their temporary home.

She settled at the dining table, and Dane brought her an entree and a glass of champagne.

"Chicken alfredo for the lady."

"Oh, hell yeah. I can get used to this."

"I follow a motto taught to me by my first company commander in the Ranger Regiment. Work hard, play hard. We were expected to bust our asses all day every day in training, but he knew we were going to blow off steam after work. He just didn't realize that Savannah wasn't ready for us."

"Well, if you mean doing spy shit like we just did and then coming back here to my private manservant waiting on me hand and foot, count me in."

Dane laughed as he put the strawberries in the fridge. He knew they would be better cold. He brought his own entree to the table, along with the bottle of champagne.

"As long as it is reciprocated." He uncovered his tray to reveal a massive ribeye steak.

"Is that it? A slab of meat? Please don't tell me that is all you are going to eat."

"It's all I need. The perfect meal for the human body."

"How about a vegetable? Or maybe even a salad. How are you going to get those nutrients? I won't even ask about fruit."

"This thing ate all that stuff and absorbed it in its meat. All the nutrients are there in this one piece of steak. Perfection. Plus, the fat is good for the body."

"You eat the gristle as well? You are too much."

After the meal, they refilled their glasses and entered the bathroom, though it would be more appropriate to call it a spa. The shower was the size of a small car with tandem showerheads. Next to it was a jacuzzi tub that could fit a whole family. To top it off, there was a small dry sauna, built from cedar, in the corner. It was the largest bathroom either of them had ever seen.

"Do I even want to know what this room cost?"

Dane chuckled. "Don't worry about it. My treat."

"Damn. A rich, good-looking spy is trying to seduce me. How did I get so lucky?"

They took an extended shower, enjoying the luxury of the space. The shower in Nairobi had been decent, but did not have anywhere near the water pressure as Amsterdam. Dane used the fancy shampoo provided and washed Nicky's long blonde hair.

"Keep it up, manservant. You might just get to stay around."

They dreaded getting out, but the jacuzzi was ready. Dane had run the tub while they enjoyed the shower. He brought the ice bucket of champagne with them and placed it beside the tub. The warm water and bubbles engulfed their bodies.

After several relaxing minutes, Nicky broke the silence. "So where do we go from here?"

"Back to reality. I am anxious to pick up the hunt with Sam when we get back. I hope you will be a part of that team."

"I plan to be. But more specifically, I was talking about us. Nothing about this has been normal."

"Oh, us?" Dane pretended to be surprised.

Nicky splashed water on his face. "Yes, us."

"Well, I think we really need to figure out logistics. My unit does have some offices up at Fort Meade, which would make commuting from your place easy. We also have NSA slots in our building. Plenty of terminals and SCIF spaces you could use. Hell, we can walk from my place together. And it is easier to link up with Charles and crew if we are in the city."

Nicky smiled and stood up in the tub. She grabbed a towel and stood before the edge, gently drying her skin and wiping away the bubbles. When she was done, she hung her towel neatly and gave Dane a mischievous grin.

"Good answer, Mr. Cooper," she said as she walked into the bedroom.

Dane quickly followed suit. He couldn't dry off fast enough. He caught her as she was pulling back the covers. They fell into bed once again. This time, they didn't fall asleep.

A while later, Nicky got out of bed and began scrounging for her clothes. Dane sat up in bed to enjoy the view. He sat with his hands behind his head.

"Don't mind me. You just keep moving around."

"Get up. Don't just sit there like a pervert. Grab your clothes. Let's head downstairs for a drink."

"Sounds like a plan. Hotel lobby bar or did you want to wander around town?"

"Let's play it by ear. The hotel bar is close in case I want to run back up here and play with my manservant again."

Dane laughed as he pulled on his jeans.

The hotel lobby was beautiful and ornate. It had what you would expect of old European charm. The bar was no different. Walnut paneling and frosted glass adorned most of the wall space. Exquisite bottles covered the entire wall behind the bar. It was only half-full, so they selected seats at the far end to afford a little privacy. They did not intend to discuss anything sensitive, but it was good practice to make sure nobody overheard them after a mission like the one they had just conducted. Details could inadvertently slip out.

"My treat," Nicky said, opening her purse. "Least I can do after you sprung for the room."

The bartender had made his way over. "What can I get you folks?"

"Can I have a vodka tonic, please?"

"Tito's okay?"

"Perfect."

"And you, sir?"

"Do you have Casamigos?"

"Sure do."

"Añejo on the rocks, please."

"Coming right up."

"Well, well, well. Tequila, Mr. Cooper? Full of surprises. You aren't going to become a problem, are you?"

Dane laughed. "Ha, nope. I have been drinking it for quite a while now. It doesn't have the stereotypical effect on me. I actually get quite mellow. I still like whiskey, but it has more sugar. One hundred percent Agave tequila is the healthiest thing if you are going to drink."

"I am sure the unit nutritionist would love to hear this one."

"We have debated a time or two. She would rather none of us drink, but she knows she is fighting a losing battle. She accepts the agave."

The bartender returned with their drinks. He turned on the overhead TV and left the remote with them. Other customers needed tending to. An American news broadcast played. Dane and Nicky became glued to the screen.

Eric: We turn now to our man on the street, Carlson Newton . We heard the police made an arrest this evening, possibly tying at least one man to a series of crimes both here in D.C. as well as in Virginia and Georgia.

Carlson: As you can see behind me, we are outside the D.C. Jail. Earlier today, Winchester County police apprehended one Sam Turner at the behest of the FBI. I am told by my sources that when this is all said and done, Mr. Turner could be implicated in twenty-two murders and one attempted murder.

Joyce: Twenty-two murders, Carlson. Was this over a long period of time?

Carlson: No, Joyce. Twenty-one murders stem from the port of Savannah shootout a few months ago. It is believed that Mr. Turner was part of a larger group that participated in that gang war.

Eric: And the twenty-second and attempted murder?

Carlson: Yes. Mr. Turner is believed to be involved in what I am being told was an execution-style murder earlier today. Mr. Tony Carter, an analyst with Alcohol, Tobacco, and Firearms, was found deceased with a single gunshot wound to the head.

Joyce: Do they believe it was related to Mr. Carter's work with firearm control?

Carlson: Although Mr. Turner is an avid gun collector who happens to own and operate a private shooting facility out in Winchester, Virginia, no motive has been released at this time. No motive has been established for the suspect's alleged assault of Pakistani diplomatic official Mr. Babak Ahmadi either.

Eric: The diplomat who was given a nearly fatal overdose of heroin in a downtown D.C. hotel room.

Carlson: That is the attempted murder Mr. Turner is also being charged with. Sam Turner is a retired Special Forces—

Dane muted the TV.

"I can't believe this is happening. This arrest is several days old."

"Dane, we need to get home quickly. We have been in a news black hole for the last several days."

"We have no way to reach Charles and Jack here. Too risky to bring our communication gear with us. Let's take these drinks back to the room. You can dig on the internet, and I will look for earlier flights."

"Actually, I can use my computer to do a one-time chat with everyone.

I know how to tunnel into the communication network. I will just wipe the computer afterward and destroy the hard drive."

"Great. Let's do it."

Nicky placed a fifty euro note on the bar. "Sir." She raised her hand. "We are going to take these to go."

Halfway around the world, Jack eased the car into the circular driveway of Charles's mansion. Once stopped, he exited the vehicle and made his way around to the rear passenger door.

"I appreciate all this, Jack, but I really can get my own door."

Jack scanned the area before moving and allowing Charles to stand. "I know, sir, but caution is needed right now."

They approached the front steps, Jack's head on a swivel. Before they reached the front door, Charles turned to Jack.

"Damn. I left my briefcase in the boot. Would you grab it for me?"

Jack nodded and returned to the car to retrieve the bag. He shut the trunk of the car as Charles opened the front door. The explosion was the last thing he remembered as he was thrown over the top of the car and out onto the front lawn.

LARRY STOPPED LEAVING NOTES. I KEEP CHECKING. I AM WORRIED. I HOPE HE DIDN'T GET SICK OR MOVE. I WILL KEEP TRYING. LARRY IS MY ONLY FRIEND, AND I MISS TALKING TO HIM. I GOT EXTRA TIME AT RECESS TODAY. IT WAS NICE OUT. I LAID IN THE GRASS FOR A BIT AND WATCHED THE SKY. I SAW SOME AIRPLANES AND WISHED I COULD FLY AWAY FROM HERE.

33

THE SUSPECTS

Dumfries, Virginia

Roger and Pat pulled away from the curb in the Springfield neighborhood. They had just left the home of the building manager for the Scottsdale Building, where Andrew Stevenson had worked. The man was distraught and willing to help in any way, but the truth was that he had very little to offer.

The building had security personnel and a general plan to deal with minor issues. Robbery, trespassing, and petty thefts, however, were the only crimes they had ever faced. Murder was unthinkable. The man had told Roger and Pat that the only violent crime they ever trained for was an active shooter in the area. "The standard procedure would then be to bolt all the doors and keep everyone away from the windows. We would then wait for the cavalry," he had explained. "My security guys are good, but not trained like law enforcement or military folks."

"Do you think Carl is giving us the boring interviews?" Pat asked from the passenger seat. "Maybe keeping all the interesting ones for his guys on the task force?"

"Unfortunately, I don't see any glamorous ones, Pat. These are just normal people with normal lives."

"I know. Guess I am just not very optimistic that we are going to find our needle in a haystack with these chats."

"Someone must have seen something useful. This killer didn't just walk in unnoticed. We are not dealing with a ghost. He got into and out of that office with nobody seeing him. Impossible."

"I know, Rog. It just seems that all the people that work there seem to keep to themselves in their own little offices. There is very little common space."

"I agree with you there. That is why we are talking with people that moved throughout the building. Folks that visit multiple floors. There is a better chance of them noticing something out of place. I actually believe Carl trusts us the most with these interviews. He has us talking to folks that may break this case wide open. The lawyer in the other office didn't see or hear a thing since he was in meetings himself."

"What about that Jack guy, the driver? What is your take on him?"

"Well, I don't think he is our killer if that is what you are asking."

"No. I mean his story. The whole secure transportation thing. It seems there is more to that story or a threat he didn't happen to mention. My gut says something is off."

"For once, I agree with your gut. Just not the sugary coffee crap you feed it."

Pat punched him in the arm.

"Hey! No hitting the driver."

"I am serious, Rog."

"So am I, and I think so is Carl. He definitely wants a follow-up with Jack and the other guy Frank and anyone else that drove for Andrew Stevenson. And I agree that Andrew Stevenson was not afraid of just a random robbery or carjacking."

"I hope he has us there for that one. I want to know that guy's story."

"I thought you said this task force was going to swamp us with too much work. Now you are hoping for more?"

"I did, but I am rested now. I want to see this thing through. Besides, you have to admit this stuff is all tied to our unsolved crimes. This started with those children appearing in the church. I want to know how they got there."

"Me, too. That is the million-dollar question."

Roger steered the car onto I-95, begging for it to be clear. They were headed to Dumfries for their final interviews. The had already spoken with all the security personnel, and now they needed to interview the maintenance personnel.

Those folks primarily kept the building running. They traveled to all floors, including secure areas where most did not venture. If the killer had used a unique method of entry, one of them might have seen something, or at least have an idea of how their ghost got in and out of the Scottsdale. Four men had been working that day. They would interview their first today and finish the final three tomorrow.

Traffic appeared to be flowing well, but Roger jumped into the HOV lane anyway. He knew that the Occoquan was coming up, and it was a bottleneck no matter the time of day. It could be two in the morning with open roads, yet traffic always slowed to a crawl between the Lorton and Woodbridge exits. That area and Stafford always backed up, and usually for no reason. At the Occoquan, one of the freeway lanes disappeared, which could account for some slowdown. *But Stafford,* he thought, *no reason at all.*

"Read to me, Pat. Who do we have next?"

Pat opened the interviewee case file and cleared her throat. "We have Victor Weber. Forty-one-year-old Caucasian male. Lives in Dumfries, obviously, since that is where we are going. Unmarried. No kids. No criminal record. And it says he is a veteran."

"What branch?"

"Army."

"Okay."

"Work history."

"Company called Dynamic Solutions Services."

"Never heard of it."

"He left the service in 2018. Looks like he contracted for a few years. Security stuff mostly. There is not a lot of information about the company."

"Does it say anything about travel or overseas work?" Roger asked.

"It does say international clients."

"Interesting. Probably means he was one of those security firms that augmented the military in protecting important people in Iraq and Afghanistan. With the reduction of U.S. forces, a lot of contract muscle was brought in."

"Well, after that, Victor got into the maintenance business. He went to a trade school before the Army." She flipped the page. "Electrician. He is a certified electrician. Looks like he is an independent contractor, but also picks up temp work."

"Like as in a temp agency?"

"Yeah. He appears kinda smart. He has his own business, but when times are slow, he sees who needs temporary specialty work."

"Agree, Pat. Kinda smart. You get to be your own boss, but if times are lean you have something to fall back on. Sounds like he was in the right place at the wrong time."

Before long they exited onto Dumfries Road, heading west toward Manassas. Victor's home was in an older community before the Manassas city limits. They found it easy enough, pulling to the curb in front. These communities were notorious for having no parking, and this one was no different. Roger threw a police license plate on the dash for any rookie looking to score a big ticket on a car in the no parking zone. A fellow officer could run the plates before writing a ticket, which would identify the vehicle as belonging to the Virginia Bureau of Investigation. But he knew they rarely did.

Pat knocked on the front door, which was quickly answered.

"Victor Weber?" she asked, showing the man her badge.

"Yes. Uh, is there some kind of trouble?"

"No. Sorry to startle you. I am Special Agent Patricia Stills and walking up is Special Agent Roger Patterson. We are with the state. We just wanted to ask you a few questions if you have the time."

Roger made it to the porch and offered Victor his hand. "We are following up with folks that were in the Scottsdale Building the other day. We are hoping that someone saw something. Just want to chat to see if you noticed anything unusual that day."

"Of course. Of course. Come in. That was a horrible day. And just my luck, the electrician was out and they needed a guy."

They followed Victor into a sparsely furnished but tidy living room. It had two small couches and a recliner that appeared well-used. It directly faced the wall-mounted television, clearly the most used piece of furniture in the room. However, Victor ignored his usual seat in favor of one of the couches.

"Oh, excuse me. Where are my manners? Could I offer either of you something to drink? I have water and soda. I could put on a pot of coffee. I don't have donuts," he joked.

Pat and Roger smiled at the lame joke but politely declined. Typically, one would lead and the other would observe when they conducted interviews. The lead would take the subject through the stages of the event. In this case, the torture and murder of Andrew Stevenson. The observer's role in this case was not to look for lies or false statement, like when they were interrogating subjects, but to identify possible threads to pull. Patricia would lead, and Roger would observe. It was their normal routine, since Roger was the senior, with far more years of experience conducting interviews.

"So, Mr. Weber."

"Please, call me Victor."

"Okay. Victor, let's start by talking a little about you. Where you grew up, your time in the service, other jobs, things like that. We like to get to know our interviewees. It helps to give perspective to their stories."

"Sure, if you think it will help. I was born in a small town in southern Indiana. My father was a mechanic, my mother a homemaker. I had two sisters and a brother. Dad wanted Mom home with us."

"Do you still keep in touch with your family?"

"Not really. Mom and Dad passed years ago. My younger brother followed me into the Army, but he was killed by an IED outside of Baghdad in 2008. And my sisters have moved on with their lives and their families. We talk occasionally around the holidays, but never any visits. They both reside in California anyway. I am never traveling to that state."

"I am sorry for your loss."

"Thank you. I had a normal childhood. Wasn't much of a student, so Dad really pushed for me to be in the trades after high school. He didn't want me to waste money on some fancy school for a bullshit degree. Oops. Pardon my language."

"It is quite all right," Pat reassured him. "Sounds like you dad was a smart man."

"He was, but he was a tough man. He was hard on us kids. Always pushing us to work hard and be good patriots. Nothing was ever good enough. He used to say our generation was weak and we had no love of country like his generation. Anyway, I went to school to become an electrician. Worked a few years as an apprentice, but I felt like I wasn't doing enough. Then, 9/11 happened."

"How long did you serve?"

"Seventeen years."

Patricia continued, but Roger made a note to circle back. It was the only note he had made. The word strange was at the top of the page. He noted very subtle quirks and tics in Mr. Weber; he just couldn't put his finger on them.

"So, after the military, back to work as an electrician?"

"Yes."

"Oh, sorry. I skipped over some contracting work for a few years. A company called Dynamic Solutions Services."

"Yes, I did a little security work, but it wasn't for me."

There it was again. The contract company's name definitely bothered him. Maybe it wasn't on the up and up. Something was strange.

"And all that brought you to the Scottsdale Building."

"That is correct."

"Walk me through your morning, what you did, anything you saw. The smallest little detail could be important."

"It wasn't anything special. I got the call the night before that their main guy had been in some sort of accident and could I work a few days while he was recovering. I came in, met the supervisor, and got my task orders."

"Were there specific locations, or did you bounce all around the building?"

"All around. First was the basement boiler room. A new furnace had been installed, but they needed the gas line run before I could take the old one offline. Then, it was weekly safety checks of all the elevators. An outlet repair on the third floor. Normal things like that."

Roger looked around the room as Victor spoke. There were no personal touches to the home. He was just realizing that for the first time. No pictures. No military memorabilia. Nothing. Roger's gut was tingling, but he still couldn't put his finger on it. Victor was giving off creepy vibes.

Roger broke his silence. "Victor, can I use your restroom?"

"Of course." He pointed to a door between the kitchen and the room they were in. "It's right there."

Roger excused himself and entered the small room. He splashed some water on his face, trying to clear the cobwebs. He stared at himself in the small vanity mirror. What is it?

Patricia was about to continue when he returned, but Roger gave her that look. She paused.

"Tell me about your military service," Roger instructed.

Victor noticeably stiffened. "Well, I joined the infantry. Did that for a number of years. I wanted to go Special Forces, but just didn't have what it took. Ended up in Civil Affairs. Finished out with the 82nd out of Bragg."

"You mean Fort Liberty?" Roger continued.

"Nope. I mean Bragg. Stupid politicians and crybaby liberals can squawk all they want about Civil War generals. It is part of our history, and we need to teach our youth, not coddle them."

Roger had definitely hit a nerve. He didn't know why he was pushing so hard. The man had done nothing wrong, but he couldn't help himself.

"Why seventeen years? Why not twenty with a pension?"

"Because I was done with the Army. The backstabbing, bureaucracy, all the bullshit."

"Did you receive an honorable discharge?"

"I received a general discharge. Politics and all."

Victor was definitely squirming. And then it hit Roger. He saw the news report this morning about a Mr. Charles Thornton that was killed by a faulty gas line in his home. Earlier investigators found evidence of tampering with the gas line. Why would he connect that to Victor? His gut said he was on some sort of path.

"So, DSS. Dynamic Services Solution. What did the company do? Were they one of those mercenary outfits running around third-world countries in places our real soldiers couldn't go?"

He didn't even see Victor's weapon until the first shot grazed his side.

Analyst: Chief. Are you out there? We are on our way home.

Analyst: President. Are you there? We are on our way home.

Analyst: Benefactor. Are you there?

Benefactor: I am. I heard the news about the Closer and our other associate. This is devastating. Are you and the Shadow safe?

Analyst: We are. Do you need us to come to you? I can't find the President or the Chief.

Benefactor: No. I am currently out of the country. We need to finish this and regroup. I will reach out to them both as well.

Analyst: We plan to end this now.

Benefactor: Good. Just tell me what you need.

34

THE RECKONING

Dumfries, Virginia

Dane and Nicky passed easily through customs. The baggage claim was faster than usual, and they were headed to the taxi stand before they knew it. The banner at the bottom of an airport television caused Dane to stop in his tracks. Nicky nearly crashed into him. They read the text as it scrolled across the screen.

ARLINGTON POWER BROKER CHARLES THORNTON WAS KILLED IN A HOME EXPLOSION DUE TO A FAULTY GAS LINE. HIS ASSISTANT IS IN CRITICAL CONDITION AT INOVA ALEXANDRIA HOSPITAL.

"Holy shit." Dane was floored.

"Oh my God. What do we do now?"

"We need to get up on comms as quickly as possible. I also think we need to avoid our places for now. Not sure if we are targets, too. Let's go to my storage unit and regroup from there. My truck is there."

They got in the first available car and Dane provided the driver with a hotel address several blocks from his unit. They each only had one small bag since they had shipped most of their stuff via diplomatic pouch. They could easily walk the few blocks with their rolling luggage. They didn't want any record of their travels from the airport, just in case.

A short while later, Dane opened the door to his unit. Nicky was the first person he ever brought there. Well, he gave Sam the code when he left for Africa in case he needed any equipment. He closed the door behind them and pushed through an opening in a false wall. He turned on the lights and watched Nicky take in the room.

"I don't know whether to be impressed or frightened that you may be the Unabomber, Dane. This place is cool, but also a little creepy."

The walls were lined with shelves and workbenches, electronics strewed about. It definitely looked like a mad scientist's workshop. Dane quickly fired up his other phone and saw the messages from the group. He then searched the back wall cabinet and found documents from Sam.

"What are those?" Nicky asked.

"Files from one of Jack's contacts. A company called Dynamic Solutions Services. We think there may be a connection between this company and our killer. It looks like they didn't get too far. Sam is now in jail. Jack is in a coma. They were only able to talk to a few folks."

He handed her the file.

She brainstormed as she flipped through the folder. "Okay. So, one of these people could be our killer or know who he is."

"That's the logic here."

"Okay, and bad things have happened since this has been passed around."

"I don't think we can assume that. Bad things were happening already. It could have been a reason for them to accelerate their plans—or maybe not. The killer probably doesn't know about this folder."

"Okay, fair. What's our next play?"

"Let's pack up what we need from here. We need a safe place to work. I have a few pistols here, as well as some clean laptops. I also have a large amount of cash and some fake IDs to go along with some credit cards. I don't want to check into a hotel as Dane Cooper."

Later that afternoon, they were in an Embassy Suites room in Springfield. Dane had collected several wireless internet pucks from his stash. He and Nicky used their untraceable internet access to do their dirty work. Dane researched DSS and their employees. Nicky hacked the FBI task force servers to cross-reference information from the various crime scenes.

"These are some nasty folks, Nicky. DSS has been accused of torture, rape, and murder in both Afghanistan and Iraq, plus several countries in Africa."

"Definitely a group that could produce our sadistic killer. Damn, these FBI servers are slow."

"Are you sure they won't know you are inside?"

"Not a chance. I piggybacked on a legitimate access route from Homeland Security. I am flowing in the normal traffic. Plus, these aren't classified data sets. Sensitive, but not classified."

"I don't understand anything you just said."

"That is why I will work on the computer security side of the house."

"What have you got?" Dane walked over and sat beside her on the bed.

Nicky shifted the computer so it was resting one both of their legs.

"First thing they did was compile all video footage from each crime scene. They are running facial recognition AI software, basically looking for the same face at two or more scenes. Nothing so far."

"What's that folder?" Dane asked, pointing to one of the marked employees.

Nicky opened the folder to a subset of several others. "They compiled rosters of everyone with access to the crime scenes. Here is the one for Jill's apartment complex. List of all residents in her building. Management. The maintenance guys. Everyone. They also have folders for the church and the Scottsdale Building where Andrew worked. Oh, and the hospital where Basker was killed."

"And they cross-referenced those I am assuming?"

"Yup. No matches."

"Did they check deliveries, packages, flowers, whatever?"

"Yup, they cross referenced those as well." Nicky paused for a moment. "Hang on. That is odd."

"What is it?"

"Well, look here on the hospital roster."

"I can see it. It's huge."

"Yeah, look here, Dane. Temp agency hired an orderly for the day, but somehow the name got left off."

"I am sure that happens sometimes."

"Yeah." Nicky scratched her head. She opened and closed files, checking names against different databases. "It's one company. Different names. One company."

"What's one company, Nicky?" She stared at the screen for what felt like an eternity to Dane.

"They didn't catch it because they didn't know. Look at the invoice records. The addresses are the same." She opened several web pages. "Anderson Janitorial Services. Advanced Electricians. Medical Support Services. They are divisions of one temp agency. Comprehensive Temporary Services. I am cross-referencing where they provided services on the days in question."

Dane stared at her work, afraid to say a thing, lest he break her concentration.

"Okay, it's coming up. Okay, here it is. Their various divisions provided workers at the Scottsdale office complex and the hospital the day of the murders."

Dane had the files from Jack in his hand with the list of names.

Nicky scrolled down. "Okay, Advanced Electricians had a Mr. Victor Weber working that day."

"Holy shit. Bingo. He is on the DSS list of potential suspects."

"Let's see if he was at the hospital." Both Anderson's Janitorial Services and Medical Support had workers there that day. It was a much longer list, but Victor Weber was not there.

"It is kind of a unique name, but you never know until you know. Let's play a hunch."

Nicky picked up the phone and dialed a number from the Medical Support Services website.

"Hello, Medical Support Services. How may I direct your call?"

"Hi, my name is Shelley Combs over here at Memorial Hospital's billing services. We are sending out invoices for payment this week and we are confirming whether Mr. Victor Weber worked the thirteenth and fourteenth or just the thirteenth. . . . Thanks, I'll hold."

Dane looked at Nicky and mouthed the word Shelley. She shrugged.

"Yes, great. You are a doll. Have a blessed day."

"So?" Dane asked

"Victor Weber only worked at the hospital or the thirteenth as an orderly."

With Victor's address plugged into the GPS, they fired up Dane's truck. He put in parameters to avoid the freeway on the way to

Dumfries. Dane knew it would be faster, but he also knew there was a greater chance that the truck would be caught on camera.

They had looked at the map before the drive to find an ideal location to park the truck. Using it was not ideal in the first place, but they had no real options at this point. Speed was necessary.

Once on Dumfries Road, they headed southeast away from Victor's neighborhood. Dane spotted the Montclair lot and turned in. He had reconned this place previously for another operation. The lot was small and didn't have cameras. It also had a path that led through the woods. He found a parking space farthest away from the main road.

"I really want to come with you."

"I know, Nicky. And you having my back would make me feel better. However, I need you to keep the truck moving away from this location. I will call you on the burner when I need a pickup. I will meet you at the Dolphin Beach parking lot."

Dane press-checked his Glock and adjusted the hunting knife strapped horizontally along the back of his belt. He gave Nicky a kiss on the check, jumped out of the truck, and entered the woods. He was not necessarily going stealth. It was nearing dusk, but people would see him regardless, and acting strange would increase the probability of someone reporting him. The object was if seen, don't be memorable.

It only took about thirty minutes to find Victor's home. The neighborhood was deserted. Not a soul on the street. *Good,* he thought. *Let's do this quick and get it over with.*

He and Nicky had debated the best approach for Victor, and they decided on the direct route. He was going to simply walk up to the door. When the man answered, a gun stuffed in his face should pay the price of admission. Dane was 99.9 percent sure this was their assassin. Further research on the ride over had revealed more damning evidence.

Victor had served only seventeen years, which was a strange number. Normally, folks went twenty if they were that far. Nicky accessed his military records. Bad conduct discharge over excessive use of force, several accusations of unnecessary violence, and some money missing during Civil Affairs missions. He received his first Article 15 when going through Special Forces Assessment and Selection. Apparently, he had punched one of the instructors when the man was correcting Victor. That mistake had cost him any chance of succeeding in Special Forces and several nights in the hospital, recovering from the beating the sergeant had given him.

Dane was nearly to the front of the house when he noticed the sedan illegally parked at the curb. Upon closer inspection, he saw the police license plate on the dash. *Crap, they beat me here.*

Just as he was getting ready to call Nicky and regroup, several shots rang out. Dane instinctively ducked and moved toward the sound of the gunfire. Crouching low, he peered through one of the front windows. He saw Special Agent Patricia Stills on the floor. She was clearly dead from a gunshot wound to the head. There was no time. He didn't know who else might be in danger.

Dane returned to the front of the house. He checked the front door handle with his left hand. Unlocked. He readied his pistol and flew through the front door. He instantly saw Roger Patterson on his side, bleeding, and he barely had time to take cover.

Victor had already been pointing his weapon in Dane's direction, firing three shots. Dane dove behind the couch. His mind was reeling. He didn't want to kill Victor outright. At least, not at first. He needed answers. But the man was forcing his hand. And then fate shined on him.

CLICK.

Dane knew an empty gun when he heard one. Without a second thought, he charged at Victor. He tackled the man, and they both crashed over an end table. Dane was first to his feet. He drove his right knee into Victor's face as he was rising. He collapsed back on the floor, but Dane gave no reprieve. He pummeled the suspect in the face and chest, but he held back. He needed answers.

He pulled Victor to his feet and threw him face-down on the one upright couch. He quickly went to Roger's side, grabbing the man's handcuffs. He needed to tend to Roger, but Victor had to be restrained. However, cuffing him seemed almost unnecessary. Victor was unconscious. *Fucking lightweight.*

Dane checked and found a pulse. He moved Roger to a seated

position. He was grunting in pain, holding his side. The bullet from Victor had torn through Roger's left hip, but he was conscious. Dane turned to Patricia, but he didn't bother to check for a pulse. Two rounds had struck her in the center of her face, creating enormous exit wounds. Nobody could survive that. Roger watched him expectantly, so Dane slowly shook his head. He retrieved a rag from the kitchen and returned to Roger's side.

"Here. Keep pressure. I will call 911."

"Pat's dead, isn't she?"

"Yes. I'm sorry."

"So am I. I didn't even get off a shot. Hold off on that 911. I can hang on. Get what you need from him. Once you are done, I will call from my phone."

Dane stared, momentarily perplexed. *Did I hear what I thought I just heard?*

"Hurry up before I change my mind. Somebody heard those shots, so I am certain a cruiser or two are on their way."

Victor started to stir. When his eyes fluttered open, the first thing he saw was Dane's face. The second was an oversized hunting knife.

"Hello, Victor. Have you been looking for me?"

"Cooper," he grimaced through blood-covered teeth. "Oh, how I have wanted to play one of my games with you. Looks like we won't get that chance now."

"Who is the Keeper?"

"Wow, straight to the point." He coughed up some blood. "Don't you want to know about all your other friends? That fat corporate fuck. That bitch. Oh, and have they found all the pieces of your boss yet?"

Dane smashed his fist into Victor's torso, feeling the satisfying crunch of his ribs snapping. A second hit made it worse. "Tell me what I need to know, or you are of no use to me."

Victor wheezed. "Time is on my side right now. Not yours."

Dane could hear the sirens from Dumfries Road.

"Get moving!" Roger yelled. "They are almost here."

Dane ran back into the recesses of the house. He found Victor's electronics in the study. He returned to the front room and removed

Victor's cuffs. The man just laughed at him as Dane removed his Glock.

"No!" He heard from Roger's location.

Dane turned toward the man, worried that he had changed his mind.

"Here," Roger said, nudging his pistol toward Dane. "Use my service weapon, not yours. No trace of you being here. Pat and I were ambushed. I was forced to defend myself."

Dane accepted the pistol and holstered his own. "I don't know why you are doing this, but thank you."

Victor was on his feet, protesting. "No, no. You have to arrest me!"

Dane didn't let him finish. He shot Victor Weber three times in the chest and once in the head.

I THINK LARRY IS GONE. I HAVE NOT HEARD FROM HIM. I HAVE NOT HEARD FROM ANYONE ELSE EITHER. MY CLASSES ARE BORING, BUT THEY GIVE ME SOMETHING TO DO. THE MAN SAID I AM COMING ALONG WELL. HE SAID I WAS THE SMARTEST HE HAD IN HIS COLLECTION. IT WAS STRANGE. THE FOOD IS OKAY, BUT IT IS BORING. I GET TIRED OF EGGS EVERY MORNING. I MISS CEREAL.

35

THE DIARY

Winchester, Virginia

Dane and Nicky returned to Dane's apartment. He immediately stripped out of his bloody clothing and headed for the shower. Nicky bagged up the clothing in a large black trash bag. They would dispose of it later. She heard the shower stop. Dane changed quickly and joined her in the small living room.

"Here, let me take a look at your hands."

"It's fine Nicky. Just a few cuts."

"Did you wash them thoroughly?"

"Yes, Mom," Dane smiled. "You want some coffee?"

"Sure, I could use it."

"Are you okay?"

"A lot to process. The coffee will help. I am just wondering if we are going to have a problem with Special Agent Patterson."

"So, he just let you go?"

"That is the rub. He was devastated over Special Agent Stills and made a decision in the moment. One I hope he doesn't come to regret."

Dane walked around the counter separating the kitchen from the living room. He filled the machine with water and ground beans. As it was brewing, he put away a few glasses that had been left on the drying rack. He had a dishwasher, but rarely used it. He fixed a meal and immediately washed the plate and utensils. He typically didn't have enough to bother with the machine. *Hmm,* he thought. *Maybe that will change in the future.*

The coffee pot dinged. Dane retrieved two cups from the cupboard. He handed Nicky a full mug.

"I did manage to grab Victor's laptop. Maybe you and the team can compare it to the others to determine how to find these guys."

"Hopefully. Hey, what is this?" she asked as she picked up a package at the end of the counter.

"Huh. No idea. Open it."

Nicky opened the small box and pulled out what appeared to be a notebook with a note taped to the front. "Strange," she said, handing it to Dane.

Dane accepted the small notebook. He opened the attached note.

Hello Dane,

It seems we have started a very dangerous game, you and I. A game with very high stakes. You have been a worthy opponent. However, this is a game I intend on winning. I will be seeing you and yours soon.

The Keeper

Dane's hands shook as he opened the notebook.

THE DIARY OF ANGELA COOPER

36

THE SAFEHOUSE

New River Gorge, West Virginia

Dane drove the truck up the long gravel driveway. The light dusting of snow crunched beneath the tires, light flurries requiring the occasional swipe of the windshield wiper. John and Jenny shared the cab with him. Neither looked happy.

They pulled up to a small mountain cabin. Although it was a picturesque location, the mood prevented a true appreciation of its beauty. The property belonged to an old Ranger buddy Dane had reached out to earlier in the week.

"Hey. What's up, Bryan? How are things?"

"Dane, man, it's been a hot minute. Things here are great. How about you?"

"I can't complain."

"Yeah? Who's listening?"

Dane laughed. "No shit, right? I had a question for you. Do you still have that rental out by the New River Gorge in West Virginia?"

"Sure do. Just did some upgrades and getting ready to get it back on those B&B sites."

"Think I could rent it for a few weeks before you put it back on the market?"

"Well, sure. Not much to do there for that long, though. Nice town and the bridge tour is cool. Get this: You actually walk below the bridge on this tiny dangling metal walkway. They tie you in like one of those zipline things, but it if that thing goes, it just ensures you follow it. It's wild as long as you are not afraid of heights. But other than that, you will probably get bored. Hell, ski slopes are over an hour away."

"Not a vacation, buddy. I need something off-grid. I am hoping no more than a month, but I would like the option to extend."

"Everything okay? I can be there in a few hours."

"Thanks, Bryan. I appreciate that, but nothing I can't handle. I just need a place for Jenny and John to lay low while I take care of a few things."

"That kinda sounds like you have a big problem, Ranger buddy. I still have all my kit. Plus, I keep a shovel in my car at all times for, uh, unexpected circumstances."

"I appreciate that. You will be the first person I call should I require mortuary services."

"Okay. I tell you what, I'll give it to you for half price."

"No. I can pay for the full three weeks."

"Nonsense. I can't make money off a buddy. I will charge just enough to keep the lights on. It's the least I can do."

"I appreciate it."

Dane unlocked the front door and felt the warmth from the large stone fireplace on the far side of the room. Bryan had obviously stopped by earlier. The fire was roaring, wood was stacked neatly against the wall, and the fridge was fully stocked when he checked inside.

Dane shook his head. *Damn, Bryan.*

The three of them quickly unloaded Dane's truck, hauling in several suitcases and groceries of their own. Later in the day, another Ranger buddy would drop off a rental car for Jenny. Dane had paid his friend cash for the vehicle, so it was not rented in his name. He wanted no trace to the cabin, but knew Jenny and John would eventually get stir-crazy. They would need wheels.

He would have turned to the club if it wasn't for everything else going on. The Keeper had forced his hand when he left Angela's journal in his apartment. The man was showing him that he and The Cabal were not untouchable.

Dane was exhausted after chasing this ghost for so long. The man had taken his baby girl, destroying his life and the lives of others along the way. It was clear The Keeper was colluding with several other monsters for their sick games up and down the eastern seaboard.

It ends now, Dane thought. But he couldn't do what needed to be done if John and Jenny weren't safe.

Dane had felt nothing when he ended Victor's killing spree with nine neatly placed bullets in his chest. He hadn't really had time to process that, since everything had moved so fast after the journal delivery.

He just wished he had gotten there sooner to save Special Agent Stills. He shook his head. *That would not have mattered. We may all have gotten killed or I would have been arrested.*

Dane knew he was going to have to deal with the Patterson situation, but that was the least of his problems. The Keeper was still out there, and his goons could be hunting them at this very moment. Dane had to remove any distractions. John and Jenny had to be safe.

Nicky, his partner in crime, was also off-grid as Dane prepared for the hunt. She had a friend with a large cabin cruiser moored in Dale City. It was the type of place where nobody asked questions. The mariners and staff kept to themselves, and there certainly wasn't any type of surveillance system. Nicky wasn't exactly thrilled he was spending time with his ex-wife, but it was his son's mother.

The West Virginia cabin had a roomy two-story layout. Downstairs was an open floorplan blending the kitchen, dining, and living rooms into one large space. Heavy wooden beams crisscrossed the ceiling, and huge glass windows covered the walls, offering pristine views of the thick forest. Considering the circumstances, Dane could not think of a better second home for John during this ordeal.

"John, take your stuff upstairs and start unpacking," Jenny said once everything was in the house.

She turned angrily to Dane while John climbed the steps. "Okay, I have played along with this bullshit long enough. What is going on?"

"Listen, Jenny, I can't get into it right now. I just need you to trust me."

"Hell, no. I am not taking your word for anything. Does this have anything to do with the overseas trip you just took? What did you do? What trouble did you bring home?"

"It is nothing like that."

"Enough, Dane. Explain. Now."

Dane nodded toward the stairs and motioned for Jenny to follow him outside. She obliged. They walked down the front steps and wandered into the woods.

"Okay, John can't hear us out here. Spill it."

"It's not that easy."

Jenny stopped and turned toward Dane with her arms crossed. "Well, make it!"

Dane had no good way to tell her, so he just blurted it out. "Angela is alive."

"Oh God, Dane, we have been down this road before."

Dane stopped her right there. "I have proof. The man who kidnapped her is taunting me."

Jenny covered her mouth in horror.

Dane continued. "I have been hunting this man and others for a while now. Several other specialists are helping me. We are getting close. Here."

Dane handed Jenny the journal. He watched as she read the small book, tears running down here face.

"I don't understand," she said between sobs. "What are the police doing?"

"Nothing new because they don't know about this. They *can't* know."

"You can't do this on your own. Are you really going to jeopardize our little girl's life so you can go play vigilante? Take this to the police!"

"That's not what I'm doing. It's hard to explain, but I work with a team."

Jenny slapped Dane on his chest. "This isn't one of your covert operations. You and your buddies can't just go running around like commandos."

"We can and we do. This is the only way, Jenny. I can't stop now. I will bring her home."

Jenny turned away from him and headed back to the house. There was nothing else he could say.

Later that afternoon, Dane and John chopped wood next to the house. They had been swinging sledgehammers on top of two large blocks for nearly an hour, breaking occasionally to stack the wood and drink water.

"Dad, what are we doing here? Are you in some sort of trouble?"

"Kinda. This is just a precaution."

"Mom seems really upset."

"She is, John. And that is why I need your help. I need you to go easy on her. I know you don't want to be here either. I promise I will make it as short as possible."

"I don't get any of this."

"I know, but it's important. One day we can talk about it. One day."

ACKNOWLEDGEMENTS

Thank you to my sister Kerri Hagerty for her insight into the procedures and techniques of police investigations. I knew I could count on her to assist with the fouling of blood samples at the crime scene in Savannah.

Thank you to Robin Mackey of Robin Mackey's Photography LLC in Copan, Oklahoma, for the wonderful book cover, website, and author photos.

Thank you to James Manzi. I appreciated your candor when discussing how the FBI investigates these types of crimes against children.

Thank you to my fraternity brother Leigh Stroh. I am not a professionally trained writer, and it helps to have a teacher as experienced as you review my work.

Thank you to my son-in-law, Ross Leventhal. I had questions about air traffic control and flight patterns along and across the Potomac River.

Thank you to my bonus daughter, Courtney Leventhal. You have shared your love of writing with me, and it has been thrilling to follow my path and intersect with your writing career.

Thank you to my bonus son, Taz Codding. Your motivation and hustle to get ahead in this world and encourage others to follow their dreams is inspiring.

Thank you to my daughter Samantha Hagerty. I don't think anyone has been as enthusiastic as you when it comes to the milestones that have been hit with this book and the prequel, *Jones Point*.

Thank you to my daughter Delaney Hagerty. You are always there to support and encourage me. I can always count on you to keep me grounded.

Thank you to my mother, Ann Hagerty. She has always been my biggest fan and does everything possible to tell everyone about her son, the author. Ha.

To my wife, Misty. I appreciate all the long hours when we talked through the flow of the book and you offered great suggestions. The final chapter idea and how it was played out throughout the book was all you babe.

Thank you to the amazing team at Blue Handle Publishing, who have shown extreme patience with all my novice questions about editing, marketing, and my enduring nemesis, social media.

And finally, thank you to all my beta readers who suffered through earlier drafts of my work to provide comments and suggestions, without which this project would never have happened.

Robin Mackey

ABOUT THE AUTHOR

Sean Hagerty is a retired Special Operations soldier with over twenty-five years of experience. He spent his younger years training and conducting combat operations with the 1st of the 75th Ranger Regiment. After nine years, in 2005, he was selected for and assigned to a Special Operations unit at Fort Belvoir, Virginia. There, he spent sixteen years and finished his military career, retiring as a sergeant major. He received several awards and decorations throughout his career, including three Bronze Stars.

Sean currently works for the Department of Defense Science Board as the senior advisor. The board tackles difficult technical issues of importance to national security for leaders within the DoD.

His wife, Misty, is an executive officer at the National Geospatial-Intelligence Agency. Their children—Courtney, Travis, Samantha, and Delaney—all live in the Washington D.C. area and are thriving, growing, and traveling along their own paths. The grandchildren Rowen, Jameson, and Wren keep Sean and Misty busy.

Sean dug into his decades of service and deep-rooted research instincts from years of academic pursuits in history to tell this story. This story was written mostly in the plush seats of the daily Tackett's Mill/Pentagon commuter bus and the shaky bucket seats of the Franconia Springfield/Largo blue metro line. However, a few chapters were written while traveling for work, taking advantage of uninterrupted thoughts on an airliner. One chapter was even written during an evening break on a business trip aboard the USS Nimitz CVN 68 aircraft carrier out in the Pacific Ocean.

Cabal all came together during evening edits in his home shared with Misty in Lakeridge, Virginia.

Jones Point was the first novel in the Dane Cooper series.

Cabal is the second.

www.ingramcontent.com/pod-product-compliance
Lightning Source LLC
Jackson TN
JSHW032155070525
84042JS00018B/116
* 9 7 8 1 9 5 5 0 5 8 3 1 5 *